HANGING ON

Awakenings 2

Michele Zurlo

MENAGE AND MORE

Siren Publishing, Inc.
www.SirenPublishing.com

A SIREN PUBLISHING BOOK
IMPRINT: Ménage and More

HANGING ON
Copyright © 2010 by Debora M. Ryan

ISBN-10: 1-60601-797-7
ISBN-13: 978-1-60601-797-5

First Printing: August 2010

Cover design by Jinger Heaston
All cover art and logo copyright © 2010 by Siren Publishing, Inc.

Printed in the U.S.A.

PUBLISHER
Siren Publishing, Inc.
www.SirenPublishing.com

DEDICATION

This is dedicated to anyone who has ever had to Take Back the Night. Visit http://www.takebackthenight.org/ to see how you can help.

Thanks to The Airborne Toxic Event for having the single best album ever. It helped create the perfect mood for writing Hanging On.

Special thanks to Laura for insisting on the chocolate and to Eric for being my DJ.

HANGING ON

Awakenings 2

MICHELE ZURLO
Copyright © 2010

Chapter 1

The soft cotton sheet pressed warm against her bare stomach and breasts, moving to let in the chill as a hot, questing hand slid over her thigh. Sophia cracked one eye open, aiming it at the alarm clock across the room. In a half hour, she had to be in the shower. Christopher was well trained enough to know this. Even five minutes later, and she would have slapped his hand away, chastising him for being so naughty.

She would still punish him for touching without permission, but they would both enjoy the process. Last night had been good, but she had to work both jobs today. Sophia didn't have the energy to waste if she wasn't going to get a reward.

Rolling to give his roaming hand more access, she drew him closer for a long, hard kiss. He had generous lips that sucked her in whether she wanted to be sucked in or not. They felt wonderful on her clit. Breaking the kiss, she pushed him down. He trailed his hot mouth over her breasts and abdomen, a grin stretching those luscious lips.

She resisted the urge to sigh in relief. Sometimes subs were so difficult to read, and she absolutely *hated* when she messed up their punishment or reward. Chris had been superb last night, and she had been exceptionally good to him.

Sophia tilted her head to watch him settle in. His cheeks, still smooth though he hadn't shaved today, rubbed against her sensitive inner thighs.

She loved the way his milk chocolate skin contrasted with her own deeply tan Mediterranean complexion. He parted her with practiced ease, his tongue darting out to tease before he got serious.

He wasn't very gentle. He knew full well what she liked and how she liked it. When she had taken him as an occasional playmate over a year ago, she had trained him first thing. He may have been angling for a punishment, but she wasn't going to give him what he wanted, not then. Soon, unhurried waves lapped through her, and he made his way up her body, begging with kisses and with soft brown eyes.

Without a word, Sophia reached into the box on the nightstand and ripped open a condom. "Slow," she warned.

He shuddered in anticipation and knelt up. The sheet fell to the foot of the bed. Reaching down, she unrolled the sheath over his thick cock and pulled it to her entrance. Trailing her fingers lightly downward, she found a fresh welt on his inner thigh and grazed her nail over it. The caress was feathery, but pressure was unnecessary.

He moaned, long and low. "Mistress," he breathed. "Oh God, yes."

When he moved, it was too fast. Sophia swallowed a grimace of pain and reached for her riding crop, which lay next to the package of condoms on the nightstand. This kind of pain might be required to drive him over the edge, but it did nothing for her.

Bringing it down sharply on the back of his thigh, she purred a warning. "Christopher, darling, *slow*."

He shuddered with pleasure and adjusted his pace. "Yes, Mistress."

Christopher's length was average, but he moved well, and he took direction with a natural enthusiasm. He was one of her best finds. Unlike many dominatrixes, she didn't keep a stable of submissives. It was too much like a relationship, which meant far too much responsibility on her part. Subs were needy. Sophia's came and went.

Being in charge of someone's pleasure was a job she didn't take lightly. She liked freedom. Submissives who enjoyed her command were free to enjoy themselves with anyone they wanted. She encouraged them to play the field, and she made no secret about the fact the scenes they played were in no way indicative of a romantic relationship.

Pressure built inside her, slow and steady, until she climaxed. Opening her eyes, Sophia watched Christopher struggle to maintain the slow, gentle pace she commanded. He would neither stop nor come until she gave permission.

"Faster," she commanded, drawing diagonal lines across his ass with the crop.

He twitched and moaned. "Yes, Mistress, oh, yes!"

It was a rather light punishment, but she needed to be careful not to overdo it. She had left his back, ass, and thighs a mass of welts the night before. Though the worst of the damage always disappeared by the morning, he would still be sensitive.

By design, it wasn't enough. He built upon the waves of her orgasm, driving her higher. She brought the whip down sharply across his thigh and ass, giving him a little more of what she knew he needed.

He cried out, and she swung again, the thin stick whistling through the air. He once told her it was the sweetest sound he'd ever heard during sex.

Frantic, he begged, "Please, Mistress, can I come?"

She waited until his whispered plea turned to a sob, reveling in the power she had over him and ignoring the power he had over her. Sophia gave him what he wanted: pain, punishment, and orgasm. He gave her what she wanted: control. Squeezing his ass tightly in her hands, she granted permission. They came together.

Later, as they scurried around getting ready for work, Sophia heard the distinct sounds of swearing coming from under her bed. Normally, she didn't let a partner stay the night after a scene. She didn't even let them upstairs, directing them to a specially outfitted room in the basement that she kept for acting out various scenarios. Christopher understood that staying the night didn't mean anything more than friendship, so she didn't mind waking up next to him. She didn't love it, either. Morning was her time to recharge and load up on caffeine, and she preferred to do it in solitude.

Kneeling carefully in the very professional-looking business skirt that was the costume for her daytime persona, she peered at him from beneath the other side of her mattress. "Problems?"

His face was twisted with aggravation, which Sophia found startling. He was usually unflappable after a night with her. His eyes met hers across the shadowed space. "I can't find my tie."

Christopher was a successful lawyer. He was handsome and intelligent. He was the only one of her submissives who knew about her day job. At night, she disciplined clients at a club owned by a friend. Three days a week, she was a corporate accountant. Chris found out by accident, but he kept her secret. Most likely, he didn't care. That wasn't the reason he texted her every few weeks.

She straightened to standing. "It's hanging in the bathroom." It was silk, and he had asked very nicely if she would refrain from using it as a gag. She hadn't minded. He looked so much better with a ball gag parting those salacious lips anyway.

He disappeared down the hall toward the bathroom. Sophia followed him out but headed to the kitchen. "Can you put on some coffee?" he asked.

The request took her by surprise. She wasn't against sharing her coffee, but Chris usually left after he showered and dressed. She always assumed he stopped by a swanky coffee chain on his way to work. "Sure," she threw over her shoulder without pausing.

"Three sugars, no cream."

The words floated down the hall. Christopher was only a sexual submissive. The rest of the time, he was bossy as all hell. Next time they met, she would punish him for that transgression. Perhaps that's why he phrased it as an order rather than a request. She wasn't a pushover outside of the bedroom, but she wasn't forceful and domineering, either.

His coffee was waiting for him when he made it to the kitchen. Lifting the mug to his face, he inhaled deeply. "God, you make good coffee. I remember the first time we were together, you made me drink coffee and sober up before you took me down to your dungeon."

The combined nostalgia and regret in his voice caught her attention. As a Dom, Sophia was pretty good at discerning the subtleties of speech and moans. "What's wrong?"

Christopher took a sip, set his mug on the table, and sighed. "I met someone."

This seized her interest. She loved dominating couples. "Are you going to bring her by?"

He laughed, shaking his head sadly. "I love that hungry look in your eyes, Sophia. I'm going to miss it. She's not into this kind of thing."

She realized he was ending their relationship. She wasn't sad about it. She would miss him, but he was rather easily replaced. She might only be twenty-four, but she was at the top of her game and generally considered hot. Sabrina, one of her best friends and one of her regular patrons, liked to refer to Sophia as exotically beautiful. Sophia didn't mind, but she did feel self-conscious when Sabrina gushed about her in front of other people.

"Sounds serious," Sophia said, smiling to let him know she harbored no hard feelings.

He blushed and studied the convection in his coffee. She knew he was thinking of his new girlfriend. "We had our first date three days ago. I can't get her out of my head, and I know she won't understand this part of my life."

Sophia didn't say anything. This was Christopher's decision. Personally, she didn't think it would work out. Chris needed pain in order to orgasm. If this woman didn't follow through for him, the sex was going to suck. More importantly, this was a major part of who he was. Hiding something this big wasn't healthy.

She wished him the best of luck and shooed him out the door so she could make it to work on time. Her boss was a jerk. If he ever showed up at the club, he better pray for another dominatrix. Sophia didn't trust herself to not exact some personal revenge for the shit assignments he shoved her way because she refused to consider full-time work. It didn't pay as well as being a dominatrix, and it didn't fulfill the deep-seated need she had to dominate.

But, God, she loved numbers. Figuring out problems that had definite answers gave her a sense of satisfaction she rarely found elsewhere.

Chapter 2

Both of her jobs were located in Southfield. Sophia took a bag with a change of clothes with her, changing in the employee locker room of the club before letting the hostess know she was on the floor.

"On the floor" was the term they used when a Dom was available to see clients. Though many clubs that offered this kind of service were sex clubs, this one was not. Michigan was pretty strict about health codes, meaning most sex clubs lasted six weeks or less. They offered bondage and discipline, but that was all. If they developed outside relationships with some clients, that was something done on their own and not on Club property.

Most of Sophia's clients were by appointment, and most of them returned regularly. These were easy jobs. She knew their bodies, she knew their needs, and she knew their limits. New clients were challenging because she didn't know how much they could take. Ellen Kubina, her boss and the owner of the club, had new clients fill out surveys. They were helpful as long as the client was truthful. New clients were frequently ashamed of their fantasies and underreported their needs.

Tonight was both easy and satisfying. Sophia lost herself in the whippings and bindings as much as the clients did. There was something about the pinkening of skin and the sobs of agonized pleasure that made her feel whole.

Sabrina was her last client. She appeared every other Friday, sometimes more often. The first time they met was in the bar attached to the club. She was short and petite and uptight. She sat up straight and crossed her legs at the ankle. Long brown hair and big brown eyes dominated her classically beautiful face. Everything about her was perfect, from her makeup and hair to the tiny stitches in her haute couture clothing. She looked like an ice queen.

If Sabrina was Sophia's boss, she'd probably have hated her. She didn't fit the type of woman to whom she imagined Jonas, her friend and mentor, would be attracted. But, as Christopher repeatedly showed her, strong people were often the best subs.

At the time, Sabrina hadn't known her husband was a Dom. She thought he was a bartender. One of the first things she asked Sophia was if she was a prostitute. Sabrina had been in shock, wanting to know if her husband was having sex with his clients when she thought he was out bartending off the tremendous debt with which his ex-wife left him. She apologized profusely after Ellen set her straight.

However, it wasn't until Ellen brought her to Sophia as a client that they became friends. She hadn't filled out a survey. The dominatrix in her was a little glad because she wanted to test Sabrina's boundaries herself. She half wanted to push her beyond them for implying Sophia charged money in exchange for sexual favors. Even when she brought subs home to the playroom in her basement, she didn't always fuck them. Dominating wasn't all about the sex. It was about the *control*.

However, she was tiny, and she was Jonas's. Given the surly and generally sour disposition he displayed at work until Ellen fired him, and the woebegone waif Ellen had plopped in front of Sophia, she deduced Sabrina and Jonas were having problems. She had ordered Sabrina to strip, tied her down, and whipped her until she sobbed and turned to jelly.

Sophia had joined her and Ellen for drinks afterward. The pair had been close friends ever since. Now that Sabrina and Jonas were split up, Sophia was torn by her desire to keep one of the few close female friends she had and by her attachment to Jonas. He was her mentor and her friend, but she couldn't talk to him the way she could talk to Sabrina. Jonas was singularly uninterested in fashion or other "chick" topics, as he termed them.

Sabrina was the last client of the day. One look from Sophia had her peeling off her clothes. The first time she came to Sophia, Sabrina hadn't been wearing underwear. Now, she wore little thongs for her to work around. Sophia didn't care either way. Sabrina was hot, but she was like a sister. Besides that, Jonas would murder Sophia in her sleep if she even tried to entice Sabrina. She hoped they made up soon. Ellen was optimistic, but Sophia knew what a stubborn ass Jonas could be.

The thong and coordinating bra were pink lace. Sophia ached to make her skin match. She turned toward the stockade, where Sophia usually secured her. Sophia narrowed her eyes, hating when one of her subs found her too predictable. When they were out in the real world, they were friends. Here, Sabrina was hers.

"No," she said, catching the petite brunette by surprise. Leaning toward the wall behind her, Sophia pressed the button to bring down a hook. Sabrina was too comfortable in this setting. It was time to change things up.

She watched the huge metal hook stop a little over a foot above her head. Those big mocha eyes darkened with fear. She trembled and tore her gaze from it, fixing Sophia with an anxious stare. From the corner of her eye, Sophia watched Sabrina wring her hands together. This was a good sign. She wanted her this way. Sabrina needed help relaxing, and Sophia was going to give that to her. It was in her power to do so.

"Hold on to it, Sabrina."

She bit her lip, the fear and the need at war. "Sophia, I really like it when you tie me down."

She couldn't ask to be tied down. Jonas had trained her to follow orders or face the consequences. Sophia wasn't that kind of dominatrix. She encouraged submissives to vocalize what they liked and what they didn't like. Some of them liked to be bound, but not whipped. Others, like Sabrina, loved the whip. She fought it. Sophia loved that she fought it, but Sabrina would yield. It was what she needed.

Sophia closed in on her, crowding her in the large, empty space of the private training arena. Sabrina shrank into herself, but she didn't move away. It confirmed her instinct to change things up. If she really didn't want to do this, she would have stepped back or used the safe word. Sophia preferred to know her subs well enough that they didn't have to use the safe word.

"Please," she begged. Her pink tongue darted out to lick at her upper lip. She was nervous, but so close to giving in.

Without a word, Sophia grabbed her wrists and forced them over her head. She was about five inches taller, so it was easy to stretch her out.

Some clients were so tall that this tactic would only highlight Sophia's lack of stature, though, at five-seven, her height was average.

Sabrina's hands wrapped around the hook.

"Don't let go," Sophia warned.

She swallowed and nodded, tears already glistening in her eyes. She trusted Sophia to give her what she needed.

Stepping back, Sophia pushed the lever the other way, forcing Sabrina to rise to her toes. Her head fell back. Her hair barely reached her chin, and this position did not put it in the way. Selecting a fuchsia cat, Sophia set to work, beginning with the stomach and thighs in front.

Sabrina settled into the rhythm too quickly. Sophia frowned. This wasn't going to do it. If Sophia didn't bring her kicking and screaming, she would never reach that place of inner peace she so desperately sought.

She switched the cat for a leather paddle, whacking rectangular patterns over her ass and thighs in back, careful not to mar her legs too low. She jerked away, and Sophia smiled, knowing she hadn't expected this. Before too long, she cried out, unable to swallow the sounds. The smacks came faster, and Sophia was rewarded with screams and tears. They coursed down her face until her body lengthened, relaxing into the punishment.

Within seconds, peace came over her. It amazed Sophia how completely Sabrina changed during those moments. Everything about her transformed, from that false ice-queen front she wore as armor to something delicate and tender. If Jonas ever saw her like this, Sophia didn't know how he could have let her go.

Sabrina nearly stole her heart, and that particular organ of Sophia's was out of commission.

She met Sabrina and Ellen in the VIP lounge of the bar for drinks afterward. Dressed in a pink satin designer halter and a skirt that fell to mid-calf, Sabrina sat gingerly on the edge of the high-legged chair and nursed one of those fruity drinks she liked. Next to her, Ellen smiled brightly. Ellen dwarfed everyone, even Sophia. They were the same size, but Ellen's forceful and dynamic personality made her seem so much larger. Plus, Ellen was curvier, but Sophia would never say that to her.

On the dance floor, Sophia spied Ginny and Lara, Sabrina's sister and her wife. Ginny looked so much like Sabrina, Sophia found them difficult to tell apart after Sabrina cut her hair. In addition to being beautiful and petite, they both had pixie cuts. The taller, sensual blonde glued to Ginny was the only telltale clue if one didn't look close enough to notice that Sabrina's hair was a couple inches longer. Well, that and the obvious soreness in Sabrina's backside. Ginny even drank the same fruity kinds of drinks as Sabrina.

Sophia took the chair next to Ellen. Ellen frequently complained that hanging around with Sabrina made her look even bigger. Her little one was eighteen months old, but she was still upset about the extra curves that wouldn't go away. Sophia didn't know why. Ellen's husband looked more in love with her now than he had when Sophia first met him. Watching the two of them together bordered on sickening. Unless an observer knew Ellen, nobody guessed she was a killer dominatrix.

A whiskey sour awaited Sophia. She smiled in thanks at Ellen, who shook her head, inclining it toward Sabrina.

"Thanks."

"You're quite welcome," Sabrina said. She was uncommonly happy. Sophia knew it was more than the recent whipping that caused her to look like she was about to erupt with sunshine and giggles. She was not the kind of woman who giggled.

"What's going on?"

She burst. "I'm getting married, and I want you to be one of my bridesmaids."

Flabbergasted, Sophia stared. "Married? I didn't think you were even divorced yet." More than that, she knew how much Sabrina was hurting from Jonas leaving. Who in the world would she marry on the rebound? She wracked her brain for a probable name.

"I'm not." Her grin lit up the semidark of the bar. "Jonas finally came around, just like Ellen said he would. I'm making him do things right this time. Vegas won't cut it. He got down on one knee and proposed. We're going to have a big wedding, white dress, five-piece orchestra, and everything."

Sophia slid to the ground, came around the table, and hugged her friend. "Congratulations. I'm so happy for you." Part of her was also unhappy. Did this mean she was losing two of her subs in one day? Granted, her relationship with Sabrina wasn't sexual, but she really liked dominating her.

Sabrina grinned a while longer before adding, "You don't have to, you know. You can say no, and I'll understand."

In her moment of self-pity, Sophia forgot the question. "Of course I'll stand up in your wedding." She turned to Ellen. "Are you a bridesmaid, too?"

Ellen shook her head, setting her brown hair skating across her shoulders. "I'm the best man."

Sophia saw Ellen so much with Sabrina, she forgot Ellen was actually Jonas's best friend.

"Best woman," Sabrina corrected with a reassuring squeeze to Ellen's wrist.

Ellen grimaced. "I spent almost a year calling him my maid of honor. He's been waiting a long, long time to do this to me."

Sabrina rolled her eyes and shook her head. Everybody knew better than to become involved in a dispute between Ellen and Jonas. Ginny and Lara joined them, and the conversation turned toward other topics.

Before they called it a night, Sabrina cheerfully reminded them there was a meeting for the wedding party at her house on Sunday. The wedding was in a little less than two months. She said she had waited long enough for Jonas to come around.

She would provide lunch and dinner. That meant it was a long meeting. Sophia sighed. It wasn't that she was opposed to spending a day at Sabrina's, just that she felt uncomfortable around happy couples. They frequently wanted to include her in their brand of contentment, but Sophia had no use for that kind of relationship.

The only truly bright spot in the day was a last-minute text from a sub she hadn't seen in several months: *Have a date tomorrow night. Love to bring him over.*

Sophia absolutely loved dominating couples. Livia had excellent taste in men, and she would expect Sophia to join in the sexual play.

Chapter 3

The doorbell rang at nine exactly. Livia had a problem with being on time until Sophia trained her. Too early and Sophia would stretch the punishment, making her wait an excruciatingly long time for what she wanted. Too late and she would send her away.

Many dominatrixes went all out, dressing in pleather bustiers or thigh-high boots. Sophia preferred for her subs to wear those kinds of things if clothing was going to be used at all. Mostly, she liked bare flesh. Something about the sight of naked skin set her juices flowing.

Sophia answered the door dressed in jean shorts and a maroon tank top. Although the air conditioning was on, she knew her activities would make her work up a sweat. Still, she left her thick brown hair flowing freely instead of securing it out of the way. It was one of her best features, falling in waves midway down her back and drawing attention away from her relatively flat chest.

Livia smiled, her eyes sidling tentatively toward her date and back to Sophia. From the way she stood next to him, Sophia could tell that, although she found him attractive, she wasn't sure about him, and she wanted her mistress's approval.

Sophia refrained from frowning. If she wasn't sure about a guy, she wouldn't ask him to have a threesome with her dominatrix.

Was Livia angry with him and looking to settle the score? Livia wasn't the nicest person in the world, and Sophia wouldn't put something like that past her. She was a few inches taller than Sophia. With her heels on, Livia was a little taller than her date. He didn't seem to mind.

They matched. That was the first thing Sophia noticed. Both of them had blue eyes and hair streaked blond by a professional hairdresser. Livia was pretty, and she took her punishments well. Her date was incredibly sexy. He was one of those perfect-looking men who invariably had a bevy of women clamoring for his attention. It made them think they were better than they were.

Usually, Sophia was immune to good looks. However, something about him was magnetic. He mesmerized with raw sexuality. It exuded from every pore in his body, especially those full, pouty lips begging to be nibbled on. Sophia wanted to push him down on the couch in the living room and have her way with him.

She struggled to resist. Tearing her eyes away, she motioned for them to come inside. Livia brushed past Sophia, her plastic breasts already pert and begging to be whipped. Her shirt showed a deep valley of cleavage, and her short skirt was slit to the top of her thigh. Underneath, she wore buff-colored leggings that matched her barely there blouse. Sophia wasn't sure if Livia dressed to seduce Sophia or her date.

Hazarding a glance at his backside, she forgot to breathe. Clad in tight, faded jeans, his corded muscles stretched and bunched under the fabric as he moved. He had an ass made for cupping, for squeezing, and for raking nails across until he cried out.

For the first time in as long as she could remember, Sophia had to pull herself together. Livia had certainly outdone herself tonight.

The good little sub waited patiently just inside the living room, knowing she was not allowed to speak without permission. Sophia closed the door with a heavy whoosh and rounded them to stand in front.

First, she inspected Livia. It had been several months since she had last seen her. It looked like she had a new nose, and the faint lines around her eyes and mouth were gone. She was over forty, but she looked closer to Sophia's age.

He couldn't have been too many years older than Sophia. She estimated late twenties, and she wondered if he knew Livia's actual age. If not, he wouldn't learn it tonight. His hair was spiked with the kind of gel that didn't leave the hair looking wet or coated. It stood up a couple of inches on the top before fading shorter on the sides.

A single tiny platinum hoop dangled from his left ear. Though he wore fairly snug pants that advertised the size of his penis, his royal blue button-down shirt was too loose to do more than hint at a broad musculature.

Sophia couldn't wait to strip him naked.

"I'm Drew," he said, shifting uncomfortably under the strain of silence. He met Sophia's eyes, though Livia remained with her eyes to the floor.

The smile Sophia gave him in response wasn't welcoming. It was gleeful and predatory.

Livia's breath caught.

"Drew," Sophia said, testing the feel of his name on her tongue. "Has Livia told you why she brought you here?"

He shrugged casually. "She said you were a dominatrix." An amused smile played around the corners of his lips, peeking out but never fully forming. His eyes sparkled.

Sophia's expression didn't change or soften in the least. "And do you know what that means?"

Again, he shrugged. God, it was a sexy gesture, and the way he looked at Sophia said he knew she was attracted to him. "You're going to tie us up, spank us, and tell us we're bad."

She shook her head. She never told her submissives they were bad. She punished and corrected, but she never talked down to them. Trust and respect were important in situations like this. Both had to be earned and reinforced.

"No spanking?" His tone was just derisive enough to reveal his relief at the idea. Was he afraid of the pain?

Sophia held his gaze and he stared at her. "Drew, do you want to be here?"

He shrugged again, as if it didn't matter.

Regretfully, she shook her head. "Livia, take him away. You may bring him back when he's sure what he wants."

Livia laced her hand through his arm, turning toward the door.

"No," he said. This whole time, he never looked away from Sophia. Something desperate came into his eyes. Already, he was submitting to her, and she reveled in it. "Wait. I'm sure I want to be here."

"You have to be sure about what you want while you're here, Drew. There is no room for uncertainties. You either need to be spanked, or whipped, or tied up, or punished another way, or you don't. When I ask you a question, I expect a clear, vocal response." Her voice was harsh, but it had to be. Softness was for later, when he let down his guard.

Those clear, icy blue eyes dropped to the floor as he thought about it. Finally, his eyes returned to Sophia. "I want to be here. I've never quite done this before, so I have no idea if I want to be tied up or whipped or spanked or anything else. I have trouble imagining what 'anything else' might look like. I'm willing to try this, all of this, whatever it entails."

She liked his voice and the cadence of his speech. It was just the right amount of husky and deep. She could listen to him speak for hours. Combined with the sex appeal that oozed from him, he could have a brilliant television career ahead of him. She nodded once, indicating to Livia she could release Drew's arm. She resumed her earlier stance.

"Rules," Sophia said. "There are rules. First, you must be honest and clear. If you like something or if you want something, you must ask for it. When I ask you a question or give an order, I expect a clear response, or I will stop whatever I'm doing. Second, if at any time you're uncomfortable and you want the scene to stop, the safe word is 'onion.' Third, this is a scene, a play. It doesn't imply a relationship between any of us. Is this clear?"

"Yes," he said. "What do I call you?"

Sophia smiled, rewarding him for asking a good question. The hitch in his breathing told her so much. "You may call me Mistress." Without waiting to see if he had more questions, she turned to Livia. "Livia, darling, take Drew into the basement and get into position. Leave his pants on, but get rid of the shirt."

Dismissing them, she walked purposefully in the other direction. She headed to the kitchen to get a glass of water. It was more a stalling tactic to give them time to carry out her orders. Damn, he was hot. She chastised herself for being so attracted to someone else's date. She wanted him to herself, which meant she couldn't have him at all. Under no circumstances would she have sex with him because she knew it would only lead to wanting more. That man was instinctively and consciously a walking sex magnet. His extreme good looks didn't even enter into it.

Sophia followed them about five minutes later, silent footsteps hiding her approach. The door to the specially constructed playroom in the basement was open, and she heard conversation drifting down the hall.

"I'm not kneeling on the floor."

"Hush, Drew," Livia hissed. "Mistress doesn't allow speaking unless it's to her."

"This will earn a punishment?"

That was the tone and those were the words of someone who doubted her ability to dominate him. Unless he wasn't a submissive at all, Drew was going to be a challenge. But why would Livia bring a date who wasn't also a submissive?

"You've already earned a punishment." Her laugh was full of delight. "You spoke to her in the foyer before she asked you to speak. I told you to be quiet."

"I introduced myself. It's called manners." He sounded a little petulant. Sophia hoped it was nerves and not the sign of a spoiled brat. She didn't mind disciplining those kinds of people, but she enjoyed them so much more when they weren't jerks.

Sophia closed the door, startling them both as she had meant to do. The room was soundproof, so their screams wouldn't be heard anywhere else, but that wasn't very effective with the door open. "Only speak when you have permission from me, Drew."

"Are you going to punish me?" he asked. Still on his feet, he had to angle his head down to meet her eyes. His fists were planted firmly on his hips.

His defensive question diverted her attention from the mass of lean muscle rippling over his chest and stomach. "Oh, yes," she said, licking her lips in anticipation. She was in full predator mode. "I'm going to punish you."

Uncertainty and the edge of fear marred his defensive position. He had the sense not to say anything further.

Livia knelt on the floor with her knees spread a little wider than the span of her shoulders. Her hands were laced behind her head, and her eyes were glued to the floor, awaiting orders.

Earlier, Sophia had laid out the paraphernalia she planned to use in the scene. Submissives had an easier time of things since the Doms had the responsibility of planning everything. It was one of the only "relationship" responsibilities she liked. Lifting a mass of leather straps, Sophia bade Livia stand.

Obediently, she rose to her feet. Sophia untangled the mass, winding it around her body. When she finished, lines of leather ringed Livia's abdomen, her thighs, and her neck. Crisscrossed straps made it so that her breasts were plumped between triangles. The straps were strategically placed to cause a discomfort that would cause her to wiggle. That tiny motion would rub the straps against several erogenous zones, heightening her pleasure.

This was one of her favorite things. Tonight, Sophia used it as a reward. On another submissive, the restrictive straps would be a punishment.

Drew watched intently. His mouth parted as his breathing sped up, and his pupils dilated. He was becoming aroused watching her outfit Livia.

"Go bend over the footboard," Sophia said.

Livia complied immediately.

"I thought you were going to punish me," Drew said, sounding both anxious and jealous. "I'm the one who broke the rules."

Sophia smiled at him. This time he swallowed in fear. She indicated a chair nearby. It was straight-backed and much more uncomfortable than it looked. "Sit, Drew. You need to learn to behave."

He narrowed his eyes but did as she instructed. Perhaps he thought he would get to watch two women having sex. Most men entertained that kind of fantasy.

Sophia left Livia alone, knowing the wait heightened the punishment/reward for her, and sauntered over to Drew. She straddled him, running her hands across his bare shoulders and down his arms.

She didn't know where Livia found him, but Drew was either a man who worked out frequently or he had a job that required manual labor. This was not the physique of a man who sat around all day. Everything about him advertised a man of action—someone who was strong, decisive, determined, not the submissive she so badly wanted.

Logistics required she sit on his lap to do what she needed to do. A bulge strained against the denim of his jeans. Centering her pussy over it, she rested her weight on him. He groaned.

Grasping his wrists, she guided them behind the chair, and he didn't resist. Her breasts grazed his chest, and she felt the sudden heat of him through thin cotton. He tensed, and she realized he felt the same jolt she felt at the contact. She used the distraction to secure the handcuffs.

The cold metal closed around his wrists, and his eyes widened in surprise. Her serene smile never wavered. She never made an effort to hide her toys. She dropped her voice so Livia couldn't hear what she said. "Tell me what you want, Drew. Your wildest fantasies can come true."

He chuckled, the sound rumbling from his chest through the peaks of her nipples. "You're not the first woman to say that to me."

Her answer might have been ill-advised, but he rattled her more than she cared to admit. "I'm the first woman who can really deliver."

He went still, and Sophia prayed to whoever was listening that she hadn't crossed a line. His blue eyes darkened with desire, and he leaned closer, trying to capture her lips in a kiss. She leaned away and put a finger to his lips. There would be no kissing, either, not with the way he made her feel, not with the things she wanted to do to him. A very large, selfish part of Sophia wanted Livia gone so she wouldn't have to share.

That would be dangerous. This was the kind of man in which she could lose herself.

"None of that," she chastised. "You don't get to touch me without permission. You get no pleasure that I don't approve. You may not come until I give you permission."

Pushing herself away from him, she bent to secure his feet. He struggled against the bonds, but they were too strong. "Sophia," he whispered.

Though he used the wrong title, the entreaty was a beginning. Ignoring him, she returned to Livia. When Sophia had dressed Livia, she ran her hands along the sultry blonde's body, reminding herself where Livia liked to be touched and how. She wanted a beating, nothing severe, just enough to heat her skin.

Grabbing a bulb vibrator and a tube of lubricating gel, Sophia approached her waiting submissive. "Spread your cheeks."

Without changing her bent position, Livia reached back with both hands and spread her ass wide. Sophia squirted gel onto the toy and some onto her fingers. Livia sighed and gasped as Sophia massaged the gel into her. She tensed when Sophia removed her fingers, knowing what was coming next. The bulb parted her, shoving hard and fast into her little puckered hole. A low moan escaped.

If they played again, Sophia would have Drew fuck her that way while she used a vibrator or clitoral stimulator from the front. She could hang

Livia from hooks in the ceiling, and they could use her body as a plaything. Livia would love it.

But that was not in the plan tonight.

Sophia turned the dial to medium, sending vibrations through Livia's body.

Livia was a good girl. She didn't move her hands one bit, even though she knew what was coming next. She liked a light whipping, so Sophia gave it to her, paying special attention to her ass. Resting her forehead on the bed's footboard, she moved in time to the rhythm of the lashes. Cries fell from her lips.

When she was a good shade of pink, Sophia stopped. The marks would fade in an hour or so, but until they did, she would be sensitive to the lightest of touches.

"Mistress, please." Her whispered words caught in her throat. The straps and the lick of the whip had worked their magic. She was primed and ready to come.

With a light hand on her shoulder, Sophia guided Livia to Drew and arranged her on top of him, her back to his front. The chair might not be comfortable, but he provided the perfect cushioning. Sophia wanted to lie on him like that, to feel his chest against her back. "Lay your head on his shoulder, and let your legs fall to the outside of his."

"Yes, Mistress."

A tap on the quick-release freed Drew's legs. "Spread your legs wider."

Annoyance and frustration thinned his lips. He hesitated before complying, opening Livia even further. Sophia rewarded him with an absent caress on the cheek. He turned into her palm, seeking to kiss her there. She pulled away before he made contact and returned her attention to Livia.

"Touch yourself," she commanded. "Outside only."

Her fingers were red and stiff from the whip. Ever so slowly, she moved them across her body, caressing her tender flesh as she found her saturated folds. The bulb in her anus vibrated, and her fingers worked quickly. Sophia watched Livia's face. She was in heaven. A pleased smile tugged at her mouth, which Drew saw.

Her eyes met his, and she realized her mistake. In avoiding looking at him, she thought he wasn't looking at her. From the expression on his face, she wondered if his eyes had ever left her. Had he watched Livia being whipped, or Sophia whipping her?

Recovering quickly, she studied his face. The punishment had been effective. He hated being restrained, restricted from the action, and he didn't bother to hide that emotion. Sophia thought he might pull at his handcuffs a little more, but he didn't, opting instead to stare at her. He ensnared her with his eyes, and electricity jolted through her body. She recognized a hunger in him that echoed in her.

He wanted her.

She wanted him to want her. She shouldn't want it, but she did, and, in that moment, he knew it. Reaching behind him, she broke the connection and released his wrists.

"Touch her."

His hands roamed Livia's body at Sophia's command, spreading sensual circles of pleasure. The pressure he used was perfect, arousing kittenish sighs and moans from the woman under his fingertips.

Sophia tamped down a twinge of jealousy. "Pinch her nipples."

He did this, too, never taking his eyes from Sophia. This slow seduction had her wet and swollen. If he kept this up, she might have to turn in her title. She never thought a man could topple her without a single touch.

Screwing in her spine, Sophia shifted her attention to Livia. She was ripe, so ready. He rolled her nipples between his thumb and forefinger, and she moaned loudly.

"Mistress," she panted. "Please, oh, please."

"Stop." Immediately, Livia halted her actions, whimpering a protest. Sophia waited, reveling in her power. Finally, she nodded. "Drew, finish her."

He reached between her legs. Fingers from one hand found her clit, while fingers from the other plunged inside. His quick mastery of her body was a clear message to Sophia. The seed of doubt inside her grew. Nothing about this man was submissive. It wasn't that she expected him to give in without a fight, but only a true submissive would fight or enjoy the process. He seemed to be tolerating it, like it was a means to an end. What end?

Sophia wasn't out to prove anything, and she didn't want someone in her playroom who wasn't going to enjoy himself. Why had Livia brought him?

She lifted, arching away from his body and toward his hand, and screamed, "Mistress, please let me come."

Sophia didn't answer. She wanted to see what Drew would do without that permission. He pumped his fingers into her without varying his pace, as if he needed to prove to Sophia he knew his way around a woman's body. Could he play *her* body that well? She shook away the recurring image.

"Mistress, please, I need to come," Livia begged, sobbing on the edge of hysteria.

Sophia waited ten more seconds. It wasn't a long time, but it was forever to a wet and swollen sub. Leaning close, she whispered, "Come, Livia. Give me what is mine."

She climaxed with abandon, but neither Drew nor Sophia paid her much mind. He held her in his arms as she calmed, his attitude less of a cuddle and more of a reticence to drop her on the floor.

Reaching under her, he removed the vibrating bulb and handed it to Sophia. She had forgotten it was there, which was completely unlike her. Of course, it was vibrating against his cock because of the way Livia was positioned. He would have been hyperaware of it.

Sophia opted not to punish him for removing it without permission.

She pulled Livia to her feet. Slowly, Sophia released the buckles on the straps she wore and slid them down, leaving her naked. "Go lay on the bed with your head toward the wall. I'm going to tie you down."

Panic flared in her eyes, and only the trust established between them over several years made Livia follow that order without protest. Livia didn't care to be restrained. She liked tight, binding clothes, but not tight bindings. She had threatened Sophia's comfort level by bringing Drew. She didn't do it on purpose. He certainly wasn't the first "date" she had brought. But Sophia did feel threatened, and she hated the lack of power and control that came with that.

Maybe it was a little vindictive, but Sophia wanted to threaten Livia's comfort level, too. Drew had seen too much in Sophia's face. This game was about control. She needed to reestablish her control.

With a crook of her finger, Sophia ordered Drew to stand. He did so with difficulty, standing in easy reach of her. She should have ordered him to strip. Guided by something foreign, she reached forward until her hands landed on the snap of his jeans. Before a thought could process in her normally quick mind, Sophia undid the snap and unzipped the fly. Free of its confines, his thick hardness grew even larger.

Drew's arms hung at his sides in anticipation. From the corner of her eye, she saw his fingers flex and stiffen. He was fighting the urge to touch her without permission. It was something, at least. She hadn't blown this thing completely.

Sophia stared at Drew's abdomen. A light trail of hair began at his navel and disappeared into his underwear. With his jeans open, the tip of his erection extended beyond the waistband of his boxer briefs.

Her chest constricted. She didn't understand how a perfect stranger could affect her so profoundly. Sophia willed her hands to not shake as she slid her fingers between the soft skin of his hips and the cotton material covering him to push his clothing downward. She crouched, following his jeans to the floor, running her hands down his thighs and over his calves. He lifted one foot, then the other, so she could completely remove his clothes.

Glancing up, Sophia saw his hunger, stronger than before. Lowering the direction of her attention, she saw that his erection was perfectly positioned. It was a good size, both long and thick. She was seized with the urge to taste him. She fought it and won, but just barely.

He held out a hand to help Sophia to her feet. She ignored it, rising on her own steam. She was so wound up just from being near him that she could have run a marathon twice.

"Go stand next to the bed." She turned and walked away to secure Livia to the bed frame. It was a specially made bed with four sturdy posts. The head- and footboards were low. Each piece of wood had places to secure the different kinds of bindings she used. On Livia, she used soft, padded bindings that held together with Velcro. This was going to be difficult for her, and Sophia didn't want to add unnecessarily to Livia's discomfort.

As she leaned over the side of the bed, Sophia felt a hand wander down the denim of her shorts to caress a bare thigh. It was strong and warm and purposeful. There was nothing tentative in what he demanded with that touch. Moisture spurted between her thighs in response. Her body and her mind wanted the same thing. Only reason kept Sophia from acting on her base instinct to push him to the bed and devour every inch of his bare skin.

Without appearing to divert her attention too much, Sophia slapped away his hand. He earned a punishment for that. Part of the fun of breaking in a new submissive—if he was one—was teaching them the rules. Drew learned not to speak out of turn. Now, he would suffer the penalty for unauthorized touching.

When she was satisfied Livia was secure, Sophia pinned Drew with one of her deadliest gazes. "Lie next to her, on your side." She settled him in position, and then she took the same position on the opposite side. Lazily, she trailed her hand across Livia's collarbone. "Mirror me. Whatever I do on this side of her body, you do on your half."

He nodded his understanding. Sophia trailed her fingertips across Livia's skin. He followed her actions. Sophia pinched Livia's nipples, twisting them hard until she cried out. He did the same without taking his eyes from Sophia's. She traced a path to Livia's pussy and parted her lips. They caressed her clit from each side, squeezing it between their opposing fingers. Livia squirmed, fighting her restraints even as she moaned in ecstasy.

When Sophia slid her finger inside Livia, Drew did the same. More than was necessary, she glanced over to him. She told herself it was to make sure he was submitting as well as following directions, but she knew that wasn't the truth. He wasn't submitting as much as he was playing along, and she just liked looking at him.

Together, they set a slow pace. Sophia inserted a second finger, and so did he, twining them with hers. She couldn't look away from him. In an unspoken accord, they increased the pace. Livia's moans went unheeded.

"Mistress," she cried.

That gained Sophia's attention. Hastily withdrawing their fingers, Sophia pressed a kiss to Livia's cheek. "Not yet, Livia. Not yet."

It was time for Drew's punishment.

Sophia pushed herself into sitting and adjusted her tank top, which had become twisted as she moved next to Livia's body.

"Sophia?"

She liked the way he said her name. His voice sent pleasant shivers down her spine. She couldn't remember the last time that actually happened.

"Yes?" Half of her hoped he would say something outrageous, earning a more severe punishment. The other half was afraid of the same thing.

"I have pleasured two women before, quite successfully."

Sophia resisted smiling at his offer. "Haven't we all?"

He groaned and closed his eyes, and she knew her response was punishment enough. The image of Sophia with two beautiful, nude women was forever etched in his mind.

"Straddle her face," she directed. "You've earned a punishment."

Color drained from his face. She knew he was dreading what was to come. "You said I could ask questions."

"Touching, you idiot." Livia stirred at last. "You cannot touch Mistress without permission." She struggled to lift her head and meet Sophia's eyes.

Sophia hadn't known Livia was aware of Drew's wandering hands.

Livia needed to see her mistress's reaction to know if she would be punished for speaking out. Sophia knew her slave's need, but she did not show a reaction.

"I'm sorry, Mistress. He seemed much more intelligent last night, and he took direction so well."

Sophia was well aware of Drew's lack of true submission. This wasn't good. If she couldn't master Drew, she would drop in Livia's esteem. Her submissive would cease to respect her.

"From whom?" Sophia couldn't resist the question. Had Livia taken him to someone else last night?

"My boss." The two words were pronounced with a finality that invited no further questions. Sophia knew better than to get personal.

She respected his boundary and returned to the business at hand. "Straddle her face. I want to see your dick in her mouth." She didn't wait for his reaction. "Livia, take all of him. He's a little large, but nothing you can't handle."

She swatted Drew on the ass to get him moving. She would take any available excuse to touch those graspable half-moons. He looked at her curiously but didn't voice his question.

Sophia kept no pillows and no bedding beyond the sheet and mattress pad, so there was nothing to get in his way. Drew knelt over Livia, leaning forward to brace himself against the low headboard with one hand and feed himself to her with the other. Sophia watched to make sure he treated her right. Plus, the sight was erotic as all hell. She wanted to taste him. She wanted to slide her tongue along the slit in his head and lick away the precome.

She had to settle for this.

Livia's color was good, though Sophia could tell she only had another half hour in her.

Drew set a steady pace. Livia caressed him with her lips and tongue. If Sophia commanded, Livia would use her teeth as well.

Turning sharply on her heel, Sophia returned to her toy box. A brief rummage produced a leather paddle. The short handle widened into a six-inch rectangle of thick black leather. Its sharp sting left a nice red mark. She hadn't planned to use it, but Drew wasn't exactly following her plan.

She needed to know how much Drew could handle before he choked. This would be as much a test as a punishment. If he wasn't a true submissive, he would lose his erection during the punishment.

The moment was perfect. Lost in Livia, he couldn't prepare for the first stinging blow. Sophia swung, loving the sound of leather against flesh.

He cried out, stiffening and pausing in his movements.

"I did not give you permission to stop." She purred with pleasure, knowing she startled him. With the slightest inclination of his head, he acknowledged his gaffe and resumed pumping into Livia's mouth.

The next blow caused his rhythm to falter, but he recovered quickly. Sophia struck him again and again. He took the punishment with grace, but she didn't see any real signs of submission in him. Yet, she wanted him with a need that made her weak. That was another caution sign. Weakness wasn't a good thing in a dominatrix.

Livia's legs were still spread wide. Lowering her aim, Sophia whacked that drenched pussy with the paddle, using a lighter hand than she had with Drew's ass. Livia moaned loudly, bucking her hips clear off the bed. Given that her ankles were tied, that amount of movement was impressive. *Whack.* Thick juices wept from her hole, making the smacks echo wetly through the room.

This was how a submissive reacted to the paddle.

Using the side of the paddle, Sophia slid it through Livia's wetness, teasing that glistening little nub. "Livia, come for me, baby." Two more sharp smacks and she did, her hips stalling high above the mattress as the spasms shook her.

Sophia dropped the paddle to the floor and watched them, hoping the sight of her submissives doing exactly what she wanted them to do would calm her.

It didn't.

Jealousy seized Sophia. She wanted to be in Livia's place, only not tied down. She wanted Drew's lips on her body. She wanted him to fuck her with all the intense ferocity she saw in his face lingering just below the surface.

She had to stop this. She had never coveted one of her submissives' dates, not ever, no matter how hot they were. "Come," she commanded, and, with a loud cry, he did.

Reaching out, Sophia guided Drew back until he lay next to Livia, with his feet near her head. She thought he would be sated, but the hunger in his eyes told a different story. Somehow, she knew he wouldn't be satisfied until he had her.

This was about control. Not only did Sophia have to control her submissives, she had to control herself. There was no way she could allow Drew to have her and remain in control. But, oh, did she want to feel him between her legs.

Hastily, and before she could change her mind, Sophia unbuttoned her shorts and let them slide to her ankles. Her useless, drenched underwear followed. Those blue eyes lit, smoldering with icy heat, and his erection grew.

She unbound Livia and helped her sit up, massaging her shoulders as she brought them forward from their bound position. Because she wanted so badly to kiss Drew, she kissed Livia hard.

Livia responded, knowing it was Sophia's way of bestowing praise upon her. Sated, her return smile was sleepy. Sophia was going to make Livia give her more than the fifteen or twenty minutes of energy she had left. Livia was a remarkable woman. Sophia pushed the limits, and Livia repeatedly met the heightened expectations.

"Lick his balls," she directed, dropping a handful of condoms on the bed. "When you feel up to it, ride him."

Ignoring the way the heat in his eyes turned to iron, Sophia moved around the bed to park her knees on either side of his head. Hovering over him, she dipped one finger between the hot, swollen lips of her pussy and rubbed it around. The hunger returned, more intense as his understanding dawned.

"Sophia." It was an adoration and a plea. She withdrew her finger and slid it between his lips. He opened for her, licking away her juices with a desperate man's thirst.

The heat of his mouth traveled through her body. She needed to feel this on her pussy. She widened her position to lower herself to his mouth. He needed no direction. Reaching around her legs, he parted her and held her in place as his tongue lapped eagerly and expertly. She came much too quickly.

Sophia waited for him to stop, but he pulled her even closer, opened his mouth wider and sealed her to him. His tongue and teeth were everywhere, teasing and pushing and fucking. The sounds of pleasure vibrated through his mouth and into Sophia. She rode his face hard and fast, losing track of the number of times he made her climax.

"Mistress, may I come?"

Livia once again pulled Sophia back to herself. "Not yet." It was more for her and less for Livia. She was close to another orgasm. Drew's tongue delved deep inside, and his teeth scraped her clit.

"Come," she breathed. "Everybody come."

She never knew if Livia came, or Drew either. She assumed they did, but she was only aware of the things going on inside her. Never before in her life had she so completely lost track of her playmates' pleasure.

She didn't know how long she lay next to Drew, trembling, before she roused herself to go get a wet towel to clean his face. He looked at her as she wiped away her juices, but she couldn't meet his eyes. She tried to keep her movements aloof and her manner detached as she cleaned her submissives.

She didn't know if she was successful.

* * * *

Drew followed Livia to his silver Mercedes. He opened the door for the attractive blonde who caught his attention with her brash attitude and promised sex that would be like nothing he'd ever experienced. Neither of them were under the impression this was going to be more than one night.

Turning the key in the ignition, Drew glanced over at Livia. He'd lost interest in her the moment that dark-haired, dark-eyed beauty opened the door. Sophia might have pretended to be unaffected, but Drew knew better. Her eyes widened, and her nostrils flared, and then she licked her lips, all signs of arousal.

"Hungry?" Technically, this was a date and Drew knew how to treat a woman, whether or not she still held his interest. Livia had shown him a good time. Buying dinner was the least he could do.

"I could go for some coffee. Maybe something light."

It was past midnight. Plymouth had nothing open, so he headed toward Detroit. Places near the city stayed open later. He found a nice little café whose kitchen was still open. He could have taken her home and impressed her with gourmet coffee and award-winning desserts, but he didn't like to bring women to his home.

Even though it was a warm June night, Livia inhaled the steam from the coffee. She sighed. It wasn't a good sigh.

Drew eyed her warily. "Something wrong?"

The cup clattered softly on the table as she put it down. Livia enjoyed a bite of strawberry cheesecake before answering. "I honestly thought she wouldn't get the best of you."

One eyebrow lifted. He had taken everything Sophia dished out. "The best of me? What do you mean?"

"I didn't take you for a submissive, Drew. That's why I invited you." She nibbled another bite daintily, disappointment marring her smooth, sculpted brow.

Drew had no idea Livia's true age, and he had no interest in knowing. He recognized good plastic surgery when he saw it, but he held firm to the belief that a woman's age was her own business. "I was your guest, Livia. What did you expect me to do differently?"

The fork stabbed the cheesecake viciously. "I didn't expect you to just sit there and take it. I thought you were the take-charge kind, but you let Sophia call all the shots. You barely challenged her at all."

He took a sip of his iced cappuccino to give himself time to figure out an appropriate response. Livia was right. He wasn't a submissive. He didn't get off on pain, but he definitely liked watching Sophia dish it out. From what he saw, Livia seemed to like everything Sophia did to her. He honestly didn't understand why Livia wasn't on cloud nine.

Drew knew why he wasn't on cloud nine. Though Sophia had allowed him to taste her, he wanted more. He wanted to have her all to himself, with no distractions, no other sex partners. When he told her he could pleasure two women, he hadn't been bragging. However, he might have failed in this instance because Sophia was all he could seem to focus on.

He wanted to touch her. He wanted to show her that he was an extraordinary lover, that he could pleasure her relentlessly. He was glad she hadn't called a halt after that first climax. She hadn't resisted him when he pulled her closer and held her to him. Livia had ridden his cock, but it was only because Sophia filled his senses that he had orgasmed at all.

Setting the half-empty cup of subpar coffee on the table, Drew leaned closer to Livia. "Let me get this straight: You wanted me to turn the tables on your dominatrix? Why? She's the one who knows what gets you off, not me. I couldn't have done to you what she did to you, Livia. You enjoyed it, all of it."

Her lips twisted in bitterness, and her fork clattered to a stop on her plate. "I didn't want to. I want to be finished with her. I want to not need her the way I do. I wanted you to topple her, to show me she isn't what I think she is. Instead, you just reinforced my dependence on her."

He stared at her, incredulous. Though his attention had been focused on Sophia, it was difficult to miss the way Livia's body writhed and arched under Sophia's punishments. Her pleas for orgasm were hard to ignore.

"Why don't you just stop seeing her?" Drew frowned, his eyes falling on the half-eaten cheesecake, though he didn't see the dessert. "Can you stop seeing her? Does she own you, or something restrictive along those lines?"

Livia shook her head. "Sophia is very clear that she only has open relationships. I can go months without calling her. Then, when I do, she greets me as if it's only been a day. She's unflappable. I really thought you would be able to ruin her perfect control of every situation."

Later that evening, after Drew saw Livia safely home, he drove all the way back to Sophia's house. The neighborhood was filled with small, silent ranch houses cut from the same mold as Sophia's. The windows in her house were as dark and quiet as the rest of the windows on the deserted street.

Drew stared at the white brick house, wishing he'd forgotten something inside, wishing he had a reason to go back, to see her again. Livia hadn't offered Sophia's phone number after she told him she didn't want to see him again, not even for casual sex. He hadn't wanted to upset her further by asking.

But he would see Sophia again. He knew where she lived. Now, all he had to do was to find a way to establish contact without appearing creepy or stalkerish.

Yawning, he started his quiet car and headed home. He had somewhere to be tomorrow afternoon, and Jonas would shoot him on Sabrina's behalf if he was late.

Chapter 4

Sophia woke alone the next morning, by design. As soon as Livia and Drew were able, she made them dress and leave. Drew kept trying to catch her eye, but she was able to avoid him completely.

For the first time ever, Sophia found herself restless after a scene's completion. Normally, she was sated and exhausted. Now, every time she closed her eyes, images of Drew bombarded her. She didn't know what his kiss felt like, but her lips tingled anyway. When she finally fell asleep, he invaded her unconscious mind. Erotic dreams made her wake up with drenched underwear and an orgasm thumping between her legs.

She slept later than she intended. Her plan had been to wake early enough to go for a run before she had to be at Sabrina's house. Things didn't work out so well. She stumbled out of bed and down the hall of her single-story ranch house to her bathroom, dropping her soaked underwear down the laundry chute along the way.

After a quick shower, Sophia flew out the door hoping Sabrina would have lunch ready when she got there. Her hair was wet, so she wrangled it into a ponytail. It was thick and dark, and it would stay damp all day this way, but there was nothing she could do about it.

She was ravenous by the time she parked in the street in front of Sabrina's large house. Loud, raucous laughter came from the backyard, so she bypassed the front door and followed the long driveway around to the rear of the house.

Sabrina had a large wooden deck surrounded by some pretty spectacular flower beds. Next to the steps, a fledgling rosebush in full bloom climbed a trellis. A quick glance told Sophia that this was going to be a large wedding party. She recognized Ellen and her husband, Ryan, lounging on a pair of chairs, hands entwined. They would celebrate their tenth anniversary soon, and they still behaved like newlyweds.

Sabrina's sister, Ginny, and Ginny's wife, Lara, shared another lounge chair. Jonas's sisters and his brother-in-law were there, as well as a very handsome black man Sophia hadn't yet met. Jonas was nowhere in sight.

"Sophia." Sabrina saw her friend and approached with her hands extended in welcome. "I'm so glad you could make it."

She was too polite to comment on Sophia's lateness, but Ellen didn't have that problem. "It's about time," she teased. "You missed lunch."

Sophia's face fell. She would have killed for a saltine. Sabrina's arm came around Sophia's waist. "I had Jonas put away a plate for you," she said, shooting a reproving glance at Ellen. "Let's go inside and see where he put it."

Excited about the wedding, she chattered as she led Sophia inside, thanking her at least ten times for consenting to be her bridesmaid. The way she spoke, she made it seem like Sophia was doing her the greatest favor in the world. More from her conversations with Jonas than from Sophia's sessions with Sabrina, she knew her petite friend was nervous. For some reason, Sabrina had a hard time believing people really liked her.

The kitchen was huge, as were the rest of the rooms in the house. Cherry cupboards dominated one side of the room, but the theme continued as trim in the rest of it. Beige-and-pink marble countertops lightened the effect of the dark wood there and on the floor.

Jonas was in the midst of loading the leftovers in the industrial-sized refrigerator. Sophia heard someone else in there, and she saw a foot peeking out, but the wide door hid Jonas's helper from view.

Jonas looked up with a smile on his face that widened when he saw Sabrina. Sophia couldn't recall ever seeing him that happy. This was the first time she had been in a room with both Sabrina and Jonas at the same time. She almost didn't believe her eyes. He gave his wire-rimmed glasses an absentminded shove as he leaned down to kiss his wife and bride-to-be.

They made an odd couple to Sophia's way of thinking. Jonas towered over her by more than half a foot. He was lanky and lean, with curly blond hair and eyes that changed from light brown to olive green, depending on his mood. She knew his build was misleading. She'd seen him wield a whip for four hours straight with no more than a five-minute break between clients. He was one of the first Doms she ever met, and he taught her the basic rules for setting scenes and controlling submissives. She'd picked up a few things since he first mentored her, but the basic motivations and rules behind the scenarios were essentially the same.

"Congratulations," Sophia said. "It's about time you realized what a good thing you have going for you."

"I'm just thankful she's patient," he said, pulling Sabrina closer for a deeper kiss.

Sophia slid onto a high stool at the other end of the large island and rested her elbows on the counter. It was freezing cold. Spreading her palm over it and pressing downward, she imagined heating Drew's backside and laying him out on this icy surface.

The quiet clatter of a plate interrupted her thoughts. "Hungry?"

She looked up to find Jonas staring with an amused smile quirking his lips. He probably had already acted out that particular scenario with Sabrina. Sophia had no doubt he guessed the drift of her thoughts. "Thanks," she said. "Nice counter."

His only answer was a grin. Sabrina elbowed him sharply.

Their relationship amazed Sophia in so many ways. She couldn't figure out how Jonas had fallen for such a strong woman. She had to be a handful in the bedroom. Though she loved to be disciplined, she fought it each time. Sophia couldn't imagine Sabrina giving in to Jonas easily. Her thoughts drifted once again to Drew. She wondered what he would be like if it was just the two of them. Would he be truly submissive, or would he try to turn the tables?

"Would you like something to drink?" Sabrina asked. "We have pop, apple juice, water..." She glanced toward the open refrigerator. "Oh, and fresh lemonade. Drew made it. It's wonderful."

"Lemonade is fine." Sophia shook her head to clear away her thoughts. Now she was hearing his name everywhere.

Jonas handed something wrapped in aluminum foil toward the refrigerator and received a pitcher of lemonade in return. Sophia had been so absorbed in watching Jonas and Sabrina, and avoiding her own thoughts, that she had forgotten Jonas wasn't alone in the kitchen. The refrigerator door closed, and Sophia saw she had been wrong. Sabrina had said Drew, and she meant *Drew.* Her Drew.

No, he wasn't her Drew. He belonged to Livia.

He wasn't surprised to see her. It was likely he recognized her voice from the few things she said to Jonas or Sabrina.

Pieces fell into place. Of course, Sabrina had mentioned him before. Drew Snow was Ginny's business partner at Sensual Secrets and a longtime friend to both sisters. She made pastries and cakes, and he handled the cooking. He had a cooking show on Food Network, and Sophia had seen the commercials. No wonder she thought he belonged on television when she first saw him the night before.

"Sophia, this is Drew," Sabrina said, oblivious to the civil war in Sophia's head. So far, the sane half was winning. "Drew, this is Sophia."

Jonas poured a glass of lemonade as Drew and Sophia nodded uncertain greetings to one another.

Sabrina continued. "If you don't mind, we have some things to do to prepare for this afternoon. Will you be all right without us?"

Sophia nodded, and Sabrina led Jonas from the kitchen.

Utilizing her avoidance techniques, Sophia buried her head in her plate, eating with wild abandon. She attacked a green salad first.

She felt Drew's eyes on her, but he watched in silence until she made it to something that looked like casserole. Sliding onto the stool next to Sophia, he closed his hand over hers, halting her fork as it went back for more and setting a million little butterflies free in her stomach.

His fingers were long and strong. Tamping down an intense wave of desire, Sophia flashed a warning look and tried to extricate her hand.

"You're eating too fast. You're going to choke, or worse, not properly enjoy the many flavors on your plate." There was nothing flirty or teasing in his eyes or in his tone. He was serious, cheflike.

"I'm hungry," she said. She felt a little stupid for being so affected by him when he seemed more affected by the rate at which she ate than the fact he was touching her. "I didn't have breakfast."

"Another crime," he said as he eased the utensil from her grasp and speared some casserole. The loaded fork hovered near her lips.

Like last night, she couldn't tear her eyes from his. Like last night, she was too entranced by him. He expected her to part her lips, to allow him this intimate act, but she could not. Taking the fork from him, Sophia was careful not to let her skin brush against his. The scorching heat from his hands radiated outward, searing her anyway.

He watched her. Sophia saw him from the corner of her field of vision, but it wasn't enough to read his expression. After a minute, he shifted to face the counter, folding his hands neatly on the cold surface. Moisture flooded between her legs as she thought about how he would look, splayed in front of her, his skin burning from the heat of her whip.

He played with his hands, a nervous gesture. There was something he wanted to say, and Sophia was sure she didn't want to hear it. She had enough trouble controlling her own inappropriately timed desires.

"You don't have to keep me company," she said, offering him a way out.

Those hands rubbed the counter absently, and she remembered the way his hand felt on her thigh. She was jealous of the damn counter.

Finally, he spoke. "Last night was incredible."

Sophia froze for a millisecond and hoped he didn't notice. "I'm glad you enjoyed yourself. It was supposed to be fun."

"It was more than just fun, Sophia. I can't get you out of my mind."

Damn. Damn, damn, damn! He wasn't going to make this easy. If she let him, he would tell her he had trouble falling asleep or that his dreams were filled with images of her astride him. He was dating Livia. She had to be careful. "It was just a scene, Drew. We played, and now it's over."

"And if I want to see you again?"

Hunger deserted Sophia. She dropped her fork. "That's not possible."

"Why?"

He wasn't looking at her, and she refused to look directly at him. His fingers gripped the edge of the counter, pressed white as lilies. Sophia relented a little, softening her tone and turning toward him. She managed only to stare at his hands, but it was better than nothing. "You were Livia's guest last night, not mine. She is one of my submissives. Trust is paramount in our relationship. I would never poach one of her dates."

"Are you dating her?"Livia was a friend, a playmate. They had a relationship with certain expectations, but they weren't romantically interested in each other. Sophia's brows dipped together. "No, you are."

She could see he was about to argue. Vanillas didn't often understand the nuances of the sub/Dom lifestyle. Hell, subs and Doms frequently didn't understand them, either.

"We're friends, sort of," she continued. "Not the kind that hangs out and shares their personal problems, but the kind who fulfill certain needs in the other. Last night wasn't meant to be romantic, only fun."

He shook his head. "No, last night was her attempt to break away from you."

How in the world had he arrived at that conclusion? For a moment, self-doubt took over. In the past forty-eight hours, Sophia had lost two of her favorite submissives. She didn't invite many over to play. It was a blow to think she was going to lose another one, even one she only saw sporadically. "I don't understand."

"She wanted you to fail with me. She wanted me to turn the tables on you."

Sophia's instincts had been right. Drew wasn't a submissive, and Livia knew that fact before she brought him over. She pushed the plate away, knowing there was no way her once-voracious appetite would return, and folded her hands in her lap.

"She told you that?" Why hadn't Livia said anything to her? Why had she behaved as though Sophia still gave her bliss? It did explain her lapse, for which Sophia neglected to punish her. Maybe Livia saw the fact that Sophia rode her date's face as punishment? Or maybe the fact that nobody licked her this time was perceived as punishment? Sophia knew how much Livia loved oral sex, and that's the one thing she didn't get, but Sophia did.

Drew released his hold on the counter and rested his hand on hers. "Afterward. Believe me, I was floored when she said it. She never once indicated that she didn't love what you did to both of us."

Afterward. After she sent them home so she wouldn't be tempted by Drew. "What about you?" she asked suddenly. "Did you love what I did to both of you?"

"No. I didn't love what you did to both of us." His hand squeezed hers, holding it in place when she tried to withdraw. "I didn't love that I didn't get to have you the way I wanted to have you. When I told you I could pleasure two women, I meant it."

He did pleasure two women, at the same time. She didn't bring that up because she knew what he meant. He wanted more, and she couldn't give him more. She would call Livia later and sort things out. Sophia didn't like knowing she failed. Livia was supposed to be safe, someone Sophia could always count on.

For now, she changed the subject.

"Look, Drew, Sabrina and Jonas are two of my closest friends. I don't want to do anything that might mess up their special day. It's best if you and I forget we met last night and make a fresh start of things today."

A delighted smile lit Drew's face. Relief flooded Sophia. He was going to make this easy. He slapped a hand on her knee. "That's the best idea I've ever heard."

Chapter 5

When Sabrina and Jonas returned from wherever they went, they were laden with bags. Sophia leapt up to help them, looking for any excuse to put distance between herself and the undeniable chemistry she had with Drew. Just because they agreed on a fresh start did not mean she could give in to the desire she still felt for him. He was dating Livia, and Sophia could not betray her like that.

The twelve of them gathered in the cavernous living room. The two chairs were taken, so Sophia was forced to take her chances on one of the two extra-long white sofas in the room. Luckily, she found a place next to the arm. Ellen, her security blanket, settled on Sophia's other side.

Drew stood behind her, resting his arms on the back of the sofa so that, unless she leaned forward, she inadvertently brushed him every time she moved. It wouldn't have bothered her so much if she wasn't trying to get the idea of him in the role of a submissive out of her head. If he were truly hers, she would have had him stand behind her or sit on the floor to await her commands. Did he mean to send this signal?

Ginny took center stage and began talking. As the maid of honor, she was running the show. Sophia sneaked a glance at Sabrina to see how well this was sitting with her. She was a control freak. She squirmed a bit until Jonas took her hand and put it on his thigh. It was a dominating gesture, designed to keep her attention focused on him. She calmed immediately, probably unaware of what he had done and why.

Sophia wondered if Sabina knew how aware she and Ellen were of the exact nature of her relationship with Jonas? She was such a private person. Would it embarrass her? Sophia shook the thought away. It probably didn't. Jonas was an exhibitionist, and she knew they had visited exhibitionist clubs around the world. There was no way Jonas would have fallen in love with a woman who was unable to help him fulfill such a profound need.

"You okay?"

The question was whispered in Sophia's ear and sent quivers rocketing down her spine. She jumped, startled, and turned her head. Drew's face was inches away. His breath smelled of sweetened lemons. The lemonade had been tasty. Sophia wanted to know if it was just as good licked directly from his tongue. Flustered, she answered quickly. "I'm fine."

"You looked at Livia the same way last night."

Sophia knew better than to react. Last night never happened. Acknowledging it now would tell Drew she couldn't get him out of her head, either. "I have no idea what you're talking about. Is Livia your girlfriend?"

His smile was brief. "No. We went out once, and then she dumped me. Apparently, I wasn't dominating enough for her." Heat kindled in his eyes.

Sophia froze, something she had never really done before, but which she seemed to be doing a lot around Drew. Was he mocking her? She knew there was a hidden message, but she wasn't exactly sure as to the contents.

"Drew, flirt later," Ginny said, interrupting the dangerous trail of thoughts in Sophia's head. "Honestly, I can't take you anywhere."

Sophia was mortified. She felt like she had been caught kissing in the supply room in high school and the principal was making her call her dad to tell him what she had done.

Drew scowled at Ginny, but she was effective. He straightened, moving out of whisper range.

Ginny noticed Sophia's discomfort. "Sorry, Sophia, it's not personal. Drew's favorite sport is flirting."

Yes, well, with someone as handsome as him, it would be.

For the next hour, Ginny acquainted them with the contents of the gift bags Sophia helped Sabrina and Jonas carry into the room. Sophia's held an assortment of personal accessories she knew Sabrina had chosen to complement her dark hair and complexion. Each of the women had something similar, but with differing color palettes.

Ginny drew their attention to one of the small boxes in the bags. "You each have a BlackBerry with two years of service. Sabrina downloaded your schedules into them already."

Sabrina was generous, and she made a good living as an advertising executive, but Sophia was surprised. There were ten of these gadgets, each with two years of service, and this was just the beginning. How elaborate would their wedding be? Sophia had been a bridesmaid before. It usually involved dress fittings, a drunken trip to a Canadian strip club, and soothing the bride's nerves on the big day. She was good at soothing Sabrina's nerves. It's the reason she thought Sabrina had asked in the first place.

After giving them time to explore their new electronic toys, Ginny asked them each to open the calendar part. Sophia looked at the myriad demands on her time for the next six weeks. Fittings were scheduled, brunches, too. Bimonthly trips to the spa for massages, facials, manicures, and pedicures were included as well. She made a comfortable living between her two jobs, but this was going to be expensive.

Then she noticed the dancing lessons.

"Dancing lessons?"

She was so glad someone else said that with the exact same level of bewilderment she was feeling. She looked across the expanse of the room to see the black man on his feet.

"Sabrina, you have *got* to be kidding. Dancing lessons?"

She smiled at him, amused. "Yes, Ty, dancing lessons. I want us all to waltz at the reception. It will look fabulous, and Vanessa will be glad you finally learned something besides the Worm."

Sabrina had mentioned Ty before. He worked for her. Since Jonas had also worked for her for a few months, he must have struck up a friendship with Ty during that time. He was wicked cute. Sophia wanted to wonder if he and Vanessa were subs, but images of Drew popped up any time she tried to imagine a scene.

As they argued good-naturedly, Ellen nudged Sophia with her elbow. "It's Tuesday nights," she whispered. "We'll have to adjust your work schedule."

Sophia's shoulders sagged a bit further. "That's the night I have Ventana and Montez." Miguel Ventana and Cherry Montez were a couple who came in every single Tuesday and would only see her. Cherry had been Jonas's client until Ellen fired him.

"Shit," she said. "I'll call them and break the news." She checked the calendar on the BlackBerry. "It's only for six weeks. Do you think you can do another night? They can do Mondays in a pinch. I don't want to overwork you. I know how important your days off are to you with working the two jobs. You need time to recharge and have a personal life."

She didn't want to give Ellen an opening to chastise her about not having a steady boyfriend. Just because her meddling worked with Sabrina and Jonas didn't mean Sophia craved that kind of thing in her life. She wasn't ready to settle down and get serious. Luckily, Sabrina saved her.

"Sophia, Jonas will work Monday nights for you. That way you won't lose any pay and Ellen won't lose any clients." She was sitting across the room from Sophia and Ellen, next to Ty, so everyone heard her.

Sophia didn't have a problem with it. Except for Ty, she was sure the rest of them knew she, Jonas, and Ellen were all Doms.

Next to Sophia, Ellen bounced up and down with glee. "Fabulous. Cherry will love it."

"You're a dominatrix?" This unexpected question came from behind.

Sophia turned to see Drew, looking a lot shocked and a little betrayed. She didn't understand. He knew firsthand what she was.

"Drew," Ginny groaned, "shut up. It's none of your business."

His mouth set in a grim line, and his eyes shot icicles into Sophia's bloodstream. Ignoring Ginny and the rest of the group, he pulled her roughly to her feet and dragged her from the room.

He was both bigger and stronger. She couldn't break his hold. In less time than she would have thought, they crossed the length of the room and the door to Sabrina's office slammed shut behind them.

"What do you think you're doing?" she demanded. She wasn't afraid of him, or even angry. She was baffled by his behavior and curious as to his explanation. If he really tried anything, she could take him down in seconds. Plus, she knew if she shouted, there were ten people in the next room who would come to her rescue.

He let go and paced from one side of the room to the other, running his fingers through his short hair.

"You knew I was a dominatrix before you met me," she said in an attempt to make him talk. She hated that he made her feel anxious.

He stopped, peering at her through narrowed eyes. "I didn't know you charged for the privilege."

Sophia's temper got the better of her. She took him down with a pinch hold Ellen taught her the first day on the job. "Listen very carefully, Drew Snow. What I do for a living and what I do with my time is absolutely none of your business. Like your good friend Jonas used to do, I work for Ellen as a dominatrix. People pay me to tie them up and whip them because I am very, very good at it."

Why did she explain after she insisted it was none of his business? She knew what he thought. He thought she was a prostitute, just like Sabrina had when she first met Sophia. Then, she found it mildly amusing. Just now, she wasn't amused. Deep down, she wanted Drew to be submissive. She wanted him to respect her as his dominatrix. He wasn't showing any kind of submission or respect just now. If she wasn't forcing him to his knees, he probably would have been doing something aggressively male and dominating, like shaking her or pissing on her.

His pallor wasn't good. Sophia released her hold on the sensitive shoulder nerve and helped him to his feet. He breathed against the pain, but she didn't care. She would likely have bruises on her upper arms where he handled her.

When his breathing evened out, he shot her a resentful look. "Jonas didn't work out of his home."

Her fist formed and buried itself in his stomach before she had time to think. Air leaked from him with a swift whoosh, and he doubled over. Blood rushed to his pale face.

"What I do in the privacy of my own home is absolutely none of your business. If this is your way of trying to piss me off, you've succeeded."

A knock sounded on the door. Jonas called through the thick wood, "You okay in there?"

"Fine," Sophia said, flinging the door open. "He might need some help." She intended to leave, but Jonas pushed her into the room and closed the door.

When two Doms are in a room as filled with tension as this one, one of them invariably assumes the role of leader. Jonas was ten years older than Sophia and had loads more leadership experience. Plus, he was her mentor. It was natural for her to defer to him.

"It seems to me the two of you have met before. I saw it in your eyes in the kitchen, but for the life of me, I couldn't remember introducing you. I asked Sabrina, and she couldn't, either." He looked from Sophia to Drew expectantly.

She sighed and spilled. If he wanted to ask either or both of them to back out of the wedding, she'd rather he did it now than after she spent all that time at the spa with Sabrina. "Livia came over last night with her latest boy toy." Sophia inclined her head toward Drew.

Jonas's green eyes lit with understanding. He looked at Drew. "I didn't think you were into that kind of thing."

Drew shrugged. It was a defensive gesture disguised as nonchalance that didn't fool anyone, except maybe Drew. "When a beautiful woman invites me to a threesome with another beautiful woman, I never turn her down."

Now Sophia felt defensive, and she hated feeling defensive. Livia had to have told him Sophia was a dominatrix. Had she framed the invitation as more of a threesome thing in order to get someone who was clearly not a submissive into the playroom? What was going on inside her pretty head that she would do something like that? Sophia needed to talk to her in the worst way.

She threw her hands in the air. "I followed protocol, Jonas. I made sure he knew exactly what he was getting himself into before I let him beyond the living room."

Jonas put a reassuring hand on her shoulder. She stiffened, but she didn't flinch. "I know." Now, he pinned Drew with a questioning gaze. "What's the problem?"

Drew locked his eyes with Jonas's, challenging his authority in this matter. "This is really none of your concern."

"It's natural to feel a strong connection to your first dominatrix, Drew." Jonas kept his tone calm and level. "If you want Sophia to train you, then you're going about it all wrong."

"Train me?" He looked from Jonas to Sophia for an explanation.

Sophia shook her head. Real submissives felt a need in their core. It was unmistakable and inescapable. A good dominatrix recognized it immediately under the right circumstances. Sophia didn't see it in Sabrina until Ellen thrust her into the training arena for her first whipping. *Christ.* Maybe she wasn't as good as she thought she was. She hated feeling insecure.

"I don't think it was anything more than amusing for him. He just wants to sleep with me. It wasn't in the cards last night."

"I have a question." Drew directed his statement toward Jonas.

Perching his hands loosely on his hips, Jonas looked to Sophia for permission. He wasn't going to undermine her authority in Drew's eyes. She wanted to smack him for being so stubbornly obtuse.

Like a good submissive, Drew followed Jonas's lead. His attention came to rest on her. She caught glimpses of this streak in Drew the previous night. She still wasn't sure he had it in him to be a sub, and she didn't want to let herself entertain fantasies in that direction. Flashes of his face between her legs made her knees weak with need.

"Ask it," she ordered. Damn Jonas. Now she was stuck with this role. There was no way to cut him loose without running the risk of ruining Sabrina's big day. A fledgling submissive needed a trainer. Sophia made a mental note with large, flashing neon letters. She was going to get Jonas back for this.

"How much do you charge for training?"

The question had an edge she recognized as jealousy. A string of curses flowed through her brain. She was going to have to deal with that unreasonable emotion first. She absolutely hated this kind of relationship with a submissive. They were so damn needy. He had to learn that this was only play and that she did not belong to him.

Jonas's eyebrows shot skyward. He pointed toward a drawer in the desk. "You might find something useful in there to help explain the price of training. We're going to take a break in the kitchen for about a half hour." Without another word, he left the room, closing the door tightly behind him.

Sophia didn't move to lock it. Nobody would dare interrupt. She looked over at Drew, noted the dangerous set of his lips, and then crossed the room to check out the contents of the drawer Jonas indicated.

They were different kinds of Doms, Jonas and Sophia. She doubted he had any of the materials she really wanted to use on Drew. She hoped he had something she could use to remind Drew what kind of punishment was coming.

Though she hadn't wanted to take on a new submissive, she knew she had already changed her mind. Her nipples hardened and her pussy pulsed with anticipation. With one impulsive act, Drew overrode her reluctance to engage in a sexual relationship with him.

God, how she wanted to fuck him!

Now, she only needed his permission. More than wanting it, Drew had to ask for it. The drawer yielded various restraint devices, illustrating the differences between her style and Jonas's. Sophia liked to use toys of all kinds. She liked to dominate multiple partners. He and Sabrina were so tame in comparison. She wasn't even fully aware of all the ways in which he dominated her, and he likely preferred it that way.

Sophia wanted Drew to know exactly what she was doing to dominate him.

Digging deeper into the drawer, she found a short whip. Lifting it, the strips of leather spilled over one another like a waterfall. She'd used a similar one on Livia the night before. She didn't want to hurt him, just teach him a lesson.

Sophia lifted the whip from the drawer and set it on the desk in plain sight. Then she looked up at Drew. He had watched silently, his blue eyes clouding with worry, probably wondering what she planned to do next. The secret she could never tell him was that she was making it up as she went along. Submissives needed to trust that their needs were going to be met, that their Dom knew exactly what she was doing. Sophia hadn't expected to see Drew today, and she had never taken on someone to train.

Rounding the desk, she stopped inches from Drew. Sparks crackled between them. He would be hers before the night was over, or they would both go up in flames. She placed her hand gently on his cheek and searched his face for consent.

"Tell me what you want, Drew." She kept her voice low and sultry, directing him in the same tone she would use to praise him during and after sex.

He leaned down to kiss her. In that second, she faltered. She hadn't kissed him last night. She knew only what his lips felt like between her legs. Her breasts swelled as he moved closer, wanting to feel him against her, wanting that intimacy.

Drawing on her reserves, she regained control before any permanent damage was done. He couldn't know how much she wanted his kiss. The hand on his cheek slid to cover his mouth. "No touching without permission." She made no attempt to move him away from her, but she did drop her hand. She needed his senses to be filled with her. "Be honest, Drew. Tell me what you want."

He shoved his hands into the pockets of his jeans, restraining himself. When he spoke, his sweet breath fanned her lips, her cheek, and her chin. "I want to kiss you, Sophia. I want to touch you all over with my hands and my mouth. I want to know the taste of every square inch of your body. I want to feel you beneath me, naked, as I thrust into you slowly and deeply. I want to watch your face when you come and know I gave that to you."

Sophia smiled, a serenity settling over her as he tried to seduce her with words. Oh, man, he was good. She might enjoy this more than she thought. She parted her lips ever so slightly. Drew's breathing sped up as the heat between them increased. "Do you want to know what training entails?"

He nodded. Remembering her earlier warning, he also vocalized his answer. "Yes."

"Take your shirt off, and get on your knees."

He slipped his light cotton shirt over his head. For the first time, she noticed it said Sensual Secrets in faded print across the chest. How had she missed that earlier?

He dropped to his knees, settling automatically back on his heels.

"Eyes on the floor in front of you." She waited for him to comply. "This is the position in which you will wait for me to discipline you."

He tensed.

"Yes, Drew, you have definitely earned another punishment. You'll get some of that now, but I'll save the majority of it for later."

His chin lifted. He gasped. "Sophia…"

"Mistress," she corrected. "You have not earned the right to use my name."

The tip of his tongue darted out, licking his bottom lip. She wanted to suck on it too badly. "Mistress…"

"Not yet, Drew. First, we have some rules to discuss. Pay attention because I do not care to repeat myself. Breaking any of the rules will result in punishment."

He lowered his eyes automatically, already submitting in small ways. It was a beginning. She could already see that sexual torture would be more effective with him than whipping.

"Four nights a week, people come to me, and they pay a lot of money to be tied up and whipped. You will never come to me there." She wanted to add that she didn't want to see him there at all, that she didn't want anyone else touching him, but that would be going too far.

Leaning over, she snagged the whip from the desk and moved to stand behind him. He tensed anew. His hands came out of his pockets to clench on his thighs.

She ran the tips of the leather tongues over his shoulders, watching them twitch at the caress. "You're special, Drew. I don't usually care to train new submissives, but I can't seem to resist this challenge." He wasn't going to submit easily. In other subs, that was a deterrent. With Drew, it was somehow different. Even now, he fed her need to be in control as he fought his need to be in control.

Sophia licked her lips, knowing he was completely unaware of just how nervous she was. "Work is purely business. My time with you is pleasure and pain. Make no mistake, this will not be easy for you. I am demanding. I expect complete obedience, and my punishments always exact a price."

He started at her use of the word "price," and a slow blush crept up his chest. Her heart sang to see he realized his mistake. She wanted there to be no question that she didn't have sex in exchange for money.

Cupping one palm under his chin, she lifted his face. "And when you are a good boy, Drew, when you do exactly as I want, the rewards are worth it."

The muscles in his jaw relaxed, and he swallowed. The clouds were gone from his eyes, replaced with smoldering flames. He wanted her.

"No matter what happens between us, there is no romantic relationship implied. You and I are friends, nothing more. You are free to date and do as you please when you are not with me, and so am I. The only restraint I put on you is that you cannot come without my permission. This means you can't have sex with your date unless I say you can, and you can't masturbate unless I say you can."

From the heat in his eyes, he didn't see that to be a problem. Sophia didn't react. He would find out what that rule would cost him all too soon. Given his reputation, she expected him to start dating again within a week after she slept with him, which she planned to do later that evening. She couldn't wait to punish him *and* his date.

"I advise you to date women or men open to threesomes, darling."

The wheels in his head were turning. He likely wanted to know what rumors she heard about him to make her leave the gender of his date open-ended. She wasn't going to tell him she was guessing. Of course, she had overheard Ginny and Sabrina talking about how Drew liked to date couples, but she wasn't going to get into that with him here and now. Neither of them knew specifics, and Sophia wasn't going to pretend she did.

She released his chin and drew the stiff handle of the whip across his shoulders. "Do you have any questions before I carry out your punishment?"

"Yes." His voice was husky and low with desire. It affected her too much.

She leaned against the desk behind him, wanting to give him safety and space, but not too much. "Ask them."

"I know Jonas and Sabrina do this kind of thing, but they keep it in the bedroom. I've seen other people who take this sort of 'friendship' public. Given my career, I can't have this public, especially not when I'm in a submissive role where I'm not sure I belong. We're in a wedding together, which means we'll be together in public. How do I know when I'll have to watch my behavior or risk your wrath?"

While she didn't hide who she was or what she did for a living, she wasn't a publicly demonstrative person, either. "All punishments will be administered privately. I expect that when we're together in public, you treat me with dignity and respect. If we're with one another, you must be next to me. You showed some natural submissiveness by standing behind me this afternoon."

He turned sharply to glare at her. "I'm standing because my ass is too sore to sit for long."

Sophia smiled in response to his discomfort. Whether he knew it or not, he had been standing next to her because he felt a bond with her. The room was vast, and there were many other places to stand. "You'd better get used to it, Drew. I'll leave you sore more times than not."

He exhaled in resignation and turned back, facing away from Sophia, just as she had positioned him. It was the price of being with her. "Mistress, you still didn't answer my question. How do I know?"

Closing the space between them, she leaned down to whisper in his ear. "The game is always on until one of us calls a time-out. It's a game, Drew.

It's sensual and sexual. It'll push you past the limits you thought you had into something unbelievable, but it's just a game. What's the safe word?"

"Onion." He was hoarse. It was a good sign.

"That's the word that will halt the action. It only starts up again when we both agree to start it again."

She dipped her head so that her breath fanned on his neck below his earring. He trembled. "This game only works when we have clear rules and clear boundaries."

He tilted his neck ever so slightly, opening himself to her. "How often will I get to see you?"

Sophia shrugged and stood up, moving away from him. "Whenever. I work. You work. I have a social life. You have a social life. I'm thinking once or twice a week."

The pulse on his neck ticked faster. "What if that's not enough for me?"

"If you want to see me, it never hurts to ask." She chuckled at her own joke. The handle of the whip itched in her hand, begging to be used. "Are you finished?"

Slowly, he turned, twisting until his eyes met hers. "May I kiss you?"

Hunger emanated from every pore of his body, knocking the breath from her. She wanted him to kiss her, but she knew she wouldn't be the one in control if he did. She needed to keep that secret from him as long as she could. The game was over as soon as he found out just how profoundly he affected her, and the damn man had yet to touch her.

"No, but I will make it part of your punishment."

Drew sighed, and his laugh was self-deprecating. "I don't remember the last time I did anything so desperate for a kiss. But, good God, Sophia, I can't get you out of my head. I can't stop imagining what your lips feel like on mine. I want to know if your mouth tastes as sweet as your pussy."

The obvious punishment would be a whipping, but she knew there wasn't enough time to make him sorry. Last night's spanking hadn't seemed to affect him much. When they rejoined the rest of the guests, most of them would look at Drew to see how he was coping with the discipline.

Sophia fixed him with an impish smile. "Are you aware that most of the people out there know exactly what I'm going to do to you?"

Anxiety made his eyes wide. Now she had him.

"Stand up and drop your pants."

With excruciating slowness, he rose, never taking his eyes from her. He fought for courage, or at least to camouflage his apprehension. The result was a total lack of emotion. She couldn't have that. The success of their games depended on him opening his feelings completely. It confirmed that whipping him was not the wisest course of action. She had to bring his emotions back into play.

She circled behind him. The tinny scrape of metal announced his snap was open. The zipper followed, and he pushed the loose denim down his legs. Hooking her fingers in the waistband of his cotton boxers, she sent them fluttering as well.

As she expected, the physical marks of his spanking were gone. The soreness was in the muscle. Since he was her responsibility, she needed to know if he was bruised or just sore. Plus, it gave her another chance to feel him up. She ran her fingertips over the smooth skin of his incredibly tight ass, keeping her touch light.

"Are you terribly sore?"

"If I am, will it make you go easier on me?" The deep-throated huskiness of his voice caught her attention. He was aroused, which was what she intended.

"No."

He ran a hand through his hair. She wanted to order him to grow it longer so she could have some silky blond locks to hold on to, but that was crossing a boundary.

"I didn't think so."

Without taking her hands from him, she returned to his front. His eyes were closed, and his cock was fully erect. The only clothing on him pooled around his ankles. He was magnificent. She traced her fingers up his chest, loving the firm feel of him and the distinct scent of his soap and aftershave.

Placing her hands on either side of his head, she tilted his face to hers. His eyes opened in surprise as she brushed a feathery kiss across his lips. It was quick. She left him no time to respond, to kiss her back.

He wasn't breathing when she knelt before him, and he gasped as she licked the length of his cock. She toyed with him, teasing with tongue and teeth. From the corners of her eyes, she watched as he struggled to keep his hands away from her. If he touched her, the punishment would stop.

The analytical part of Sophia stayed in control. She could not afford to lose herself in his flavor and texture. This was a punishment. She closed her mouth around him, taking him deep and sucking hard until he moaned.

Then she stopped.

She pushed herself to standing. Drew gazed at her through half-closed eyelids. His face was flushed, and his breathing was abnormal. She smiled. Before she could tell him to get dressed, he pulled her to him, crushing her in his arms as his lips claimed hers in a kiss that singed Sophia to her bones.

He kissed with his whole body. Completely wrapped in his arms, she felt safe and exposed at the same time. She couldn't have stopped that kiss if she wanted, and she sure as hell didn't want to.

When he released her, they were both trembling. She stepped out of his arms, needing distance in order to gather her thoughts and catch her breath. "Get dressed."

A cocky smile lifted the corners of his lips and lit the brilliant blue of his eyes. He lifted his pants over his still-erect penis and snapped them into place. "I suppose I've earned another punishment for that?"

"Yes," she said regretfully. She scooped his shirt up from the floor near her feet and tossed it to him. "I'll see you tomorrow night."

His jaw dropped, and he froze in the midst of pulling on his shirt. "Tomorrow?"

She smiled serenely at the underlying desperation there. She had planned to have him over that night, but she couldn't reward this kind of behavior. She paused with her hand on the doorknob. "Don't forget, Drew: no masturbating."

"If I do?"

"You do seem intent on learning the hard way," she said, opening the door. "Care to try me?"

He followed her out a few minutes later and took his position behind her. He was quiet for the remainder of the afternoon.

Chapter 6

Sabrina cornered Sophia after most people left. Her coral shirt perfectly matched her lips and nail polish. Sophia was amazed at how well put together Sabrina always appeared. She frequently wished she was as self-possessed, but she wasn't. Everybody hides an insecurity. Sophia lived in mortal fear that someone would find out that she wasn't in complete control and that she spent more time running from relationships than anything else. Even friendships made Sophia uncomfortable.

She wrapped a tentative hand around Sophia's upper arm. "Sophia, what on earth did you do to Drew?"

Before she could say a word, namely, that it was none of her business, Jonas interrupted. "Honey, I can't believe you actually asked that."

Sabrina turned on Jonas, impaling him with a look that shut him up. Sophia really didn't understand their relationship. How could Sabrina be the submissive but still have such power over Jonas? How could he be a dominant and be okay with that?

"He looked so lost and desperate. I've known Drew for almost fifteen years, and I've never once seen him so...so...upset."

Sophia repressed a proud grin and met Jonas's eyes over her head. "I told him I was too busy tonight to see him." Then, she closed her eyes and swore, her moment of pride gone. Tomorrow was her brother's birthday. She had plans to meet Daniel and their parents for dinner. These things always ran late, and she had to get up early Tuesday for work.

The white brick ranch house was empty when Sophia got home, not that she expected anything else. Flipping through the channels on her television, she stumbled into an airing of Drew's show. She watched the last ten minutes of the episode without moving.

Those ice-blue eyes stared out of the flat screen, ensnaring her. Sophia was certain he was looking directly at her, that his flirty smiles were meant exclusively for her. Of course, they weren't. He hadn't even known her when he taped these episodes. His smiles were meant for the masses. The knowing glint in his eye was for someone else.

Climbing into bed later that night, Sophia quelled the possessiveness she felt toward Drew, burying it deep inside with the rest of her shameful secrets. Yet when she slid her vibrator deep inside, it was the feel of Drew's body against hers that propelled her to orgasm.

Sabrina had thoughtfully loaded the numbers of each member of the wedding party into the BlackBerrys, having had each of their cell numbers transferred to the new account. Sophia waited until the next morning to text Drew. She turned on the phone to find three messages.

The first was from Sabrina. She apologized for being so presumptuous. Sophia and Drew were adults, and she very much hoped they could be happy together.

Sophia knew Jonas hadn't put her up to it. She would never make one of her subs apologize to anyone but her. She'd learned that from Jonas. Every successful relationship respected boundaries.

The hesitation in Sabrina's voice made Sophia wonder if she doubted Sophia or Drew, or the two of them together.

The second was from her mother. She wondered what Sophia was getting Daniel for his birthday, and she wanted to remind Sophia to be at the restaurant at six sharp. She didn't call her mother back.

The third was a text from Drew: *I would rather have had you whip me.*

The grin on her face didn't fade as she showered and dressed. On the way to the mall, she tried to figure out the best way to break the news to him without driving him away. She didn't want him to think she was playing the wrong kind of games. How could she establish the necessary trust if he couldn't rely on her?

Sophia was in agony. Even thinking about how successful her unorthodox punishment had been didn't cheer her up. The only time she had free in the next three days was Thursday during the day…unless he could come over today before she had to meet her family. Her grin returned. She sent him a text and hoped he got it in time.

Change of plans. I'm busy this evening. I can't see you today unless you can be at my house by one.

She hit send and left it in the hands of fate.

Daniel wanted the complete collection of Bruce Lee movies on Blu-ray. If she hadn't been so invested in her procrastinator status, Sophia would have shopped over the Internet and had them delivered to her house. Now, she was stuck with whatever she could find at Twelve Oaks Mall, which was not a complete collection. Hopefully, it would be enough. She and Daniel had always been close. He was a good person and a good friend. He owned his own karate studio where she taught a women's self-defense class on Wednesday nights.

Traffic made her late in arriving home, and pessimism made her sure Drew hadn't received her text in time. He hadn't responded.

Nobody was on her porch when she pulled into the driveway, and she had no idea what Drew's car looked like. However, she did recognize Daniel's truck in the street out front. He had a key to her house. She expected to find him waiting inside, but she was baffled that he didn't call or text to find out what time she planned to return home. Sophia had a notorious reputation for being late.

Sophia parked in the garage and entered through the door to the kitchen. Since she also stopped by the grocery store, her arms were laden with bags. Daniel rushed to help when she opened the door.

He was tall, nearly six feet, and thickly muscled, taking after their father with his larger build. He mirrored their father in other ways as well. Like Sophia, he had their father's thick, dark brown hair that looked black in certain lights, and deep brown eyes that were sometimes hard to read.

He clipped his hair short, letting his cowlick stick straight up over his right eye. On him, it looked charming. When they were younger, Sophia used to tease him mercilessly about it, to the point where he kept his head shaved through most of high school. Enough of his girlfriends had commented on how sexy it was since then that he let it grow.

He was ten months older than Sophia, and she couldn't remember a time when they hadn't been close.

"Don't look in the bags," she warned. "You'll ruin the surprise."

"I can see you put a lot of thought into this," he teased.

"Well," she explained, "I knew what I wanted to get, but I haven't had the time to get to the store."

"Yeah, that stable of submissives requires a lot of maintenance." He dug into a bag of vegetables she set near the refrigerator, automatically helping even though she hadn't asked.

Sophia knew he was teasing, but she wasn't feeling up to it. She'd lost two subs over the weekend, she had no idea what was going on with Livia, and Drew wasn't waiting on her front porch when she got home. "I'm down two subs, Dan. Christopher got a girlfriend."

The pair made short work of her shopping excursion. He cracked open a can of pop and regarded her solemnly. "When you started doing all this stuff, I didn't say anything, Sophie. I'm your brother and your friend. I love you no matter what. However, I do have to say that I don't understand why you can't settle down with one person. You and Chris were together for what? A year?"

She nodded. That sounded right. It was useless to tell Daniel that she had never dated Christopher. They played, that's all.

"You don't even seem upset that he dumped you for someone else. Something else is bothering you."

The sound of a car pulling into her driveway distracted them both. Daniel was in a better position to look out the front window. A car door closed, and his expression turned grim.

He set his half-empty can on the counter and grabbed his keys. "Looks like another one of your 'friends,' Sophie."

Her heart leapt into her throat, and her eyes flared. She didn't need a mirror to know the depth of the transformation Daniel saw in her demeanor. His curiosity was proof enough. The doorbell chimed. Daniel beat her to it. He wasn't usually nosy about her sexual exploits, and she afforded him the same privacy. He held open the door, beckoning Drew inside.

The two studied one another intently. Though they had similar builds, the two men were a study in surface contrasts. Drew was blond and light. Daniel was olive-complexioned, just like Sophia. However, delving deeper brought to light a similar reputation for playing the field. If Ginny and Sabrina had told her nothing else about Drew, they definitely let her know he had a new girl on his arm every time they saw him. Ginny rarely bothered to learn their names.

Drew said absolutely nothing to Daniel. He was probably grateful for her rule about staying silent. From the myriad expressions that crossed his face, she could tell he was sizing up Daniel and trying to figure out his place in her life.

Daniel dismissed Drew pretty quickly. He turned to Sophia, his expression serious. "I'd love to stick around, Mistress, but I have things to do. Don't be late tonight. I guarantee you will not like the punishment."

Sophia rolled her eyes. "Drew, wait for me downstairs."

Drew tore his gaze from Daniel with obvious reluctance. Narrowed eyes containing a thinly veiled warning pinned her briefly as he brushed past her.

She waited until he was safely out of earshot before she gave voice to the glare she shot at Daniel. "That was mean."

He looked at her funny. "That's ironic coming from the woman who is going to strip him naked and make him look like a candy cane."

She hadn't decided if she was going to whip him or not. Maybe he wouldn't kiss her like that again if she did. "You never said why you dropped by."

"I was going to ask you for relationship advice, but I decided against it." Without waiting for her reaction, he pushed open the door and left.

The idea that Daniel would ask for relationship advice took Sophia by surprise. Daniel hadn't stuck with one woman for more than a couple of months for as long as she could remember. Their parents were going to celebrate thirty years together in the fall, and neither of their children spent any time looking for a permanent relationship.

Maybe they both knew something like what their parents had was impossible to find.

Sophia shrugged away those concerns. Drew Snow was naked and waiting for her. She locked the doors and hopped down the stairs with an extra spring in her step. Except for the three rooms her father helped her build along the far side, her basement was a wide-open space. One room was for laundry, one was a bathroom, and the other contained Drew.

Pushing open the door, she found him kneeling in the center of the room, naked. Hard, tense muscles corded his entire body. Those lush lips pressed together, not quite hiding his jealousy. Nostrils flared, and thick lashes hid the fury in his eyes.

Instantly, Sophia was wet. This did not bode well for her ability to hold out against him for very long. She had wanted to get home before him so that she could change into something sexy. When she dressed to go shopping, she did so for comfort. She wore a cream-and-brown patterned cotton dress that came down to her knees and brown leggings that covered her to the ankles. She looked cute in earth tones, not sexy.

She leaned against the door frame. "You're late."

"You didn't look like you were hurting for company." He growled the words to the floor.

His vehemence had the effect of pouring ice water over her head. She snapped out of sex mode and into dominatrix mode. It was a good thing, too. He could have seduced her so easily, rendering her domination of him ineffective. "If you're ever late again, I will send you home. I do not tolerate lateness."

"I don't suppose, *Mistress*, that you know I work over an hour away from here. I didn't get your message until after twelve. A little more lead time might be nice." Again, he growled.

He had a point, but she wasn't about to concede. She needed to deal with his attitude first. "Next time, you may call or text me if the time is inconvenient." She planned for them to have three hours together. They might get two now, if they were lucky. She longed to bind his wrists and ankles with thick leather just to see those muscles straining for freedom.

Drew lifted his eyes to her for the first time. "I don't know if I can do this."

He was nervous. Sophia almost sagged with relief. She could deal with nervousness. Impertinence was something else altogether. Given his behavior, she thought she wouldn't be able to fuck him. Now, she knew she could. She just had to punish him first.

She closed and locked the door. Daniel wasn't the only family member with keys to her house, and her parents had no idea what she did down here. They thought it was an odd place to put another guest bedroom. It was soundproof and sparsely furnished. The bed was bare, and the single set of shelves held various-sized boxes where she kept her tools and toys. The walls were a warm dark beige, designed to melt into the background.

Eyeing the shelves, Sophia shook her head. She didn't want to use toys with Drew, not their first time together. She wanted him to appreciate her without the toys before she blew his mind with them.

She let her hands wander over his shoulders and chest. Muscles rippled and twitched beneath the gentle glide of her fingers, and his cock lengthened. He felt so damn good. A soft tap under his chin and he responded, lifting his face to look at her.

"Did you enjoy your punishment?"

A skirmish waged behind his eyes, and she had no doubt as to the cause. He wanted to deny that her refusal to see him last night mattered. She ran a single fingertip over his lips. They parted ever so slightly, and his moist breath heated her.

Finally, he opted for honesty. "No."

Though sending him home had been just as hard on Sophia, it was an effective punishment. He hadn't reached for her once despite the strong desire defined in the tense lines of his body. She favored him with a sympathetic smile, tilting her head to the side ever so slightly. "But you learned your lesson. You're being very good right now."

"Thank you, Mistress."

"Stand up." She wanted to check his ass. "Are you still sore?"

He didn't tower over her. They were the same height, but he was in his bare feet, and she wore heels. She stood inches from him. The heat of his body fed a need she'd never felt before. He lifted his eyes to meet hers. "No."

She kissed him. She couldn't remember the last time she found it so hard to keep her hands away from a sub. She could go weeks without touching a sub and still end the scene with orgasms for everyone.

Like last night, he wasn't passive. He allowed her to control the kiss, but somehow he made her feel things other than attraction and desire. Something tingled deep inside, spreading through her abdomen and making her weak. She didn't want to think about what that meant. She just wanted this from him. She wished he would wrap his arms around her, but he didn't.

Drew made a little sound in the back of his throat, the beginnings of a moan. An answering mew came from Sophia, jolting her back to reality. If she didn't watch out, he was going to seduce her into forgetting the only reason she consented to have sex with him in the first place. She wanted him to look at her and know she owned his soul.

She couldn't recall ever needing anyone to submit to her so profoundly, but she needed this with Drew. She needed to know she had control. She crossed to the shelves where she grabbed four leather cuffs. When she had them securely buckled around his wrists and ankles, she led him closer to the bed.

The bed frame was blocky on purpose. Posts rose seven feet in the air from each of the four corners. The footboard connected the bottom two posts with a thick square beam of polished wood. Sophia connected his wrists to the bedposts with short chains, and then gave his ankles the same treatment.

When she had him positioned how she wanted, he didn't move. She wanted him to test his bonds, but she refused to ask him. A predatory smile, which he could not see, curled her lips. She snatched a riding crop from a hook near the shelves and went to kneel on the bed in front of him.

"You're very handsome, Drew, but you know that already, don't you?"

His eyes were glued to the small rectangle of leather on the end of the riding crop. Lifting it to his shoulder, she caressed him gently, tracing patterns over his skin.

"A snap of your fingers or a lazy smile of invitation is all it takes, isn't it? Women flock to you." She looked him up and down, the whip following her sightlines. He was magnificent. "Men, too, I bet."

She began tapping the tiny bit of leather against his pectoral muscles, watching them jump and twitch, reacting to the tiny sting of the slaps. He stared at her, those clear blue eyes never wavering, not even when his skin sensitized to the repetitive slapping.

"Things come too easy to you, Drew. You don't have to work for it."

His eyes burned into her, answering her accusations without words. Whether he worked for his earlier conquests or not was irrelevant. He was working for this, for her.

"Easily gotten, easily forgotten," she muttered as she slid from the bed to escape his penetrating, knowing stare. She was saying too much. "You won't forget this."

She switched whips, opting for her fuchsia cat with the braided nylon falls. He flinched at the first blow, and the second, and the third. After a while, his back, his ass, and his thighs were stained pink. He relaxed into the rhythm she set.

He had yet to cry out or gasp. When she was sure the gentlest caress would be magnified a thousand times, she gave his front the same treatment. He wasn't the first submissive to watch her intently, but he was the most disturbing. She hated that he could disturb her with just a look, especially a look that was so inscrutable.

Sophia had a heavy hand, which the subs who came to her liked. Drew wasn't someone who sought pain or who needed it to achieve orgasm. It frustrated her. It meant he could never truly be hers, and she wanted him. God, how she wanted him.

Between her anger and the effort it took her to keep the whipping light, she worked up a sweat. Without breaking rhythm, Sophia lifted her dress over her head, removing one arm. She switched hands expertly, something she had practiced for hours to get right, and freed her remaining arm.

Drew's eyes lit at the sight of her dark brown, lacy bra. She had far sexier lingerie in silk and leather, yet heat kindled in him at the sight of this polyester blend.

She realized this was the first time he'd seen her topless. She wasn't naïve enough to think there was anything special about her body. She was athletic and curvy about the hips, with breasts that could swell to a boring B-cup when she retained water. But the way he looked at Sophia made her think that maybe he saw something she missed.

His arm twitched, the bicep flexing mightily, and she realized he was fighting the restraints. The sight of her body tortured him more than the whip, which she hadn't intended. She was getting nowhere this way, so she deemed him done. Exhaling heavily, she rolled back on the bed to remove her leggings. His broad, tanned chest rose and fell as his breaths came shorter and shallower.

His dick hardened, growing before her eyes, reaching out as if he could touch her that way. He wanted her.

Though Drew had been open about wanting Sophia, something deep inside doubted his truthfulness. With a lazy smile that disguised her insecurity, she lay across the bed, inches from his reach if only his hands were free. She slid her panties down and kicked them away. Then she parted her lips and roamed the slickness there with two fingers.

She had been wet since she heard his car door slam in the driveway.

He jerked against the bonds now, fighting them with all he had. The sturdy bed frame shook. She was glad she hadn't used the Velcro cuffs. With the force he used, he would have pulled free.

Pressing lightly, she rubbed her clit faster. Tension coiled low in her belly, and she arched against it, stretching her body to accept the pleasure as a low moan rolled from her throat.

"Mistress," he breathed, begging for release.

She focused on the fever in his eyes, getting off on it as much as from the stimulation of her own hand. A short cry, and she came.

With closed eyes, she reached for his cock, the fingers of her hand still freshly wet from her own juices. It was lubricant enough. He cried out in protest at the simple contact.

"Don't you want to come?" Her breathing hadn't returned to normal, making her question breathy.

"Not like this," he said, shaking his head once, slowly. "I want to be inside you, Sophia. I want to know what you feel like coming on me."

Shifting to bring her feet underneath, she rose to her knees. The position put her inches from his face. "And you always get what you want, don't you?" An edge of bitterness crept into her question.

Drew didn't hide his surprise. It flashed momentarily, displaced by urgency. "No. I want you. I've wanted you for so long. Damn it, Sophia, I need you."

She might have snorted. "You've known me for three days."

His pained expression didn't change. "I've known you since the beginning of time. I've needed you since the day I was first created, only I didn't know it was you."

She laughed, a short, mirthless sound. "Does that line work on every woman who gives you a hard time? It has all the hallmarks of a 'spotted and inconstant man.'"

His smile didn't reach his eyes. "That's the first time I've been the victim of a Shakespearean insult."

She was impressed he'd caught the reference. It softened her a little but not enough to let him skip his punishment. "Yes, well, if you start comparing me to a summer's day, I have plenty more where that came from."

He jerked his arm violently. "Then I'll speak plain English. I want you, Sophia. Untie me, and let me have you."

Lazily, she caressed his hard cock, drawing her fingertips up and down his length. "I won't let you come, you know." The warning was softly spoken.

"You're going to kill me."

"Perhaps," she said, "but you'll never forget to call me Mistress again."

"Mistress," he begged, dipping his head nearer. She scooted to the edge of the bed to release the cuff from his wrist. He did not grab for her, which, given the look in his eyes, cost him much.

She released his other arm and threw him a cheeky smile. "Take off your ankle cuffs." She crossed the room and snagged a handful of condoms from another box.

He crouched, making quick work of the buckles. "'When at your hands did I deserve this scorn?'"

The panic in his rapidly spoken words brought a brief frown to her face before she realized he was unfamiliar with the contents of that particular box.

Sophia returned to the bed before he finished, lying on her side in an inviting pose and scrambling to find an appropriate quote for a reply. When he stood to face her, she showered the condoms on the bed. "'Seest thou this sweet sight? I shall do thee mischief.' Come to bed, Drew. There are things I want to do with your mouth that don't involve talking."

He approached cautiously to kneel next to her. "Mistress, may I touch you?"

She praised him with a smile. "Oh, yes, Drew. Make me come."

In less than a second, she found herself engulfed in his body. His lips and hands were everywhere. She felt the sweet heat of his mouth at her neck, and then it was gone, moving down her body. He left her quivering, yearning for the return of his kiss and caress. Her bra disappeared. She writhed beneath him, trying to recapture the caresses that kept moving.

With a swiftness of motion illustrating his frustration and need, he wrenched her legs apart. She wanted him inside her, but she wasn't stupid. She wasn't on the Pill, and he wasn't wearing a condom. She grabbed his dick, halting his intention.

His eyes grew wide. "Mistress," he breathed. "Please."

She groped to the side for a small, cool plastic package. "Condom, Drew. Always use a condom. I'm not on the Pill, and I have no idea if you've been tested."

He snatched the square from her hand and ripped it open with his teeth. She took it from him and reached between them to roll it around his long, thick cock. She hadn't been exaggerating when she told Livia he was large.

Then he was inside her. He filled her completely, and in a way she had never imagined. Something about him just *fit*, and it scared the hell out of her. Drew didn't allow time for panic. He set a frenetic pace. With the whirlwind of things he made her feel, instinct made her hang on to his shoulders.

His tongue plunged into her mouth, licking and sucking so vehemently all she could do was lie there and take it. She wanted to drive him there. She wanted so badly for him to want her with such abandon he couldn't control himself. He granted her wish, but took her prisoner in the doing of it. She didn't mind, though she knew she would hate herself later for letting him take over so completely, for taking control from her. Not only had she lost control of him, she didn't have control of herself.

She felt things, intense things, so much more than the heat and tension coiling inside. She hadn't wanted this. She knew the way he made her feel wasn't unique to her, to this situation. Women flocked to him. He made them all feel this way. It was his gift and her curse. She had to regain control.

All of these thoughts whisked through her mind and left to hide for the time being. They would return to haunt her later. Now, all she knew, all she felt, was Drew.

He murmured her name, and it tore at her soul. Why couldn't he have given her this one telltale sign that she wasn't special to him, that her name was inconsequential? She'd instructed him to call her Mistress for a reason.

Her body writhed and arched, fighting the inevitable. He increased his pace, but he did not hurt her. As frantic as he was, as much as passion ruled him, he remained gentle. A tear escaped the corner of her eye, and she screamed as she climaxed.

The orgasm washed over her, wringing violent spasms that echoed in him. He collapsed on top of her, and she was too weak to push him aside.

She wasn't sure how much time passed before they both regained the ability to move, but Drew soon rolled to the side, taking her with him. Before she could protest, his lips were on hers, feasting with slow motions that rekindled her sated passion.

His hands roamed over sensitive places that arched to him. He played her body with practiced ease, and she let him push her over the edge again and again, until they both lay there, panting and exhausted.

Sophia slept. She hadn't meant to fall asleep, not in that room and not with Drew. She woke later with the vague sense that all was right with the world even though most of her front was freezing cold. Drew had curled his body around her backside, holding her close with one arm draped over her waist. Her head was pillowed on his firm bicep. The soft glow from the recessed lighting reflected from the lines of his arms, evident even in rest. She reveled in the feel of him for far too long.

This couldn't happen. She couldn't allow this to happen. The only possible outcome for becoming emotionally involved was heartbreak and lots of pain. Just thinking about it hurt. She did not like pain of any kind, especially not the kind that wouldn't go away with a couple of aspirin.

As if he sensed her withdrawal, Drew woke. The hand on her stomach began to move in slow, gentle caresses. She picked it up and gave it back to him. "You need to get dressed and go home." Without waiting for a response, she slid to the floor and dressed. She threw his clothes on the bed next to him.

He sat up, unembarrassed in his natural state, and watched her. "Are you angry with me for some reason I don't know about?"

Sophia frowned as she finished dressing without looking at him. "I'm not angry with you. You did fine. The scene is over. I have plans tonight."

Finally, he pulled on his jeans and shirt. She leaned over to grab the extra, unused condoms, but his hand on her wrist halted her actions. Unauthorized touching set off alarms in her head. He hadn't learned. He had only humored her.

"With the man who was here earlier?"

"Yes."

"Sophia." He brought her hand to his lips, but she snatched it away before he could kiss it. His eyes widened in shock. After what they shared, he thought she was his.

She had to show him he was wrong. "We're finished for the day," she said. "You need to leave."

His lips parted to say something, but he rethought whatever he might have said. He nodded thoughtfully, never taking his eyes from her. She hoped he couldn't see the panic or the utter lack of control she felt.

"Will I see you again?"

She managed what she hoped was an offhand smile. "We're dancing tomorrow night, remember? I figure you're going to be stuck with either Samantha or me." She hoped Sabrina would pair him with Samantha. They were both tall and fair-haired. Sophia and Ty were both darker. Aesthetically, the four of them matched better that way. However, one could never tell with Sabrina. She wasn't the kind of person to stick her nose in another person's business, but she wasn't exactly predictable, either.

Drew sighed, but didn't force the issue. "Yeah, I remember. I guess I'll see you tomorrow, then."

She closed and locked the front door behind him. Groaning, she rested her forehead against the hard wood. She stayed that way for far too long. Her domination of him had failed. He hadn't responded to anything she did to him by submitting. He put up with it, he played the game, but his heart wasn't in it. The only thing she did that got to him was masturbating while he was restrained. Somehow, she knew she would have elicited the same reaction if he hadn't been tied up.

He was dangerous. Now he was gone. It had to stay that way. She couldn't keep this up until the wedding. That man would destroy her.

* * * *

Drew sped along the interstate, heading in the general direction of his house. Sensual Secrets wasn't located too far from his home, and he needed to stop in to make sure they had the supplies they needed in order to fulfill their catering contracts for the week. He needed a shopping list.

He could have assigned the shopping to any of his employees, but Drew preferred to choose the ingredients he used himself. If something wasn't right, he altered the menu for the event. Clients who chose to work with him were required to sign a contract permitting reasonable substitutions. Drew's reputation assured an excellent meal, and most clients signed without complaint. Those who refused were encouraged to contract their catering elsewhere.

However, fresh produce wasn't on his mind as he navigated rush-hour traffic in the heavily populated Oakland County. That honor went to the chestnut-haired vixen who rocked his world and kicked him to the curb.

Her manner after sex was mechanical, impersonal. Sophia had shown more care and concern two days prior when she cleaned her come from his face before handing his clothes over and instructing him to dress.

At least he wasn't as sore now as he had been after she finished with him Saturday night. She had gone easy on him. After watching her with Livia, he knew she had it in her to hit much harder than she had.

She knew he didn't enjoy it. He'd meant to hide it from her, but he failed. This presented a problem. Sophia enjoyed—maybe even needed—disciplining her sex partners. Drew hadn't known how long he could keep up a façade of enjoyment. Now he did, and he was disappointed in himself. He couldn't have lasted more than fifteen, twenty minutes under the sting of her lash.

There had to be another way to do this. There had to be a way he could have Sophia and she could have a willing slave who loved being dominated, bound, and disciplined. Drew didn't mind being tied up, and he didn't mind being tortured sexually. The problem came when she introduced the ideas of pain and submission into the equation. It just didn't work for him.

It didn't stop him from enjoying himself, but it didn't further his pleasure, either.

With a sigh, he parked behind the bakery next to Ginny's BMW. It was unusual to see her there that late. She was responsible for opening things up and overseeing the baking aspects of the business. Drew's clients usually wanted service in the afternoons, so he was frequently required to work in the afternoon or in the evenings.

The familiar sounds of the kitchen greeted Drew as he opened the door and stepped inside. Sniffing the air was an automatic response, as was the mental dissection of the spices contained in the smell wafting from the stove.

Something was off.

His sensitive nose led him closer, to a pot filled with a simmering tomato-based sauce. "What the hell is this?"

Sophia's cold post-coital response contributed greatly to his soured mood. The sex had been fantastic for both of them. How could she brush him off as if they hadn't just shared something profound?

A five-and-a half-foot-tall fireball flew across the room. Maya, his *sous-chef*, hustled over to shoo him away with one hand. "It's not done."

"Too much garlic," he said. "It's ruined."

"I'm cooking for Italians. They have a high tolerance for garlic."

Drew's eyes narrowed. Everything that left the kitchen carried his name and rode on his reputation. If he didn't approve of something, it wasn't going anywhere. However, Maya, who was a whole year out of culinary school, had her own opinions, and she seemed to like arguing with him. More than once in the past six months, Drew had regretted making her the kitchen manager.

"That crap isn't leaving my kitchen, Maya, not for any ethnicity."

From the way her eyes narrowed in response, he knew the fight was just beginning. Sophia had thrown him out of her house, and she was probably at that moment dining with another man, and there was nothing he could do about it. Given the easy manner he'd observed between them that afternoon, she was no doubt entertaining him in her little room, or even in her bedroom.

If Maya wanted a fight, Drew was more than ready to deliver. He had angst, jealousy, and frustration to spare.

The shouting brought Ginny. Drew and Maya both ignored her.

She parked her hands on her hips, and her cute, little cheerleader smile turned icy. "I have a client in the bakery whose amusement over the noise coming from here has turned to serious concern."

Maya blushed and stared at the floor, embarrassment superseding anger. "I'm sorry, Ginny." She didn't offer an apology to Drew, her actual boss. Muttering under her breath, she killed the heat under the pot and dumped the sauce.

Responding to the curt jerk of Ginny's head, Drew followed his business partner into the hallway that separated the bakery from the kitchen. At one end was a lone door that neither of them liked using. The stairs behind led up to a shared disaster area bearing the title of "office." While both Ginny and Drew were world-renowned in their fields, neither of them was very organized when it came to the business side of their business.

Lifting a stack of unopened mail out of a chair, Drew threw it on the cluttered desk and sat down. "Don't start, Gin. It didn't smell right."

Ginny waved away his opening. "That's not what's bothering you."

In the fifteen years he'd been friends with Ginny, Drew had never once voluntarily sought her advice on anything relating to women. The pair had commiserated, sure, but he'd never asked her for her take on a woman or a situation, and he didn't intend to start now. Of course, that never stopped Ginny from voicing that opinion.

"Spill," Ginny said, emptying another chair and sliding it closer. "You spent the afternoon with Sophia, and now you're in a bad mood."

He leveled an even stare. "Don't you have a client downstairs?"

Tilting her head, Ginny's mouth scrunched, and one brow rose in confusion. "No, and neither do you. Stop stalling."

Her comment had been designed to shut Maya up, nothing more. Drew exhaled in relief. While a lost client or two wouldn't kill them, he didn't want his reputation smeared for any reason.

His mouth twisted with bitter jealousy. "Sophia has a date tonight."

Ginny nodded and stated the obvious. "And not with you."

Drew jerked his head in assent.

"That's funny." Ginny grinned, but she didn't laugh. "Usually, the shoe's on the other foot. I recall you doing the same thing to lots of women over the years, Drew. Now you're upset because you've met one who won't put her entire life on hold just to see you."

"He was over there when I got there, Gin." He ran a hand through his hair, his default gesture for any emotion he didn't particularly like. "She slept with me, and then kicked me out so she could go out to dinner with him. How long have you known her?"

Ginny shrugged. "A few months. She's Sabrina's friend."

"How well do you know her?"

This time, she shook her head. "We've had drinks a few times, hung out, but nothing touchy-feely. I'd put her more in the 'acquaintance' category. As much as Sabrina likes Sophia, I don't think she knows her very well, either."

Drew's brows knit together. "She's standing up in Sabrina's wedding."

Ginny shrugged again. "Sabrina doesn't have many close friends. I think Sophia is good friends with Ellen and Jonas, and that's why Sabrina feels closer to her."

It was useless to pump Ginny for further information. His shoulders slumped.

She slapped his knee. "Cheer up, buddy. I'll do some digging and see what I can find out for you. From the sound of it, I think you met your match."

Chapter 7

Sophia worked the next day. She hadn't planned to work, but Jeremy, her jerk of a boss, called at five in the morning. Anna, one of his full-time accountants, had gone into labor a week early. They weren't quite caught up enough for her to be gone yet. Since Sophia chose the three days she worked each week, it wasn't a big deal.

Daniel's birthday dinner had gone well, and she had stayed out far too late. Several more hours of sleep would have been nice, but that wasn't going to happen. Once she woke up, she was awake for good.

"I'm taking Friday off," she informed Jeremy as she strolled into the office a half hour late. She could have been on time, but she decided against it.

"No, you're not," he said without looking up from whatever he was reading. "And you'll stay a half hour later today to make up for being late."

Tall, blond, tan, good-looking, and athletic, Jeremy Monticello had it all, and that was his problem. He thought his looks were a free pass to treat women as chattel. Most of the women in the office nursed little crushes on him and let him get away with pretty much anything. He'd say, *"Get me a cup of coffee, sweetheart,"* like adding a false and demeaning endearment made up for the fact he asked a woman with an MBA to wait on him.

He made the mistake of asking Sophia once. She poured a cup of coffee for herself and returned to her desk. Since she hadn't wanted coffee, she wasn't drinking it. He thought to take it from her desk, so she spit in it, smiled her deadliest smile, and said something not very nice.

Most men who considered themselves dominant weren't jerks. They showed a woman, or a man, respect and care. Sophia's problem with Jeremy wasn't that he was dominant. Ellen and Jonas were two of her best friends, and they were both Doms. There was a difference between dominating someone for mutual pleasure and dominating someone to grind them down and keep them in their place.

She used to want to get Jeremy under her whip to see if he was sexually submissive, as were many men who were dominant in a professional setting, but she abandoned those fantasies. His appeal faded quickly.

She shook her head at Jeremy. "Prior commitment, sweetie." She could be a jerk, too, but only when provoked. After working under him for a year, just the sight of him provoked her. "And that wasn't a request."

He put down the file he had been perusing and followed Sophia to her desk. The open design of the office meant all eyes were on them, waiting for the show. He followed her behind the desk and leaned against the side to block her access to the drawer where she kept her purse. She plopped it on the desk and leaned next to him. Their backs were to everyone else, making them look more like colleagues. From the way his jaw ticked, she knew it bugged the hell out of him.

"You're treading on thin ice, DiMarco."

"Am I?" She wondered just how far she could push him. After dealing with Drew yesterday, she wasn't in the mood to deal with another man who wouldn't submit. "Then fire me."

Jeremy exhaled a long breath. "You're one of my best accountants. I put up with your shit because you're good. But you are replaceable, Sophia. If you don't show up on Friday, then you don't have a job."

"Then I guess tomorrow's my last day," she said. The only reason she hadn't quit already was because she couldn't be the one who walked away from this battle. She turned around and addressed the office. "Tomorrow's my farewell party. I'll bring the cake."

Productivity for the day was highly compromised. Everyone spent their time planning what dish they were going to bring and speculating on whether Sophia was fired or quit. She spent the day working. While she wouldn't miss working for Jeremy, she would miss her job. She loved working with numbers and solving problems. Numbers were predictable and reliable and honest. Frequently, she preferred accounting to having sex.

Though she hadn't planned on it, she did work the extra half hour. She hated leaving something unfinished. She knew she'd spend the night obsessing about that last project. That meant she didn't have time to change before dancing lessons.

Sabrina was waiting by the door to the studio to direct the wedding party to the right room as they came in. She gasped when she took in Sophia's smart skirt and heels. "You didn't have to dress up for this." She, of course, looked even better.

Sophia smiled and accepted her hug. "I came from work. I didn't have time to change."

"I'm sorry," she said, a blush staining her cheeks. She blushed more often than anyone Sophia knew. "I thought Tuesday was the day you had completely free. It looks like I've really messed this up."

Sophia squeezed her hand reassuringly. "Don't worry about it. It was unscheduled."

Sabrina brushed an invisible strand of hair away from her eye and peered up at her friend. "I put you with Drew. Jonas said that was probably best for everyone involved, but I'm not so sure."

The friendly expression on Sophia's face didn't change. She hoped. "Why?"

"Jonas seems to think you're dominating Drew, but I've known Drew for a long time. He's not a submissive." She didn't have to say the rest. Sophia had already failed with Drew. She just didn't know the temperature of the situation.

"It'll be fine," she assured Sabrina. "We're both mature adults."

Of course, telling Drew their experiment was finished didn't go as planned.

"Why?" He whirled her around the floor, comfortable with the dance from the moment the average-looking female instructor demonstrated the moves with him. Sophia was no slouch herself. It didn't take much time or practice to find an easy rhythm.

"You didn't enjoy the scene," she said. Why did he need a detailed explanation? He had been there, too. "I don't think the whole Dom/sub thing is for you."

"I agree," he said, "but I fail to see why that means we can't still see each other."

"Drew," she warned without missing a step.

"You look incredible tonight, Sophia. I can't believe you dressed up to break my heart." The warm, strong hand on Sophia's back pressed her closer. Inches separated their bodies, inches she wanted to close. "I think you want me to beg."

"No, I don't want you to beg. I'm not into playing head games like that. I'm a dominatrix, Drew. I really like control and submission and whipping. It's who I am. It's what I need in a sex partner." She refused to use the word "relationship." Though she had made things clear from the beginning, Drew was a boundary-pusher. The lines had already blurred for him.

"You can still tie me up, Sophie, and do whatever else you want. I'm open to any kind of sex you want to have, and any kinds of toys you want to use. I just don't enjoy the whipping." His head dropped the slightest bit to direct his husky whisper closer to her ear. His lips brushed the outer edge. Her knees weakened. "I did, however, enjoy watching you work over Livia. You mentioned threesomes. I love threesomes. There is a perfect solution here."

Shivers shimmied up and down her spine. "Wasn't last night enough for you?"

"No. Do you need proof?" Hard proof his desire hadn't dimmed was inches from her abdomen. "What are you doing tonight after we get out of here?"

He regarded her with a smug smile. He knew the way he affected her. He was too adept at reading her body's reactions. She took great satisfaction in being able to deflate his ego. "I'm seeing Livia."

The hand holding hers and the one on her waist tightened painfully. It was his only reaction, but it was enough. He wasn't the only submissive in her life. "Is she bringing a date?"

"That's none of your business." Under no circumstances would she tell him that she was meeting Livia for drinks. She needed to talk to her about what Drew said. If Livia wasn't happy with their friendship, Sophia needed to know.

Drew pressed his lips together so hard the area around them turned white. "Stupid question. She always brings a date to you."

He said nothing more the rest of the night, and his eyes avoided her face. When the lesson ended, she bade farewell to the rest of the group, apologizing for not keeping the evening free to go out for drinks with them afterward.

Ellen followed Sophia to her car. "Sophie? Is everything all right?"

Sophia opened the door and threw her purse inside before giving Ellen undivided attention. Ellen had been there for her from the beginning. Sophia had never kept an important secret from her. "Yeah, why?"

Ellen studied Sophia in that way she had of dissecting people. Sophia used to find it unnerving, but then she learned to perfect the technique. While Ellen was perceptive, she relied more on making people spill information than on discerning it for herself. "Drew bothers you. I just want to make sure you're all right. Do you want me to talk to Jonas about you standing up with Ty instead? He'll understand if you're not ready to try something like this."

Sophia shook her head, the denial coming before she thought about it. Watching Drew dance with anyone else would have been worse torture than doing it herself. She didn't want to feel the way he made her feel, but she didn't want to watch him working his magic on anyone else, either. "I can handle Drew."

Ellen's lips pursed in a way that said she didn't believe Sophia, but she wasn't going to challenge her. "If you need me, I'm here. You can call me anytime."

Without waiting for a response, she hugged Sophia tightly. Sophia hugged her back with equal emotion. Almost five years ago, Sophia had been raped in the parking lot near Ellen's club. She had been underage, but her boyfriend was older. He tried to get her into the club. When that failed, he shrugged it off, and they went back to his car and made out. He didn't stop when she asked him to.

When he finished with her, she ran into the alley behind the club, which probably wasn't something she would have done if she hadn't been so distraught. He came after her as if they had only argued, his hands spread wide in apology. Sophia pounded on the nearest door.

Ellen happened to be in the hallway near the door and heard the noise. The door opened, and Sophia fell in, clinging to Ellen in terror. She didn't clearly remember everything that happened after that. She remembered bouncers watched over Charlie until the police arrived. Ellen went with her to the hospital and held her hand through the entire ordeal. She had been too ashamed to call her parents or Daniel.

Other than emotional trauma, nothing was medically wrong with Sophia, so the hospital released her. Ellen drove her home. At the time, she had lived in a tiny apartment with three other college students. Sophia never expected to see Ellen again.

She called or stopped by every single day. She didn't do it from a sense of guilt. The parking lot belonged to the city, not her club, so there were no liability issues. She helped Sophia find the courage to tell her family what happened. She held Sophia when the news came that the case wouldn't go to trial due to lack of evidence. She had been relieved she didn't have to testify, but the fact he was going free made her feel violated all over again.

By chance, the door she pounded on at the club that night opened to the members-only portion. Sophia caught a glimpse of the main room as Ellen ushered her to the public part of the building to await the police. As their friendship developed, Sophia asked Ellen about what she had seen. Ellen's explanation was candid. That kind of control appealed to Sophia like nothing else ever had, and she had been looking for a way to reclaim control of her life.

Ellen introduced Sophia to Jonas, and he became her mentor.

After a year, Sophia no longer felt guilty, but she didn't feel in control of her life. She started at Ellen's club, hoping to salvage what was taken from her. It worked, and she was loath to tamper with the formula.

Drew didn't fit into any of the molds she'd created in her life, and that's why she'd needed to end this thing with him. Livia did, and that's why Sophia needed to talk to her.

They met at a coffee bar midway between Livia's house and Sophia's. Livia was dressed in white slacks cut to show off her long legs, and a peach blouse that coordinated perfectly with her makeup. As always, she was immaculate.

Sophia, however, suffered from spending all day dressed as an accountant. Her clothes were wrinkled from sitting so long, and her feet were sore from dancing in the wrong kind of shoes. She wasn't in the best mood when she joined Livia.

One of Livia's pale brows rose. "Tough day?"

"Long day," Sophia corrected as she poured four sugars into her coffee.

"We can do this later."

Sophia recognized Livia's nervousness. If she had more energy, she might have teased the information from Livia so that she would never suspect Sophia had spoken to Drew. "It turns out that Drew Snow is friends with a friend of mine."

Livia fiddled with the handle of her purse, probably wishing she still smoked so she would have something to do with her hands. "Is he?"

"Yes. We're standing up in a wedding together."

Relief flooded into Livia's face. "Oh, I've finished with him, Sophia. Really, he was just an amusement for a couple of days. I haven't seen or talked to him since we left your place."

"I know," Sophia said as gently as she could. She needed to catch Livia off guard if she was going to get the truth from her. "It's what you said to him after you left that concerns me."

Her hands fluttered again, moving to her throat, and then back to close around her coffee cup. "That wasn't supposed to get back to you."

"Livia, if you aren't enjoying our scenes together, you're under no obligation to come back for more. I won't be upset with you for dissolving our game."

She studied the pattern of black specks on the white table. "I like our games, and I hate them, too."

A heaviness settled in Sophia's chest. She never meant to make Livia feel like this. "Livia, stop treating me like I hold all the cards. We're equals, you and I."

Her head snapped up. "Are we?" Round spots of anger stained her cheeks. "I let you tie me up and whip me until tears run down my face. Even then, I don't want you to stop. You always use the men I bring you too well. I've tried to replicate the way you make me feel. I've tried to find a lover to replace you, but I can't. Every try is a failure. I hate the control you have over me."

Sophia was careful to not touch her. Any physical contact couldn't help but be a controlling move, even if it was meant reassuringly. "I do those things because you want me to do them. Livia, if our scenes make you feel this way, then we're done with them. They're supposed to set you free, not make you hate yourself or me. It's supposed to be fun, that's all. You aren't in love with me."

She shook her head. "I'm not even attracted to you. I like the scenes you make. I wish I could make them without you."

"Maybe you want to switch sides," Sophia suggested. "Maybe you want to give being dominant a try."

A strange light glinted in her eye, bringing strength with it. "Maybe I do," she said. "I suppose that means we're done with our games."

"The fact that you aren't loving our games means we're through with them," Sophia corrected, downing half of her cooled coffee. "The suggestion is a friendly one. You're a fabulous-looking woman, Livia. There is no shortage of submissive men and women out there." She held her breath, hoping Livia wouldn't ask her to be a mentor as she trained to become a Dom. She wasn't the generous teacher-type like Jonas.

Thankfully, Livia did not. They chatted a while longer. Sophia helped Livia determine her next course of action. Before they parted, Livia hit Sophia with a parting shot. "You know, Sophia, there were definite sparks between you and Drew. I would be okay with you hooking up with him."

By the time Sophia got home, she was dead on her feet. She slept through her alarm and showed up for work late and without a cake.

She had completely forgotten it was her last day.

When she walked in, Jeremy looked over at her. Their eyes met for a second. He sighed and went back to what he was doing. Screwing in her courage, she walked into his office without knocking. He saw her coming through the glass divider.

"I'm sorry I was late," she said. She always admitted when she made a mistake. "I can't stay late to make it up. Did you want me to come in tomorrow morning?"

He stared at her for ten full seconds without speaking, his brown eyes round with incredulity. "You are amazing, DiMarco. I thought you might show up on time today and beg for your job." He shook his head slowly. "I think, under other circumstances, we would have gotten along better."

Sophia's brow lifted. She knew where this was heading. He had refrained from hitting on her for a whole year. She wanted to give him the opening just so she could turn him down. "Other circumstances?"

He pushed his chair back and stood to face her. "Yeah, other circumstances. Like, if I was a woman or if I wasn't your boss. You have a problem with male authority. I don't know what guy screwed you over, Sophia, but we're not all like that."

This time, her jaw dropped. "You call women 'sweetheart' and 'dear.' I don't have a problem with having a male boss. I have a problem with having a chauvinist for a boss." If he was going to open this door, she was going to take the opportunity.

He smiled. It was laced with bitterness. "I haven't done that in a long time," he said. "A fact that has obviously escaped your notice. I admit I haven't always been the most enlightened of men. However, I always thought I was approachable. Out of all my employees, I thought you would have been the one to take me to task for stupid behavior like that."

Still shocked, Sophia sat heavily in the chair opposite his desk. She stared at Jeremy with new eyes. He was right. He hadn't said or done anything chauvinistic after the first six months. Management sent him to some kind of retreat, and he stopped those behaviors half a year ago. "You're right," she said. "Perhaps an apology might have helped."

"Admit I was wrong?" he said, coloring slightly. "I'm not that big of a man."

Sophia laughed. "But you just did it."

He nodded slowly. "That's because I fired you. I don't have to face you after today, knowing you know I know my behavior was wrong."

She rolled her eyes. "Jeremy, your employees like you for some reason. They'll only think better of you if you come clean. Do it individually, and don't make a big deal out of it. People appreciate heartfelt apologies."

He eyed her for a long, long time. She met his gaze unflinchingly. "I'll be sorry to see you go."

It was an opening. If she wanted her job back, all she had to do was ask. Maybe if Drew hadn't been screwing with her perfect little world, she might have. "I'll stay until you can replace me." It was the best she could do.

"That's generous." Jeremy's smile and tone were both dry.

Sophia shrugged. "You're shorthanded with Anna gone. Do you want me to stay until you can complete the interview process or not? It should take you two weeks, tops."

"I don't need you to train anyone. I'm recalling someone we laid off a few months ago." He held out his hand to her, and she shook it. "I'm gonna miss you, DiMarco."

Chapter 8

Drew called or texted every single day. After Sophia overcame her surprise that he wasn't going to let the fact she had been with Livia Tuesday night or with Daniel on Monday deter him, she ignored every message.

Sophia taught a class at Daniel's karate studio on Wednesday, and she helped out whenever he found himself shorthanded. She also handled his accounting, but it didn't take very long. She billed him for about three days a month. He didn't say anything when she let the phone go to voicemail the first night.

Saturday, one of his regular girls came down with a nasty flu. It was a beautiful day outside, and Sophia suspected the girl had the kind of flu that was only cured by a day at the lake with a bunch of friends. Still, she didn't mind. She liked working with the older teens and the women who came in for Saturday classes. Daniel handled the younger kids, and they co-taught the multiage classes.

Her phone rang every couple hours. At first, Daniel ignored it. Then, he began looking at it whenever it rang, even though she told him to turn it off.

"It's Drew, Sophia. Don't you think you should take it?"

They were between classes. Both of them were wet with sweat. Sophia swabbed a towel over her face. "Stay out of it, Daniel."

"Is this part of the domination game?" he hissed. "I have to tell you, Sophie, this is a head game. When I call a woman and she doesn't answer the phone, it tells me that she's either not interested or she's a bitch. Either way, the relationship is over."

She snatched the phone away and turned it off. "Here's hoping he takes the hint."

"Maybe you should just tell him straight out," he suggested, lowering his tone as the seven-to-nine-year-olds began to wander in. "It would be the decent thing to do."

"I did," she said. "He doesn't want to be a submissive, and he doesn't want to stop seeing me. He can't have it both ways."

Daniel stared at her as if she had lost her mind.

Tuesday, Drew glared with his icy blue eyes while they danced. He held her closer than necessary for the variation of the dance they learned that night. Sophia struggled against the smell of him and the heat of his body next to hers. His lips stayed nearby the entire time, torturing her with their proximity and their silence.

He didn't mention the fifteen messages she hadn't returned, and he left as soon as the lessons were over. She went out for drinks with the rest of the group.

Ginny managed to snag a spot next to Sophia. She knew she was in trouble when Ginny smiled that sweet Breszewski smile as she offered the sugar. It was the smile the popular girls in high school flashed right before they made someone's life miserable.

She brushed a stray strand of her short hair behind her ear. "Drew's been a bear this whole week."

Sophia had forgotten they owned a bakery and catering business together. "And you blame me."

Her smile gentled, but it wasn't at all apologetic. "I know Drew has a reputation as a player, and he's definitely earned it, but he's a good guy. He's had a few serious relationships, Sophia. He's a faithful boyfriend. I've never seen him like this before."

Sophia stirred six sugars into her coffee, wishing she had opted for something much stronger. "I can't help that."

"Yes, you can," she said, pointing a heated look that scorched Sophia's clothes, but didn't penetrate the skin.

She had much to learn about playing control games with a control freak. Sophia met her look with ice and put out the fire. "I might be the first woman to ever turn Drew down, but I won't be the last. He'll learn to accept it and move on."

An herbal tea came down between them, the sweet apple-cinnamon scent competing with the strong smell of overly sweet coffee. Sabrina wedged her little body onto the edge of Ginny's seat. "Ginny, how about you go sit down by Lara before she thinks you've dumped her for Sophia."

Ginny rolled her eyes in an "as if" gesture. She might not have responded to Sabrina's words, but she did respond to the accompanying look. With a huff and a warning look, she retreated to the other end of the three tables someone had shoved together to accommodate the large group.

Sabrina turned to Sophia. "I'm sorry about that. Ginny and Drew have been the best of friends since high school. She's a little protective where he's concerned."

Sophia didn't think Sabrina was any less protective.

"It was a bad idea to even start something, I tried to make a clean break, but he won't stop calling me."

Sabrina frowned. "If you don't mind my asking, what's wrong with him that you don't want to go out with him? You're both single, and you're obviously attracted to him."

Sophia shrugged and opted for partial honesty. She wasn't about to reveal that the idea of being in a relationship scared the hell out of her, especially one where she didn't have absolute and complete control. "I'm not looking for a relationship. I made that clear from the start, but Drew seems to only hear what he wants to."

Clutching a hand to her heart, she burst out laughing. "Oh, this is ironic. For years, Drew has used that same excuse. I'll talk to Drew. He should leave you alone after today."

It was a nice gesture, so why did Sophia's heart suddenly feel like icy fingers were squeezing it?

Mercifully, nobody mentioned Drew for the rest of the night.

Wednesday night, Sophia taught her self-defense class for women. Most of the clients were victims of violence. She didn't charge for the class, and she used money from a grant to pay for counselors to be on hand afterward. It made her feel like she had more control over her life, like she could help prevent horrible things from happening to other women. When it was finished, she locked up for the night. Daniel's class had ended fifteen minutes earlier, and he had disappeared up the stairs to his apartment above the studio for a shower.

Sophia joined him after locking up. The loft was large, with an open plan. The kitchen, living room, and dining room shared one space. The couch converted to a bed when Daniel had the inclination to pull it open. He usually just slept on the sofa. The only private room was the bathroom.

As she closed the front door, he strode out, hair water-slick from the shower, already on the phone. They usually ordered out for dinner. Sophia turned on the TV and scrolled through the channels while he talked.

"We'll be there in about a half hour," he said into the phone.

She wrinkled her nose at him. She didn't feel like going out. She liked ordering in. She thought he would want to watch one of his Bruce Lee movies with her. He hung up and threw the phone into her lap. She glanced down to see he had been using her cell. "I hope this means you're going out alone to pick up something greasy and fattening to bring back here."

"Nope," he said, tugging at her hand. "Get changed. That was your dominatrix friend, Ellen."

Sophia hated when he did that. She only knew one Ellen, and she was perfectly aware that he didn't approve of his little sister working for her.

"Apparently, we're missing poker night."

Sophia glared at him through narrowed eyes. "You answered my phone."

"It wasn't Drew, so I figured I was safe. You like Ellen. I like Ellen. She promised pizza, chips, and salsa. Food and poker, Sophie. Unless there are a bunch of bikini-clad women bursting out of their tops to wait on us, it doesn't get better." His grin was crooked and disarming. Unfortunately for him, she was immune.

"You go. I don't feel like it."

He punched her in the arm, the gesture more reassuring than violent. "Drew's not coming. I checked, little sister."

Sophia gave in. That had been her only objection. Last night hadn't been pleasant unless she closed her eyes and pretended there was no tension crackling between them. She had done it far too much to feel good about it. If just once he showed up at her house instead of calling, she would have melted in his arms.

Ellen's house wasn't far from Sabrina's. The group gathered in the basement consisted of Ellen and Ryan and their friends. Sophia recognized a couple of teachers Ryan and Jonas taught with that she had met before. Jonas was there, but Sabrina wasn't.

"Jake is with the grandparents," Ellen said with a huge grin. "We can be as loud as we want." She lifted an empty glass in Sophia's direction, and then frowned into it. "Ryan, honey, my glass is empty."

He frowned into it. In the dimness of the finished basement, his freckles seemed to run together, making him appear much darker than his fair skin should allow. "Is it? How about some coffee?"

"Coffee?" she spat the word at him. "I'm not looking for sobriety."

He rolled his eyes and took her glass. "You better not end up with a hangover."

She blew a kiss in his direction. "He's hoping to get lucky," she announced.

Sophia took the seat next to her, and Daniel slid in on the other side. Completely ignoring her comment, Ryan filled Ellen's drink. He watered it down quite a bit.

"Care for a drink?" Ryan asked, quirking a red eyebrow at Daniel and Sophia.

"I'll have what she's having," she said. "And water it down just as much."

Daniel turned to study the bar. It was nicely done in solid mahogany. "What's on tap?"

Ryan laughed. "You want regular beer or something fancy? I bought a bunch of Blue Moons for Sabrina, but she's not drinking anymore."

It had been a little over a week since she'd come to Sophia. She shot a glance at Jonas. "Any news you want to share?"

He took a swig of light-colored beer and shuffled the cards. "We're trying to get pregnant. I told her I want two before I turn forty."

The idea of having kids was foreign to Sophia. She liked Ellen's little guy, but she mostly avoided children. She didn't say anything in response.

Daniel indicated Jonas's bottle. "I'll have one of those."

Jonas introduced Daniel around, which was a relief because Sophia hadn't remembered his friends' names. "Aces and eights are wild. Ten-cent minimum to ride this train."

She lost herself in the cards and conversation. It was nice to hang out with friends and have a good time. An hour later, they heard noises coming from upstairs. Jonas swore and chugged his third beer, and then pushed the empty bottle over to Ryan.

"Sabrina has cut me off from alcohol and caffeine. She says if she can't have it, neither can I," he said by way of explanation.

"Since you're making her get pregnant, I think it's only fair," Ellen returned. "I'm surprised she's still marrying your sorry dictatorial ass."

Jonas suggested something rude and physically impossible. Ellen ignored him, so he tried another route. "Drink up, Elle. I'm sure you two will be throwing each other baby showers by Christmas."

This was a sore subject with Ellen, who often lamented not being able to quite lose the weight from her last pregnancy. In the middle of sipping her drink, Ellen choked and turned a murderous glare on Jonas. Ryan pounded her on the back. "Settle down, you two. I refuse to referee if I'm not getting any action tonight." He put his cards down and leered at Ellen. "Though, if you do want to have another one, I'm all for it."

Disgusted, she pushed his face away. "You just like how big my boobs get." She looked down at her cards, blushing.

Sophia watched this all with wide, wary eyes. Turning to Daniel, she wrinkled her nose. "This makes me not want to get married or have children. Ever."

Daniel shrugged. "I'm in favor of large-breasted women, but I prefer them not pregnant."

Sabrina finally made it down the stairs. She was still dressed from the office. Her hair was up, twisted around a hairpiece that made Jonas wince. When Sophia first met her, it was long, spilling halfway down her back. She looked cute with it short, but Jonas had a thing for long hair.

Jonas stood to greet her. The kiss and the way he looked at her was so intimate Sophia felt like she should leave the room, though he most likely preferred the audience. "You look wiped out, honey. You didn't have to come tonight."

"Someone has to drive you home," she said with a tired smile. "Besides, this is the only way I'll get to see you today." She greeted everyone at the table by name, even Daniel, whom she had not met before. Taking Jonas's seat, she waved in the general direction of the stairs. "The food is upstairs. Why don't you guys bring it down?"

Jonas jumped to do her bidding. He dragged the two teachers, Daniel, and Ryan with him. As soon as they were out of earshot, Sabrina turned to

Sophia with a sad, apologetic frown. "I'm sorry, Sophia. They didn't tell me you were coming tonight."

Before she could ask anything, footsteps thumped down the carpeted stairs. Through the din of chatter, Drew's distinct voice stood out. Sophia glared at Ellen. "You told Daniel he wouldn't be here."

"No," she said slowly, rattling the ice in her drink. Triumph sparkled in her dark brown eyes. "I said he wasn't here. He wasn't. Now he is."

Sabrina threw a chip at her, nailing Ellen in the forehead. "That is sneaky and underhanded. I can't believe you sometimes."

Ellen added the chip to her pile. "I fail to see why you're surprised."

Drew stopped suddenly when he saw Sophia, and then he turned away. The lines of his body were stiff and tense.

The men set up the food. Daniel grabbed a plate, but Sophia grabbed his arm. "Danny, we have to go."

Daniel looked from her to Drew and back again. "I'm hungry, and I've had two beers. Let me eat and sober up a bit. Then we'll go. If he gets out of line, I'll kick his ass, okay?"

"I can kick his ass, Daniel." She leaned in closer. "Thanks for nothing."

Instead of answering, he shoved a plate in her hands. "Eat, Sophie. You're much more pleasant when you're not paranoid and hungry."

"I'm not paranoid," she said through clenched teeth.

Daniel spooned some food onto her plate. "Yes, you are. Nobody here is going to let anything happen to you. Eat. If you sober up first, you can drive home."

She let him heap her plate with different foods, refraining from denying she was drunk. She wasn't. She had no idea what half of the dishes were, and the pleasant aromas were wasted on her.

She returned to the table to find Jonas once again shuffling. Drew sat at the other end of the table, next to Sabrina. Sophia wedged herself firmly between Daniel and Ellen, her support system. Ellen might have finagled things so that she and Drew were both there, but she wouldn't force them to talk.

Conversation picked up, and Sophia did all she could to avoid meeting Drew's eyes.

Still, she could feel him looking at her. Though it was impossible, she could smell the subtle mingling of his cologne and soap and shampoo with the scent that was uniquely him. If she concentrated, she could feel his lips on hers and the warmth of his hands as they caressed her bare skin. The food was delicious, but she didn't pay it much mind.

Daniel did. "Sabrina, did you make this? It's incredible."

Jonas laughed, guffawing so hard he almost fell from his chair. Sabrina pushed him the rest of the way. He hit the floor with a soft thud. "I don't cook," she explained daintily. "Drew made the food."

Daniel looked at Drew with a fresh perspective. "This is pretty good. Do you cook professionally?"

Drew's nostrils flared slightly as he glared at Daniel. His response was terse. "Yes."

"Where at? I'd love to bring Sophie by for dinner. She's very amenable after a good meal."

Daniel was toying with Drew. Sophia hated it. She put a restraining hand on his arm, but he was in full big-brother mode. Tonight had a double benefit for Danny. He annoyed his sister and took potshots at a man who fucked her in that little downstairs room.

Those blue eyes darkened. "It's just down the street from Ellen's club," he said. It was three cities down the street. "You know, where Sophia works her magic."

The muscles in Daniel's forearm tensed under her hand. "Yeah, I've been there." Daniel visited one time after he first found out the exact nature of Sophia's job. He had never been back.

Ellen, probably to avoid a fight, chimed in. "Drew's never been to my club. No matter how many times I invite him... Well, that's his loss. On the other hand, I've been to his shop frequently. He co-owns a catering company and bakery with Sabrina's sister. Her desserts are responsible for at least ten of the pounds I can't seem to lose."

For once, Ryan didn't say anything. Like Jonas, his eyes flicked from Drew to Daniel and back. Sophia pushed her plate away, suddenly full. The beginnings of a headache pressed against the back of her skull.

Daniel took another bite and chewed thoughtfully. "What's it called?"

"Sensual Secrets," Drew said.

He might have answered Daniel's question, but he directed the words, and the meaning, to Sophia. Her mouth went dry. She excused herself and fled, like the coward she was, to the bathroom upstairs.

It was a large bathroom, with granite countertops and plush rugs. She paced the length of it, stopping every few turns to splash cold water on her face. How could she want him so badly she ached and not want to want him? Why couldn't he just sleep with her until they worked it out of their systems?

Sophia wasn't sure how long she spent in there trying to convince herself to pull it together long enough to collect Daniel and make her excuses. Finally, she opened the door and stopped cold. Leaning casually against the wall across from the bathroom, Drew waited for her.

His hands were in the pockets of his jeans, and his blue Sensual Secrets shirt stretched across his chest, emphasizing his defined physique all too well. The shirt was the exact same blue as his eyes. He held out a hand to her.

She stared at it stupidly, wanting more than anything to take it. Slowly, she watched her hand slip into his, and then she felt his chest against hers. He kissed her. It happened in slow motion, but far too quickly for Sophia to formulate coherent thoughts. Her mind took a hiatus, leaving only the chaotic feelings swirling through her body.

His lips captured hers, fanning irresistible sensations as he coaxed her mouth open. He moaned, and she caught the vibration in her mouth. It was another way in which he drugged her. She was jelly in his arms, powerless to resist his charm.

A door opened, and they fell through it. It closed behind them, but she was too caught up in Drew's kiss to wonder how it happened. At last, he broke away. His lips moved to tease the sensitive places on her neck and shoulders. She sighed, shuddering in his arms.

Weakly, she pushed at him, her hands clutching his shoulders in case he tried to let go. "Drew, I can't do this."

He paused, locking his eyes with hers. "Then tell me to stop, Sophia. Tell me you don't want me as much as I want you."

She didn't want him to stop. She wanted him to tell her this meant nothing and that he was her slave, awaiting her whim. But he wouldn't do that. He made it clear he didn't want to play that role. He wanted more from her than she had to offer.

She couldn't speak. Then his lips took possession of hers again, and she didn't want to. She let her hands rake through his hair, and she pressed her body against his. She wanted him to push her back onto some surface so she could feel his weight on her, pressing her down and holding her prisoner.

His hands stroked across her back and teased under the hem of her shirt. "I want you, Sophia."

The words were whispered against the hollow of her throat. She pressed her eyes closed, trying to put off the decision, trying to ignore the question in his statement. She gripped his shoulders, tightly curling her fingers into the tense muscles there. "I…I want you, too, Drew."

The kiss was slow, reverent, and gentle. Waves of violent heat spiraled through her, radiating from his body into hers. She pushed his shirt out of the way, lifting it over his head and tossing it to the floor. She needed to feel the texture of his skin under her palms and against her body. The kisses deepened, demanding instead of giving.

His caress was everywhere at once, twisting and turning her body to allow him access. Wet and wanting, she trembled in his arms.

He turned her so that her back rested against his chest. She opened her eyes to see that they were in Ellen's den, standing behind the large sofa positioned in front of the television set. Their silhouettes reflected there. His lips grazed her neck as his hands loosed the button and zipper on her jeans. The denim slid down her legs, taking drenched panties with them.

One arm banded across her waist to hold her upright. His fingers found her wetness, circling her swollen clit, rubbing around and over it, faster and harder, until she cried out. The tangy smell of orgasm filled the air.

With languid slowness, he bent her over the back of the couch. It was a vulnerable position. She had never let a lover take her like this. She quivered as she waited for him to lower his pants and slip on a condom. Then his hands were on her again, lifting her hips, rotating them forward and down to position her to receive him.

The tip of his cock nudged her opening. Just as slowly as he did everything else, he entered her, not stopping until he was buried completely. Sophia gasped at the feel of him inside her, filling her. Her fingers dug into the sofa cushions. She wanted to fight him, to fight herself, but she didn't have the will.

He thrust into her, and she arched, pushing against him. He set a slow pace, and she whimpered, wanting more and faster. His strong hands gripped her hips, prohibiting her from hurrying him. Heat built, coiling deeper and deeper. She bucked against him in protest. Each thrust wrung a moan from her, a noise she didn't want to give him. He didn't vary his pace in the slightest.

The orgasm took her by surprise. It was strong and deep and slow. She cried out and collapsed, unable to face the enormity of what he made her feel.

Behind her, Drew cried out and fell against her. He controlled their fall, pushing Sophia over the back of the couch so that she landed on the cushions. He landed on top of her. Limbs entwined of their own will, seeking to keep the physical link.

When she could move again, Sophia lifted a weakened hand to his cheek. He kissed her tenderly, and then sat up and straightened his clothes. She fixed hers as well.

"I don't want you seeing other people," he said, breaking the silence. "You'll leave here with me tonight. If you want to have threesomes with your submissives, that's fine. You'll need to do all your disciplining on them. If you want to have your boy toy follow us home tonight…"

Sophia put her hand over his mouth and stifled the twin urges to laugh and vomit. This game had to end. "Drew, under no circumstances should you suggest we have a threesome with my brother."

Drew frowned. She fought the urge to kiss away the lines. "Brother? He called you Mistress. He said he'd been to Ellen's club."

"He was being nasty," she explained. "Daniel doesn't approve of my work there or of my sex life." Her hand rested on her own knee. Drew's fingers twined around them and squeezed lightly. She stared at the place they came together. The gravity of what Drew asked washed over her.

"That explains why he took an instant dislike to me," Drew said. "I was jealous, so naturally, I assumed he was, too."

"I didn't sleep with Livia." She swallowed, not wanting to come clean. She had to be honest with him, even if it meant removing some of those protective barriers. She hadn't limited herself to one lover since the disaster that was her last boyfriend. At least he wasn't asking her to dinner, or to meet his parents. The decision was made. She had to see this through. "We only met for coffee."

His laugh was short and ironic. "I haven't slept very well because I keep imagining you with other people. I wake up every morning wanting to murder someone new."

Sophia needed rules, boundaries. "Can I still tie you up?"

"Yes," he said, moving her hand to his knee, turning it up to trace patterns on her palm. "But don't expect me to call you anything but Sophia, no matter how much you torture me sexually." He turned her face toward his and dropped a kiss on her lips. "I know you too well to think you'd want to suddenly go vanilla. I like that you're adventurous and that you like your toys. I'm looking forward to seeing whatever else you have up your sleeve, Sophie. But don't shut me out like this again."

She looked away and took a deep breath, but it was ragged and unsteady.

"I know you're scared. I'm well aware of my reputation, but I've never lied to you, and I won't start now. I only want you."

He had no idea how terrified she was, or why, and she wasn't about to tell him. Let him think his reputation mattered. She chewed her lower lip. She had no choice. Once she got him out of her system, she would have her carefully controlled life back.

He stared at her pensively. She knew better than to ask what he was thinking.

Chapter 9

Sophia didn't go home with Drew. Her car was parked at Daniel's studio. He was quiet for all of two minutes on the drive back to his place.

"Drew seems like a good guy." Daniel's statement was a question. The rest of the evening had gone well. When Sophia and Drew returned, the tension was gone. Daniel had thrown her a concerned look, and she knew the only reason he hadn't come after her was because someone, probably Ellen, convinced him to wait until she came back of her own accord.

"He does," she agreed. Drew wasn't the problem. The rumors about him didn't matter. He admitted to playing the field. He admitted to liking threesomes. He asked her not to sleep with anyone else.

That brought her to a screeching halt. How did he expect to have a threesome if Sophia wasn't allowed to have sex with the third person and he didn't want to? A groan escaped as she realized he meant he had no problem with her dominating and disciplining someone else as long as sex wasn't involved. He would even watch and sleep with her afterward. That wasn't a threesome, and it wasn't fair to the sub.

"What's wrong?" Daniel asked anxiously. "If he hurt you…"

Slapping a hand on Daniel's tense forearm, Sophia interrupted the thought with a reassuring squeeze. "He's not like that." Drew was gentle and generous, even when she wished he was rough and greedy. So far, the only bad quality she could find in him was that he wanted more of a commitment than she wanted to give.

"Then why don't you want to go out with him? It's obvious you're attracted to him, and he has it bad for you. I don't see the problem."

Sophia chewed her bottom lip and tried to control her breathing to tamp down the panic that just the idea of having a relationship brought to the surface. "He wants more than just sex."

Daniel glanced over at her, doing a distressed double take before gluing his eyes back to the road. "You say that like it's a bad thing."

She didn't reply. This was an old road. She didn't wish to rehash the old arguments. It took time to rebuild her life, to make it so that she felt safe. Maybe her life was stuck in the status quo, but she liked it that way. There were no complications and no surprises. Like numbers, she needed her life to be concrete and predictable. She needed to be prepared for what happened every day. She needed to be in control.

"Sophie, maybe it's time to let someone in."

Her volume was just as muted as his, but the iron could not be missed. "No."

Wisely, he let the subject drop. He chose something else she didn't want to talk about. "So, what happened with your other job? You know, the one Mom and Dad know you have? The one they tell their friends about?"

Exhaling a stream of air, she rolled her eyes. She wanted to kick herself for making the mistake of telling Daniel how she came to be unemployed. Then she relented, letting herself off the hook. Invariably, she told Daniel everything important in her life.

"Sophia, how are you going to make your mortgage payment? I know you like being a dominatrix, but it isn't a career. There will come a point when you're too old, you lose your looks..."

She cut him off. "You're such an asshole."

He ignored her, continuing as if she hadn't spoken. "I'm just saying, you gotta have a plan. As much as I love you, my place isn't big enough for the two of us to live together and not kill each other." His mouth pursed in careful thought. "Mom would love to have you back home. She and Dad could monitor your activities much more closely, and I wouldn't have to explain why you're never home in the evening, yet you don't have a boyfriend."

Sophia pinched the bridge of her nose and cursed the higher powers for giving her a brother who was adept at pushing her buttons. She snapped at him. "I'm going to start my own business." After she said the words, she stopped, frowning. The idea had never before occurred to her. Daniel owned his own business, but their grandfather passed that on to him when he retired. It had already been established.

"Accounting?"

"Yeah," she said, warming to the idea. It didn't fit into her carefully constructed schedule, but it seemed so right. "I already do your accounting, and I help Ellen out a few times a month. It's a start."

Daniel stopped the car, having arrived in his parking lot without Sophia realizing where they were. He killed the ignition and turned, resting a hand on the shoulder of the seat behind her. A lone streetlight filtered through the windows, casting long shadows that distorted his face. "I think that's a great idea. I can refer a couple of clients to you. I'm sure Ellen can do the same thing."

Sophia's hopes began to rise. Being her own boss was an idea she could really embrace. It brought even more control into her life. She could work out of her house. The extra bedroom on the main floor would be easy to convert to an office. "I need to research how to set up my company."

Daniel caught her excitement. "You could pick up extra classes at my studio if you need money to make ends meet while you're getting this off the ground."

With a wide smile, she kissed Danny's cheek and exited his car. She drove home with mental lists spiraling through her thoughts. The energy that had flagged at this late hour returned with a rush. She wanted to get to work.

By the time she pulled up in her driveway, she was so preoccupied with her plans that she nearly missed noticing Drew perched on her front porch. The wooden bench on which he rested was more for decorative purposes than anything else. It appeared delicate and fragile beneath his sturdy build. He was brilliant in the sweep of her headlights, a sexy god swinging his keys in a circle as he waited for her to come home. She groaned, and her breath caught.

He was on his feet by the time she parked in the garage and made it back out to the front of the house. The expression on his face was both stubborn and hopeful.

"I didn't expect you tonight," she said. Really, she wanted to know what he was doing at her house at two in the morning, but she couldn't bring herself to ask the question. He had her not three hours before. Afterward, he treated her with friendly respect, not flirting overtly, but not hiding his attraction, either. She didn't want to give him an opening to say things that were sweet or romantic.

He shrugged. "I told you I wanted you to come home with me tonight."

A snort of laughter escaped through her nose. That was when he thought she was sleeping with her brother. "It's a little late to go all the way to your house. I have an extra bed. Why don't you come in?"

Once they were inside, she ignored him. She kicked off her shoes and threw her purse and keys on the kitchen table. The lists in her head weren't going to go away until she put some of it on paper. She whipped out a stack of sticky notes and started writing.

Drew watched her for some time before he broke the silence. "If you don't want me here, why did you ask me in?" The irritation in his voice was raw. He made no effort to disguise it.

She glanced up at him briefly, taking in the tense way he filled the doorway of the kitchen. Broad, well-muscled shoulders tapered to slim hips. If he turned, she would see the strong back, powerful thighs, and that deliciously rounded ass. Taking a breath, she hoped he couldn't hear the effort it took to stay where she was. "I have some chocolate in the freezer."

"Chocolate?" It wasn't in the realm of possible answers, so his mystified question was completely justified.

"Chocolate and a vibrator do it for me," she explained without looking up. She didn't need to see him move to know he stood right next to her. The musky, masculine scent of him filled her senses, damning her. "If I'm horny and sex isn't going to happen, I go for the chocolate first."

Without another word, he snaked his arms around her waist and pulled her close. "Don't worry, Sophia. You won't need chocolate tonight." Then, his lush, full lips devoured hers.

He wasn't holding her close enough so that much more than their lips touched. Heat raced, generated by his tongue and the way his firm lips molded to hers. Her nipples hardened where they brushed against his shirt, the thin cotton of the material between them not significant enough to matter.

His hands moved up to thread through her hair and tilt her face to give him better access. He cupped the back of her head with one hand and explored the tender skin of her neck and cheeks with the other. The urgency from earlier in the evening was gone. He wasn't going anywhere for a long, long time.

She reciprocated by taking her time, letting her hands lazily explore him over the barrier of his clothes. He was hard everywhere—his arms, his shoulders, his chest, stomach, back, ass, and thighs. Everywhere her hands roamed, she met unrelenting muscle.

He pulled back, regarding her with that piercing, sensual stare he used as a weapon. Though she would never admit it to anyone, she had watched his show several times in the past week. She loved watching him flirt with the camera, knowing he meant the casual come-on for millions of viewers, not just for her. It was safe to know he was a player. The way he looked at her now wasn't safe. She was a fire that burned in him, and he evoked the same response in her. She was terrified, but she couldn't push him away.

"Am I still staying in the guest room?" His voice rumbled through her chest, though his body barely touched hers.

Sophia slid her hands from his chest to rest on his shoulders. With the slight tilt of her chin, she locked on to the heat in his icy blue eyes. He affected her far too much. She enjoyed having sex quite a bit. Being with Drew wasn't like being with other men. The fire he ignited when she wasn't looking wouldn't seem to go out. Now it consumed her. If she fought it, that thing would destroy her. This was a matter of self-preservation. Her admission was nearly inaudible. "I need to get you out of my system."

He pushed a strand of her hair away from her face, the gentle brush of his fingertips sending tingles to places that yearned for his touch. Following the curve of her cheek downward, he traced her lips lightly. "I won't go willingly," he whispered as he lowered his lips to hers, brushing them against her gently, seeking permission to take things further.

She opened her mouth and gave it to him. She flexed her fingertips, digging them into his shoulders, and she pressed her body into his, loving the way they fit together.

They were going to have vanilla sex. There would be no domination or submission, and no head games. She wouldn't torture him by teasing and withholding orgasm, and she knew he wouldn't ask permission before he came, not that he had before. For the first time since her fateful mistake, she led a man to her bedroom without clearly stated rules and clearly delineated boundaries. It was dangerous, but she didn't care. She wanted Drew more than she had ever wanted anyone before. She was willing to compromise her own rules for a night in his arms.

She promised herself it would just be one night. No matter what he said, it would just be one night on his terms.

Gently, he laid her down on the bed, holding himself over her while his lips roamed the exposed areas above the collar of her shirt. The places he abandoned quivered and cried out for his return, and the places he had yet to visit trembled with anticipation. Her breasts swelled as he nipped at the skin just above them. He knew just how to touch her. Never had her body responded to a man the way it did to Drew.

She moaned when he shifted position, moving lower to close his wet mouth around her hardened nipple, toying with it through the fabric until she gasped. He knew his way around her body too well for someone she had fucked only twice before. She wasn't shy about what she liked, but she never divulged her secrets completely. Drew seemed to find all the right places and pressures without direction.

Her shirt disappeared, and so did his. Sophia closed her eyes, concentrating on the feel of his skin brushing over hers.

Drew captured her lips again in a searing kiss. He pressed himself against her and bit the fleshy part of her shoulder. She gasped as the smoldering heat in her core turned into a full-blown blaze. Her clitoris swelled, the small nodule becoming a mass of nerves that responded to the pressure of Drew's body through the thick cotton of her jeans.

Hands flat against each shoulder, she pushed against him until he rolled, taking her with him. It was her turn to explore. With light fingertips, she let her hands lead and followed with her lips and tongue. She savored the taste of him, a mix of clean masculinity and tangy muskiness. He gasped when she traveled down and across the dips and planes of his stomach, her dark hair trailing over his lightly tanned skin, blocking the light so that she had to feel her way. The hand he put on the back of her head was tentative and encouraging, accepting what she gave without demanding anything more.

Sophia sat up, straddling Drew to be further tantalized by the sight of him beneath her. His hair was mussed, light and wild against the navy pillowcase, his eyes heavy-lidded with desire. He looked like sex should look. He said nothing as he watched her, and she silently thanked him for that. She wanted to just be with him, to feel without thinking about the consequences.

Deftly, she loosed the five buttons on his jeans, freeing his erection from its confinement. When she rose up on her knees to remove his pants, he sat up, capturing her waist in his hands to hold her still while his tongue laved her breasts. He closed his mouth around a nipple. The pull of his sucking reached to her core. Kittenish moans sounded in the back of her throat. She felt his hands at the snap of her jeans, and then she was naked and beneath him, his mouth never having left her breast.

He hovered over her, resting his weight on one elbow. His free hand drifted lower, parting the folds of her pussy to glide over the wetness there. He pressed harder, gently scraping away the thick moisture. The nub was dough under strong, hot fingers. Then he moved lower, slipping two fingers inside. She gasped, arching against him. His thumb rotated around her throbbing clit as he slowly thrust his fingers in and out, in and out.

He leaned up, watching her face while he worked her body. She writhed, pumping her hips in time with the pace he set. Her breathing came faster, and he increased his tempo, upping the ante until she cried out, lifting from the bed in orgasm, her eyes locked to his.

He rolled away from her, missing the surprise in her eyes at his sudden absence. She wanted him back, on top of her and inside her. It was gone when he rolled again, condoms in hand, and slid out of his boxer briefs.

He slapped a plastic rectangle in her hand. "I like when you put it on me." He settled onto his back, and she rose to her knees, which were still trembling, next to him.

She unrolled it slowly, enjoying the way he jerked and pulsed under her light touch. Straddling him, she positioned that thick cock at her opening. She intended to glide down him just as slowly, but he thrust suddenly upward and pulled her down at the same time.

He chuckled as her mouth opened in surprise. She flexed, tightening around him in a way that turned his chuckle into a husky groan. "God, Sophia. I've never wanted a woman the way I want you."

She concentrated on the feel of him inside so she wouldn't have to think about what he said. He would say things like that to all of his lovers. Drew would have no problem meaning it at the time. His feelings would change when he left in the morning. It was a passing thing. It had to be.

Wordlessly, she rocked on him, once, then twice before stopping. She was too close to coming. She needed to pull back a little, or she wouldn't push him over the edge with her.

Drew sat up, kissing her as she began to rock on him again. He was too close, inhibiting her movements, so she pushed him back against the bed.

She wandered the length of his chest with one hand as she leaned forward for leverage.

Tension built, coiling tighter and tighter inside her, until she burned. Beneath her, Drew lifted his hips, thrusting to the rhythm she dictated, his hands squeezing her hips as tiny moans slipped from between his swollen lips. Even though they weren't playing a scene, he let her have control, knowing instinctively she couldn't surrender to him. Throughout it all, he watched her, never closing his eyes to concentrate on the sensations inside or to block her out. Instead of distracting her from her goal, his intense interest drove her higher. She liked being watched by him.

She slipped her free hand between her legs, rubbing against her pulsing clit until he pushed her hand away to take over. He was gentle and considerate, giving her everything he had. She didn't know how much more she could take.

She altered the rhythm, lifting herself to slam down along his length. Sounds of her cries and his mixed with the soaked slapping of the wetness between them. The cries came faster and louder as the tension climaxed and exploded. Sophia convulsed, squeezing him until he cried out, lifting her from the bed. She collapsed against him. It was her last coherent action until her body cooled.

Awareness returned. His chest was warm and damp beneath her cheek. The masculine smell of him assaulted her senses. She could have drowned in him and not minded. Gingerly, she lifted herself from him to crumple on the bed. She was immensely glad that he didn't try to caress her skin or kiss her or talk to her. Now that she was sated, she wanted to have no use for him. She wanted him to fade into her memory.

After a little while, he got up and disposed of the condom. Dimly, she heard the toilet flush. When the bed dipped next to Sophia, she opened her eyes to look up at him. His lips were swollen, and his eyes were still heavy-lidded with passion. He regarded her possessively. She resisted the urge to trace her fingers along the line of his jaw. His sky-blue eyes wandered over her body, his gaze caressing her and turning her on again.

She did nothing to encourage him, returning his stare dispassionately, as if she felt nothing. She wanted to feel nothing. If he reached for her, the lies in her eyes would be revealed.

Something flickered in his eyes, determination, desperation, and defeat. When he turned away, she slid her hand down her stomach. She reached between her legs to finish what he started. She had ridden him hard and enthusiastically. Her orgasm had pulsed around him, milking him for all he was worth, and now she was masturbating. Never had a man given her so much and left her wanting so much more. A soft sigh escaped, and he turned back.

Drew watching her masturbate drove her higher than she could have achieved on her own. Her brow creased in concentration, and her rhythm became erratic. He hardened watching her.

Her eyes roamed his face. She took his hand in hers and guided it between her legs. She finished masturbating using his hand as her prop.

The light he'd left on in the hallway spilled over his face, highlighting the planes and angles there. "I want you again."

Sophia ran her hand over his thigh and traced the length of his erection with her nail. "You can have me until I pass out from exhaustion, but you'll probably pass out first."

Drew lifted a brow at her challenge. "I have amazing stamina."

Sophia propped herself up on one elbow, recalling that last time they had been limited by plans she had made in the evening. Now they had all the time in the world. "So do I."

He kissed the tip of her nose. "Is your vibrator downstairs?"

"That's cheating." The small smile on her face cushioned her accusation.

The smoke in his eyes didn't hide the flames. "Not if you're using it while I fuck your breasts."

Looking down, Sophia regarded her chest skeptically. There wasn't much there. "I'm not sure that's possible."

Drew's smile was wicked. "Trust me, Sophia, it's possible."

She motioned to the drawer in her nightstand. "I keep one in there."

He extracted it and a tube of warming gel. Reading the side of the label, he asked, "Is this okay for men to use?"

She laughed and took it from him. Squirting a generous amount on her palm, she coated his erection and used the extra on herself. Instantly, her sopping pussy heated. She arranged herself on the bed with her knees up and legs spread wide.

"Are you going to watch?" She wanted him to watch.

Drew nodded, his eyes never leaving the vibrator. He watched as she slid it inside and turned the dial. She moved her hips, languidly thrusting against the machine. With her free hand, Sophia grasped his cock, sliding her palm up and down the shaft, slowly working the gel into his skin. He fondled her breasts until her nipples pebbled. Then he straddled her, positioning his erection between the swells there, which he pushed together until they enveloped him tightly.

He was right. It was possible.

Thrusting slowly, he matched her rhythm. He moved faster, and so did she, her cries growing louder and louder until she came.

She pushed away his hands and held herself around him, adding firm caresses to his experience. Drew leaned forward, resting his weight on his hands above her head. She reveled in the power she had over him. It was a woman's power, not exclusive to a dominatrix, but something she had because he wanted her.

She watched him, fascinated by the way his lips parted and moved, as if they had something to say that he didn't know about. On a whim, she spoke to him, her voice just above a murmur. The words meant nothing, but the effect was tremendous. He breathed faster, his cheeks stained magenta as he strained and her words drove him higher.

Watching someone come had never touched Sophia so profoundly.

Chapter 10

Sophia woke to the familiar bass line of "Under Pressure." Without opening his eyes, Drew scooted to the edge of the bed. His arm reached to the floor, groping for his phone.

"Drew Snow." His voice was a hoarse croak. Given all the shouting he had done until the early morning hours, Sophia was only surprised that his greeting wasn't grouchy.

Sliding from bed, she stretched sore muscles. He hadn't lied about having stamina. She could wield a whip for hours, but rarely did she have anyone between her thighs for very long.

"I told you not to put that on the menu. It's not ready." Now he sounded grouchy. "I haven't perfected the recipe."

Sophia headed to the kitchen and put on the coffeemaker before she jumped into the shower. The hot spray loosened some of her overworked muscles. Her night job was physical, and she taught self-defense classes, but it had been a long, long time since she had been this sore. Drew's sexual appetite was voracious. She could easily see how he had come to have the reputation he had. One woman wasn't enough for him. Already her brain was choreographing scenarios for threesomes.

Every single one of them ran headlong into the limitations he put on them. Ten minutes later, she twisted her hair into a wet knot at the nape of her neck and headed to the kitchen for coffee. The smell of something warm and inviting wafted around the corner into the hallway, hurrying her. The house was a modest-sized three-bedroom ranch, though the third bedroom could double as a walk-in closet. The kitchen was only steps from the hallway.

Rounding the corner, she stopped in the doorway. Drew stood in front of the stove, wearing only his jeans, which he hadn't bothered to button. The trail of blond hairs leading from his navel disappeared into his boxers. Her eyes fastened on the barrier, and she fought the urge to touch him there.

"I have to go to work," he said as he lifted the pan to shake it the way practiced chefs do, with just a dish towel around the handle for protection. Sophia tried it once and ended up with a huge mess to clean and a mild burn on the heel of her hand. "My *sous-chef* is getting a little too big for her britches. She wants to put my Hawaiian Chicken on the catering menu, and it's not ready." He set the towel on the counter and sipped at the mug of coffee he had poured. "Maybe I should let you put her in her place for me. It'll save me a few dozen arguments."

Sophia tore her eyes away from his pelvic area. He faced the stove, so his side was to her. Luckily, he hadn't noticed the way she had been staring at him. His eyes were glued to whatever was in the pan.

"You don't owe me an explanation."

Now he looked at her. She avoided meeting his eyes. Propelling her feet forward, she slipped in on the other side of him to pour some coffee.

"Sophia..." His voice trailed off. "I'm making crepes."

That wasn't what he was going to say. She was glad he decided not to force the issue. "I don't expect you to cook, either."

His arms came down on either side of her, resting his hands on the counter to block her in. She felt his breath on her neck, but he didn't touch her at all. "'Thank you' is the correct response. Maybe later you can move on to something like, 'I've never had anything so heavenly in my mouth before,' or 'You've earned that five-star chef rating, Drew.' You can even offer to cook breakfast next time."

Sophia swallowed. He was right. Intimacy like this made her edgy. It wasn't his fault, and she was behaving badly. "I just don't want you to think I expect you to cook for me." It was a poor apology, but Drew accepted it anyway.

"I'm perfectly aware that you only want me for my body." He squeezed her ass in an exaggerated display of making a pass and turned back to the stove. "Go wait at the table like a good girl. Later, you can brag to all of your friends that the hottest chef on TV made breakfast for you."

She laughed out loud at that. Many of her pitifully few friends had already reaped the fringe benefits of knowing Drew. Before she was seated, he plated the crepes, rummaging with uncanny accuracy through her cupboards for things like sugar and toothpicks.

He set the plate before her. Crepes weren't in her vocabulary, so she didn't know what to expect. They looked like thin pancakes wrapped around a fruit filling. The energy she expended the previous evening had been considerable, and she was famished. She dug in. They were heavenly, just as he predicted. Her plate was clear before he was half finished.

Drew stared at her dubiously. "I think I need to feed you when you're less hungry. There's no way you tasted anything."

"It was good," she assured him.

He let loose a long-suffering sigh. "Remind me not to let you write my reviews."

She smiled, again. That was her first glimpse of his sense of humor. It had been far too long since one of her lovers made her laugh. Given the serious nature of her usual "relationship," the lack of mirth wasn't surprising.

"Mouthwatering," she teased. "A sensual feast, perfect for the morning after."

"It's afternoon," he pointed out between bites. "And if I didn't have to go to work and murder Maya, then this would just be a refueling break. We're not out of condoms yet."

She waved away that concern, a smile never leaving her face. "That's only cause for a run to the store."

Drew's mood shifted, suddenly somber. "Should I stop by the store on my way back here tonight, or are you going to come to my house?"

The way he looked at her stole her breath. It was as if nothing in the world mattered to him more than her answer, her assurance they would be together again. "I work until two tonight," she said. "I heard you tell Jonas you had an early call tomorrow."

He closed his eyes and rubbed at his forehead. "In New York. I'm cooking for Matt Lauer, and then doing a couple of book signings. My flight is tonight at nine. I completely forgot."

It was a heady feeling to know that being with her made him forget a national television appearance. Growing panic made her snap out of it relatively quickly. "I'm teaching a class Saturday morning. Then Sabrina has us all at a spa for most of the day, and I work Saturday night. How about Sunday?"

Not seeing him for seventy-two hours should be enough time to acclimate to not having a lover on her usual terms. She needed time to rationalize the anxiety she felt at not being the one completely in control. Drew, as she found out, liked a variety of sexual positions. Some of them cast her as the leader, and some of them did not.

Outside of the bedroom, he was different as well. The few lovers she had allowed to sleep in her bed after a night's passion were ejected early the next morning. Drew was behaving more like a boyfriend. She needed to find solid ground. He wasn't going to let her do that if he stayed too long.

He nodded to her suggestion. "I'd like you to come to my place," he said. "I want to make dessert on you and lick it off slowly."

Heat rushed between her thighs. She clamped them together tightly, intensifying the sensation. Restless, she jumped up to clear away Drew's cooking mess, which wasn't very much. He cleaned as he cooked.

She needed things to be less intense. "Drew, last night you said you wanted to have threesomes, but then you said you don't want me sleeping with anyone else and that you had no interest."

He joined her, handing over his empty plate to be rinsed and loaded into the dishwasher. "It doesn't count if I'm there," he said. "I understand that you not only like to dominate your sex partners, but that you need to do it. That's a need I can't fulfill for you in the way you would like, Sophia. Invite your submissives to join us. I like to watch you do your thing, and I'd love to join in the sex play."

"Most of them are men," she warned. He had only seen her with Livia.

Drew shrugged and leaned against the counter next to the sink. "I'm bisexual, honey. It won't be my first time."

She'd heard rumors, but she didn't like to rush to conclusions. "Are you a top or a bottom?"

"If there are three of us," he said, watching her closely, "I can be a top and a bottom. Whatever turns you on more."

The image of him inside one of her subs while she took him from behind ruined her panties for the day. Sophia closed her eyes at the rush of desire, opening her mind to a dozen more sexual combinations possible for two men and a woman. Mostly, it was the things she could do to Drew that heated her.

The rush of water from the faucet ceased. Her eyes flew open, and she stared uncomprehendingly at the place from which water should have been flowing. Slowly, Drew's hands on her arms turned her toward him. She felt his breath tickle her neck. His teeth grazed her earlobe, sending jerky shivers to her core.

She sighed his name. "I thought you had to get to work?"

He pressed her pelvis to his, rubbing the thick bulge there against her as his hands kneaded her ass. "When you look at me like this, Sophia, I can't seem to go anywhere."

Passion exploded through them. She didn't bother with seduction or teasing. Thrusting her tongue into his mouth, she mastered him, bending him to her will. She wanted to shut him up before he started praising her beauty and telling her how she made him tremble. She wasn't clueless, she could see the way she affected him. Comfortable with his attraction to her, he didn't bother to hide anything.

He lifted her, carrying her the few steps to the kitchen table on which they had just dined. His large, strong hands ripped away her shorts and panties before laying her across the hard surface. She needed this roughness, this completely untamed and unromantic fuck. She needed to know he saw her as a sexual object, not as something more.

Drew fished a condom from his pocket and pushed his open jeans down just enough to free his engorged cock. The table was pushed against the half wall that separated the kitchen from the living room. Raising her hands above her head, Sophia braced herself against the wall just in time. Drew's first thrust was that of a man possessed.

Gone was the gentle lover whose lips and hands roamed her body tenderly the night before. In his place was the fierce not-a-sub she'd teased to frenzy. She had the power to drive him up the sheer face of the cliff or deny him that sweet release. She was in complete control, and they both knew it.

For Sophia, there wasn't a more powerful aphrodisiac on the planet. She came in seconds, the seizures in her vaginal walls holding him tightly and pulling him deeper. He lifted her legs, hooking her knees over his shoulders to meet those demands.

The orgasm lengthened, intensifying and wringing loud cries from them both.

"The things you do to me," Drew gasped, his thrusts coming faster and faster, lifting her from the table. "Oh, God, Sophia, the things you do to me."

Heat spiraled out of control. Flames consumed her. Blackness closed in, obscuring her peripheral vision, and then stealing her sight completely. She screamed as the next orgasm took her, a monsoon washing over her very being.

Sometime later, her senses began to return. The table was cold and hard against her back. Drew was both inside and on top of her. His face rested between her still-covered breasts. He wasn't moving. Her dominatrix instincts kicked in. Tilting his face to the side so he could breathe, she checked his vital signs and took his pulse.

"If you pry open my eyes, I will bite you," he warned, raising his head to meet her eyes with his warm ice-blue stare.

She checked his pupil response anyway. The habit was too deeply ingrained.

Drew lifted himself, reaching out a hand to help Sophia up. She snatched her panties and shorts from the floor and put them on. Being soaked, they were a temporary covering.

He turned away to dispose of the condom and swore.

"What's wrong?" she asked as she buttoned and zipped.

"Condom broke."

Her breathing stopped. She licked at her lips and stared at Drew's back. It only took a couple of seconds to pull herself together, but time slowed so much that it seemed a couple of hours. "Broke as in I should pay close attention to my next period, or broke as in you spilled semen all over the floor?"

He washed his hands before turning to face her. She didn't know what he saw, but she was doing her damndest to hide any emotion. "The first one."

She glanced at the calendar hanging from the refrigerator. She was due for one in a little over a week, which put them in a questionable position, but she wasn't about to tell him that. "Have you been tested for STDs?"

He nodded, watching for a reaction she wasn't going to show. "I'm clean."

"So am I," she said, affecting a nonchalance she didn't feel. "I'll pick up a different brand for Sunday. Do you have any preferences?"

Incredulity wrinkled his brow. "You *are* on the Pill." It was an accusation.

Sophia shook her head. The nightmare that was her interview with the prosecuting attorney reached its claws from her past to clamp around her heart, rendering her ice inside and out. She had been on the Pill, then. It only gave strength to the defense's claim that it was consensual, preplanned. The accusation was her revenge for being dumped afterward, or at least that's how the defense had framed it.

"But you're not the least bit worried?"

She shrugged. "There's no point in worrying. I can take a morning-after pill if it'll make you feel better." She hadn't known about those before. When Ellen had gone to the hospital with her, she asked the nurse to give Sophia one *"just to make sure."*

Hands firmly fisted on his hips, Drew studied the ceiling. His lips moved, and she deduced he was counting to rein in his temper.

"If it will make *me* feel better." He muttered the phrase under his breath several times before locking eyes with her. "What about *you*, Sophia? What do *you* want?"

It was her turn to be perplexed. "I've known you for two weeks, Drew. I don't want a relationship with you. Sex with no strings attached. This is supposed to be casual and fun. *That's* what I want."

He grabbed his cell and keys from the counter. The expression on his face was dark, and storms clouded his eyes.

She reached for him, placing a tentative hand on his arm. "I think it's premature to get upset over something like this."

"You want me to...what? Put it on the back burner? Pretend like it didn't happen?" He wouldn't look at her, and she began to panic. She didn't want this to be serious, but the idea of not having him in her life constricted her chest painfully.

"For a little while, yes," she said as calmly as she could manage. She didn't want him to hear her panic. It had been three years since she had a panic attack. She wasn't even on antidepressants anymore. "At least for a week. I'll take a pregnancy test in a week, okay? I just…I just don't want this to ruin what we have."

He looked down at her hand on his arm, and she followed his gesture. Her fingers were white with the pressure of the grip she had on him. Suddenly self-conscious, she released him and apologized.

Relenting, he took her face in his hands. "I don't want to lose what we have, either. You're right. It's premature to worry. I'll give it a week."

Her lips parted in surprise. He treated her admission as if it confirmed she had some hard-core feelings for him and for some random egg that might be floating around inside her, running from his sperm the way she ran from his affection. Before she could think of anything to say, he continued.

"Set up something with one of your subs, honey. I'm free Monday evening, and so are you." He dropped a brief kiss on her lips and walked out the front door.

Chapter 11

Sophia spent most of the day Thursday setting up her company. She already had an independent license. It was just a matter of filing some more paperwork. Since she owned all the programs and equipment she needed, she had no real start-up costs. Now all she needed to do was find some clients. Luckily, she had already downloaded her lists of contacts onto the BlackBerry Sabrina so thoughtfully supplied.

Friday afternoon, she was contemplating whom to call first when the damn thing rang, startling her into dropping it. Christopher's name showed on the caller ID.

"Hi, Chris," she said brightly. "How are you?" The question was casual, but she was dying to know how his relationship with his new woman was going. She didn't see how a man who needed pain in order to have an orgasm was going to have a successful relationship with a vanilla woman.

His rich laugh, something she was not frequently in a position to hear, sounded on the other end. "Actually, Sophia, I was calling to see how you were doing. I called your office to see if you were up for some work from my firm, and some helpful lady gave me all the details as to how you had a melodramatic fight with your boss and stormed out, fist in the air, vowing never to return."

She laughed, easily picturing the face of Jeremy's secretary who loved Jeremy and gossip. "Sounds interesting. Did I yell and throw things?"

Christopher laughed in understanding. He knew how tightly controlled she was. Public yelling and screaming would never happen, not again. "You broke the poor man's heart and left him an empty shell."

"The shell was decorative," she explained. "And expensive. I thought he could put some bath soaps in it." They shared a mercy laugh. Chris didn't sound overly happy. Concern softened her voice. "What's wrong, Christopher? Why are you really calling?"

He didn't hesitate, switching to a purely business tone. "Really, we're looking for an accountant. I've worked with you before, and I know how good you are. We'd like you to put together a proposal. I can bring over the specifics right now if you have time." From the way his cell phone crackled, she could tell he was on the road. His next warning confirmed it. "I'm heading into a tunnel…"

Static buzzed the line, and then she heard nothing. She hung up. Before she could wonder how he knew she was setting up her own business, he called back.

"Sorry about that. I'm about five minutes from the exit that'll take me to your place. Are you interested?"

"Yeah," she said, looking down at her jean shorts and ratty T-shirt. Chris had never seen her look unkempt. "I'll see you in ten."

Her transformation was impressive, even if she was the only one around to appreciate it. The clothes were easy. She put her hair up in a twist and dabbed on some light makeup. It was strange to dress in a business suit to meet Christopher at her house.

She greeted him at the door with a brief kiss on the cheek. After she took care of the pleasantries and poured him a cup of coffee, they settled down in the living room and got to business.

"So, tell me, Christopher, how did you know I was starting my own business?"

He laughed, a deep and genuine rumble escaping his chest. "I was hoping to convince you to do just that. But I can see you've already thought this through."

"You know me so well," she said. It was a snide swipe, and she felt resentful. The beautiful part about being a dominatrix was that her submissives never knew much about her, while she knew a great deal about them. Christopher's assumption made her uncomfortable because it made Sophia doubt her armor. Maybe Drew had found that chink, too. Maybe he was using that to break her.

His laugh turned tiny and nervous. "I know you like to be in control." He shook his head, denying the boundaries he might have overstepped. "I don't pretend to know the details of your life, Sophia, but I know you. Don't be upset. It's not a bad thing, you know, for someone to *know* you."

Yes, it was. Knowing her meant she would have to face their pity and indignation. Knowing her meant the fragile shell that barricaded her from hurt was shattered. She didn't want to be open, raw, and broken. She had seen how much it broke the hearts of the people who loved her. Her parents still tiptoed around too many subjects. Daniel still blamed himself because Charlie had been his friend. Ellen never questioned her need to work at the club. Jonas pushing her toward Drew was the first forward thing anyone had done around her.

She squared her shoulders and took control of the conversation. "You mentioned something about handling an account?"

The proposal he invited her to write was for the contract to handle the billing and accounting for his law firm. The partners themselves had been handling it all, but the firm was growing too large. They needed someone to keep everything organized.

It was pretty straightforward and would keep her fairly busy. She assured Chris she could have something for him Monday by two. When he rose, she expected a few pleasantries to fall out of his mouth as he made his exit, but he only moved closer.

"Now that the business is finished, there is a reason I came to you instead of inviting you to my office." His big brown eyes were somber and sad. She hated seeing him like this.

She tried to keep it light. "You thought I'd bring my whips with me?"

His smile broke her heart. "Things didn't work out with Janelle."

She nodded in understanding. "You told her the way you like things, and she judged you."

"I couldn't bring myself to tell her. We tried to have sex a couple of times." Chris studied the ground. "I couldn't get there. She thought it was her and ended it."

Sophia put her hand over his, something a friend would do.

"I need you, Sophia. You're the only woman who really understands me."

She blinked. She expected begging, not what bordered on a declaration of romantic interest. "Christopher, we've been through this. You're not in love with me."

"I could be," he said, turning to face her and capturing her hands in his larger ones. "We could date, get to know each other outside of the bedroom. We're both professionals with common interests. It could work."

Biting her bottom lip, she struggled not to recoil. She didn't even want that with Drew. A grain of doubt wedged itself under the edge of her shell. She did want that with Drew, and it terrified her. "I'm seeing someone," she admitted. "He's asked me not to sleep with my submissives unless he's part of it."

Chris shook his head. "It's not like you to let someone else call the shots."

"He's not a submissive." Her lips twisted ruefully. "He likes watching me dominate others, but he doesn't like to be dominated himself."

Fascination lit in Christopher's dark eyes. His full lips puckered with the possibilities. Livia loved threesomes, which was why she frequently brought her dates to Sophia. Christopher had never once hinted an interest. She could see the questions in his eyes. The dominatrix in her waited, making him voice them.

"So, he would watch you discipline me, and then we would both have sex with you?"

She shook her head. "The rules aren't that stringent. All of the possibilities are on the table, Chris. You might be a bottom or a top. You might find your face between my legs and his dick in your ass. I may instruct you to fuck him while I whip you. I won't know until I choreograph the scenario."

Christopher's pupils dilated. His lips parted, and his breaths came shallowly. He was interested, and he trusted her to make sure he got what he needed. "Yes. I want this. You wouldn't happen to be free tonight, would you?"

She laughed. "Be here Monday at five, Christopher. You need to hit the lab and get tested again. Janelle isn't part of our circle."

When Christopher was gone, she texted Drew, asking something that would have been phrased as a command if he were a sub: *3some Monday at 5. My house. You okay with that?*

He texted her back moments later, attaching directions to his house: *I'm still dipping your ass in chocolate Sunday. Bring your vibrator.*

He didn't answer the question directly, probably to make her bristle. He knew how much she hated inexact consent. She wondered if he was back from New York yet. She knew Jonas, or more likely Sabrina, had scheduled all the groomsmen for some of the same spa treatments that the bridesmaids were getting. Sunday suddenly seemed so far away. Sophia wondered if she would run into Drew at the spa the next day, wanting it with a sharp pang that made her chide herself for acting like a hormonal teenager.

Sabrina showed up that evening at City Club, her last client. It was a little after one in the morning. She wore her customary thong and bra, sky blue this time, crossing her arms over herself to shield her body from prying eyes. Sophia swallowed her amusement at Sabrina's shyness. How could she travel the world with an exhibitionist and still be shy about her own nudity?

Maybe because she was so absorbed in her own life, Sophia was hyperaware of how Sabrina was shielding her body. Unconsciously, she protected her abdomen, not her breasts or pussy.

The argument Sophia had with Drew replayed fresh in her head. Did he want her to be pregnant? What did he think that could accomplish?

Sophia took a deep breath and dropped her dominatrix persona. "Sabrina, what are you doing here? Does Ellen know you're here? Does Jonas?"

"Jonas has known for some time that I come to you," she said quietly. "What he does to me is different."

Sexual, was what she meant. Her interactions with Sophia were not charged with any kind of sexual tension. While Sophia wouldn't turn Sabrina away from her bed, she knew Sabrina didn't share the sentiment. Her eyes were focused squarely on Jonas. Nobody else existed.

It made Sophia ache with jealousy for something she would never have.

"That's not what I meant," she said gently. Sophia could tell the shedding of the dominatrix attitude bothered Sabrina.

She bristled anxiously. "Are you mad at me about Drew? I know you're still seeing him. He came to see me this evening."

Sophia shook her head, keeping things focused on Sabrina. "No. I question your sanity at showing up here pregnant. It's not safe." And she wanted to know why Drew went to see Sabrina. They had been friends for years, since he and Ginny met in high school. It wasn't unusual for him to spend time with either Sabrina or Jonas, but something in the way she offered up that piece of information made Sophia think his visit had been to ferret out information about her.

Her lips parted, and then snapped back closed. Drawing herself up fully, she affected the haughty demeanor Sophia loved to whip out of her. "You can stay away from my stomach."

This time, Sophia shook her head with regret. She could stay away from the abdomen. She could make sure she concentrated only on Sabrina's ass and legs, but she would never forgive herself if something happened, and neither would Sabrina. "Go home, Sabrina. Nobody here is going to whip you."

Tears glistened in her eyes, sparkling in the dim light. "How did you know? We aren't telling anyone until after the wedding."

Sophia put her arm around Sabrina, a gesture designed both to comfort her and guide her back to the changing rooms. "My lips are sealed, but the signs are obvious. You're tired, eating healthy, and not drinking anything but water and fruit juices. I'm happy for you both. I know this is something you really want. I'm not going to jeopardize your pregnancy just because you want to relax a bit. Go home to Jonas. He can do other things to relax you."

She burst into tears and threw her arms around Sophia. God, she was tiny. "Did Jonas call you? I didn't tell him I was coming tonight."

"We'll keep this between us," she promised. "Go get dressed. There's a nice non-smoking bistro in the hotel next door, and I'm starving."

They stayed out far too late. It was just the two of them, and Sophia never got up the nerve to ask her about why Drew had stopped by her place that evening. She told Sabrina about starting a business. Sabrina confided her pregnancy fears, and Sophia listened, pushing her own fears to the back of her mind.

Sophia had a self-defense class to teach at nine the next morning, and then she had to rush over to the spa for several hours of pampering. Manicures, pedicures, massages, and facials were not something in which she regularly indulged. Hell, she'd never had a pedicure in her life. The last facial and manicure had been a pre-prom gift from her parents. Her last massage had been erotic.

As she drove her freshly showered self to the spa the next morning, Sophia found herself wondering what kind of prowess Drew might have in the massage department. His hands were large and strong, with long fingers. She grew wet just thinking about the things he could do to her. She could be putty in his hands while he relaxed her muscles, slowly making his way to her sopping pussy where those lush, firm lips would take a turn massaging until she screamed. He could make her come repeatedly, and then use her body for his own pleasure.

Sophia gave herself a mental shake. Those thoughts were very submissive, and that wasn't like her. The whole relationship with Drew wasn't like her. They were equals in bed, true partners giving one another pleasure and greedily taking their fill. Did she have it in her to give herself over to him?

No. It was better to stop thinking like that.

Late as usual, Sophia was the last one to arrive at the spa. Drew awaited her in the lobby, sunglasses twirling between his thumb and forefinger, a slow grin lighting his face.

He wore his usual light blue jeans, slung low on his hips, and a charcoal Sensual Secrets T-shirt. Ice-blue eyes perused Sophia with false casualness. He didn't have to meet her gaze for her to recognize the heat there, but he did. "Ellen said you're always late."

She knew where this was going. "You find this ironic."

"I know the punishment for tardies. I'm just thankful you were never my teacher." He closed the distance between them but stopped short of actual contact.

"Me, too," she agreed. "Otherwise, my plan to fantasize about your hands all over my body while I'm getting a massage would be highly unethical."

Color rushed to his cheeks, fanning the flames in his eyes, and his lips parted. "My house isn't far from here. How about we skip this thing and you won't have to pretend it's me touching you?"

Her legs and lungs stopped working. Thankfully, her knees froze instead of collapsing. Sparks arced the tiny distance between them. His lips were inches away, and she ached for that kiss.

"Sophia! You're finally here."

Drew rolled his eyes at Ginny's timing, and then turned to her with narrowed eyes. "Isn't there some kind of Food Network Challenge you should be at?"

She twisted her lips at him in distaste, a graphic expression that would never mar her sister's serene face. "My assistant, whose ego was already over-inflated, went into the catering business and got his own show, leaving me high and dry on the competition circuit."

Their sparring was lighthearted. The two of them behaved very much like siblings. Sophia never saw Ginny take pot shots at Sabrina like this, though she did fire some shots at Ellen. She liked to see Ellen wrestle with her inner dominatrix.

Stepping behind Sophia, Drew enfolded her in his arms. She stiffened in shock before relaxing into his possessive embrace. God help her, she liked it. "You plan to exact your revenge by stealing my girlfriend?" She stiffened anew at that title. There was no way she was going to relax now. "You own half of the show, Gin. I'm not letting you have Sophia, too."

She hadn't known Ginny owned half of his show. She hadn't known a show could be owned. Carefully peeling away Drew's arms, Sophia stepped away from him.

"Sophia?"

Her name was a loaded question, filled with all sorts of messy, emotionally loaded innuendo. She pasted on the biggest smile she could, which was quite pitiful by any standard. "Sorry, Drew. This is a girl thing. I'll see you tomorrow."

She expected Ginny to stick her tongue out at Drew in a victory gesture, but all she did was look from Drew to Sophia and back again, concern wrinkling her brow. "Are you two still fighting?"

With a brief shake of her head denying Ginny's asked and unasked questions, Sophia turned to follow the attendant through the door into the women's changing rooms. Knowing hesitation would only fuel Ginny's probing questions, she didn't hang around to hear them.

Ginny joined Sophia before too long. Sophia knew the fact they had joined the others in comfortable chairs to await manicures wouldn't stop Ginny from asking.

"If you're not still fighting, what's wrong?" Ginny had settled into her chair and was thoughtfully perusing nail colors. "Lesbians avoid nail polish," she informed her specialist. "Just make them look good without the chemical paint."

She didn't have to repeat the question because Ellen took up her cause. "I thought things were going well between you two. Not everyone has the balls to go at it in my den with a roomful of people downstairs who know exactly what you're doing."

Sophia busied herself with choosing her color. She liked bold, vibrant colors that contrasted with her naturally olive complexion. From the corner of her eye, she saw Sam and Amanda exchanging glances. With her curly blonde hair and changeable olive eyes, Amanda looked much like a feminine, pretty version of Jonas. Her curvy build attracted her husband's attention in eighth grade, and it never wavered.

Samantha's hair was darker, with auburn highlights that shone brightly in the sun. She was taller than Amanda, and she had a boyish, lanky build. Sophia didn't know Sam, who spent much time traveling, as well as she knew Amanda, who lived locally. Both of them had no scruples about following Ginny's lead. *Christ.* Lara wasn't there to keep Ginny in line. Sophia wasn't going to get out of this.

With a heavy sigh, she gave them something. "Drew and I are not fighting. We have plans for mind-blowing sex tomorrow and Monday."

Ginny chimed in next. "He called you his girlfriend, and you gave him the cold shoulder. That's obviously a sore spot." Selecting a subdued peach, she handed it to her manicurist. Apparently, she had changed her mind about lesbians eschewing nail polish. "Drew's not a cheater, if that's what you're worried about. He gets around, but honestly. When he wants no stings, he makes it clear beforehand. If he called you his girlfriend, he meant it."

Sophia hoped the massages were private.

Amanda studied her curiously. "He's really cute, Sophia, but I thought you were already seeing someone."

Even as pressure built at the back and top of her head, Sophia affected nonchalance and waved away her concern. "I don't do relationships. I have lovers, affairs. Entirely stringless."

All the pairs of eyes turned to Sophia, not only those of her supposed friends, but those of the manicurists as well. She wondered if they knew exactly who they were talking about. She hoped this didn't end up on the

Internet or some trashy TV pseudonews show. Drew already had enough publicity from that front. "I am not his girlfriend."

Silence greeted her vehement announcement. Sabrina was the first to break it. "But you've agreed to not see other people. That's a commitment people in a relationship make."

Nausea churned Sophia's stomach. She fought the beginning of a migraine. "Can't we talk about your wedding? Aren't there dresses to complain about or flower arrangements to discuss?"

Ellen finally got the message. She had witnessed several of Sophia's meltdowns. "Sure," she said a little too enthusiastically, "let's talk about how the neckline needs to be lower on my dress."

Sabrina gasped, her big brown eyes growing saucerlike. "It already shows most of your cleavage."

"Honey, that's the only hope I have of deflecting people's attention away from my massive thighs. I've got a wicked set of breasts, and I intend to use them." Ellen's dry declaration produced some laughter and succeeded in changing the subject.

Sophia rested her head against the back of the chair and closed her eyes. The chatter faded to background noise, and her nausea subsided.

* * * *

Drew watched as the pretty, petite manicurist buffed his nails. Due to the demands of his show, manicures were something in which he indulged every week. Nobody wanted to see close-ups of a cook with dirty nails handling food. It tended to detract from the visual attractiveness of the dish.

His mind, however, was a million miles away. Sophia had seemed glad to see him. She had been close to accepting his invitation to return to his house for an afternoon of steamy sex. Then Ginny interrupted. Sophia stiffened at his touch. Did she have a problem being touched in front of Ginny?

"I don't want a manicure, either, Drew, but I'm not scowling about it."

Jonas's voice broke through, interrupting Drew's puzzled thoughts. He looked up suddenly, focusing on olive-green eyes that were laughing at him. "If you don't want a manicure, why are you getting one?"

Sabrina's lanky husband shrugged, a gesture of surrender. "Wife says, husband does."

"You do everything she says?" Drew found that difficult to believe. Sabrina had always been on the bossy side, but he'd never seen her try to boss Jonas around.

"Absolutely." He grinned. "Every successful marriage is built upon a few simple rules. Doing what your spouse says is just one of them."

Ryan, even taller and lankier than Jonas, threw in his support. "It's the most important one. 'Yes, dear' is the most important phrase to learn in a marriage."

A deep laugh came from behind Drew. Ty added his opinion. "You also need to learn 'I'm sorry' and 'Prettier than who? I only notice you.'"

The three married men in the room laughed. Drew looked at them one at a time. Two weeks ago, he would have felt sorry for the poor bastards, and now he was jealous. At long last, Drew understood why it would make a man happy to repeatedly bend to the same woman's wishes. Sophia had only to ask something, anything, and he would move heaven and earth to make it happen.

"It does work both ways," Richard added quietly.

Drew started before leaning back to look at Jonas's quiet brother-in-law sitting unobtrusively on the other side of Ty. He hadn't noticed Richard. "Both ways?"

Richard smiled widely. "Happy spouses make for happy homes. If you keep her happy, she'll keep you happy."

Jonas's groan came from behind Drew. "Drew, do not ask him to be more specific. Rich and I have an unspoken agreement to never talk about his sex life."

"I'm sleeping with his sister," Richard said, an evil light glimmering in his friendly brown eyes. "We've been together for seventeen years, but talk of anything more than kissing brings out his big-brother instincts. It gets messy, but Amanda doesn't make me sleep on the couch for kicking her brother's ass."

Ryan made a knowing noise. "He's the same way about Ellen. Very brotherly."

The dripping sarcasm wasn't lost on anyone. Jonas's mouth twisted in disgust. "Ellen tells me enough, Ryan. She doesn't censor anything, no matter how much I beg. I don't need that from you, too."

Before Drew could ask, Jonas held up a hand. "Don't even think about getting technical about Sophie. She's like a little sister to me."

"Remind me to keep you away from Vanessa," Ty said dryly. "It sounds like you have enough sisters."

"I don't think that'll be a problem," Drew said, addressing Jonas, but avoiding actually looking at anyone. "I think she just dumped me again."

Ryan's carroty brow rose. "You think?"

Drew's scowl returned. "She's hard to read."

"That's a dominatrix thing," Ryan said. "It'll get easier the better you get to know her. It took me about six months to crack Ellen."

The manicures ended. As a group, they made their way to the pedicure chairs. Drew sank into the cushion and neglected to acknowledge the way the woman massaging his foot used her eyes to throw invitations his way.

"Did you ask her to give up her submissives?"

A question like that from Richard shocked Drew.

"I wish this was a completely different discussion," Ty said. "I saw the Tigers play at Comerica Park yesterday. Good game. My boss thinks I was sick."

"No, she doesn't," Jonas, who was married to Ty's boss, said.

Drew closed his eyes and answered Richard. "No."

"Why not?" Ryan asked. "That's the first thing I made Ellen do before we got serious. She made like it was painful to let them go, but I could tell she really wanted to be with just me."

"I don't want her to give up her submissives," Drew said. "I can't play that game with her. She needs them. And, truthfully, I like to watch her work them over."

"What, then?" Jonas said. "Sophie's pretty clear about what she wants and doesn't want."

"I don't know." Drew opened his eyes and stared at the ceiling. This male-bonding afternoon wasn't supposed to turn maudlin, but he needed information about Sophia that she didn't seem inclined to provide about herself. Most women couldn't wait to spill their life story. Sophia seemed to pretend she didn't have one. "I waited for her in the lobby. Things were fine.

I was joking around with Ginny, and Sophia just…changed. She stiffened up and pushed me away. Then, she disappeared into wherever they keep the women."

"Joking?" The tone in Jonas's voice left no doubt he was frowning. "About what?"

The pedicurist pressed a point in Drew's foot that momentarily stole his breath. He glanced down at her, and she smiled up at him in a way that dared him to make a big deal out of it. "Did that hurt?"

"A bit," he said, ignoring the warning. "Just be careful." Sighing, he turned his attention back to Jonas. "Ginny came out to take Sophia back to where Sabrina is. I grabbed Sophia and accused Ginny of trying to steal my girlfriend."

"Well," Ryan said, "there you go. She's not your girlfriend."

"Yeah," Ty added, giving up on a sports-related conversation. "When she's still sleeping with other people, it's not an exclusive relationship."

Drew resisted the urge to roll his eyes. "She agreed to not see them when I'm not part of the action."

His proclamation was met with silence.

"I'm okay with it as long as I get to play, too," he added. "Sophia doesn't have a problem with that. I think she was willing to let them go until I told her I was okay with her keeping them."

"I'm amazed she gave you that much," Jonas said quietly. "But Ryan is right. She's not your girlfriend."

"We're not seeing other people."

Jonas leaned forward, reached out, and squeezed Drew's arm. Sympathy blazed from him. "You have to take it slow with her, Drew. She's been through a lot. The fact she's agreed to have any kind of a relationship with you at all is significant. I've never seen her do that with anyone before. Go slow, and be patient."

Drew glanced over, meeting Jonas's eyes. Unspoken words told Drew that Jonas wasn't going to say more about Sophia. Drew also understood the look to mean he did have a significant chance with her if he followed Jonas's advice.

"And don't use the *G* word," Ryan added. "Let her get used to the idea first."

* * * *

Thank goodness the massages were private. Sophia lingered afterward, hoping the rest of them would assume she ran out of there to avoid them. The firm hands pressing into her muscles made her forget about life for a while. Everything left her head, allowing her to just exist in peace. She was already looking forward to the two others Sabrina had scheduled in the coming weeks.

Sophia straggled to her car afterward.

Her unhurried exit did help her to avoid mostly everyone. Drew waited in the parking lot, leaning casually against the driver's side door to Sophia's Fusion. He looked just as good as he had four hours ago. She didn't know what spa treatments Sabrina planned for the men, but whatever they did suited him. He was relaxed. A light smile rested on his lips and echoed in his bright eyes. His body language clearly stated that he wasn't going to let her leave without talking to him.

She approached, stopping out of his reach when all she wanted to do was press her body to his and lose herself in his kiss. "I have to go to work."

His expression didn't falter. "Not for two hours." He held a hand out, just as he had three nights ago when he followed her to the bathroom at Ellen's house. Sophia saw the beginnings of a game she didn't want to play.

She didn't want a man who waited for her, holding out a figurative olive branch whenever she distanced herself from him. She wanted to be with him, but she didn't want the complications he required.

She glanced at his hand, dismissing it outright when she felt like doing the opposite. That was the dominatrix inside, always in control, denying herself what she wanted because it would compromise what she needed. "It'll take me that long to get home, change, and get there."

He withdrew his hand and shoved it into his pocket, not bothering to hide his anger or his disappointment. "You keep a change of clothes in your car. You have no pets waiting to be fed or watered. Let me buy you dinner. I promise I will adequately apologize for unauthorized use of the *G* word. From now on, we're just friends."

Sophia blinked at him, mystified. "*G* word?" Even as she asked the question, she wanted to kick herself. *Girlfriend.* She harbored the hope they could both pretend he had never uttered the word or the sentiment. She put up a hand before he could answer. "Wait. In the same breath, you asked me to dinner and apologized for calling me your girlfriend."

Mirth sparkled in his eyes, transforming his face from something perfect into something spectacular. Breathing became difficult. "I frequently buy dinner for my friends. I cook for them, too, a benefit you seem to resent." He ignored her reference to the *G* word and the fact he had not actually apologized for using it.

She wasn't going to lose her composure with him. "Yet I'm the only one you asked."

Her sarcasm didn't dent his humor. "The Spencers are having their brood over for dinner, Ellen and Ryan's babysitter has a date tonight, Ty has plans with this wife, and Ginny is going home to reap the benefits of her massage. It's just us left."

His reasoning checked out, but the two of them alone together tended to not do friend things. Drew's headlights flashed as he unlocked his car, startling her. She hadn't realized she parked next to him.

"Come on," he urged, rounding the front of his car. "You can follow me."

He didn't open a door or otherwise do anything gentlemanly to facilitate her entrance to her own car. His engine purred to life, and he glanced over, lifting his brow in a hurry-up gesture.

With a sigh, she followed him to what turned out to be a sports bar. The drive was only fifteen minutes, but she spent every moment alternately listing the reasons she should or shouldn't have dinner with him. He was going to try something. She wanted to be sure she would rebuff his advances, but she was learning not to trust her reactions around him.

The inside was neither dark, nor well lit, but something distinctly in between. No smoke hung in the air, stale or otherwise. He held the door open for her to enter. She told herself it was in deference to her sex, not to her. Even Daniel held doors for her.

In a sweep of the room, she noted pool tables, video game machines, pinball machines, and a trivia contest. Drew signaled to a guy in the back to put his name on the board for pool, and she rolled her eyes. His plan was to watch her bend over a pool table and stare at her ass. That was subtle.

Well, two could play at that game. She had no trouble staring at his tight, squeezable ass, either. She did it as she followed him to the bar, where he promptly ordered onion rings and a burger with extra onions.

It had to be his way of assuring her that he wasn't planning to try anything tonight. Nobody ate that many onions on a date, not if they wanted to get lucky later.

The barkeep turned to Sophia. He was an older man who was either ignorant of or unimpressed by Drew's status. "What'll you have?"

Taking her cue from Drew, she ordered a burger, minus the onions. She had to work, and the last thing she needed to do was sweat out the odor of onions. As a certified Italian, she had to be careful where powerful spices and vegetables were concerned. Sophia and Daniel spent a considerable portion of their teen years experimenting with the amount of odor they could make seep from their bodies. She could hold her own with him or anyone else.

Drew glanced over at her. "I heard you play pool."

She shrugged. "I've played pool." She hadn't picked up a stick in years. Once upon a time, she had been pretty good. She had no idea how her dormant skills fared.

"Are you a wagering kind of woman?"

"What are we betting?" She steeled herself. He couldn't suggest strip pool in a public place, but it wouldn't surprise her if he wanted to barter something sexual.

"Five bucks a game."

"Fine," she said. "Get me a water. I'm going to use the restroom."

When she returned, her water was perched on the edge of the table, whose wooden ledge attested to a past filled with many other sweating drinks. Drew gestured to it with an offhand glance. Standing with a long stick in his hands, his real concentration was on the triangle of colored balls at the other end of the table. "I'd give you first break, but then you'd think I was coming on to you."

He broke. Drew sank three balls with seemingly effortless grace. He made his way around the table, sending four more into the pocket before he made it around to her side. She sipped her water and wished she'd worn a short skirt or a top with a lower cut. That man needed a distraction.

She adjusted her bra, fondling her breasts in a manner that was both overt and discreet. In a pinch, anything would do. Her breasts might not be huge, but Drew seemed fascinated by them anyway. It was a long shot, as he was standing next to her and his attention was centered on lining up his next shot. Anything he saw would be from the corner of his eye.

He missed. Straightening, he narrowed his eyes at her. "That's not friendly warfare."

"Friendly warfare? That's an oxymoron." Sophia selected a cue from the rack next to the table and lined up her first shot. She played conservatively, taking the easy shots first only because they'd leave the white ball in position for another shot.

Drew adjusted himself.

"Taking off your shirt would be more effective," she suggested. "Rub some baby oil all over your chest so it glistens and tug your jeans down low to show the beginning of your happy trail. You'll have every woman in a square mile clamoring for your attention, and a goodly amount of men."

He paused in the midst of lifting his beer bottle to his mouth, staring at her in mild astonishment. In the two weeks she'd known him, she had commented on his physical attractiveness, but she'd never grouped herself with those who wanted him.

The next shot put her near him. He stepped back to allow her room to pass. She turned her body sideways to squeeze through, keeping her back to him. Electricity crackled in the space between. She marveled at how much he affected her when she didn't want to be affected, by him or any man. Her standoffishness wasn't personal.

"Except you." Did she imagine the desperation in his whispered words?

Completely lacking in mercy, she bent over the table. The jeans she wore hugged her ass nicely. She had three pair, all exactly the same. As difficult as it was to find jeans that fit right, she knew better than to buy just one pair when she finally found them. She heard Drew's intake of breath as the heat of his stare penetrated the denim of her pants.

The slow grin stretching her lips was hidden from him. "I already have your attention." It was an excellent shot. She sank two balls and established her control of the situation.

"You do realize that friends don't flirt like this," he pointed out.

Definitely desperate, she decided. This game was hers to lose. Butterflies invaded her stomach, and she couldn't breathe. *Which game?* Some games, she couldn't afford to lose. Still, she couldn't stop now. That would be acknowledging she was flirting, seriously flirting. Flirting meant interest. She had no interest in Drew. She was there because they had a friendly relationship. They had friends in common. Tomorrow, she would go to his house because they were sleeping together. It didn't mean anything except that he was good in bed. If she kept repeating those words, she might convince herself.

"Most of my friends don't find it distracting for me to adjust my bra." She congratulated herself on keeping an unaffected air.

The waitress brought over red plastic baskets filled with their burgers. Drew's was littered with onion rings, Sophia's with fries. She set it aside and sank two more in one shot. Then she leaned back, studying the table. All the simple shots were taken. Unless she got fancy, Drew was going to get a turn.

He leaned in close, brushing his arm against hers. Sparks flew at every point of contact. She wished she could jerk away, but she found her body leaning closer, pressing against Drew's warmth. She doubled her efforts to concentrate on finding the next shot. Finally, she found it. She would have to bank both balls. Damn. This was the point in the game where she got her ass kicked.

As if sensing his opening, Drew made a pretense of stepping back to allow her room to maneuver. Once she bent down, he leaned closer and burped.

It wasn't the sound so much as the smell. Extra onions on the burger and onion rings were not date food. If she was under the impression he meant this as a date, that illusion was shattered. Her eyes watered, but it had the opposite effect from what he intended. That was too much like something Daniel would have done to be distracting.

Sophia focused with iron concentration and sank the shot. With a satisfied smile, she straightened and regarded Drew with superiority. "I have a brother, Drew. It would have been much more effective to start stripping."

She won the game—one of them, at least.

When he walked Sophia to her car later, he didn't try to kiss her. She drove away feeling like something was missing.

Her heart wasn't in her work that night. She went through the motions, affecting the proper tone and demeanor, hoping nobody noticed her mechanical delivery.

* * * *

With a satisfied smirk on his face, Drew watched Sophia's Fusion drive away. She was coming around. He wasn't sure waiting for her and forcing her on a date was the right course of action. Ellen had advised against it, though Jonas had only shrugged and said it wouldn't hurt to ask.

There was something more going on here, something Ellen and Jonas knew about, but they had no plan to share with him. His only clue was Jonas's cryptic statement about Sophia having been through "a lot." What did that mean, exactly? Obviously, Sophia had been hurt before, but by whom? And how?

He would get the truth from Sophia eventually. It would take time, but he would prove to her that she could trust him.

Of course, burping in her face like that was a definite gamble. Drew had never let himself have fun like that with someone with whom he was planning to have multiple sexual encounters. He'd dated models, actresses, and heiresses. Not one of them would have had dinner with him at a bar while playing pool. None of them would have been amused by his attempt to be gross.

Sophia was different. Her initial reaction had been surprise, followed closely by enjoyment. She'd laughed at him. He liked her laugh and the unpretentious smile that went with it.

Drew climbed into his silver Mercedes. He had some errands to run before he headed to his parents' home, which happened to be just down the street from his own house.

Miranda Snow was in the kitchen pummeling dough when Drew strolled in and kissed her on the cheek. His mother cooked to relieve stress, and she was very good at it. Many of Drew's early recipes were ones his mother taught him. However, she only made bread when she was exceptionally upset.

"You okay?" He knew she wasn't.

She blew a strand of her short blonde hair away from her face. "Peachy," she lied.

"Want to sit on the couch and talk about it?" Not knowing the extent of his mother's emotional upheaval, he tempered the threatening smirk. "I could write on a clipboard and sip some brandy while you rant and rave."

Miranda shot him the look of death and punched the white mass in front of her. The couch joke was something between Drew and his sister, Lila. As the children of a very successful psychologist, they spent many afternoons being urged to talk about their problems. Those sessions invariably took place in the kitchen and were punctuated with instructions to *"add more garlic"* or to *"cut those peppers into smaller cubes."*

"I'm making sourdough." The words came out in grunts.

Drew dragged a high stool closer and sat down. He didn't offer to help, knowing the look she just shot him would be nothing compared to the explosion that would follow an offer of help when she didn't want it. Miranda's volatile temper was also a joke between Lila and him. Their mother was all talk and no action, so her explosions were safe and often fun to watch.

"Really, Mom, what's wrong? Where's Dad?"

She looked around the kitchen, as if she was surprised to find her husband absent. She grunted again. "Packing."

His parents' marriage was rock solid. Drew wasn't overly concerned. "You just got back from Brazil."

Miranda's expression turned dreamy as she remembered Brazil, and her violent actions halted. Her smile was short-lived, as was the cease-fire on the dough. "Lila thinks she's staying in Minnesota."

That explained everything. Miranda and Jonathan encouraged their children to travel. They were proud when Drew was accepted into culinary programs in Switzerland and Paris. As long as the absence was temporary, the Snows didn't have a problem with their children leaving.

Drew, ever the good son, not only returned, but he purchased a home just down the street. Lila, ever the independent daughter, lacked a driving need to return home.

"Mom, Lila's twenty-six. You can't have Dad fly to Minneapolis and haul her back to Michigan." The dough was ready for the oven. Drew rose to his feet, pulled out a bread pan, and sprayed it before setting it on the counter. Then he came around behind Miranda and put his hands on her shoulders. "She's won a very prestigious fellowship. You should be proud of her."

"I am proud of her." The violence left Miranda. She slumped, defeated, and let Drew envelop her in a hug. "She's not coming home for the Fourth of July. I miss my baby girl." She sniffled a bit, and then looked up at her son. "If you would stop tomcatting around and settle down, I'd at least have a daughter-in-law."

The idea of settling down with Sophia did appeal to him. Referring to a woman as a girlfriend wasn't something he did lightly, or often. When he did, he meant it. With a tiny laugh, he released his mother and washed his hands. If he was reading the situation correctly, this was going to be a long night filled with pastry making.

"I'm trying, Mom. If it's possible, I found myself enamored of a woman who has commitment issues."

Miranda arranged her dough into the pan Drew prepared and slid it into the oven. Facing her son, she handed him a clean towel. "Let's make baklava, and you can tell me all about it."

"After you tell Dad to stop packing."

Chapter 12

Sophia hated feeling like this. Drew sent directions to his house again—in case she deleted them the first time. When she checked her messages after work, her airways closed off, choking with emotion. She wondered how he would take it if she went directly from work to his house. Technically, it was already Sunday...

Shaking off the feeling, she forced herself to breathe and drive home. It was just sex. If she kept telling herself that, she might eventually believe it. The alternative was unacceptable. She couldn't have these feelings. Not again. She swore it would never happen again.

She worked on the proposal for Christopher's firm, but that didn't stop thoughts of Drew from invading her mind. They weren't just sexual thoughts. Never once did she picture him naked. Okay, maybe she did a couple of times. Mostly, she thought about him. She pictured him reclining on a lawn chair in her backyard, a cold glass of lemonade in his hand as they relaxed and talked about nothing at all. She pictured him surprising her with tickets to see a Shakespeare play. She wondered if he would participate in the pickup softball games she and Daniel seemed to find all over this time of the year. She wondered if he would volunteer to help demonstrate to victims of violence how to fight back against an attacker.

Sophia shook away that last thought. Even if everything else went well, that wasn't a part of her life she wanted to share with him. She didn't want him to know.

He was generous, thoughtful, and fun. He had a sense of humor and not much of a temper. Even when he was angry, it was a calm anger, like he accepted the emotion and he knew what it took to work through it.

He wasn't ashamed of anything. Her lovers were all submissives, each with some kind of shame to hide, some kind of shame to mask what she carried. She envied him, and she wished he were there with her. Somehow, she knew he would lie in bed with her, hold her in his arms until the panic subsided. Without too much imagination, she could feel his arms enveloping her in warmth and safety. She wanted him there with her, and that was a dangerous thing to want.

Sophia ran on the treadmill in her basement until she couldn't stay awake, and then she dragged her sweaty, exhausted ass to bed and slept a deep, dreamless sleep.

The shrill ringing of the phone woke her. She sat up slowly, blinking at the shaft of light that peeked from a gap between her curtains and beamed her in the eyes. In no hurry to answer the phone, she rolled from bed and made her way into the bathroom for a shower. She would change the sheets before she left. A glance at the clock predicted that her late start would make it a late night.

She called Drew from the road. He hadn't lied when he mentioned he lived and worked an hour from her house. The messages in her voicemail were both from him. The call that woke Sophia was his second attempt to reach her.

When she did make it to his subdivision, she stopped cold. The stop was literal because the entrances to the exclusive area were gated. She hadn't even known they had places like that in Michigan. It wasn't California or New York or Miami. The biggest movie star lived in Chelsea, located somewhere in the middle of nowhere, and she could never remember who it was, but she had been to Chelsea once. It was a cute little town.

Drew lived in an exclusive area of Bloomfield Hills, which was itself an exclusive area. Even Sabrina and Ellen, cloistered away in their big houses in Milford, weren't this inaccessible. If this didn't bring to light the economic disparities between Sophia and Drew, she didn't know what could.

The uniformed guard at the gate was unarmed, which made her feel better. He sauntered casually to her car and stopped under the awning that guaranteed trucks over a certain height could not gain entrance there, clipboard in hand.

"Good afternoon, Miss. Can I have your name?" His eyes raked over her relatively new Fusion, the expression in his eyes clearly stating she didn't belong inside as a guest. She qualified as domestic help, maybe, but not as a guest. She had never even noticed what kind of car Drew drove. She only knew it was a silver sedan.

"Sophia DiMarco." God help her, she was self-conscious about giving her name. Tension settled in her chest. Everything about this was wrong. This was the Fates reinforcing her trepidation, telling her that being with Drew was dangerous. She battled the urge to flee. How could she explain to Drew that she got all the way to his gate and turned into a chicken? She tried dumping him before, and it hadn't worked out too well. Now that he knew how he affected her, she knew he wasn't going to let her go without a fight.

"Ms. DiMarco, Mr. Snow is expecting you. I have a gate key for you." He slid a card with a magnetic strip from his clipboard and handed it to her. "It's a guest pass, good for the rest of this month. You can use it at any unmanned entrance. Just slide it in the reader, and the gate will lift. You'll need it to exit from those areas as well."

Now she knew the real reason for her trepidation. This was the equivalent of giving her his class ring. He might have apologized for calling her his girlfriend, and he might have taken her to a bar as a friend, but his attitude toward Sophia hadn't changed. If he gave her the key to his house, she would run as fast as she could the opposite way. And then, in a shaking, sweaty mass puddled on the floor in defeat, she would add it to her key ring.

The gatekeeper gave her directions to Drew's house. As she drove through the quiet, tree-lined streets, she gawked at the glimpses of the mansions set deep in what she estimated to be five-acre parcels. Some of them had to be at least ten acres.

Even with the gate around the entire subdivision, most of the homes had another gate at the driveway. They must have been remote-operated because she didn't see anyone getting out of their cars to open them. Some houses with gates kept them open. Drew's house was one of those.

She parked in the curve of his driveway near the door. His landscaping was immaculate. Beds of manicured foliage and blooming flowers were tastefully scattered, accenting the beauty of his mansion. The house itself was brick and cedar siding, done in warm earth tones. Dread settled its cold self in her stomach. Everything about Drew's house underlined how mismatched they were. Then, the worst of her trepidation lifted, and with it, her spirits.

She didn't belong in his world. This was just sex, nothing more. He was slumming. When he was ready to settle down, he would find a woman from a "good" family who would please his parents.

The door opened as she climbed the steps, and she hoped to hell he didn't have a butler. Sun glinted through the trees near the entrance, temporarily blinding Sophia. Her next step moved her into the shade. Drew stood on the porch wearing only jeans, the ornate, dark wooden door open behind him.

Her smile widened as she came closer. He was barefoot and shirtless, his naked chest glistening in the sunlight. She wore a short skirt and a lacy top that accented the curves of her breasts and made her waist seem thinner than it was. The gleam in his eye was pure lust.

His hands rested casually on his hips until she was within reach. They were on hers before she knew he moved, pulling her closer until her hips were nestled against his.

"I missed you," he whispered. The words brushed over her skin, and she was trembling before he kissed her.

It was a light kiss, the kind that invited something deeper, but didn't demand. She needed this kind of gentle approach, this reassurance that she still called the shots, even if it wasn't true. This instinctual understanding was yet another thing she liked about him.

"I'm glad you came. I was starting to think you changed your mind."

"You promised chocolate and told me to bring my vibrator. No woman could resist an invitation like that."

The smile he gave her was affectionate, an appreciation of her sense of humor instead of something lustful. She would have been more comfortable with something lustful. He reached around to hold the door with one hand while the other found the small of her back. His gentle touch guided her into his home and fed a need for tenderness she couldn't seem to shake.

She wanted him to take her straight to his bedroom and tear off her clothes, but he didn't. Her "lovers" were never given such courtesy. She directed them to the basement straightaway. Some made it to her bedroom later, but they all started out in the same place.

"Would you like a tour?"

The foyer could easily have swallowed half of her house. It was a wide room with twin curving staircases that led to a second-floor balcony. The room was a study in contrasts, dark woods and creamy walls. The detail in the woodwork was exquisite. A giant crystal chandelier hung from the ceiling.

"You live alone?" She meant it as a joke. She knew he lived alone, but the house was far larger than anything she had ever seen.

Her parents were working-class people. Sophia's father owned his own landscape company, and he still did much of the physical work. Her mother stayed home with Daniel and Sophia until they were both in middle school, and then she went back to work as a nurse. They weren't poor, but they never had anything like this. She had no business being there. She felt like an impostor.

"Until you're willing to move in." His qualification was quiet and serious.

She ignored it and answered his original question. "A tour isn't necessary. Just promise me you haven't been eating onions and take me to your bedroom."

He grinned widely. "I see you missed me, too."

Unwilling to answer, she looked away, tracing the banisters with her eyes, following the upward curve. She had only seen the foyer, but she couldn't help thinking it was an awfully large house for one person. "Do you get lonely here?"

She regretted the question immediately. She couldn't seem to stop herself from asking personal questions. They had the effect of encouraging Drew in ways she didn't want to encourage him.

"My parents live just down the street," he said, pointing in the direction of what she assumed to be their house. "My sister moved to Minneapolis last fall to finish her PhD, so they have nothing else to divert their attention. Ginny's mom lives a couple of streets over. We all grew up in this neighborhood. I know pretty much everyone."

She understood the parts he wasn't saying, too. He liked being close to his past. Emotion choked her before she shook it away. She wished she could be close to her past. She wished her life wasn't broken into two distinct before-and-after sections. The part she was in now alienated her from the part she wished to be in—that ignorant, innocent place she would never know again. Even Drew was a part of the "now" instead of the "then." She wouldn't know him if she hadn't met Ellen.

"Have you had lunch? Or breakfast? It's after two, but you seem to sleep late on Sundays."

Drew had been the cause of her sleeplessness both times she had slept excessively late on a Sunday. Heat rose to her cheeks. "I had breakfast before I came. You won't have to worry about me passing out from hunger. I'm up to the physical exertion."

His chuckle was a low rumble in his throat. "In that case…" He gestured to the set of stairs on the left. The light pressure of his hand at her back guided her through the wide hallways.

The master suite was larger than her entire house. Double doors opened to an elegant sitting room decorated with accents of strong blues and browns. She had never thought those two colors were very compatible, but they worked here, giving the room a classic, yet homey feel.

At the far end, another set of French doors opened to a wide balcony, where it looked like he had a hot tub. Across the room, a third set of French doors, flung open to invite further inquiry, opened to the actual bedroom part of the suite. The blue-and-brown theme continued into that room.

Sophia stopped in the doorway, her eyes fastened on the king-sized bed. The comforter, patterned with blue and cream blocks, was folded clumsily across the bed. It looked more as if he'd tossed it aside during the night than purposely placed there. The sheets were rumpled from use.

Her gaze swept the room. From what she had seen, the rest of the house was tidy and clean. This room, where he must spend a significant amount of time, was messy. Clothes were strewn everywhere, some on the furniture, some on the floor. The vast size saved it from being a complete disaster.

"My housekeeper doesn't come in until tomorrow," he said by way of explanation. There was no note of apology in his voice.

"You can't pick up your clothes or make your bed?" She meant it as teasing, but she was locked in a sense of overwhelmed incredulity at the opulence of his house.

"My kitchen is immaculate," he said. "If I clean my room, she'd be out of a job."

There was more to cleaning a house than picking up clothes or making a bed. "She doesn't complain?"

He laughed and reached for Sophia. "She has a boss who is almost never here. I cook for her when I am home and leave leftovers for her when I'm not. She's not allowed to touch my kitchen, which is a major cleaning area, when I'm not here to help her. She knows a sweet deal when she sees one."

Before she could think of anything else to say, he kissed her. His mouth devoured hers, demanding a response. It was a far cry from the way he kissed her on the porch. Her anxiety melted, and she forgot her surroundings as he led her to a place where only they existed. It was a dangerous place, but she was powerless to resist his call.

She pressed her body against his, reveling in the hardness of his chest against hers. With her hands, she roamed the broad, well-defined muscles of his shoulders and back.

His probing thumbs created a gap between her shirt and skirt. She expected him to go straight for her breasts, which were already puckering in anticipation, but he didn't. Instead, his strong hands gripped her waist. One slid to her back to caress the smooth skin there. No bra impeded him, yet he took his time, letting them savor the flavor of her kiss and the simple eroticism of his body against hers.

She drowned in the liquid heat rising to meet their demands. His tongue wrapped around hers, probing deeper until she couldn't breathe, couldn't think, and didn't want to. Without breaking the cadence of his control over her, he picked her up and, shoving aside the rumpled sheet, set her carefully on his bed.

Drew followed her down, his weight pushing her into the softness of the mattress beneath. Only then, when he had her where he wanted her, did he break the kiss. She protested against the loss, but her sigh was quickly replaced with a moan as he found the sensitive places on the curve of her neck and just below her earlobe.

She wanted him to hurry, to rush to stroke her everywhere at once. She wiggled under him, writhing in her need to touch and be touched. Passion smoldered, but he refused to let her rush things, to transform the smoke to flames. He wore no shirt for her to remove. She tightened her fingers, searching the smooth planes of his shoulders and back for a handhold.

Desperately questing, Sophia slid her hands up to his hair, but it was too short to be of any use. She cried out his name, her voice wretched and frantic even to her own ears. This wasn't her. This wasn't her place. She wasn't at her house, and she wasn't in control.

As if he sensed her panic, his lips left her neck. He drew back to look at her, those sensual blue eyes warm and tender. Silently, he stroked the sides of her face, pushing hair away from her cheeks and wiping away the tears she hadn't known were there.

"I dream of you, Sophia. I dream of making slow love to you, of exploring every inch of your body with my lips and tongue, of hearing you cry my name as you lift from the bed with the force of yet another orgasm." His thumb slid across the curve of her jaw to caress her lower lip. She trembled under him, but he held her with the hot plea in his eyes. "I've wanted you in my bed from the first moment I saw you. Give me this, Sophia. Let me have you here, on my terms."

He was asking her to trust him. The rules she used with her lovers were in place so that trust was defined. From the beginning, Drew rejected her strictures, tossing aside her safeguards. He wanted things from her that she gave to no one.

"Just today, honey. Let go and trust me. I promise you won't regret it."

Gradually, Sophia relaxed, lulled by the honesty in his voice and the gentleness of his caress. The trembling didn't go away. She was hyperaware of it as she raised her hand to his cheek, bringing his lips back to hers. The kiss was slow and deep. When at last he moved down her body, her internal storm was calmed, replaced with the hurricane he generated.

This time, when his name escaped her lips, it was a sigh.

He undressed her slowly, lingering over each inch of skin as if discovering it for the first time. By the time his tongue slipped between the folds of her pussy, she was drenched and tight with need. Even then, he took it slowly, kissing and licking her reverently. His tongue swirled lazy circles, playing as she writhed beneath him.

When he finally caved to her frantic pleas, locking his lips around her swollen clit and sucking forcefully, she came immediately. True to his word, he didn't stop. The waves of her orgasm weren't given a chance to recede.

A thick finger slid into her, followed by another and another, pumping a rhythm that matched the way he sucked. Her hips lifted, and he captured her, caging her with his free arm so she couldn't escape. She pushed against him, begging for more.

He mastered the tide, luring it back again and again. It rose a little each time, lifting her higher without ever quite leaving. The first orgasm became a stepping-stone, stretching out and lengthening as the intensity grew.

Sophia's moans turned to screams, and she turned to jelly, unable to do anything but lie there and let him control her body. Oral sex with Drew had been incredible before, but not like this. This time, he didn't allow her to hold back.

Blackness dotted the periphery of her vision as another orgasm took her prisoner. He moaned as she came in his mouth, lapping up her juices with an eagerness that defied reason. Fingers pinched her clit, plumping and pressing while his tongue fervently fucked another orgasm from her.

She felt like a thing. The pieces that made her separated, each too preoccupied with the pleasure thrumming through her entire body to be anything more than primal need. He sucked harder, fingers joining his tongue while other fingers twisted and rubbed her glistening nub. There was no longer a need to hold her down., She had submitted completely.

Her body was his. Even as a wayward finger slowly invaded her virgin anus, she did nothing to stop him. The pressure in her pussy increased. Her hands wrapped around the edges of the pillow so tightly it hurt.

Sophia orgasmed quickly on a normal day, but the orgasms were generally just pleasant and enjoyable. This was so much more. Drew pushed her, treating the first few as foreplay. She teetered on the verge of something earth-shattering. With nothing holding her back, she fell, trusting Drew to catch her.

The last thing she remembered was her body lifting from the bed, the movement so violent and sudden that she ripped his mouth from her.

When awareness returned, she was nestled in the crook of his arm. The soft silkiness of the sheet covered her bare body. Her cheek rested against his chest. She lay there for a moment longer, savoring the feel of his fingers stroking her hair near the temple.

Finally, she opened her eyes. "I was right about you."

"Were you?" She couldn't see his expression, but his surprise was hard to miss.

"Yes," she said. "Your face belongs between my legs."

This time she felt his smile, and the shaking of his chest betrayed the laugh he tried to swallow. "I like it there, too."

"Tell me what else you like." It was a standard line she used with her submissives, but she meant it in a completely different way. With them, these deep, personal confessions were part of the breaking-down process. With Drew, it was because she wanted to know about him. She wanted him to share himself with her.

The hand tracing a path through her hair dropped to caress her shoulder. "I like hanging out with you. I like flirting with you and watching you eat. I love listening to you talk, though it's hard to get you to say much. I love to look at you."

She put a finger to his lips. The entire time Charlie raped her, he had gone on and on about how attractive he found her. Sickness twisted low in her stomach. She hated how he could violate her now, years later, ruining what could have been a stunningly romantic moment. "Tell me what you like *in bed*."

The wry way his lush lips pursed let her know he was aware she was steering the conversation to less relationship-oriented waters. "I liked when you straddled me the other night and rode me slowly, stretching your orgasm out for a long, long time. I liked bending you over the back of the couch at Ellen's and taking you from behind. I could see your face reflected in their TV."

He shifted, rolling to his side without releasing her. Now that she was pressed against the length of him, she realized he was naked. She wondered how long she had passed out. She wondered if he knew exactly what he had done to her. Several of her submissives had achieved this level of orgasm before. She knew to check their pupil response, breathing, and pulse.

Unaware of her thoughts, or of how he brought her back from the edge of a panic attack, Drew continued. "I love watching you come. I love hearing you come. I asked you to bring your vibrator so that I could watch you pleasure yourself. Sophia, you have no idea what you do to my insides when you get that look on your face."

Her eyes were still heavy-lidded. The sincerity of his answer and the graphic picture show playing in her head combined to heat her from the inside. She couldn't remember ever wanting a man like this. The smile that slowly curved her lips was flirtatious and inviting. "What look?"

He touched her chin lightly, catching her fire. "This look, honey. With this look, I am putty in your hands. There's nothing I wouldn't do just to see this look on your face."

She moistened her lips, darting her tongue out quickly. The move was functional, not sensual, but the effect was the same. Drew was rock hard against her stomach. His eyes were glued to her lips. "And to think I wasted all that time whipping you when all I had to do was look at you like this."

"What can I say? You're better at wrapping me around your finger than you thought. You had me from the first moment I saw you."

He kissed her, and she knew exactly where it was leading. She stopped him. There was something she needed to know first. "Drew?"

"Yeah?"

She looked away, suddenly shy. He waited in silence. With a deep breath, she plunged ahead. "Men who aren't submissives, which you clearly aren't, have a difficult time...performing...when they're being whipped or spanked. For most submissives, the pain sharpens the pleasure, intensifying it or bringing it into focus. Some submissives can't orgasm without it."

"You're wondering how I was able to keep it up when you spanked me?"

She nodded.

"Easy." He smiled. "I knew if I failed, I wouldn't have a chance in hell with you. My dick might have been in Livia's mouth, but it was you I pictured beneath me. When you ordered me to touch her, I was really touching you. Sophia, I never once took my eyes from you. I knew from the moment I saw you that I was going to have to prove myself to be with you."

Her brows lifted in surprise. He was right. If he failed that first night, or if he had approached her wanting vanilla sex, she would have dismissed him outright. "But you had an orgasm."

He shrugged. "You don't hit very hard, Sophie. I ignored it for the most part."

That was the wrong thing to say to a dominatrix who prided herself on her heavy hand. Pushing him back, she rolled them until she was on top. "I went easy on you because I knew you were a virgin."

Grinning up at her, he grasped her hips in both hands and repositioned her so that she straddled his cock. She rocked back and forth, grinding against him until he groaned and stilled her hips. "I'm far from virginal,

Sophie. However, if you want to tie me up and torture me sexually, I'm okay with that. Livia, Ellen, and Jonas all raved about your ability to set a scene. I've seen firsthand how incredible you are. I just don't go for the violent stuff."

Her jaw dropped. "Ellen and Jonas? You've talked to them about me?"

"I tried," he said, sitting up and holding her close. "Neither one would say much, and neither of them told me anything I didn't already know."

Sophia wanted to ask for details, but he was kissing her. Unable to resist the scorching flames, she melted into him. He rolled her across the bed and felt for the box of condoms on his nightstand, never once pausing for breath. They fell to the floor, spilling out and across the polished oak flooring.

Breaking the kiss, she vaguely noted the beauty of the flooring as she snatched a handful of foil packets. She threw all but one to the sheet next to them with a practiced efficiency. Sophia tore open her prize and pushed Drew down on the bed.

Sheathing him was fun. She did it slowly, letting her fingers explore the thick length of him as he groaned and growled his impatience.

"'Thou driv'st me past the bounds of a man's patience.'"

She scooted back to add her tongue to the mix. She liked when he spouted Shakespeare. She wasn't a fan of all his plays, but she loved *A Midsummer Night's Dream*. Her entire relationship with Drew was nothing more than a fantasy, so it was even more fitting. One day she would wake up to find it all a fairy-drug-induced dream.

"'If you were civil and knew courtesy, you would not do me thus much injury.'"

"Injury?" The condom was completely on. She stroked and mouthed his balls, injuring him to the fullest.

His hips lifted to thrust helplessly into empty air. "You're killing me, Sophia."

Finally, she rose above him and swung her leg over his hip to straddle him. "'I believe we must leave the killing out, when all is done.'"

"Thank God," he said as she seated him deep inside.

She rode him slow, thinking only of her pleasure as she snapped and gyrated. True to his word, her first climax drove him higher. The second made him rise from the bed with the force of his orgasm. He wrapped his arms around her as he came down, holding her so tightly she could barely breathe.

Breathing was overrated. She didn't want him to let go.

Chapter 13

Drew smacked her on the ass. Compared to what Sophia dished out, it was nothing more than a love tap. Cracking open one eye, she peered at him through the slit. He stood next to the bed, a towel wrapped around his waist, grinning.

"Now that I've spent an hour pumping you full of endorphins, you should be relaxed and amenable to anything I suggest."

The languor to which she surrendered was fast vanishing in the face of her interest in his next proposal. She opened both eyes. "What did you plan to suggest?"

"Hop in the shower and rinse off. It's time for dessert."

He'd promised chocolate. Sophia padded into the cavernous bathroom to find everything she might need arranged on a low bench next to the shower. The shower itself was almost as large as her entire bathroom. Pushing aside serious thoughts, she stepped into luxury and enjoyed her time under the warm spray.

When she returned to the bedroom, he wasn't there. Sounds from the sitting room pulled her in that direction. Naked, she leaned against the doorway and watched Drew set out bowls on the low table in front of a long, wide ottoman. He hummed as he worked.

* * * *

Working with liquid dessert toppings was always a messy undertaking. As a precaution, Drew covered the ottoman with a sheet of plastic, which he cleaned before setting down. He wanted nothing but the best for Sophia. After all, she was the main course. The toppings were just for fun.

She might play sex games all the time, but she seriously lacked the playful attitude that was supposed to mark all kinds of games. She had definitely played with him the day before when they were shooting pool. It was that attitude he wished to recreate with her today. She'd been serious from the moment she stepped through the door. Now that she was relaxed, the fun part of the day could begin.

Glancing toward the door to the bedroom, he froze. His eyes raked up and down the figure standing there. Long legs led to where hips flared before curving in at the waist, then out slightly where there were breasts of the perfect size. Drew appreciated all types of bodies, but he preferred women with smaller breasts. Sophia's were perfect. He was glad she hadn't taken the surgical route to achieve society's ideal.

She watched him. The expression on her beautiful face was both sensual and curious. He was glad he'd only pulled on his boxer shorts.

"A blank canvas," he said. "My favorite kind."

Crossing the room, she came to stand next to him. Her smile was playful. "Now you're an artist?"

"Actually," he said, "I nearly chose art school over pastry school."

Her head tilted to the side. "Why didn't you?"

Grasping her hands in his, he pulled her closer to drop a kiss on her lips. "I like food a lot more than paint." Guiding her to the ottoman, he pushed her down onto the plastic. "There are so many things you can do with food that you can't do with paint."

Sophia's gaze dropped to the table, checking out the contents of the bowls before rising to meet his again. She was amused. "Such as?"

He dropped another kiss on her lips. He couldn't seem to resist. "Lie back, honey, and I'll show you."

Shadows of skepticism clouded her brown eyes, but she banished them quickly. He'd asked for her trust, and she was determined to make the effort. He could see what it cost her. If he ever found the bastard who hurt her, well, it was a good thing he was wealthy. He could afford a good lawyer.

She draped her body across the length of the ottoman, lifting her chestnut hair so that it flowed over the side of the cushion. He loved her natural grace and beauty, and he adored how comfortable she was with her body and nudity in general.

The chocolate was room temperature, but it wouldn't solidify unless he cooled it down. He had brought white, milk, and dark chocolate, as well as whipped cream and diced fruits. Sprinkles were just for fun.

Grabbing the white chocolate, he straddled her hips. The ottoman wasn't overly wide, and he wanted to be comfortable. Decorating always took some time if it was done well. He wanted to impress Sophia with his artistry. He might be a chef, but he was also very good with pastries. He and Ginny had built their company with sweat and talent. He wanted Sophia to know that side of him.

He started with her stomach. Her skin was a deep honey color. The white would stand out in sharp contrast. Working quickly, he used a brush to paint swirling patterns that curved upward to spiral around her breasts. On top of that, he layered the milk and dark chocolates.

Glancing up, he caught the amusement in Sophia's eyes. The curve of her lips beckoned for another kiss. He obliged her.

"I thought you'd go straight for the nipples," she said when he released her lips. "Or I thought maybe you'd eat it off me as you went along."

He smiled down at her. "We'll get to that, Sophie. Are you impatient?"

She raised her arms, running her hands up his chest until they rested on his shoulders. He loved the way she touched him. "When you said you wanted to dip my ass in chocolate, the picture in my head was much messier and less…deliberate."

"I'm always deliberate with food, honey, even the kind I'm going to lick off your delicious body." He watched the wheels turning in her head. One thing was certain with Sophia: she was always thinking, always looking for the angle.

Her hands moved to caress his pectoral muscles. "Would messy bother you, Drew?"

He laughed, a quiet sound. "Not at all, Sophie, but beauty needs beauty. The picture in my head is an erotic feast for the palate and the senses. A true Sensual Secret."

Suddenly uncomfortable, she shifted under him. "So, if I was ugly, you'd just dump the chocolate on me and lick it off?"

"If you were ugly, we wouldn't be having this conversation." Before she could say anything more, he kissed her, claiming her lips for something hard and deep. She needed a distraction, and he needed a taste of heaven. "I'm a typical male, Sophia. I wouldn't have pursued you if I didn't find you incredibly attractive. Your looks caught my interest, and your strong personality keeps it."

She studied him intently, with that look she used on her subs. It was disarming, but he wasn't going to let her see that, not while she was still jockeying for dominance. He liked equality, and he didn't care for power games, not when he also wanted a relationship outside of the bedroom with her. His eyes flickered to her stomach and back. There was a very real possibility she was already carrying his child.

When it first happened, he thought he would be filled with dread. Instead, the idea held great appeal to him. The timing was bad, but he knew without a doubt that he wanted that kind of future with Sophia. He thought falling in love would be painful. He thought he'd fight it with everything he had. He was wrong. He would fight *for* it with everything he had.

A smile transformed her face, bringing him back to the present. Drew caught his breath. "That's okay," she said. "I noticed your looks first thing, too. I guess we're both shallow that way."

"We're not shallow," he said as he moved down her body and pushed her legs apart. "We're just both attractive people."

Anything she might have said in response was lost in a gasp when he parted her lips and placed pineapple, strawberry and watermelon between them.

Moving up her still body, he arranged the fruit along the chocolate trails. Every few pieces, he popped one in her mouth, covering the strawberry with chocolate. He didn't trust her to have eaten more than a Pop Tart before arriving at his house.

Lastly, he topped the fruit with strategic squirts of his favorite canned whipped cream.

"Don't chefs hate that stuff?" Sophia shivered as he coated her inner thighs with the cold cream.

Drew chuckled. "I can't speak for everyone, but I love this stuff." To prove his point, he opened his mouth and squirted some inside. She watched him, careful not to move.

He started at the sensitive places he discovered behind her ears, licking the thin trail of chocolate painted on her neck first. Drew moved slowly, taking his time and savoring every inch of her body. Her hands roamed his head, searching for something to hold, but his hair was too short. As he moved lower, Sophia trembled and clutched at the plastic covering the cushions.

"Drew."

His name was a sigh on her lips. He liked when she said it that way.

She screamed when he moved from her inner thigh to greedily lick and bite at the fruit and toppings he had carefully placed in her pussy. Her cream mixed in to create the ultimate dessert. She rocked her hips, demanding more.

When she cried out, lifting her hips from the ottoman completely, he didn't want to stop. She tasted like ambrosia and felt like silk. He could have stayed there for days.

But Sophia had other plans. Sitting up, she locked her fingers on the short hairs she could grasp and pulled his mouth to hers. The next thing he knew, he was the one lying on the plastic, and she hovered on top of him.

"My turn," she said, a wicked grin curving her lips and lighting her eyes.

Sophia's actions were not slow and deliberate as his had been. She didn't bother with complicated or layered designs. She grabbed the bowl with the most chocolate left and poured it down his stomach. Her tongue began licking his chest before she finished pouring the sweet liquid over his erect cock.

When had she removed his boxers? Damn, she was good.

Drew lost himself in the feel of her lips and tongue, and of her body moving down his. She licked his dick and his balls, cleaning much of the chocolate away with erotically firm strokes.

When that luscious mouth closed over him, he lifted her hips, turning her so that he could lick her pussy while she worked him over. She fucked his mouth to the same rhythm she sucked his cock. He thrust his hips, unable to resist the need to move in time with her mouth. She sucked him deeper and deeper, sounds of muffled pleasure issuing from the back of her throat.

He squeezed her ass to let her know he was about to come, though he doubted she would pull away. His Sophia took what she wanted, and she wanted him. Musky juices flooded his mouth seconds before his come shot into hers.

As he held her body against his afterward, his arms flexed, subconsciously pulling her closer. There was no way he was going to let her go, no way in hell.

* * * *

After a shower, they lounged in his bed, cloaked in post-coital languor. He ran his fingertips lazily over her skin. Still sensitive from his earlier caresses, she quivered where he touched. She expected his caresses to grow steadily stronger as his desire returned. Surprisingly, Drew didn't want to spend the afternoon in bed.

With a quick kiss on her shoulder, he leapt from bed and strode to what she assumed was a walk-in closet. He returned with two silk robes. He put the blue one on and threw the red one to her.

She held it up, scrutinizing it warily. It was a woman's robe. He kept a woman's robe in his closet. A shard of ice stabbed deep inside.

"If you don't like it, I can take it back. Do you want a shorter one? Longer? A different color? I thought you'd like that red. It matches your nails."

Like an idiot, she held out her hand and stared at it. The color of the robe was almost identical to the nail polish she had chosen at the spa the previous day. She looked from the robe in her hand to Drew. "You bought a robe for me last night?"

He shrugged, more a reaction to her incredulity than to her question. "I didn't think you would bring your own."

He bought a robe to match her nail polish. He arranged a guest pass so she could come and go through security as she pleased. This was too much.

He must have known because he came to her, halting anything she might have said by taking hold of her hand. "I just want you to be comfortable here, Sophia. I know this is difficult for you."

She snapped her eyes to his, searching those pale blue orbs for the deeper meaning. "Difficult?" She forced the word, but it only came out as a whisper. What had Ellen or Jonas told him? He stopped her from asking before. She couldn't let him do that again. "What did Jonas tell you?" Since they spent part of the day together yesterday, Jonas seemed the logical traitor. He'd obviously been the one to let Drew in on the fact that he shouldn't refer to Sophia as his girlfriend.

Emotions and thoughts flickered across Drew's face. "He said you had a hard time trusting people. I should be patient, give you time and space."

He should give her time and space. "So you bought me a robe?" What was wrong with her? She was upset at the thought he might keep an all-purpose women's robe in his closet for the myriad naked women he had visiting his home, but the knowledge the robe was for her set Sophia on course for a full-blown panic attack. Why couldn't he have lent her a spare robe of his *own*?

His dark blond brows drew together. "Yeah, and I bought my mom a pair of diamond teardrop earrings. I don't see the big deal."

"I don't want you buying things for me." The beat of her heart thundered in her ears, drowning out her words and making them echo hollowly in her head.

"Get over it, Sophie." He took the robe and put it on her, turning her so he could tie the belt in front. "We get along pretty well, and we're very compatible sexually. If I'm out shopping and I see something I think you'll like, I'm going to buy it for you because that's the kind of person I am. I plan on having you over often and for prolonged periods of time. It's inevitable that you'll have a toothbrush in my bathroom and several changes of clothing in my laundry."

"Inevitable?" She felt like an inane echo, unable to think of her own words.

"Yeah, inevitable." He straightened the shoulders and visually checked the fit. "It looks good on you."

"Drew..."

He took her hand. "Time for that tour. You should know your way around the house. That way, if you want to surprise me by swimming naked in the pool when I come home, you'll know where to find it."

That kind of surprise would entail having the key to his place and the alarm code. He must have guessed the drift of her thoughts because he answered them.

"Of course we're not to the point where we would exchange keys yet. I'll wait until Thursday for that."

She didn't want to know how he decided on Thursday. Wordlessly, she walked beside Drew, her hand tucked into his, as he explained each room.

It was a house like any other. It had a few more bedrooms and bathrooms and living rooms, but the overall result was the same. He did have an indoor pool, three hot tubs—two indoor, one outdoor—and a basketball court. With the addition of a center net, it could also be used for tennis or volleyball.

In his walk-out basement, he had a room set up with two massage tables, a weight room, and a game room, complete with a pool table at one end. If she brought Daniel there, he would never leave. It was a bachelor's paradise.

"You have your own pool table, and I still beat you?" She regarded him suspiciously. "I haven't played pool in years."

He shrugged. "I'm not stupid, Sophie. I know better than to beat a woman at pool. I kept the higher purpose in mind."

"Higher purpose?"

"Yes." He grinned. "In case you haven't noticed, I did manage to get you into my bed today."

She caught the tenor of his mood, banishing the last of her anxiety. "By your logic, if you had won, we would be at my house right now."

"Where your vibrator is," he added dryly.

Waving away his concern, she said, "Those are in the car." She didn't add that she was so intimidated by the size of his house that she completely forgot the bag where she had packed assorted sex toys and a change of clothes.

"Those? How many do you have?"

It was her turn to shrug. "Lots. I brought the most likely candidates, some for you and some for me."

"Some for me?" He was interested and excited.

"You said you were a top and a bottom, Drew. I have toys for that."

This definitely piqued his interest. "I didn't know. This kind of thing is unquestionably a benefit to dating a dominatrix."

She wanted to argue with his claim that they were dating, but she refrained. If they weren't seeing anyone else, dating was a loose enough term. He understood they weren't actually in a relationship, hopefully.

He fingered the felt on the top of the pool table. "So, what kind of scene do you have planned for tomorrow?" His pose strove for casual, but she heard the worry in his question.

"I haven't planned it yet. There are some things that have to happen. Is there anything specific you would like for me to plan?"

Tugging on her hand, he led her out of the gaming room to a small sliding door. It looked like an elevator. When the doors opened, she saw that it was, indeed, an elevator.

"What things have to happen?"

Telling him wouldn't ruin any surprises. "Well, Christopher can't keep an erection without pain, so I'll have to work him over pretty well. I can do that before you come over if you don't want to watch."

"Do you wear a tight black leather outfit?"

She shook her head. "I'm a T-shirt-and-shorts kind of girl. What you saw me wearing is my standard uniform."

The door opened again, and they were in what was easily the largest kitchen she had ever seen. It swallowed half of the first floor of his house, or so she guessed. Castles and mansions on those History Channel shows were meager in comparison. Everywhere she looked, she was met with pale marble, stainless steel, or dark-stained wood. It was stunning and impossible to take in with one sweep of the eyes.

"I designed it myself. The kitchen is the most important room in any home. I can cook a seven-course meal for fifty people or a simple breakfast for two. I can fit all of my family and friends in here during the holidays."

She would have thought he would use the dining room, but she didn't say anything. Watching Drew talk about his kitchen was captivating. As he pointed out the features, she watched his eyes light with a passion she recognized. It was the same look she got when she talked about finance. The effect was devastating. She felt a tug and a give in her heart.

There were too many sinks for her to memorize the purpose of each one. His cutting boards were built in, but some of his counters were moveable. Pots and pans and mixing bowls of all sizes hung from hooks. All of his cooking paraphernalia was arranged in the open for easy accessibility.

Sophia lost track of time as she listened to him explain why one counter was heated and another was cooled. He expounded on the making of desserts as much as about cooking in general.

Parking herself on one of the stools at the central counter, which was square and high, she watched as he began unloading foods and spices from various cupboards and from the industrial-sized refrigerator. He had a walk-in freezer and refrigerator, but they were on the other side of the kitchen. They were only for special-occasion cooking.

He eased her into the conversation as he worked, chopping vegetables with dizzying speed and amazing precision. There was a mathematical beauty about the evenness and symmetry he achieved with his cuts.

"Do you have any food allergies I should know about?"

She shook her head, and then remembered one. "I'm lactose intolerant. I can handle cooked cheeses, but the soft ones give me problems."

Then he was off again. He talked her through the steps of preparing the Hawaiian Chicken recipe he was still trying to perfect until she couldn't stop laughing. He looked up, suspending his activities as he stared at her quizzically.

"You sound like you do on your show. Are you practicing, or do you always flirt with your audience when you cook at home?" A home, she realized, that looked suspiciously like the set of his show.

He opened his mouth and closed it again. "You watch my show?"

She shrugged as if she had caught it casually. Truthfully, she recorded the episode that aired the day after she met him. Even though she didn't think she would ever see him again, she set the DVR before she went to sleep and watched the show when she arrived home from Sabrina's pre-wedding meeting that Sunday. After she ended things with him, she watched his show because she missed him.

"I've seen it."

His look said he didn't believe the nonchalant spirit she tried to affect. Thankfully, he let it go. "This dish is good, but something is missing. It's your job to help me figure out what isn't quite right."

His chatter changed after that. As he cooked, he told her about his parents, Miranda and Jonathan, who lived just down the street. "You'd think I would see them every day, living this close, but I don't. They travel all the time. Ginny's mom is the same way. House-sitting is an actual career for some people in this area."

"Are you close?" She bit her lip after asking. Inquiries like this invited personal questions about her own life.

"Yes. I talk to my parents a few times a week. I talk to my sister, Lila, about every other day. Her name is actually Delila. My parents liked names they could shorten by dropping the first two letters. I've always been amazed that they didn't make people call them Randa and Nathan."

Sophia speedily put those pieces together. "Your name is Andrew?" He didn't seem like an Andrew.

He nodded, claiming the name dismissively, and continued. "I see Gin pretty much every day, but I don't see Sabrina so much now that she's married."

"But you're friends with Jonas."

Drew shrugged. "Only because he's married to Sabrina. Don't get me wrong, I like him. He's a great guy and a good friend, but Sabrina is like a big sister to me. Although, I did have a brief crush on her in high school after I realized it was never going to happen with Ginny." He set a plate of sliced veggies in front of her.

She selected a julienned carrot. "Because she's a lesbian?"

"Because she kicked me in the balls when I tried to kiss her." He tossed a bunch of cut tomatoes into a pan and set it to boiling. "That was freshman year of high school, when we were the same height. She didn't start dating chicks until college."

"So you moved on to Sabrina?" She hadn't realized how hungry she was. She munched another carrot.

"I tried. She had a boyfriend at the time, Stephen Galen, Star Quarterback, so she didn't even notice." He laughed. "I hit on her and Jonas last summer, and she thought I was kidding."

That should have been disturbing. Sophia found it funny. "Were you?"

He shrugged. "I've spent a good amount of my life dating couples. I liked the lack of commitment it required on my part because they were already committed to each other. All the fun of a threesome with none of the headache."

That was food for thought. They were more alike than she cared to admit. She wandered over to the pot of tomatoes that he was reducing for a sauce. She wasn't part of a couple, and he put conditions on their friendship right away. "What changed?"

Without looking up from whatever he was skillfully doing to boneless chicken breasts with a very large knife, he grimaced. "I met you."

There was nothing she could say to that. She stirred his sauce instead of replying.

"What about you?" he asked. "Are you close to your family, and why do you run from commitment?"

She choked on that one, coughing so hard he turned to pound her on the back. When she regained control of herself, she ignored the question she didn't want to answer. "I'm extremely close to my family."

Wisely abandoning his second question, he returned to his chicken, moving it to a sink. "I've met Daniel. Do you have any other siblings?"

"No, it's just Danny and me. We're ten months apart. Irish twins."

"I'm Irish on my mother's side."

"My parents are both Italian. Mom didn't think she could get pregnant so soon after giving birth. She made Dad get a vasectomy right after I was born." She fished in his cupboards for red wine and cinnamon. Without consulting him or measuring in any way, she added them to the sauce. It was the way her mother taught her to make tomato sauces. She didn't even think about the consequences of messing with the contents of a professional chef's pot.

They talked as they cooked, their movements falling into perfect synchronization as he ceded control of the sauce. She barely noticed as he guided the conversation to the kinds of stories about the past that reveal things about who a person is deep inside. Before she knew it, Sophia told him about how she used to put makeup on Daniel while he was asleep and the way her family still gathered together the last Sunday of each month for a huge dinner and a gluttonous quantity of dessert, which they had both before and after the actual meal.

She couldn't remember the last time she felt so relaxed around anyone.

With practiced panache, Drew plated the meal and they dined, sitting on the high chairs at the counter. He had a ton of wine in his fancy wine rack, and a large wine cellar in the basement, but he poured water for them both. She didn't question his action, deducing he saved the wine for special occasions.

His Hawaiian Chicken was delicious. It was more than chicken smothered in tomato sauce and garnished with pineapple. She didn't see everything he did to it, but there were a lot of steps. She couldn't imagine making it after watching a half hour tutorial.

The expression on his face morphed from trepidation to surprise pretty quickly. "This is perfect." He lingered over the next mouthful, analyzing the sauce with his taste buds. Finally, he looked at her. "It's the wine. It gives the sauce a tanginess that goes well with the sweetness of the pineapple."

She nodded slowly. "It's how my mom makes spaghetti sauce."

He kissed her, hard. "I knew there was something I liked about you, other than the embers that shimmer from you every time you look at me."

They cleaned up after dinner. Mostly, Drew told her what to do, and she did it. If she had known her way around his kitchen a little better, she would have bristled under his direction.

Then again, maybe she wouldn't have. He was a natural leader, exactly the type of person Sophia usually avoided. There were so many things about him she liked, both in and out of the bedroom. It should have scared her more than it did. She felt the subtle shift in her psyche, the temporary easing of her need to be in control.

He asked her to trust him. Little by little, she was giving him pieces of something she kept locked inside, safe from the world at large.

This wouldn't last.

Dressed only in his thin, blue robe, he made the trip out to her car to retrieve the bag she left on the floor of the backseat. He'd asked her to stay in the kitchen. She nursed a cup of the mint tea with honey he insisted she have instead of the coffee with lots and lots of sugar she wanted.

Before too long, he returned. One by one, he laid out the selection of toys on the counter. "You must have planned to stay for a week," he muttered.

She might have taken offense if he hadn't sounded so pleased about it. "A week? Who would feed my imaginary cat?"

He laughed and rubbed nervously at his shoulder. She was adept at reading that kind of body language.

"Drew? You never answered my question earlier."

Glancing up, he raised his brows. "If we're keeping score, you avoided several of my questions, too."

She sipped her tea to cover a grimace. "Mine was in regard to Christopher tomorrow," she prompted. "Did you want me to get him started before you come over, or do you enjoy watching me dominate someone else?"

He shrugged, his eyes never leaving the array of toys spread on the counter. "As long as you don't fuck him, I don't care what you do to him before I get there."

"Drew? What's wrong?"

He picked up a short toy with a bulbous head. "I've seen vibrators before, but I have no idea what this one is. It doesn't look like the one I pulled from Livia's ass the other night."

With a gentle smile, she rounded the counter and explained the selection she brought. She hadn't chosen them with any degree of care. Running short on time forced her to dump an entire box into her carryall bag. The device Drew held was a clitoral stimulator, as were several of those on the counter. Others were regular, no-frills vibrators. Then there were combination toys, vibrators with clitoral stimulators.

"What's this?" He handed her a combination toy. The parts that were the phallus and the clit stimulator were easy to identify. Another spike curled away from the base, one-inch beads stretching the length at intervals.

"That's for anal stimulation."

He regarded it thoughtfully. "Have you ever used this?"

Sophia shook her head. For all the kinky things she did to her submissives, she was a virgin when it came to many of them.

Next, he lifted a set of adjustable straps. "What's this?"

"That's for the strap-ons," she explained, pointing to several phalluses that lacked battery power and to a couple that were dual use.

He quirked his eyes at her. "That was thoughtful, honey, but I come equipped with the built-in model."

She ran a suggestive finger down his chest, loosening the front of his robe until it hung open. "That's for me to use on you. I don't think you know how much the idea of fucking you from behind turns me on." Reaching between her legs, she dipped a finger into the wetness there and raised her fingertip, full of thick cream, to his lips.

Without hesitating, his mouth opened. He sucked the evidence of her arousal from her finger, scraping it clean with his teeth. He released it to answer her challenge. "It probably turns you on as much as watching you masturbate makes me have to strain not to come in my pants, or my robe, as the case may be."

Without breaking eye contact, she eased herself onto the cold marble in front of him. It was a split-level counter. The side at which she had been seated, sipping tea, was higher. The side where Drew arranged the vibrators was hip level for kitchen work.

She settled her rear on the higher counter and braced her feet on the lower one. Licking her lips to moisten them and drive him crazy, she tugged at the tie on her robe. The pliant silk slid from her shoulders to lay forgotten behind her.

Using both hands, she pushed her knees apart, spreading them as far as they would go. Drew wasn't breathing, and his dick stood at attention.

"Put your hands on the counter," she said. Without hesitation, he did as she directed. "Good. If you lift them or move them at all, I will stop."

He didn't move or speak. She wanted to love that he was so well trained, but she had a sinking suspicion that he would be compliant only as long as it suited him.

With one hand, she fingered the folds of her pussy. Drew's attention centered there, watching as if she had ordered him not to move his eyes. She moved her other hand along the length of her inner thigh, caressing the sensitive skin there. Fingers splayed, she continued up her abdomen to cup one breast. She pinched the nipples lightly, tweaking them to peaks with a gentle pressure.

She brought herself to the panting point before letting her hands drop away.

Drew made a sound of protest, which she quickly silenced by reaching forward and snagging a pink silicone vibrator. She held it next to his hard-on, comparing sizes. Drew's dick was long and thick. While the vibrator was comparable in length, it wasn't as thick. She replaced it and selected another, one as close to his size and shape as she could find.

The one she ultimately chose was bright blue. Drew's eyes smoldered, and the thick, corded muscles of his neck and shoulders stood out with the effort it took to keep his hands still.

The tube of lubricant was out of reach. She would have to abandon her pretty pose in order to get it. With the tilt of her head, she indicated it. "Would you be so kind as to hand that here?"

"You said if I move my hands, you'll stop." He sounded as if he had just run a marathon.

Visually, she remeasured the distance. There was no way he could reach it with his mouth. "One hand for this one purpose."

He held the tube out to her, unscrewing the cap with his thumb and forefinger, as if she needed a reminder of how good he was with his hands. She held up the length of blue silicone while he squeezed the clear gel along the shaft.

With slow-moving fingers, she spread it, thoroughly lubricating the entire thing. The excess found its way to her entrance. She rubbed the edges of the little, pink hole until she gasped involuntarily, and then slid her slippery fingers inside, though she didn't really need the extra wetness. The look on Drew's face was reward enough.

Sophia's vibrators were her best friends, quiet lovers that did exactly what she wanted without questions or expectations. More than that, she loved the feel of them inside. She rubbed the slippery, pulsating tip around her clit before plunging it deep inside with one powerful stroke. Both of them stopped breathing.

Drew's fingers curled, pressing into the hard, flat surface until the tips turned white. Strain showed on his face. She positioned the shorter arm of the vibrator against her clit and turned the dial to medium. Drew's lower lip disappeared into his mouth. Knowing the exact extent as to the magic skills residing there, she envied that lip he bit and sucked.

She moved the phallus around inside her, concentrating the tip and the vibrations against the places that made her knees tremble and sent electricity through her synapses. Her breaths came faster and shallower as her hips thrust harder and faster. Bracing her weight behind her on one hand, she let her head fall back.

"God, Sophia, you are so unbelievably beautiful. Delicate and strong, fragile and tough. You're open to me, yet completely off-limits. I want to spend the rest of my life peeling back your layers, discovering all your secrets."

His voice was low and reverent, tight with need. The tone drove her higher, though the meaning of his words wouldn't penetrate until much, much later, when it would be easy to dismiss them as the ramblings of an aroused man.

The heat spiraled out of control, coiling her body tighter and tighter until she cried out. Rigid, and in the throes of an orgasm, Sophia didn't protest when Drew reached for her. Strong hands gripped her hips as he lifted her closer. One hand cradled her head, fingers threading through her hair to hold her still while he nipped at her docile lips.

The other hand brushed hers away from the vibrator, which he now controlled. Turning it to a higher setting, he pushed it into her steadier and with more force than she had been able to muster. Her senses overloaded, and she beat against Drew with her fists, fighting for control.

Kisses rained on her temple and brow. "Don't fight it, Sophie. Hang on to me, and let it come. I've got you, honey. I've got you. All you have to do is hang on."

That kernel of trust she loaned him earlier returned, bigger and stronger because he hadn't abused it. She buried her face in his neck and dug her fingers into his biceps. Colors exploded behind her eyelids, and she screamed.

Feeling left for a little while, but she was hyperaware of certain sensations. Drew's arms were around her, stroking the hair at her temple as she quivered against him. He murmured words against the top of her head, nonsense about her beauty and strength. His chest was pressed against hers. His erection waited patiently against her thigh.

Finally, she lifted her head and kissed him slowly. She meant it to thank him for using her trust well, but it morphed into something more. If she wanted to face facts, he was telling her with every fiber of his being that he loved her. But she didn't want to face facts. They were cold and hard and led only to devastation. She had survived a betrayal of these proportions before, but she didn't have it in her to do it again.

Still, her traitorous body returned his affection until she finally broke the kiss.

Drew regarded her with a lopsided grin, and he held up the strap-on harness.

She wasn't overly surprised. He was bisexual and a switch-hitter. The kinds of sex they'd been having for the past two weeks wouldn't fulfill all of his needs.

"Are you sure about this?" She wasn't hesitant, but she did want clear consent.

He nodded. "If you're going to be everything to me, then I want you to be everything to me."

She stepped into the straps of the harness and secured it around her legs, hips, and waist. He handed her the dildo he wanted her to use and turned, positioning himself against the counter.

"By that logic, you're going to want to do the same thing to me." She managed to sound composed, but in reality she was nervous. She enjoyed his touch at her back entrance earlier, but it was a relatively small intrusion.

"Yes, but not until you're ready."

He sounded so sure, so confident about something she had done to others, but she had never allowed to be done to herself. Not even one of the plentiful back-door pleasure vibrators still arrayed on the counter had been inside her own anus. She was thankful he hadn't caught the shock on her face. "Tell me how you want it, Drew. Tell me what you like."

"Start slow. Work your way up to faster and harder."

She reached for the tube of lubricant and coated the dildo. Then, she squirted some into her hand to slowly massage into his puckered hole. He moaned, and she slid a finger inside, testing his tightness and his give.

"Jesus, Sophie. You are the perfect woman."

With a soft chuckle, she withdrew her finger to position the tube just inside him. He inhaled sharply as the cool gel entered his rectum. She wanted him nice and slippery.

Dropping the now-empty tube to the floor, she worked the head into him. It entered him easily, and she slid it all the way inside, slowly stretching him to take the full length of the long, thick dildo he had chosen.

Because he was a couple of inches taller than her, she tapped the back of his knees and instructed him to lower himself. She wouldn't have as much leverage if she rose to her toes, which she could have done.

He moaned, and her swollen clit throbbed in response. The thought that she wanted him again, that she would consider allowing him to touch her in this hypersensitive and still-swollen condition, was daunting. She'd already given him too much control.

Determined, she shook away the thought and concentrated on him. She was in control now. This was what she wanted—utter and complete domination of Drew. This was the image that sent her spiraling out of control the other day in her own kitchen, prompting Drew to throw her to the table and have his way with her.

She withdrew almost completely, and then rammed him. His head fell forward, and he moaned. "Yes, Sophie, yes. Like that, honey. Don't stop."

She didn't. Again and again, she rammed him. When she established a good rhythm, she reached around to palm his rock-hard dick. Lubricant coated her hand. She had purposely not wiped it away.

He jerked, his cock twitching in her fist. She didn't waste time petting or teasing. With her hand wrapped around his thickness, she pumped him to the same rhythm she fucked him. Her hand moved harder and faster as she fucked him harder and faster. She was in complete control. She was mistress of the man who mastered her over and over, despite the objections in her head and heart. She marveled that he could give over so much to her without thought, trepidation, or regret.

She was floored by his complete trust.

He came, shouting her name before collapsing against the counter.

Chapter 14

After a leisurely soak in his very large bathtub, where he initiated her into the pleasures of partially submerged love, he challenged her to a game of pool.

"Now that I've gotten laid, I don't have to throw the game," he teased. "I'll clean the floor with your ass."

She grabbed sweats from her bag, tugged one of his Sensual Secrets shirts over her head, and snorted at his comment. "Sounds like someone doesn't want to get laid again."

He pulled her to him and dropped a loud, smacking kiss on her lips. "I sound like someone who is secure in the knowledge that you're addicted to me. I've hooked you, babe. You couldn't stop lusting for me if you wanted to."

He had no idea how right he was. She wanted to stop the tingling between her legs whenever he pierced her with those pale blue eyes. She wanted his magnetism to vanish. That wasn't unique to her. During the tour, she spied the mountain of unopened fan mail in his office. Some of the bulkier ones, she was sure, contained panties. She was one of thousands who felt his pull.

Drew finished dressing and turned that grin on her. He lifted her soggy mass of hair. "Did you want to use my hair dryer?"

She couldn't stop her eyes from lifting to regard the short spikes in his hair. After their bath, he toweled it dry and massaged in some product that left it sticking straight up. "Why do you have a hair dryer?"

That question probably should have remained unasked. If he bought a robe for her, he might have bought a hair dryer to keep there for an ex-girlfriend or for the parade of women volunteering to warm his bed.

"I used to have longer hair. I cut it after Ginny and some of the other producers told me it looked unprofessional. They thought it would adversely affect the ratings."

With a concentrated stare, she tried to envision him with long hair. It might look unprofessional, but she thought it was probably damn sexy. It would be something she could hold on to during sex. She shrugged, indicating she would withhold judgment on that until she saw proof.

"Plus, my mother insisted I have things like that for the guest bathrooms. I have tampons, too, if you ever need them."

"Thanks," she said, expressing it as more of a question. "I'll just take the hair dryer for now."

He did kick her ass at pool. His skill left her no doubt he purposely missed shots at the bar. The conversation during play didn't help her to concentrate, either. It vacillated between serious topics like politics and organized religion, where she revealed a lack of faith in either system, to stories about their childhoods, both funny and serious. She learned more about Ginny and Sabrina than either woman would ever tell her voluntarily.

After he shut her out of yet another game, her inner imp went into survival mode, which was never a pretty thing. She pushed all the balls she was supposed to have shot, but wasn't given an opportunity to do so, out of the way. Draping herself on the felt, she struck a deceptively inviting pose. Something strange happened inside her head. She was out of her body, looking down at the scene below. Though she was filled with dread, she was unable to stop herself from making a huge mistake.

"I can kick your ass, too. Take your best shot, tiger. See where it gets you."

A knowing gleam lit his eyes as a slow, sensual smile curled his full lips. "Maybe I should have used this strategy the other night. Who knew you responded so well to humiliation?"

One step put him in easy reach. He extended an arm, and she put him on the floor before he knew what hit him. She smiled at his confusion. "That was your best shot? I know ten-year-olds who have better moves than that."

He rose to his feet slowly, watching her cautiously. "I didn't know I was supposed to use those kinds of moves."

Then, she was back in her body, ashamed and embarrassed. A shadow crossed behind her eyes, a bit of her dark past come back to haunt her. She blinked to hide it, but Drew must have seen it. She stepped back to evade his attempted embrace. "Sorry. That was unfair." She had training he didn't even know about. More than that, she knew better. He hadn't attacked her with anything but good intentions.

She wanted to flee.

"Don't worry about it," he said quietly. "Sophie, are you angry with me?"

Yes. Yes, she was angry with him, but she was angrier with herself. He was too handsome, too charming, and she liked him too much. He stirred feelings she thought were dead and buried, feelings that scared the hell out of her and kicked her into an unnecessary survival mode. There was no way he would ever understand.

Pressure built behind her eyes. She shook her head and turned toward the door, envisioning the hallway and the stairs, trying to remember the exact location of her bag and her purse. She had to stop when he slid his arms around her from behind and rested his forehead on her shoulder. She wanted to melt into him, inhale his clean, masculine scent. She wanted the memories of something similar, but far darker, to go away.

"Can we talk about this?"

Again, she shook her head. Any minute now, the pressure would either turn into a panic attack or a migraine. She needed to get away from him. It was bad enough she threw him to the floor. She didn't want him to see her lose it completely.

The ache spread behind her jaw and to the back of her head. Nausea made her stomach roll. Blood drained from her extremities, leaving them tingling from the loss. Her face was probably green. "Please let go," she whispered.

The moment his arms reluctantly released her, Sophia ran for the nearest bathroom and lost her dinner.

Drew was there to pull her hair away from her face. He carried her to a nearby chair—his tenth spare bathroom was large enough to contain furniture—and set her down gently. Her throat burned, and a headache pounded in her ears. She hated the way she behaved toward him, and she hated that he was seeing her in such a vulnerable state.

A cold cloth wiped away the beads of sweat from her mouth and brow. He folded a second cool cloth and placed it on the back of her neck. The nausea disappeared.

She opened her eyes to see Drew watching her. It was the first time she'd ever seen him look scared. Snatching the cloth away from her neck, she stood. "I need to leave." Did he notice her legs trembling, or did she successfully cover it?

Drew stood with her. "I'll take you to the emergency room if you want, but other than that, you're not leaving until you feel better."

His tone was gentle, but there was no mistaking the steel behind his words. Sophia lacked the physical and emotional strength to fight him. These headaches took everything from her. She wasn't going anywhere. Weakly, she nodded and let him lead her to the elevator. It was that or let him carry her the two flights of stairs to his bedroom. Her legs weren't going to last much longer.

He gave her two Tylenol and tucked her into bed. "I don't suppose you're hungry? I can make some chicken noodle soup."

"I'm not sick," she mumbled. The sound sent shock waves of pain through her body. She winced. "Sorry."

"Shhhh," he said, settling next to her. One hand trailed through her hair, soothing her until she curled into his side. "Every man secretly hopes for a woman who can kick ass. Tell me you have a black belt, and I'll worship you for life."

She tried to laugh, but what came out was a pathetic substitute. Real martial artists didn't use a belt system. She couldn't tell him that because she slipped into blessed unconsciousness.

Her migraines were a direct result of stress. Taking down Drew wasn't the first stupid thing she had ever done, but it seemed like it at the time. A million admonitions rocketed through her head, most of them variations on the idea that he wouldn't want to see her again. She should have been happy that she might have succeeded in sabotaging what was morphing into the first serious relationship she entered into since the man she had planned to spend the rest of her life with raped her.

She had been young, but she really loved him. Charlie had been friends with Daniel for years. She should have been safe with him. They had everything in common and a plan for the future.

She didn't know what she was doing with Drew.

She woke to a completely dark room. A sliver of light spilled through the door to the bathroom, where she found a nightlight masquerading as a light switch. Gathering her courage, Sophia turned it on. It would be a true test of whether this was a light migraine or one that was going to set up camp and stay for a week. It had been years since she had one of those kinds.

To her utter relief, the light made her wince, but it didn't send her reeling in pain. She raided Drew's medicine cabinet, muttering questions to herself about what would possess him to give her Tylenol when he clearly had stronger medications available. Halfway to the Aleve, she stopped, debating the relative merits of the different medicines. She opted for two more Tylenol.

She freshened up, only because if she didn't, the sight of her looking like death warmed over was going to be his last memory of her. Also, she needed to brush her teeth and gargle in the worst way.

Gathering her things didn't take long. Slinging her canvas bag over one shoulder, she took the back stairs, reasoning that she would most likely find Drew in the kitchen.

She was wrong.

A woman was bent over the sink nearest the stove, filling the teakettle and humming something that sounded suspiciously like a disco tune. She was on the short side. Sophia would tower over her by four or five inches. Her blonde hair was perfectly coiffed in a short style. Her figure was neither fat nor thin, but something in between that proclaimed a healthy woman who had borne her share of children.

When she turned, she caught Sophia from the corner of her eye. A warm smile broke the lines of worry in her face. "Sophie, you're awake, and you look so much better. Drew will be so relieved."

It didn't take a rocket scientist to recognize Drew's ice-blue eyes and million-dollar smile in this woman's face. The last person she expected to see tonight was Drew's mother. Hadn't he said they were on vacation somewhere?

She placed the kettle on the stove and turned the knob for the gas. "I'm Miranda Snow. You can call me Miranda. I'll make us some tea. Chamomile will settle your stomach."

Caffeine guaranteed her headache would go away, and the substance had never kept Sophia from sleeping. Moreover, it would fortify her for the drive home. "I'd like some coffee, if it's all the same."

She smiled regretfully. "Sorry, dear. Drew would shoot me if I let you have something with caffeine in it."

The dots finally connected. He served water with dinner. He gave her decaffeinated mint tea afterward. He took her to a nonsmoking bar and never offered a beer. Sophia sighed. "I'm not pregnant."

She sat at an oak oval table taking up space on the far side of the kitchen. Patting the seat next to her, she ignored Sophia's statement. "Come sit with me, dear. I've never seen my son lose his mind over a woman before."

Sophia's eyes darted toward the doors leading out of the room, as if some last-minute reprieve would burst through at precisely the right moment to save her from having to spend time with Drew's mother. Now was the right moment, but nobody came.

As if sensing her thoughts, Miranda smiled and patted the chair next to her again. "I sent Drew to the store. It's best to give a man something to do when there's nothing he can do."

"I really should go," Sophia said. "It's late, and I didn't plan to stay the night." She wasn't saying that because she was speaking to Drew's mom, either. Spending an entire night with a lover was never on her list of acceptable outcomes for an evening. Though, before she lost her mind, she could have been easily persuaded.

She laughed. "Andrew warned me you were a slippery one. I assured him I wouldn't let you leave while he was gone." The kettle whistled. With a broad gesture, she indicated two cups with tea bags already in them. "Why don't you be a dear and pour the tea?"

She was trapped. Curiously, the walls didn't move in on her, and she didn't feel the telltale twinges of a panic attack coming on. Sophia did as Miranda asked and brought the teacups to the table.

Miranda inhaled the fragrant steam rising from the surface before pushing it away. "Let it steep for a while, my dear Sophie. We have so much to talk about."

Oh, no, they didn't.

"To begin with, can you explain those items on the counter over there? They look so interesting."

Sophia stared at Miranda without looking in the direction Drew's mother indicated. She knew exactly what was on the counter. After they had played in the kitchen, Sophia had washed the toys they used and put those away, but the rest of them were still on the counter. She took a deep breath. "I don't suppose you want to pretend like you never saw those?"

She laughed, her smile and mirth every bit as infectious as Drew's. "Sophie, at my age, things like that are items one wants to see more and more of. I know what they are, dear. I just don't know what some of them do."

With the tilt of her head, Sophia invited Miranda to follow. Some of her clients were Miranda's age, and some were older. Because the discussion was with Drew's mother, it was a little uncomfortable, but Sophia quickly moved past that. There was no way Drew would want to see her after tonight.

Over the course of the next quarter hour, Sophia explained the concepts of clitoral and anal stimulators to Drew's mother. By the time they sat down to sip their cooled tea, Miranda had two unused vibrators tucked away in her purse. Although Sophia explained how to sterilize them, she did gift them to Miranda. She had plenty, and two would not be missed. As she dumped the rest of them into her bag, Miranda admonished Sophia not to say anything to Drew.

"Andrew would never understand," she said. "He was plenty interested in talking about sex right up until he realized his father and I still have a wild time in the bedroom. Jonathan kept the lines of communication open, but it's become a father/son issue."

Just when Sophia became comfortable talking to Miranda and assumed she would keep the topics neutral, she changed the subject.

"Tell me, Sophia, do you get these headaches often? It sounds like a migraine."

"It was," she said, sipping her tea and putting Miranda off as long as she could. "Not a bad one, though, thank goodness."

She leaned forward and put her hand over Sophia's. "Andrew told me what happened to bring it on, dear. Were you in an abusive relationship?"

Wow. She brought out the big guns pretty quickly. Sophia narrowed her eyes suspiciously. "Are you a shrink?"

"I was a practicing psychologist for thirty-four years, Sophie. You can talk to me."

Sophia leapt up so quickly, she knocked into the table and spilled her tea. She was going to have one hell of a bruise on her thigh. She didn't care. She rubbed her temple as she backed away from the table. "This is unbelievable. He called in a therapist."

Miranda stood, but she didn't approach. "No, Sophie, he called his mother because he wanted to know if he should respect your wish to not take you to the hospital, or if he should call an ambulance."

"And you want to psychoanalyze me." Sophia shook her head again and picked up her bag and purse. "This is a bad idea."

"You show all the indicators," she said quietly. Her voice benefited from years of talking to crazy people. It was kind and nonjudgmental. Sophia felt drawn to her, connected in a way she hadn't connected with any of the shrinks she had seen in the past four years. Was it because she was sleeping with Miranda's son? Because she had the same caring blue eyes that Drew used to turn her to jelly?

"I don't want to discuss this with you." Calm, firm statements played through her head. *I am angry. I am terrified. I hate myself. I want to die.* Some of those she had voiced in therapy, but most of them she kept to herself.

Her smile was serene, sympathetic. "I understand, Sophie. Just know I'm here if you need a confidential ear or a sympathetic shoulder."

"Sophia? Where are you going?"

She closed her eyes as dread closed over her. She hadn't heard Drew come in. The tenderness and concern in his voice nearly undid her. "Home," she said at last. "It's late, and I have to work tomorrow."

The frown was the first thing she saw when she turned to face him. "You don't work on Mondays."

"I started my own business." Her throat constricted to see the anxiety in his face. "I have to finish a proposal that's due tomorrow afternoon."

He threw a plastic shopping bag on the counter. "Stay the night tonight. Something tells me you won't let me drive you home, and I don't want you attempting such a long drive by yourself tonight."

"Or you can stay at my place." Miranda placed a light hand on her arm. "I have plenty of extra rooms."

"I have extra rooms." The look in Drew's eyes made her ache deep inside.

Sophia closed her eyes. Daniel would come if she called. He would take her to his apartment. No questions would be asked, but a strong shoulder would be offered.

But she didn't want to be away from Drew. She didn't want to leave things this way. "I'll stay." She had to force the whisper.

Miranda gave Sophia's stiff shoulder a reassuring squeeze and pressed a card in her hand. "You call if you need me, dear. I'm just a stone's throw away."

Sophia wanted to thank her, but she only managed a nod.

Drew walked his mother to the door. Sophia heard the low murmur of their argument. Never once was she tempted to eavesdrop. Whatever they had to say was most definitely about her. She already had enough on her plate. As it was, she needed to unload a few items.

She followed Drew up the stairs, unsure if he meant for her to sleep in a guest room or with him. He paused outside of his door with the same dilemma.

"Where do you want to sleep?" There was no pressure in his question. It was completely up to Sophia.

"If you don't mind, I'd like to sleep with you."

Relief washed over his features, and he swept her into his arms. The gesture was affectionate. He held her against him tightly, pressing his face into her neck. Without thinking, she relaxed into his embrace and let his strength flow through her.

They got ready for bed, sharing the bathroom clearly meant for two with an ease that left her even more shaken. There was a time when she wouldn't have given it a second thought. They somehow choreographed their bedtime rituals well. So what? Now things were different. Using only actions and reactions, Drew let her know she meant more to him than she wanted.

Her instinct was to body-slam him again and head for the hills. A bit of stubbornness deep inside wouldn't let her off so easily. He spent the night at her house only four nights ago, and she had missed his presence in her bed every minute of every night since then.

His bed was huge. They could have slept on separate sides and never once come into accidental contact. She settled onto a portion of her half, and he turned out the lights. The bed dipped gently as he climbed into the other half, and then the room was dark.

She waited a long, long time for him to fall asleep.

"Drew?" She whispered his name, not wanting to wake him. He didn't say a word, so she felt free to continue. "I don't understand you at all."

He said nothing. She felt safer and safer. Even if he wasn't a solid sleeper, the events of the day had surely worn him out.

"I've tried very hard to sabotage this thing, to make you tired of being with me."

Quiet, even breathing greeted her confession.

"You're nothing at all like I thought you would be. The gossip shows and magazines show you with a different woman every time. You have a reputation for playing hard and fast. You flirt with a million people every week. You make a million women feel special because they think your smile is for them alone."

Her voice was barely a whisper. She needed to say these things out loud, to him, without him being aware. Otherwise, it would eat her up after she finally did something horrible enough to end the relationship. Despite her objections, that's exactly what this was developing into.

"But you mean it when you look at me, I know you do, and it scares the hell out of me. It scares me more to know I mean it when I look at you. You were supposed to be just another affair. I'm going to hurt you, and I'm sorry for that. Each time you choose not to walk away from me, it'll just get worse. It's the only thing I know how to do, the only way to stop you from making the worst mistake of your life. I was nasty to you tonight, and you responded with kindness. I don't know what I'm supposed to do with that. I wish you'd yelled, said vicious things, or hit me. God, I wish you had hit me."

Tears ran down her cheeks, and she let them flow unchecked. It was dark and quiet. She wasn't alone, but he couldn't see her weakness. He was blessedly, blissfully asleep.

A stifled cry escaped when he pulled her to him, sliding her across the gulf as if she weighed nothing. His body curved around hers, and he held her tight, as if he expected her to fight him. She didn't have the strength to mount any kind of defense.

"Is that what he did to you?" The words were muffled by her hair. "Did he hit you, Sophia?"

Her brain processed his questions as it tried to get over the shock of realizing he probably heard all of what she said to him. Safety was an illusion. Had he hit her? She tried to remember. Yes, a few times. "Just to calm you down."

Next to her, Drew trembled. She'd never seen him come close to losing his temper, but she knew fury when she felt it shaking next to her. "Just to calm you down?"

Had she said that out loud?

He shifted, looming above her, a dark shadow in a dark room. His hands were on her shoulders, and he shook her. "He hit you to *calm you down?*"

Sophia squirmed away, her breaths coming hard and fast. She wasn't afraid that Drew might hit her. She was terrified that he'd make her talk about the rape. He reached for her, capturing her wrist in the dark. She pulled away, frantically trying to dislodge his grip. *"No!"*

It was the magic word. She was free. Then a pool of light flooded his side of the bed, sending shadows to reveal the mess that was Sophia. She crouched on the edge of the bed with her back to him. Her knees were drawn into her chest, and she rocked back and forth, willing the remembrance and the pain away.

Drew stood in front of her. She looked up to see him, wearing the boxer shorts and Sensual Secrets T-shirt he put on before coming to bed. He was perfect, a feast for the eyes. Why couldn't he be a shallow jerk like someone that gorgeous was supposed to be?

"Sophie, honey…" The combination of the plea in his voice and the way he sat so carefully next to her had Sophia on her feet faster than anything else could have.

"This was a bad idea. I have to go." She paced in front of him. One glance repeated his objection. "I'll call Daniel. He'll come get me. He always comes."

He studied her silently. Her stomach turned, and she ran for the bathroom. She had the presence of mind to close and lock the door. Thankfully, nothing came up. The coolness of the marble tiles against her bare feet and the distance from Drew and any judgments he might be inclined to make combined to chase away the nausea.

Maybe showing him how unstable she was would finally get him to understand that he had no place in her life, and she had no place in his. It took a long time to find the courage to face Drew again.

When she opened the door at last, she found him sitting on the edge of the bed, waiting. He looked up as she exited. "Did you call Daniel?"

Her brows knit in confusion, and her glance fell on her bag, which had her purse and cell inside. "Not yet."

"It's after one in the morning, Sophie. Do you really want to wake him up?"

Knowing Danny, he was awake and with a pretty woman. He would drop her like asbestos if Sophia called.

"I can drive you home, if that's where you really want to be."

Understanding, patience, and something she didn't want to face emanated from him. In her heart of hearts, Sophia wanted to be there with him, curled up in his arms with all the bad memories erased. She said the only thing she could think to say. "I'm not pregnant."

"That's neither here nor there," he said gently, unwilling to argue. She envied his vast pool of inner calm. Even before the rape, her temper had been easy to set off. "It's late, and you're upset, and now it's raining. I don't want you driving in these conditions."

She could leave. She could pick up her bag and go, and he wouldn't stop her. He was asking, not insisting. "Drew, I..."

He held up a hand. "Look, Sophie, I don't know what exactly happened to you, but I know it was bad. You rebuilt your life, constructing every facet so that you have complete control of everything. I'm not judging you, honey. It's how you're surviving."

She was surviving, not living, just existing. That was her. She didn't know how to do anything else.

When he stood and came closer, she flinched, drawing her arms tightly across her body. He stopped an arm's reach away. "I've fallen for you, Sophia. I'm not going anywhere, no matter how badly you try to sabotage this thing between us."

Was that a challenge? Did he not think she could drive him away? When the choice was him or her sanity, she chose her sanity.

Besides, she wasn't fixable. Sooner or later, he would tire of trying and realize just how broken she was.

Chapter 15

Daniel came to get her. Drew waited with her in the foyer. He had chairs there, perfect for just this kind of thing. She was probably the first woman to use them to flee his presence. Sometime during the long, silent wait, he had slipped on a pair of jeans. His hands alternated between being stuck in his pockets and running restlessly through his hair.

"I'm filming tomorrow," he said at last. "If you call or text, it's likely I won't get it immediately."

Sophia didn't respond. It was unlikely she would call him tomorrow.

"If you call Ginny, she can reach me. She's one of the producers, so she'll be on set. She always has her phone." Fingers went through that blond mane again. The thick mass stood on end, but he had successfully beaten down tracks.

Ginny was a producer? She hadn't known. Now Drew's crack about her owning half the show made sense.

The flash of headlights poured through the tall windows in the front, bathing them both with brightness. The smudges under Drew's eyes showed with strain. Sophia didn't want to think about what she looked like. Her golden Italian complexion made tanning easy, but the dark circles that appeared under her eyes at a moment's notice were hereditary as well. She stood, but Drew beat her to her bag.

"Are you sure about this, Sophia?"

She nodded. "It's best if I leave."

He chewed that bottom lip again, resisting the urge to argue. It was useless. He wouldn't make any headway. Dropping the bag, he scooped her into his arms. "I'm here, Sophie. I'm here for when you need me."

She needed him now. That's why she had to go. Lifting her lips, she pressed a light kiss to his stubble-roughened jaw and backed away. The doorbell chimed, sending bells echoing through the house.

Drew greeted Daniel at the door. The two eyed one another unflinchingly, reminding Sophia of their first encounter.

Daniel looked away first, his gaze sliding to his sister. "You ready to go?"

She nodded once. Drew handed her bag to Daniel. She tried to ignore the pain in his eyes and the silent plea tensing his entire body. "He won't let me drive."

Daniel took the bag, one brow rising in surprise. "Has she been drinking?"

Drew shook his head. "She's upset, she's had a migraine, and the roads are wet."

Throwing the bag to Sophia, Danny indicated his truck. "Give your keys to Alaina. She'll drive your car to my place." He watched her cross the brick-and-cement porch, waiting until she was out of earshot before he continued speaking to Drew.

Inside Danny's truck was yet another beautiful woman. She was short, which was different, and had dark hair. Usually, he liked tall, leggy blondes with big breasts and tight dresses. This woman's outfit was attractive, but tasteful. That was different, too. She eyed Sophia sympathetically. Immediately, her hackles rose. What had Daniel told his one-night stand about her that he had no business sharing? And why did she look familiar?

"Hi," she said, sliding to the ground from the high seat. "Dan is pretty worried about you."

So he had told her about the messed-up little sister who can't take care of herself. "I'm sorry if I interrupted your date." She wasn't sorry. Daniel wouldn't remember this woman in a few days.

"It was over anyway," Alaina said with an ironic laugh. "We were in the middle of a pretty big argument when you called. I agreed to drive your car back. Otherwise, I'd be at home, showering off the stench of a bad date."

She made Sophia smile. This wasn't the first one of Daniel's dates Sophia had met. It wasn't the first date she'd interrupted. She had faced some pretty irate women in the past five years. Alaina was the first one who seemed relieved to find her night cut short.

"Danny's dates don't usually thank me for this," she said. "Or complain about going out with him. He usually treats women very well."

Alaina shrugged. "We're just not compatible."

"You're not his usual cup of tea," Sophia agreed.

She didn't seem upset by the comment. A smile brightened her face. "No, I'm not. I imagine he prefers blondes, the taller and sluttier the better."

Sophia laughed. "You aren't in the usual mold, that's for sure. Women who flock to Daniel are usually too enamored of his looks to give him a hard time about anything."

The clomp of boots announced Daniel. He eyed the two women suspiciously. "What's so funny?"

Taking Sophia's keys and her own purse, Alaina raked her eyes over Daniel in a way that left no doubt she found him lacking. "We were just discussing how you can't handle a real woman."

Sophia winced. Daniel's preference for shallow, plastic women wasn't her business. Except for Drew, her lovers were all submissives. Drew was supposed to be shallow and plastic, but he wasn't.

A subtle tightening of his jaw was the only indication her barb struck a nerve. His temper was every bit as volatile as Sophia's used to be. Before he could say something mean, she reached for his hand. "Danny? I'm tired. Can you take me home now?"

With a curt nod, he growled something at Alaina. It might have been an order to follow him, but Sophia wasn't sure. He stomped around to the driver's side.

She faced Alaina. "Thank you for doing this. He's not usually such a jerk."

Alaina sighed. "You don't remember me, do you?"

Taking a closer look, Sophia searched her memory for a match and came up empty. "I'm sorry."

She set a gentle, sympathetic hand on Sophia's shoulder. "That's okay. You have a lot to deal with right now."

Before Sophia could say anything, Alaina was in her car, starting the engine. Involuntarily, she glanced back to Drew's front door. He stood there, a lonely figure framed by the light spilling in from the porch. Her heart lurched and her arms ached with wanting to be around him. Turning, she climbed into Daniel's truck and buried her face in her hands.

He didn't speak to her. She recognized the anger rolling from him in waves as something that had nothing to do with her. The drive to his place was only twenty minutes. She hadn't realized he lived so close to Drew.

Sophia thanked Alaina again. The petite woman climbed into her car and left without uttering a single word to Danny.

Baffled, Sophia followed him up the stairs to his loft apartment. "What happened? You're usually so suave with the ladies."

"I see you two bonded over your mutual dislike of men. I'm not surprised."

Her brows shot into the air. He hadn't used that caustic tone with her since before...

"Danny? Are you okay?"

He ran a hand through his hair. Like hers, it was thick and dark brown. His curled to just below his ears, falling in a messy look that most women couldn't seem to resist. "Yes. No. I'll be fine."

Tentatively, Sophia put out a feeler. "She's a feisty one. I like her."

"She's feisty, all right," he mumbled. "How about you tell me what happened with Drew? I thought you liked him."

Kicking off her shoes, Sophia flopped down on his bed. The sofa was already converted in anticipation of the night ending well. "I do."

He flopped down next to her. "He's crazy about you, Sophie. I don't see the problem."

"That is the problem." Her voice was soft, barely above a whisper. "The last guy I felt strongly about was Charlie."

She hadn't said his name out loud in almost five years. Next to her, Daniel flinched.

"He's nothing like that son of a bitch."

"No, he isn't."

"Then what?" It wasn't like Daniel to press her, to force an issue. Why the about-face tonight, when she just needed to get away from it all?

"I can't be in that position again, Danny."

His hand closed over hers. "I hate seeing you like this. I hate what that bastard did to you, Sophie, but you can't let it destroy what you have with Drew. He loves you."

Walls closed in, which was pretty significant in the wide-open space of Daniel's loft. She couldn't breathe. She knew exactly how Drew felt about her, but even he hadn't framed it like that. "I have to end it."

The tears started, but she didn't know if they were more from the idea that Drew was in love with her or the thought of not having him in her life. Daniel's arms closed around her. He held her as she sobbed and somehow babbled the disjointed details of everything that had happened with Drew. She probably told him more than a brother wanted to know about his sister and her boyfriend, but she wasn't in control.

Drew stripped that away from her, bit by bit, from the moment he first stepped through her front door. Now she had to find a way to regain it.

The sun was high in the sky by the time she stirred. Daniel hadn't moved to the other sofa. It wasn't that either of them had a problem sleeping in the same bed—they'd shared a mattress more often than not until he hit puberty—but Danny was a bed hog. None too gently, she shoved his arm off her face and his knee away from where it pressed into her kidney. He muttered something and turned onto his stomach.

She crept over to his coffeemaker and set the magic potion to brewing before hopping in the shower. Daniel kept a drawer for her clothes since she often stayed the night after her Wednesday class, so she had fresh clothing to wear.

Her brother was a sound sleeper. She didn't bother to be quiet because she knew almost nothing was going to wake him. Tackling the pile of dirty clothes in the large pantry he used as a laundry room, she started a load for him. He was pretty good about keeping his place clean, so she knew the clothes wouldn't sit there for two days, waiting for her to return.

She helped herself to some cereal and left. It wasn't until she was halfway home that she realized she hadn't poured herself a cup of coffee.

Worries threatened her for the rest of the ride home. Something about seeing her house helped push the thoughts of *what if* and *how the hell could I be a good mother when I was so messed up* far away.

She finished the proposal for Christopher's firm by three. Ginny called as she was collating the printed pages into a booklet. It was at this point she missed Grace. She might have been Jeremy's secretary, but she had done things like copying and collating for the entire office.

"Sophia? How are you doing, girl?"

Her upbeat tone beat back the suspicion that Drew had put her up to calling. While they had hung out together quite a bit, Sophia and Ginny weren't good friends. They were friends through Sabrina. Every time she saw Ginny, it was because Sabrina had invited them both someplace at the same time.

"I'm fine," she lied. "What's up?"

"Well, I'm calling for three reasons. The first is that I'm planning a surprise bachelorette party for Sabrina. Technically, she's an old married lady, but we'll overlook that for now."

She emitted the requisite chuckle. Personally, Sophia didn't think Sabrina wanted a bachelorette party, especially not the kind Ginny would plan. Sabrina was more of a sedate-get-together kind of girl, while Ginny was more of a drinks-and-strippers kind of party girl.

"The wedding is three weeks from this Saturday. I want to do it the weekend before. Sabrina has some weekend getaway planned for all of us in the Bahamas. I want to do it the night before we leave."

Grabbing the BlackBerry into which their schedules were loaded, Sophia punched up that weekend. She hadn't realized Sabrina planned to take them all to the Bahamas. This didn't bode well. If she didn't get the account with Christopher's company, then her job at Ellen's was her only income.

While it paid well, Sophia didn't work enough hours to take the time off. She toyed with the idea of picking up Sunday and Monday nights. That would give her Tuesday for dancing lessons and Wednesday for the self-defense classes. She sighed. This was the worst time to have quit her accounting job.

"I can't do it, Ginny. I have to work." Before she could say anything, Sophia continued. "I'm already losing my Tuesdays, and I'll lose Saturday that weekend to the trip."

"I thought Jonas was working Mondays for you." Her tone was tentative. Sophia could envision her on the other end, the flurry of activity around her forgotten as she focused her undivided attention on the phone call.

That was another mistake. She could have used the money. "I told him not to worry about it." Ginny was still silent. "Look, I'll help organize it and set it up. I just can't be there for the actual party."

"I've got it under control." She started doing whatever she had been doing again. Sophia heard voices raised in frustrated anger. "Try to swing it, Sophia. Sabrina really likes you. She doesn't feel warmly toward very many people, so that makes you special."

"I'll talk to Ellen." It was the best she could do.

"Great. Second thing. Ellen tells me you do her books."

"I help out. She does most of it herself."

"Sabrina told me you started your own firm, and Ellen, she says you freelance. I'm not sure what that means in the financial world, but I'm hoping it means you'd be willing to help me out."

Now she had Sophia's interest. Sophia listened while Ginny prattled on about merchandizing and how Drew's show killed them with the taxes last year. Finally, she interrupted. "It sounds like you lack a financial plan."

Ginny laughed. "I just want to make cakes and assorted pastries. Drew and I used to tackle this together, but with the show and all the appearances..." Her sigh was tired. "He's leaving tomorrow night for Los Angeles, and he won't be back until Sunday or Monday, depending on the number of engagements his agent confirms. But I'm sure he told you all about that."

He hadn't.

"I'm producing, which is a fancy term for dealing with the director, editors, and anyone else who tries to stick their hand on this thing. Luckily, Drew writes his own material. Give that man a camera, and he's good to go." Another sigh. "The bottom line is that we're busy. I'm tired. Drew's tired. We're both working so much, and none of the books are getting done. I'll pay you anything to straighten this out."

Sophia's thinking must have been too quiet for Ginny. Her laugh on the other end was nervous.

"I talked to Ellen last night. When she mentioned you were an accountant, I think I heard angels singing."

Something clicked. "I thought Lara was in accounting."

"Corporate accounting. It fits with what we need done, but she refuses to work for me. The last time she tried it, we fought and fought. So now she's wicked serious about keeping our work lives separate from our personal lives. This would necessarily cross those boundaries."

"Does Drew know you're offering me a temporary job?"

"No, but I can't see that he'd have a problem with it."

After last night, she honestly didn't know where they stood.

"Oh, and the third thing," she said. "Before I forget. Drew showed up at the set four hours late, which is saying a lot because it's in his kitchen, and it's been downhill from there. Anything that could go wrong has gone wrong. He said to tell you he won't be able to make it over tonight."

That took care of where they stood. He couldn't even call himself. Air whooshed out of her lungs. She felt like someone had punched her in the stomach, and she'd been punched in the stomach before, so she knew precisely how it felt. Ginny babbled on as Sophia struggled not to lose control. The last thing she needed to do was burst into hysterical tears. She'd lost enough face the previous night in front of Drew. She didn't need Ginny witnessing just how unhinged she could become.

"We're likely filming tomorrow, too. Oh, please say you'll at least look at the books. I can meet you at the bakery whenever you have a free day."

"I'm free tomorrow," she said. If Drew was going to be filming tomorrow, and then in Los Angeles for the rest of the week, this would be the perfect time to get started. Ginny was likely exaggerating the extent of their problem. "I can meet you at the bakery at nine."

"Can you make it seven? I have to be on set at nine, but I'll be at the bakery bright and early. Thank you so much for this, Sophia. If I was single, I'd give you sexual favors for this, show you all the ways women are better lovers than men."

Well versed in having sex with both genders, Sophia laughed. Quality wasn't so much about the gender as the person. "Money is fine." They talked for a few minutes longer, discussing the terms of the agreement. Sophia would bring a contract with her in the morning, and Drew would be safely in the studio instead of at the bakery.

Sophia's feelings were mixed after Ginny's call. She was happy to actually have a client, even if it was just a temporary job. More pressing was the fist crushing her heart. He hadn't even bothered to call himself to cancel. Likely, he didn't want a repeat of last night. She didn't blame him.

At least Christopher would be over in an hour. They could both escape from the grief caused by their failed relationships with vanilla partners.

Chris was prompt, but then, he knew better than to be late. They took care of the business first.

"Do you have a proposal for me, Ms. DiMarco?" The respectful tone lost a little luster to the twinkle in his eye.

She handed over the package she put together. He stuffed it into his bag without so much as lifting the front cover. She narrowed her eyes at him. "Chris, is this an honest bid request, or did you just want to get into my torture chamber?"

"Both," he laughed. "I'll be honest, though, you're not the only one, and some of the others that have come in look pretty good. The committee meets Friday. I'll have a decision for you by Monday."

She nodded, understanding the bureaucracy of the corporate system. "Head downstairs."

He looked toward the door, then back at her. "Is your boyfriend already here, or are we starting without him?"

"I don't have a boyfriend." Saying that statement stung, and the fist squeezed even tighter. "It's just us tonight."

Christopher headed for the stairs, any questions he might have asked squelched by her tight expression. This was a drill he knew well. She disappeared into her room to change into something with a little more give than her smart power suit.

He was in position when she arrived, naked, kneeling with his knees spread wide apart, and his hands positioned behind his neck. Chris had a magnificent body. He was lean and whippet thin, all muscle. She loved the way he rippled and bunched under the sting of her lashes.

She walked around behind him to choose a whip, trying with all her might to ignore the longing for someone with bigger muscles and broader shoulders that made his hips seem even narrower than they were. She bit her lip and shoved Drew, and the feel of his arms around her, far away.

Christopher was hard from the moment she trailed the falls of the cat across his shoulders. In a moment of sheer perversity, she made him move to the foot of the bed. She secured him to the posts with Velcro handcuffs in the exact same position she had put Drew in. She had failed with him. She would not fail with Christopher.

She started with easy blows, tempering them to short licks of the lash. She didn't see Christopher's dark skin in front of her. She saw Drew's sun-kissed, paler skin, the tiny freckles dotting his shoulder blades. The pressure of her whip increased. Red streaks marred his backside. The lash curled around his thighs, raising welts on the sensitive flesh between his legs.

In front of her, Christopher moaned in ecstasy. Tears streamed down her face. Her cat fell to the floor. She yanked the Velcro loose, hysterical hiccups escaping as she fought for breath.

"Sophia?" He caught her as she fell and carried her to the bed. He sat her upright and put her head between her knees. "Breathe, Sophia. Just breathe."

"I'm sorry." She gulped for air and tried to raise her head.

He pushed her back down. "Just stay like this until you're done hyperventilating."

Long moments passed. He rubbed her back, and she thought about how this was the first time she had a panic attack about something other than the memory of the rape. Was this progress, or was she getting worse?

By the time she pulled herself together, Christopher was dressed. He sat next to her and draped his arm across her shoulders. "You know, this only worked for me because I was pretending you were Janelle. I don't think I could have gone through with this, Sophia. I think we're both in impossible situations."

She nodded weakly, the numbness setting in to anesthetize the pain. "Ain't we a pair, raggedy man?"

He laughed. "I'd ask if you want some dinner, but I don't think either of us has much of an appetite."

She shook her head. "I'd invite you to stay and get drunk with me, but I might be pregnant, so that's not an option for me."

"If you don't want to be alone, I can stay," he said. "We could watch TV and hate everyone who looks happy."

"That sounds nice," she said.

He surfed through the channels, and she cried during a commercial for *Sensual Secrets*.

Chapter 16

Before he left, she threw an idea to Christopher. She couldn't teach Drew to be a submissive if he didn't want to be one. However, Christopher hadn't even brought up the subject with Janelle.

"Why don't you ask her if she is interested in dominating you, Chris? You could bring her by, and I could give her some pointers."

"My old lover teaching my new lover what I like in the bedroom." His brows rose at the dramatic irony. "I don't see anything wrong with that situation."

Sophia rolled her eyes. "Don't tell her we were lovers. Tell her I'm a dominatrix friend who is willing to teach her how to hurt you without damaging you."

"You wouldn't...give that away? She wouldn't understand about how we're just friends who sleep together." He sounded hopeful. She wanted to give him a happy ending.

"My lips are sealed. Bring her by the club. I'm working Thursday, Friday, and Saturday. She could watch me work you over."

He wouldn't commit to the idea, but she could tell he liked it. "I'll think about it."

Sophia actually slept well that night and arrived at Ginny's bakery promptly at eight. Due to the popularity of their show, the bakery wasn't open to the general public. An appointment was needed to come inside. She parked in the city garage, careful to keep her receipt for tax purposes, and trudged the three blocks to Sensual Secrets.

"Can I help you?" The woman who answered the door was on the far side of fifty. She had the kind of body that hinted at a reluctance to say no to carbs. Lines creased her eyes and the areas around her mouth, marking her as someone who laughed often. In short, she reminded Sophia of her mother.

"I'm Sophia DiMarco. Ginny is expecting me."

She smiled regretfully. Her colorful shirt hung nearly to her knees, covering dusty polyester-blend pants. "Ms. Breszewski doesn't have appointments scheduled today." She handed Sophia a card. "You can call for an appointment."

Sophia held a hand up. "Give me a minute." She speed-dialed Ginny, grateful Sabrina had programmed the numbers into their phones.

In less than thirty seconds, Ginny threw the door completely open. "Sophia, thank God you're here. Ellen told me to tell you to be here at seven if I wanted you here by eight. Do you know how to do payroll, too?"

Whoops. And here, she thought she was on time for once. With a smile, Sophia assured Ginny that she knew how to do it all. Ginny gave Sophia a tour of the bakery. It wasn't what she expected. The door opened directly into the kitchen. There was no storefront or customer area. At one end, nestled under a bank of windows that were covered on the bottom half to protect them from prying eyes, was a long table. Several chairs were set up around it. Every seat was occupied except one.

Ginny pointed out people and said their names by way of introduction. In full accountant mode, Sophia would rather they were assigned numbers. If Ginny wanted her to do payroll, that was how she was going to get to know them anyway.

She flashed a pleasant smile as Ginny introduced her.

"This is Sophia DiMarco, Financial Goddess. She's going to wade through that mess upstairs and get it all in order."

"It needs to be computerized." This helpful suggestion came from a heavily tattooed man with a boyish smile and a rail-thin build. Sophia was 80 percent sure Ginny said he was their baker. Or maybe she called him a sculptor. She didn't know bakeries needed sculptors.

A true smile cracked the corner of her lip. "You don't have your records on computer?"

"There is a laptop up there with some stuff on it. Lara set it up for us a couple of years ago, but like I said, she won't go near the finances for this place."

That didn't give Sophia hope this would be an easy job, but she liked the idea of a challenge. They made cakes. How bad could it be?

The rest of the room had an open design. She spied various workstations, and Ginny explained what some of them were for. Fondant was rolled in one area. Icing was done in another place. Airbrushing was done in yet another area.

Mouthwatering aromas poured through a doorway to the rear of the building. Ginny laughed at the way Sophia's head swiveled to catch the scent. "That's the bakery kitchen. Drew has his thing going on in the other half of the building."

The thing that amazed her most was the lack of cakes. In her experience, most places that made wedding cakes had them shellacked and displayed all over the place. Ginny had a few pictures on the wall. The artistry and design were amazing. Sophia could certainly see where she earned the various titles she had picked up around the world. But where were the cakes?

"Drew isn't here," she said, doing her best to whisper it in Sophia's ear. Sophia was about six inches taller, so she had to bend down to hear Ginny's words.

"Actually, I was looking for the cakes. I smell them, but I don't see them."

She laughed. "We have a book full of pictures for clients to see. We make all of our cakes fresh, so you won't see a finished cake until the day it's due. Most of our deliveries are for the weekend. You'll see more and more as the week progresses."

Ginny led Sophia through a door to a set of stairs. A closed door was the only other thing in the hall. A sign on it warned anyone going through it to make sure it was tightly closed.

"That's where the culinary stuff is done. I don't understand how someone can spend so many years doing pastries, and then suddenly decide he likes to cook more than he likes to paint fondant."

Sophia had experienced his painting abilities. Plus, he had a display case in his basement full of trophies and medals and awards for his baked goods.

"He's an incredible artist. I'm better at the overall design, but he's great at the detail work. We're a great team, and we're not too proud to admit when we need help." She smiled up at Sophia with her head cocked to the side. Sophia wondered if Ginny was aware she was flirting. "You guys really do just have sex, don't you?"

If that had been the case, Sophia wouldn't be praying Drew wasn't on the other side of that door. "We've talked, just not about work."

With a dramatic roll of the eyes, she climbed the stairs. "It's a mess. I'm warning you now, Sophia. If you're going to ask for more money, now is the time to do it."

They had settled on a fair rate. Since Sophia didn't know what she was getting into, and neither did Ginny, she was charging by the hour instead of for the job.

Ginny paused two steps ahead of Sophia. It added enough inches to her height that she could look down on the taller woman. She shook her head. "Drew's right. You don't laugh enough."

Sophia didn't know if the sympathy or the fact that Drew criticized her to his friend hurt more. "I laugh when there's reason to laugh." Maybe it was a bitchy thing to say, but she wasn't full of warm, mushy feelings right then.

Chastened, Ginny continued.

The second floor was a wide open space. Boxes and equipment were neatly lined on shelves or stacked on the floor. A broken mixer, industrial-sized, was disassembled on a table near the back of the building.

"Ethan thinks he can fix it," Ginny supplied.

"Ethan?" She probably should know who that was.

"Skinny guy with all the tattoos? I keep telling him that ink and muscle are two different things, and that having an abundance of one doesn't make up for lacking the other."

Sophia winced. Ethan was young, probably a few years younger than her. Some men took a little longer to add bulk to their bodies. Ginny's jab was a low blow. "Don't you have a few tattoos yourself?"

She smiled, a catlike curl of the lip that was dangerously attractive. If Sophia wasn't numb from the inside out, she might have been moved. The differences in these two sisters amazed her. Sabrina and Ginny could have been identical twins if Ginny wasn't three years younger. Both could be insensitive and catty. However, Sabrina tended to stumble on it by accident. When she realized the implication of what she said or did, she was mortified and genuinely sorry. She worked hard to be tactful.

Ginny, on the other hand, was as ballsy as they came. She was vivacious, lively, and caustic. If she felt she needed to say something, she said it, voicing her opinion without concern for the consequences. Only when Lara was around did Ginny's bitchy exterior sweeten, and it did so considerably.

Sophia would love to get her little wiggling ass under her whip. Sabrina came to her because she liked pain. It was a secret few knew about her. It calmed her, purified her soul. Like Christopher, she probably liked to mix pain with sex. It made Jonas a good match for her. He knew the boundaries. He could hurt her just enough to take her to that place of mindless pleasure.

Ginny wasn't a natural submissive. It made Sophia want to dominate her all the more. Sex didn't have to be involved. Given her relationship with Lara, that wasn't even on the table. But the vision of her naked body writhing and bouncing under the tongues of a whip called to Sophia's dark need.

Then, she remembered the disaster with Christopher last night. Dominating him had reduced her to tears. It wasn't Chris she wanted. It wasn't Ginny. It was Drew, only Drew. She didn't want to whip him. She just wanted him. She closed her eyes against the flood of pain and longing the thought of him released.

Oblivious to Sophia's internal storm, Ginny indicated a single door. "This is the office." Producing a key from the pocket beneath her apron, she shoved it in the keyhole and twisted sharply. "I hate this room."

Immediately, Sophia saw why. It was a disaster area. Piles of papers were strewn over the desk, spilling to a nearby table. A few steps in the room revealed additional stacks behind the desk.

Ginny pointed to a laptop. "Lara set something up on that. I know we should have kept it up, but I make cakes, Sophia. I love to bake, and I love to decorate. I'm good at it."

Sophia was still processing the mess of invoices, receipts, and miscellaneous paperwork. "What's Drew's excuse?"

She must have heard the underlying censure, the anger lying just below the surface. There was an edge to her answer. "When he's not busy being a damn fine chef, he's filming the show or helping me with the cakes. He might concentrate on cooking now, but he's one of the best decorators I've ever worked with. He has a great mind, an incredible eye, and skillful hands."

Don't I know it. "So, you want me to sort through this, enter your data in Lara's program, and straighten out your billing?"

Teeth came out to tug at her generous lower lip. "Ellen said you do it all, Sophia. I need you to check our tax returns for the past three years." She snapped her fingers and flared her big brown eyes. "An audit. Lara said you need to do an audit. And then fix all the stuff that's wrong."

Sophia's mouth opened and closed. "Ginny, what you're asking will take at least a month, and that's if I can find all of your records and organize them today."

She nodded absently. "Take as long as you need." She scratched at the spot on her cheek where a wisp of hair tickled. "I know you have other clients, but we're in a bad way here."

With a feigned casualness, she drifted to the desk, opened a drawer, and drew out a stack of unopened mail. Words like "overdue" and "final notice" were stamped on them. Her confidence vanished.

"I have no idea how this happened. I thought we were paying our bills. I don't want to be one of those tragic success stories, the kind where everything is going right and we blow it because neither Drew nor I paid much attention to our suppliers." Again, she worried her bottom lip. "Lara doesn't let me near the finances at home."

"Yet Drew trusts you with them here?"

She shrugged. "He thinks I'm competent. I have this huge trust fund, so I must know how to manage money, right? The truth is that my grandfather set it all up with someone to oversee the money. He looks after my mom's money and Sabrina's, too. They all assure me things are fine, but I have no idea."

Sophia felt a surge of sympathy. She knew what it was like to feel out of her depth with something. Finances and dominating were the only places in her life where she didn't feel like she was drowning. She had control in both places.

"Sophia, you're not a neutral party. Drew trusts you. Everyone I know has a high opinion of you, and nobody doubts your integrity. I want you to do this because I know you'll do right by us."

With a nod, Sophia set her own laptop case down next to the desk. She wouldn't need it for some time. "Is everything out in the open? Is anything in here off-limits to me?"

She shook her head. "You'll need stuff in the files and in the drawers. Honestly, I don't know what is where, but it's all in here."

"I'll try to have a timeline for you by the end of the day."

With a devilish grin, she shook her head. "There's no rush. Lara told me this should take you at least six months."

Sophia could see where Lara wouldn't want to tackle this problem in her spare time. "It might," she admitted.

"She also told me I should keep you on afterward, at least three days a week."

Her smile was weak. "We'll cross that bridge when we come to it."

Ginny left her alone, and she got to work. There was no rhyme or reason to anything in the room. Customer orders were mixed with supplier orders. The only thing that made sense was that the payment information for their customer orders was stapled to an itemized invoice.

By noon, Sophia was on the floor with several piles growing around her. Because she hadn't known what to expect, she wore a summery dress with a long skirt. It wasn't strictly business apparel, but Ginny didn't seem to mind. If she was going to be shut away in the dusty office and on the floor, it was a good choice. She had wanted to wear jeans, but her sense of professionalism nixed that idea.

The first order of business was to separate things into months and topics. Preliminary piles included supplies, employee-related and customer-related. Ginny had customers who bought from her regularly. It would be helpful to have computerized files with their past orders because they tended to order similar things each time.

Sophia got into a rhythm that only a light-headed feeling and the growling of her stomach interrupted. The smell of cake and bread combined with the spicy scent of whatever was on the catering menu for that evening. It drifted upstairs to tempt her. She didn't expect them to feed her, but she was hungry. It was time for a break.

Purse in hand, Sophia made her way down the stairs and into the bakery. Things were in full swing. Ginny had a staff of at least ten, each of them chattering away as they worked. It was a happy environment, where people liked each other and they liked their jobs. Sophia wished she could smile at the sight, but all she felt was a vague jealousy mixed with anxiety.

Ginny was bent over a table, pencil in hand, gesturing wildly. Next to her, Drew listened intently. After a moment, he took the pencil from her to sketch something. His movements were quick and decisive. Both of them had their backs to Sophia. She thought they were on the set, filming today.

"I like to stare, too."

Sophia jumped. A small, pretty woman with dark eyes and a bouncy brown ponytail smiled up at her. She appeared to be around the same age, which put her in her mid-twenties. "Stare?"

"Drew has a gorgeous ass, the kind meant to be squeezed and teased. I could sculpt it in modeling chocolate all day long and never get tired of running my hands over it." She winked. "It's only one of the perks of working here."

Sophia's heart was in her throat. She wanted to run away, hide upstairs until he was gone. She hadn't meant to invade his workplace. Visions of carting all that paperwork home temporarily made her feel better. Then she jettisoned the idea. She would need boxes and boxes to move everything she would need in that room. No, she was stuck there.

Squaring her shoulders, she delivered a weak smile to the admiring decorator and approached Ginny. She tried to knock Drew to the periphery of her vision and of her awareness, but it didn't work entirely.

"Ginny?"

Drew whirled, a surprised smile lighting his face. "Sophia?"

She couldn't find a smile, even a small professional one, to return to him. Focusing her attention on Ginny, she took another deep, cleansing breath. "I'm taking a break. I'll be back in an hour."

His smile faded. She felt the shift in his mood as palpably as a punch in the stomach. There was a good chance she wouldn't be hungry for lunch, but it would take at least an hour to convince herself she could sneak back in without encountering Drew.

Ginny looked from Drew to Sophia, a frown pinching between her eyes. "Okay."

"A break? From what?" Drew's mouth was a grim line. Her eyes were drawn to it immediately.

"I hired Sophia to straighten out that mess upstairs."

The grim line turned down at the corners. "You need an accountant for that."

Ginny stared at him. "Sophia is an accountant."

Stunned disbelief and a flittering of betrayal crossed his face. His eyes never left Sophia's. "You're an accountant?"

"I have a degree in finance," she clarified. "Accounting was my minor." She watched the play going on behind Drew's eyes as he fit this new knowledge into his incomplete understanding of her.

"You never told me that." It was an accusation.

She shrugged. "You didn't stop to ask for a résumé when you were stripping off my clothes. I didn't think you were interested in my brains."

Color drained from his perfect face. "Sophie, don't do this."

Ginny looked worriedly between them. "I thought things were going well with you two."

Ignoring both of them, Sophia repeated her intention to go to lunch, and then she walked away.

Royal Oak was an old town. Sophia didn't need anything but her feet to find a small café where she could find something good to eat. She wanted to find someplace where she could get a stiff drink, but with the fleeting pass of her hand over her abdomen, she settled for decaffeinated tea. Damn that man. She wasn't pregnant. She could pee on a stick today for confirmation.

Sophia returned at the time she said she would, stopping briefly at a pharmacy for an early pregnancy test. When she knocked at the door, the same woman answered it again. This time, she beamed and opened the door wide.

"Well, you certainly have stirred things up around here."

It was Sophia's turn to be surprised. Ginny had asked whether she knew how to do payroll. "Why? Hasn't Ginny been paying you regularly?"

Her smile widened. "We've all been wondering about the woman who swept Drew off his feet. Now we know."

Sophia patted her shoulder as she brushed past. "He's still standing."

Just barely standing, thanks to the way she knocked him on his ass, both literally and figuratively. She did warn him. She hadn't meant for him to hear it, but he did. He canceled their plans last night because of it. She didn't blame him, but that didn't make it hurt less.

She was on the floor, knee-deep in piles of papers and muttering to herself, when a shadow fell over her. Startled from bliss, she glanced up. His jeans stretched over his thighs in a careless caress as he shifted restlessly.

"Are you pissed at me for canceling last night? The shoot ran long. We didn't finish until this morning. Ginny said you understood."

She stared at him for a full minute, waiting until he squirmed just a bit more. Subconsciously, he had to know she was in control of the situation. She had already learned her lesson about overt domination with him. "I'm not mad at you."

He came closer and squatted next to her. "You could have fooled me."

Again, she stared at him, registering no emotion whatsoever in her face or demeanor. "I thought I was very honest with you."

A mirthless laugh barked from him. "You're not even honest with yourself."

Sophia shrugged, unwilling to discuss this with him. "Consistency has always been one of my strong points."

"I'm not going to let you walk away from this, Sophie."

The slight narrowing of her eyes was her only response. She couldn't stop herself. "I didn't end this." She couldn't end this. She wanted desperately to end this, but she couldn't. "You did."

His temper flared, chilling those ice-blue eyes until they burned with cold fire. "Canceling one date isn't ending a relationship. Are you pissed that you didn't get your threesome last night? Is that what this is about? You didn't get laid, so now you're pissed at me?"

It wasn't a date. "You wanted the threesome, Drew. I set that up for you."

"You wanted it, too, Sophia. You want someone you can whip into submission because you can't get me to fall in line the way you'd like." His eyes narrowed even more. "Is that what's wrong? Did you not get the domination fix you needed last night? Are you looking for a whipping boy?"

She reveled in the heartlessness of her next comment before it left her mouth. Something had to break him. Something had to drive him away. "Christopher didn't cancel on me, Drew. You did."

She thought he was angry before. She meant to push him, and she did. He grabbed her by the arms and hauled her to her feet. Papers scattered. Her neat stacks were ruined. Even as her heart pounded in fear, she held her ground. She needed this. She needed him to be angry, to mistreat her. She needed him to show her he was no different.

He shook with the power of his fury. She watched him with expectant, wary eyes. His mouth worked as he struggled for the words. "Tell me you didn't sleep with him, Sophie. Tell me you didn't do something stupid."

Some people might define the way she pushed away a man who was so obviously in love with her as stupid. She wasn't about to point that out to Drew. There was a reason for everything she did, and she wasn't obligated to explain herself to him or anyone else.

When she didn't answer, his hands tightened on her arms painfully. She thought he might shake her, or throw her, or hit her, but he just stared at the hands biting into her flesh and slowly released her. "I'm sorry, Sophie. I'm so sorry."

He thought she had been with another man and *he* was apologizing? What did she have to do to make him hate her? She rubbed at her arms and watched the little white fingerprints disappear. She wouldn't even have a bruise to show for her efforts.

She closed her eyes, sickened yet again at her behavior. It wasn't his fault he was a decent man. "I didn't have sex with him. I whipped him, and that was all."

He was silent for a long time, studying her misery even though she refused to look at him. Finally, a gentle hand tilted her chin upward, forcing her to meet his eyes. "You weren't kidding, were you?" His thumb caressed her lower lip, and she felt the sharp prick of tears behind her eyes. "I'm not going to walk away from you, Sophia. I'm not going anywhere. I know it will take some time to prove that to you, but I will."

"If you were a smart man, you'd cut your losses now." Her voice was a whisper. She wanted him to leave as badly as she wanted him to stay. She wanted him to hit her as much as she wanted him to kiss her. Either action would unravel her.

He held her, folding his arms around her, wrapping her in the safety and security of his embrace. "I love you, Sophie. I'm not giving up on us."

Chapter 17

They took on the tango that night. Sophia couldn't fathom what Sabrina was thinking in having them all learn that dance. Even the simplified version they learned contained intricate footwork that had them tripping and stumbling all over the dance floor.

Every time they messed up, which was frequently, Amanda and Richard shot Jonas and Sabrina evil looks. Ty and Samantha didn't do badly. Samantha had formal training, and she kept Ty looking respectable. Ginny and Lara had obviously done this before. The instructor clapped her approval and pointed enthusiastically. Ellen and Ryan made the best of it, using the closeness of the dance to grope one another shamelessly.

Jonas led Sabrina around the floor with confidence and panache, leaving no doubt that he had chosen this number, not Sabrina. They laughed and stared into each other's eyes, a big, gooey mass of sappiness.

Drew held Sophia close, swearing under his breath every time something went wrong. On the surface, he seemed to be taking it all with grace and dignity. From the expression on his face, no one could tell he was actually whispering an incredible stream of curses, ranging from colorful to raunchy.

"I didn't realize you were so well versed in the art of swearing."

He stepped on her toes, issuing another curse instead of an apology. "I'm well-versed in a lot of arts you don't know about. I can't believe you didn't tell me you were an accountant."

"Would you have hired me sooner?" she teased, not at all sorry about withholding facts about herself. "Tried to woo me with lists of numbers instead of all those roses? Oh, wait. You never sent roses."

He planted a loud smooch on her cheek. "You got pouty when I made you breakfast. I had to force you to let me buy you dinner. I bought you a robe, and you nearly killed me. I think I should take this slowly, let you acclimate to the concept of receiving gifts first. If you smashed them in my face, the thorns would hurt."

A mischievous glint lit his eye.

"What?" she demanded. She was still in awe that he was with her after all she had put him through over the past two days. Deep down, she was starting to think he meant what he said.

"If I dip you and we fall over, can we stay on the floor and make out?"

"Save it for later. Livia called me today. She'll be at my house at nine thirty unless I text her otherwise."

He was quiet, avoiding eye contact.

"Drew? If you don't want to do this, just tell me. I can cancel."

They both stumbled. She fell against Drew as he lost his footing. He broke her fall with his body, but they both hit the ground anyway. Sophia thought she knocked the air from him until the cursing began anew. He whispered the words in her ear with the same sexy tone he used to say things that were actually sexy. She giggled, inappropriate laughter causing Sophia to bury her head in his neck as her body was wracked with paroxysms.

"Get a room," Ginny yelled from across the polished floor.

Drew stroked a hand over her hair and across her shoulder. The sweet nothings continued to pour from his mouth.

She laughed harder. Tears poured from her eyes. "I take it you're not hurt?"

"The woman of my dreams is lying on top of me and shows no signs of moving. Even if I was hurt, I would deny it."

Feet stopped next to them. "You guys okay?" Sabrina's concern floated down.

Sophia felt the smile stretching Drew's lips. "We're fine. We figure the longer we stay like this, the less time we have to spend tripping on our own feet and stepping on each other's."

Pushing herself to kneeling, she moved so Drew could get up. Jonas lifted Sophia from the floor and set her on her feet. She turned to thank him, but stopped when she saw the anger compressing his mouth into a thin line. "What's wrong?"

Reaching out, he used his thumb to wipe away a few stray teardrops.

Behind Sophia, Drew got to his feet and threw an arm around her waist to pull her closer. "If I knew swearing was the best way to make you laugh, I would have tried it long before now. I'm fluent in five languages."

Jonas frowned. "You were laughing?"

"Yes," Sophia admitted, a rare smile lingering on her face. "Drew says some pretty amusing things when he's frustrated."

Jonas looked from her to Drew and back again. His face softened. "Then don't let us interrupt." He swept Sabrina away, but not before she saw the brilliant smile Sabrina bestowed on her and Drew. She refused to let herself think about what Sabrina saw.

Stepping back into Drew's arms, Sophia took a deep breath. "I guess we have time to try this again."

"Always, Sophie. With us, there's always time to try again."

She didn't respond except to ask again if he wanted Livia to join them later.

He shrugged.

"That's not an answer."

"I want to watch her lick your pussy." He dipped her low and brought her up slow, running his fingers softly down the length of her body and back up. "Or am I not allowed to make requests like that?"

As her eyes came level with his, Sophia smiled her craftiest smile. "You can make requests like that. Anything else?"

He shook his head. "I'm sure you'll surprise me."

As they danced, Sophia planned likely scenarios in her head. This was the first time she was going to have a threesome where she didn't dominate the couple. Though he probably didn't plan to play the role, Drew was going to help dominate Livia. He needed to do it. She couldn't seem to plan a scenario in which he was just a neutral party.

Livia wanted to up the ante in their game. Expecting Drew to dominate Sophia was her cry for help. She didn't want to become a dominatrix. She wanted the unexpected. Sophia suspected Livia needed to have her boundaries pushed further, to help her find the next thrill.

Being smaller than most of her submissives, Sophia relied on mental intimidation more than anything else. Perhaps having a man as part of the equation could change the game enough to make it more interesting for all concerned.

"I hope that incredibly sexy smile has something to do with me." Drew's low-toned observation made her toes curl and her pussy throb.

"It does," she assured him before whispering a request of her own in his ear. They spent the rest of the hour massacring the tango and planning their evening.

As they left the studio, Ellen eyeballed Sophia with a puzzled expression. "Given the way you two have been glued together, I'm guessing it's pointless to ask if you're going out to dinner with us."

Drew turned that charming smile on Ellen, melting her with ease. "We have other plans."

* * * *

Sophia chose a black leather skirt to wear with her white camisole. It matched the black leather wrist cuffs that caused Drew's jeans to tighten. He watched her change with undisguised interest.

"How do you decide what to wear?" he asked. "You obviously dress the way you do for a reason."

Brushing her hair into a ponytail, Sophia twisted it up and secured it with several pins. "Reason one: comfort. Reason two: I look hot." Leaning closer to the mirror, she darkened the eyeliner around her eyes. Drew's fascination distracted her, as did the way her second reason didn't draw a comment or a discernable reaction of any kind. She met his eyes in the mirror. "Take off your shirt."

"Why?"

"Same reasons previously stated." She flashed a flirtatious smile and painted her lips.

"How will me being shirtless make you look hot or affect your comfort?"

She dug in the pile at the bottom her bedroom closet for strappy black heels. "Are you fishing for compliments, or did you want me to offer baby oil? It's under the sink in the bathroom." Sitting on her bed, Sophia detangled the straps and secured the shoes to her feet. "Though I should warn you that too slippery has its drawbacks and that oil gets everywhere. It's like sand at the beach."

He threw his shirt on the bed next to her. "There is something anticlimactic about the way you get ready for this."

She raised a brow at him. "You object to clean sheets?"

"I completely agree with stripping the bed after each time, and disinfecting it, too. It's just not romantic." He sat down next to her. "And the way you choose which toys to use…"

Laughing, she planted a kiss on his cheek, the first spontaneous sign of affection she'd ever shown him. He sobered immediately, all thoughts about her arbitrary 'I haven't used this one in a while' selection process forgotten. He stared at her with such intensity she had trouble sitting still. Her heart pounded with equal parts hope and dread that he might say something sweet or romantic.

She bit her bottom lip. "Have I ruined the fantasy for you?"

He shook his head. "Never." He leaned closer, and his breath fanned across her lips. "I have so many fantasies about you."

The kiss was light, feathering over her lips. He didn't deepen it, yet it affected her more than if he had. When he drew back, she took a shaky breath.

"Most of them aren't sexual."

She blinked. "What?"

The doorbell chimed. Drew rose to his feet and held out a hand, ignoring her question. "What would you do if I tossed you over my shoulder, carried you down to that soundproof room, and tied you to the bed?"

No one had ever said something like that to Sophia before. Unlike many dominant personalities, she hadn't started this part of her life as a submissive. Cold fear and panic should have had her in their grip. She expected his words to chill her, to penetrate the numb place she kept inside for just these kinds of occasions. Her heart thumped in her chest, slow and loud, and her nipples hardened.

"I don't know," she said truthfully. She didn't feel a need for him to do it, but if he had, she knew she wouldn't have an anxiety attack. Not if she was with Drew.

He tugged at her hand. "How long do we keep her waiting?"

His question jolted her back to the present. "I'll get the door. Wait about a minute and follow me out."

Livia looked wonderful as always. Sophia didn't notice what she was wearing, but the expression on her face was tight and petulant. It confirmed her assessment of the situation. Livia needed to feel completely owned. Sophia could do it by herself, but she thought Livia craved the violence Drew could bring to the bedroom.

Sophia gripped Livia's hair tightly, pushing her to her knees and pulling her head back. Then, she kissed her slowly and deeply.

Kissing a woman wasn't all that different from kissing a man. Their lips tended to be softer, but not always. Livia had firm lips, and she knew what to do with them. The lips of Sophia's pussy thickened in anticipation.

She released Livia, bestowing a pleased smile when she saw her disappointment. Livia hadn't wanted tenderness, but she needed it. Sophia would make her see that. With perfect timing, Drew strode from the hallway leading to the bedroom, that stingy, sensual smile on his lips.

"Livia, it's good to see you." He reached out, and she responded by lifting her arms, ostensibly to hug him in greeting. Ignoring the intention, he bent and scooped her up, throwing her over his shoulder and hopping down the steps as if he carried nothing more substantial than a pillow.

Sophia followed, noting with satisfaction that he'd knocked some air from her. She sputtered at the unexpected greeting. When he threw her on the bed, she stared up with wide eyes, struggling with the urge to demand answers and with her excitement over the change in the rules of play.

Working together, Sophia and Drew stripped Livia naked and shackled her wrists and ankles to the bed. Hands on hips, Drew stood back to watch as Sophia double-checked the security of the cuffs. Having him in the role of muscle and assistant was different for her, but Sophia was loving it already. She planned to push Livia's comfort level tonight. There was definitely going to be a struggle.

Already she squirmed. "Sophia." The name spilled from her lips, a plea. She hated being restrained.

Sophia smacked Livia's thigh. "Mistress."

Lifting her head, Livia stared at Sophia. Her lips trembled. The pupils of her blue eyes dilated in fear, and the scent of her arousal filled the room, but she said nothing.

Sophia smacked her again, leaving the imprint of her hand to stain Livia's inner thigh. "Mistress. Say it."

"M-Mistress."

Sophia's answering smile wasn't a form of praise. It was cold and wicked. She wanted to induce fear. Livia needed this. Sophia needed this.

"Mistress, please untie me."

Drew traced a path along the underside of Livia's arm, down to her waist. "Not until you've learned your manners."

Livia's eyes widened. Even though he had carried her down the stairs, she relegated him to the role of muscle. Having him in authority brought home exactly how much the rules of the game had changed.

Sophia fetched the riding crop from a hook on the wall. "I wanted to thank you for introducing me to Drew." Really, she wanted to punish Livia for that. This was Sophia's chance to exorcise some of the frustration she felt over the changes in her life she couldn't control, and all of those changes centered around Drew.

Tracing the tip of the crop lightly from Livia's feet to her fingers and back again, Sophia had her trembling before one circuit was completed. From behind those short blonde curls, the lips of her pussy swelled and glistened.

"Do you think you could do this to someone else, Livia? Could you give them the kind of pain and the sweet release of pleasure you want so badly?"

The scent of her arousal permeated the air. Drew lay on the bed next to Livia and traced light patterns on her stomach with his fingers. A tear escaped the corner of her eye, and they hadn't done much more than caress her. He pinched her nipple, twisting it the way Sophia showed him last time.

Livia cried out. The taut muscles of her inner thighs spasmed.

He twisted the other one, keeping the pressure constant. "Answer your mistress."

Livia cried out again as Drew pulled harder. Sophia was impressed at the way he caught on so quickly. He had never been anything but gentle when he was with just Sophia.

Livia's back arched, lifting her upper body from the mattress. "No. Please, Mistress, I would be too jealous."

Sophia brought the small leather patch on the end of the crop down hard on Livia's inner thigh. She orgasmed.

Drew's head jerked up, and he peppered Sophia with silent questions. She shrugged in response. In the entire time she'd known her, Livia had never orgasmed so quickly, or without her pussy being touched, and especially not without permission.

They were doing something very right.

"Livia." The single word was a chastisement. She needed to be punished for losing control without consent.

Her breaths came in short pants. It had been a small orgasm. "Mistress, please don't be angry with me. I didn't mean it."

Sophia tsked her disapproval. "I see we need lessons in self-control."

Livia's eyes widened, following Sophia as she turned away. "Mistress, please. I'm sorry. I'm so sorry."

"Not as sorry as you will be." Drew's eyes twinkled with excitement. Combined with Sophia's disappointment, it was enough to make Livia panic.

When Sophia returned with a blindfold, Livia strained against her bonds, fighting them furiously. Sophia secured the scrap of black cloth in place before cautioning Drew to wait. If Livia was going to use the safe word, now was a likely time.

Pleas issued forth from Livia's mouth, nothing more.

A hook dangled from a chain in the ceiling. The simple system was screwed into the support structure for the house. Sophia used a step stool to adjust the height of the chain. This was part of the process Livia would never see. With a brief nod to Drew, Sophia indicated the position she wanted Livia forced into. Words were not required with him, either. They had discussed the probable scenarios in detail while they had danced.

His muscle certainly helped expedite things. Sophia had no need to use verbal commands or mental intimidation. With minimal effort, he released the cuffs and carried Livia to the other side of the room. Sophia tied Livia's wrists to the hook. The height was perfect. The submissive dangled, balancing precariously on the balls of her feet. There was no way she could protest her position.

Climbing down from the step, Sophia found herself enveloped in Drew's arms. He plundered her mouth with his tongue and pressed her body against his. "I love watching you work. You are so fucking sexy." He whispered in her ear, low so Livia heard only the sibilant sounds and no words.

Sophia pulled a cat from her belt loop and motioned Drew out of the way. She started low, well below Livia's thigh, almost to her knee. Light licks alternated with sharp ones. Livia moaned and cried out. Her body jerked as she struggled to fight her natural inclination to move away from the pain. If she did that, she would lose her balance.

It didn't take long to turn Livia's skin a brilliant shade of salmon. The screams of protest turned to sobs of apology. "I'm sorry, Mistress. I'm so sorry."

The whip halted. Now, Livia would be sensitive to the slightest pressure.

Turning, Sophia slammed into Drew's solid chest. His arms came around her again. This time, his lips fastened on her neck, sucking and biting the reactive skin there. "I want you now," he whispered in her ear. "I can't wait, Sophie. Don't make me wait."

Pushing him back, she held up one finger. She had one more thing to do to Livia before she could leave her submissive to contemplate the consequences of coming without permission.

Sophia fished the complicated system of straps from the bin she kept exclusively for Livia. Last time, she had used them to reward Livia. Now, she would use it to torture her. Placing the straps carefully over Livia's pink skin, Sophia arranged them so that they would force Livia to wiggle in discomfort. In doing so, they would rub against several erogenous zones, but not enough to bring her to orgasm. This was the punishment for unauthorized climaxing.

Drew waited impatiently, condom in hand. As soon as Sophia had everything how she wanted it, he dragged her from the room and closed the soundproof door firmly behind them.

He shoved her against the door, lifting Sophia to grind against her pussy. "You are so unbelievably hot, Sophia."

Sophia would have smiled, but his hand joined the bulge pressing against her core. No underclothing impeded his questing fingers. She gasped, bucking against him, asking for more. She planned to let Drew have Livia, but that couldn't happen for some time yet. As a dominatrix, Sophia was used to waiting, to putting off her own pleasure for the sake of her submissive.

Drew made the wait unnecessary. His lips landed on hers, hot and demanding. She pushed his jeans out of the way and helped him roll the condom over his engorged cock. He impaled her, and all she could do was wrap her legs around his hips and hang on to his shoulders.

He fucked her hard and fast. Sophia clenched around him, the orgasm rocking her within seconds, forcing Drew to follow her. It was intense, but over quickly.

He let her down slowly, pressing his body into hers, reluctant to sever contact. "Last time, I wondered how you could delay for so long," he said. "I was impressed with how you held off, even when I knew you wanted me."

She had been that transparent? It was too late for regret. "Delaying orgasm usually leads to bigger orgasms."

"Is that what you're doing for Livia?"

Sophia nodded. "Punishment and reward go to the same end. Everything leads to surrender. Surrender leads to orgasm."

"Clever. But that's all for her. What do you get out of it? You aren't subject to punishment or reward. You aren't forced to surrender."

"Control," Sophia said with a grin. "I am in complete control of her pleasure, and of mine." Trailing a finger down his chest, her grin widened. "And of yours."

"I still want to see her lick your pussy."

She laughed. "Patience, Drew. All in good time. Now, head upstairs and get some ice. Livia's punishment is just beginning."

Entering the room alone, Sophia took a long moment to study Livia. The woman squirmed, shifting her weight from one foot to the other and trying to move the leather straps abrading her sensitized skin. Sophia knew Livia heard the door open and close twice. Her whimpers increased in volume, the only speech she was allowed.

"How are you doing, Livia? Have you learned your lesson yet?"

"Yes, Mistress," Livia sobbed. Tears of frustration trailed down her cheeks.

Sophia reached between Livia's legs, stroking her wetness, teasing Livia to test how well she learned her lesson. Her breaths came faster, and she shook with the effort it cost to resist the lure of another orgasm.

Drew returned with a bowl of ice cubes. They were the old-fashioned kind, two inches wide and three inches deep. Sophia glanced over at Drew, smiling in welcome. His cock hardened as he watched her tease Livia.

Reaching up, Sophia released Livia's wrists and removed her blindfold. Livia blinked, her eyes adjusting to the soft glow of the overhead lights. She looked from Sophia to the bowl in Drew's hand, struggling not to ask questions.

This was so very different from the usual game. Normally, Sophia was the unchallenged mistress with no assistant to help her dominate. The chain of command hadn't changed. Sophia still called the shots. However, Drew was definitely an unknown element. Livia trembled.

Sophia's hand exerted a firm pressure on the back of Livia's neck as she guided the taller woman to the bed and forced her to bend forward. Motioning Drew closer, Sophia selected one ice cube, which she worked into Livia's dripping vagina. Drew's brows rose in surprise. His gentle approach to dealing with women was so at odds with Sophia's controlled violence.

"Don't drop it, Livia."

Shivers ran through Livia's body. "It's cold, Mistress."

"Greedy women who steal orgasms don't get off so easily." Sophia chuckled at her joke, a low sound meant to alarm Livia. It did the trick.

"Please, Mistress. I haven't come again. I've been very, very good."

"But you're close," Sophia said regretfully. "You need a distraction."

Fetching the riding crop from the edge of the bed where she'd left it, Sophia delivered a series of sharp blows to Livia's ass and thighs. Moisture trickled down her legs, a combination of her cream and the melting ice cube. Shoving her fingers deep inside, Sophia extracted the tiny cube, rubbing it along the crease to tease Livia's puckered pink hole.

Her ass lifted in offering. Sophia didn't oblige her. Instead, she took another cube and shoved it roughly into Livia's pussy. "You have a long, long wait, my darling slave."

Tears coursed down Livia's cheeks. "Please, Mistress. Please use my body."

"I will," Sophia said. Shedding her skirt, Sophia knelt on the bed next to Livia, drawing her slave's head onto her lap. With gentle caresses, she smoothed away her tears. The combination of pain and tenderness was lethal, more so when it came at the same time.

"You're going to lick your mistress, sweetheart." The way Drew used the term was not endearing. He reduced her to something not worthy of a name. It was exactly what she wanted, to forget herself.

Drew snagged the handcuffs and locked Livia's wrists behind her back.

Sophia settled back on the bed and spread her legs. Livia was positioned at the side of the bed on her feet, bent over the mattress. Grasping her hips, Drew issued his command. "Make her come with your tongue."

Reaching down to her pussy, Sophia held her vaginal lips open so Livia could have full access. Livia locked her lips around Sophia's clit and sucked it hard. That hot tongue flicked back and forth until Sophia arched, gasping.

She moaned, a kittenish sound tinged with desperation. Her tongue delved deep into Sophia's opening, fucking her. No doubt the ice cube was completely melted by now. Lacking the use of her hands, she rocked her body to the rhythm. Sophia came in her mouth.

"Don't stop." The order came from Drew.

Livia gasped, losing her hold on Sophia. Sophia lifted her head to see why, and she saw Drew naked. His hard dick was covered with a condom, but his hand was on her ass. It didn't take much to extrapolate that he had several fingers inside her anus.

"Relax," he ordered, rubbing a hand down her pink ass. "Nobody told you to stop. I want to hear Sophia come again. Show her how much you appreciate what she's done for you. Show her you've learned your lesson."

Livia obeyed, attacking Sophia's pussy with renewed determination. She moaned, sucking and swallowing juices flowing from Sophia. Heat coiled inside. Reaching up, Sophia gripped the edge of the mattress, digging her nails in deep. Tension built. Another orgasm loomed close, but she held it off.

Between her legs, Livia whimpered and moaned as Drew worked her anus with his fingers. They toys Sophia used on Livia weren't as wide as Drew's penis. He needed to stretch her, but not as much as he did. He was playing with her, punishing her for coming without permission. He was enjoying dominating her.

Sophia smiled and let go, welcoming the orgasm that washed over her. She moaned loudly. Her hips jerked involuntarily, seeking respite from the constant stimulation.

Drew reached forward and grasped Livia by her tangled mass of white-blonde hair. Gently, he pulled her head up and away from Sophia. "I'm going to fuck you, but not until you ask nicely."

Her eyes took a minute to focus. She looked at Sophia, puzzled. Sophia knew the likely drift of Livia's thoughts. "Nicely" could mean so many things. The gears of her mind churned behind those blue eyes as she searched for his likely meaning. Finally, she settled on something. "Fuck me, Master. Please fuck me."

Reaching under her, he pressed his fingers into her clit. She moaned and lifted her ass to him, but he didn't respond.

Sophia took pity on Livia's desperate whimper. "You came without permission, my little slave. Drew is going to fuck you up the ass. You don't get to come, not until you've earned it by pleasing us both."

Livia loved anal stimulation. Sophia's directive was her undoing. He touched the tip of his engorged penis to her puckered hole. She shoved herself toward him, lifting higher. "Oh, yes, Master. Please use me."

Drew reamed her, burying himself in her with a thrust that would have moved the bed if it hadn't been bolted it to the floor. Livia's eyes nearly disappeared into her head. She screamed, orgasming again. At that moment, Sophia realized she had been far too gentle with Livia. She should have chosen larger and harder toys, and she shouldn't have eased them into her. Even when she fucked Livia this way, Sophia was gentle, demanding her slave masturbate to orgasm.

Behind her, Drew was just getting started. His hips moved backward, and he rammed her again. Livia fisted the sheet in her hands, pulling it free everywhere she and Sophia weren't holding it in place. The throbbing between Sophia's thighs, fed by the sight of Drew pumping into Livia and by Livia's uninhibited enjoyment, gathered steam.

Sophia scrambled off the bed, grabbed a double dildo, and returned. Drew understood enough to lift Livia and let Sophia slide under her. Positioning herself carefully, Sophia slid the hard plastic phallus into herself. The other end, she slid into Livia. A flick of the wrist, and vibrations pulsed through both women.

Drew watched Sophia's face, and she watched his. The whole evening, with the exception of when he needed to look elsewhere, his eyes hadn't left Sophia. Livia was a toy, an amusement, nothing more. Faster and faster, he pumped into her. Twice, Livia begged for permission to come. Twice, she came. Sophia's climax took longer to achieve. Drew watched her, waiting and shouting his release only after Sophia screamed hers.

Livia, not surprisingly, came as soon as Sophia gave her the command. She collapsed on top of Sophia, who wrapped her arms around her good little slave and stroked her hair.

Drew disposed of the condom and disappeared into the bathroom.

Livia and Sophia lay in stunned silence, listening to the shower running. Sophia would have to talk to him about caring for a sub after a session, especially when her legs were too jellied to move.

"Jesus, Sophia. That was fucking incredible. I can't remember the last time I had that many orgasms, and good-sized ones, too."

Though she agreed with Livia's assessment, Sophia didn't comment. Reaching down, she removed the dildo from both of them.

"You two are good together. I don't mean to say you aren't good by yourself, but Oh. My. God. I could feed off the sexual tension you two generate forever." She sat up and looked at Sophia. "I think I'm in love with both of you."

Sophia was too shocked to speak.

The silence spurred Livia to explanation. "I mean, together. I don't think I'd care for either of you separately. I'm saying I want to belong to both of you."

Sophia had always been very clear about her policy against relationships. Except for Drew, she held to it pretty successfully. With silent finality, Sophia rose from the bed and held out her hand to Livia. "Let's get you cleaned up."

She had intended for this to just be a break, but if she kept the scene going, Livia would take it as a promise of something more. Sophia wouldn't mind longer, more involved scenes, but she wasn't about to take on another serious relationship. One was more than enough.

By the time she got Livia dressed and up the stairs, without Drew's help, tears streamed down Livia's face. She hiccupped and clutched at Sophia. "Sophia, please. I'll do whatever you want me to do. This is what

I've needed for so long, and only you knew that. You dominate me so well, and Drew takes direction from you flawlessly. Please don't send me away."

Sophia hugged Livia, a hand cupping the head buried in her shoulder. Behind Livia, a newly showered Drew cast troubled and questioning looks at Sophia. "Livia, I'm glad we were all able to have a good time, but that's all this is. I'm not looking for a relationship. You know that. Put some time and distance between us. It'll help you put this into perspective. Don't call me for at least a week."

Struggling to control her sobs, Livia nodded and slipped out the front door. Sophia closed and locked it.

"Do they always get clingy like that?" Drew asked from the kitchen.

"Sometimes," Sophia said. "After a really good session. We broke her down. She's emotionally sensitive."

Drew chuckled and shook his head. "I was right about you," he said as he set something on the table. "Come eat, Sophie. I made us a snack."

She eyed the sliced fruit on the platter and sat down heavily, snagging a sliver of juicy, ripe pear. The sparse offering of pear, apple, and grape was all she had left in the refrigerator. Between working, the wedding, and Drew, her weekly shopping schedule was shot to hell. "What were you right about?"

"You make a habit of breaking hearts." He popped a purple grape into his mouth. "I won't complain as long as you don't break mine."

A small smile escaped. Sophia covered it with a grape of her own. "She gives up more easily than you."

He selected an apple slice next. "I took a cold shower."

She nearly choked on another pear. The intensity of his expression as he thrust into Livia and looked at Sophia was burned into her memory. Conjuring up the disquieting image made her wet for him. "Why?"

He didn't look at her. "Because I wanted to bury myself in you."

Never had a confession sounded so angry and bereft. She wanted to reach for him, to comfort him. She didn't want him to feel he had to hide an emotion just because she found it uncomfortable. "Why didn't you?"

He ran an uncertain hand through his hair and scratched at the rough, pale stubble on his chin. Finally, he met her patient gaze. "Because I want more from you than you're ready to give. I don't want to push you too hard,

Sophie. I don't want to scare you away. And I don't want to take it from you with someone else present."

Breath left her body, but not because she connected the dots and realized the details he wasn't saying. He had already said he wanted back-door sex with her. That wasn't the shocking part. It was more the way he looked at her, as if he could see her secrets, as if he knew the parts she never intended to reveal. And he accepted it.

Certain a panic attack was minutes away, she jumped to her feet. She grabbed the glasses of water he set on the table and refilled them, though they weren't empty. "I—We—I would be okay with that," she stammered. "I would ask you to go slow, just because I've never done it before."

Every single one of her subs enjoyed it. Even Christopher, who wouldn't verbally acknowledge it or ask for it until she made him, liked anal sex. When Jonas had first introduced the concept to Sophia, she had been reticent to go there. He insisted that it was a necessary part of her repertoire as a dominatrix, and then he introduced her to a sub willing to let her experiment.

Behind her, Drew rested his forehead in his hands. "I don't want to go slow, Sophia. I want to throw you on the bed and hook your knees over my shoulders and not let you go anywhere until you submit to me completely. What we did tonight was new to me. I've never made a woman submit to me before. I've had threesomes, but I've never…"

He broke off, lifting his head to stare deep into her eyes, as if the right words were there somewhere. She began to think she had been wrong about what he was asking.

"When I told her to lick you, she was eager for it. She wanted to taste you, to make you come, but she didn't submit, not then. I felt it when she did, Sophia. The moment she gave herself over completely—I *felt* it."

She knew the feeling he struggled to describe. The rush of power generated by total submission was an incredible, potent, and unparalleled aphrodisiac. It's what rendered sexual attraction genderless for Sophia. The person didn't matter nearly as much as their ability to submit. As profound as the experience had been for Livia, for Sophia's purposes, it could have been anyone.

"I want that from you. I want that level of trust between us."

Sophia wanted that, too. She wanted to have such a profound place in his life. As much as she fought it, he already occupied a profound place in her life. But then, he had already given to her the thing for which he asked.

For the first time in five long, dark years, she saw a glimmer of light, of hope, at the end of the tunnel. It was still so far away, but no longer unreachable. In that moment, some of her scars began to heal.

Drowning in the compelling blue of his eyes, she drifted around the arc of her oval table and settled on his lap. "I want that, too."

The next move was hers. Lifting a trembling hand, she caressed his cheek and temple before spreading her fingers to hold him closer for the whisper of a kiss across his lips.

Passion unfolded low in her body, beating a slow rhythm that traveled through her bloodstream until her entire body shook. She was terrified, but she wanted this intimacy with Drew more than she wanted anything else.

Pushing herself to stand on weak legs, she held a hand out to him. The gravity of the situation reflected in his eyes, and she knew she was right to trust him.

Words she'd never uttered tumbled from her lips. "Make love to me, Drew."

He rose and crushed her to him. His kiss was rough and demanding. She jumped up and wrapped her legs around his waist so he could carry her down the hall to the bedroom. He set her down gently and lifted the hem of her shirt.

She needed to tell him he misunderstood. She didn't want a gentle lover, not tonight, not with the intensity of the feelings flowing through her body. Words wouldn't form in her head, and nothing but a low moan made it past her lips. With a growl, she pushed him to the bed and tore at his clothes.

That was all it took.

She heard her shirt rip, and she had to help him remove her skirt because he hadn't unzipped it enough to make it over her hips without shredding skin. Within seconds, they were naked, rolling over the mattress with abandon, each seeking to suck, lick, nip, and flick tender spots on the other.

She bit his pectoral muscles and sucked his fingertips, working her way down his body. He kept pulling her back up to work his way down her body.

She solved the problem by flipping around to position her saturated pussy over his mouth. He sucked her hard, thrusting fingers into her opening.

Rocking on his face, she leaned down to taste him the way he tasted her. He was hard. Beads of moisture shimmered from his large oval head. She licked him, swirling her tongue around the tip and dipping into the slight depression leaking precome.

He moaned and bit her clit, bringing her attention back to the sensations mounting inside her. If she didn't get to work, he was going to taste her orgasm before she accomplished anything with him.

She licked his length and laved his balls with her eager tongue and lips. He thrust toward her, seeking the heat of her mouth around his cock. Wrapping her lips around the head, she slid him into her, sucking him deeper and deeper to the same tempo with which he sucked at her. When the tip nudged the back of her throat, she swallowed, drawing him as deep as she could, and then she wrapped her hand around his base to enclose the rest of him.

Her hips pumped, pushing her pussy into his face. She fucked him hard and sucked him even harder. Liquid heat pooled low in her abdomen, drawing muffled moans and cries from deep down.

Then, with a sudden violence, he ripped her from him, tossing her to roll on the bed next to him. She panted, winded and frustrated. "What the hell was that?"

"I don't want to come in your mouth," he said, panting just as hard. "Not right now. I want to own you, Sophie." Sitting up, he leaned closer to her face. "Can you give me that, honey? Can you surrender to me?"

Honestly, she didn't know. One surety remained. His question didn't make her panic. She didn't edge away from him. Reaching up, she pulled his face to hers and licked her juices from his lips before capturing him in a searing, demanding kiss. "We'll see."

Before she could register a response in his face, he had her bent in half. Her feet rested on the floor, and her breasts pressed into the coverlet they hadn't bothered to remove. Drew stood behind her, his fingers spreading the wetness from her pussy to her ass. Each swipe was a little more intimate than the previous.

Kicking her legs further apart, he lifted her hips and positioned himself at her unused entrance. She felt him, soft and hard, pressing against the tight muscle there. He wore no condom, and she was okay with that. He had been tested. She knew she was going to need to get on the Pill, and she knew he wasn't going to have unprotected sex with any of their submissives.

"Relax, Sophie. The stretching is going to hurt at first, but once you're used to me, it'll be fine."

When she prepared her subs for this kind of first experience, she spent several sessions stretching them with different-sized dildos. She knew she was unprepared. She knew it would likely not be pleasant at first. She was prepared to masturbate while he fucked her, knowing it would help train her body to equate the sensation with pleasure. It might take some time, but she would orgasm. She didn't mention any of this to Drew.

Breathing deeply, she relaxed and pressed into him to let him know she was ready and willing. He pushed, but nothing happened. With a grunt, he lifted her until she knelt on all fours on the bed, and then pushed her head and shoulders to the mattress.

When he pushed again, she exhaled, relaxing enough so that he was able to stretch her. As lubricated as he made her, it still burned. She breathed through it, pressing back until she felt the telltale pop indicating the larger head was inside.

He reached around to caress her clit. "Hard part is over, honey. You did well."

She wanted to laugh at the way he praised her. Being in the dominant position came too naturally to him. Praise, encouragement, and punishment was an effective training cycle. But she couldn't laugh. He knew just how to touch her. Before long, she gasped, moving against his hand as he eased himself farther into her.

Then his hips were against her ass, and she knew he was fully inside. He pulled back slowly, moving in and out by inches, increasing the depth of his thrust each time. The palm of his hand scraped against her clit as he pumped several fingers inside her pussy, the thrusts alternating.

Heat like she'd never felt before coiled in her hands and feet, traveling through her bones until her core was on fire. This wondrous fullness claimed her, making her his. As if he sensed the moment of her complete surrender, he went wild. His thrusts came at the same time, deeper and deeper into both holes, filling her like nothing she'd ever known before.

Sweat trickled down her back and itched between her breasts. She pushed against him, meeting his rhythm. Sobs, desperate pleas for harder and faster tore from her. She came, but he wasn't close to finished with her. The orgasm stretched. Her sensitized clit wanted to be left alone, but he didn't allow her that control.

"Sophie." He whispered her name reverently, over and over. It became a sob and a howl as he lost control. She came again, screaming and buckling, her knees too watery to hold her up.

Strong fingers dug into the sweaty flesh of her hips as he came with a mighty roar. Hot semen shot into her.

Drew collapsed, his weight pressing her into the mattress. Several minutes passed before he rolled to the side, taking her with him. Their sweaty bodies folded together, and though he separated himself from her, he didn't let go.

Sophia clung to him, wanting to preserve the closeness they felt. For the first time in her life, she felt part of another person. The oppressive loneliness that was with her all the time lifted, dissolving into the past. Hanging on to Drew, she fell asleep.

Chapter 18

Sophia woke feeling warm and safe, utterly sated on a soul-deep level. It was a foreign feeling she really liked.

Drew slept facing her. The bulky muscles of one arm pillowed her head. His other arm and the leg he twined with hers held her close.

She watched him sleep, seeing past the handsome surface features of his face to find the beauty of the man he was. Now that she knew him, the relentless tenacity, limitless strength, and the generous soul were easy to see.

Sophia loved this man. The terror was still there. The fear he would run from her secrets, disgusted with the dark parts of her soul, was still there. She tried to push him away because she knew what he could make her feel. Five years ago, she promised herself she would never be this vulnerable again.

Silently, she resolved that he would never find out about that dark night she wanted to forget. She couldn't risk losing him.

"Serious thoughts should always wait until after breakfast."

The raw baritone rumbled more from his chest than his mouth. She hadn't realized he was awake. Heedless of the consequences, she took the plunge. "I love you."

The smile that curved his lips was utterly cocky. "Those kinds of thoughts don't have to wait for food." He planted a sleepy kiss on her lips. "I love you, too, Sophie."

His hard-on pressed against her stomach. Glancing down, she raised a brow.

He flexed his fingers around her hip and pressed closer. "I wake up naked with the woman of my dreams in my arms, and she tells me she loves me, and you expect me to *not* be aroused?"

"We have to go to work," she protested as his lips found sensitive places on her neck. It was well past time she was up and in the shower.

"Your boss won't mind if you're a little late." He pushed Sophia onto her back and kissed lower. "He isn't exactly planning to be there early. Maybe not at all."

"Client," she corrected. Her hands explored every part of his body she could reach, putting lie to her protest. "I'm the boss. And Ginny's my client, not you." He pressed a finger into her and spread moisture to her clit. She gasped and spread her legs, automatically granting him more access.

"Gin and I are fifty-fifty on everything," he assured her. Fingers delved deep, eliciting a croaking moan from Sophia. "Besides, she's late for this reason all the time."

She lifted her hips, thrusting against his hand. "It's only my second day on the job."

"We'll miss the traffic and get there at the same time we would if we got up now."

She tried to protest, but he hushed her with the demands of his lips on her body.

A lot later, he made breakfast. Sophia didn't object to the domesticity of their new situation, but she couldn't help wondering how long it would last. She hadn't been kidding when she told him she would sabotage the relationship. Whether she wanted to be with him or not was irrelevant. The damaged parts of her were all intact. It was a matter of time before the world closed in again, forcing her to push away everything or lose herself completely. But she would enjoy him for now. She would allow herself this short bout of happiness.

Things were much more critical than they had ever been. She actually submitted to Drew. She gave herself entirely over to him, something she hadn't done with a lover in over five years. She fell in love with him. Somehow, she would find a way to punish herself for slipping.

Sophia hated the way her feelings vacillated.

Oblivious to the darkness inside Sophia, Drew whistled as he worked his magic at the stove. She had no idea what he was making, but it smelled good.

"If I give you a shopping list, will you run to the store sometime soon and replenish your food supply?" His dry question pulled her from the shadows.

The contents of the pan on the stove were questionable. She didn't have much food in the refrigerator, and her cupboards were painfully bare. "I've been busy," she laughed. "And I didn't know you'd be cooking this morning. I planned to grab a coffee and eat a peanut butter sandwich in the car."

"Yes, well, if you'd stop breaking up with me, then you could plan your meals better." Humor suffused his words, but his message was clear. Her attempts to break from him were a source of frustration. "Maybe I'll stop at the store on my way over tonight. Unless you want to stay at my place. I'm fifteen minutes from the bakery, and my kitchen is fully stocked."

"Your housekeeper shops for you." It was a guess, something she would have a housekeeper do if she had one. It would be nice to have a fresh bottle of shampoo appear in her shower when she ran out, or milk in the refrigerator even though she didn't have a chance to stop by the store.

"Yes, she does. And as soon as she figures out what you like, she'll shop for you, too."

Did the fact he asked her to stop by the store put her on par with a housekeeper in his life? She shook away the thought, knowing full well what she was to him. "Ginny said you were going out of town today, and that you'll be gone until Monday."

Drew turned slowly, his attention drawn away from the magic on the stovetop to Sophia. He swore. "I forgot."

Her brows shot upward in disbelief. It was an excuse she could buy once, and even feel smug about. But twice? "How could you forget something like this?"

His pale blue eyes were serious when they met hers. "When I'm with you, I can't seem to remember things that will take me away from you. Come with me."

She would have laughed if he hadn't been so earnest. "I have to work."

"Call it a business trip. You can be my assistant."

Not sure whether she should be flattered or not, Sophia cocked her head to the side. "Did you just offer to pay me to have sex with you?"

A blush crept up his neck. "Sorry. Marry me. You'll never have to worry about work again."

Her breath caught, but not in a good way. Automatically, her eyes shuttered and the wall slowly crumbling around her was stronger than ever.

Recognizing the signs, he backpedaled. "At least keep Sunday night open? Monday isn't a firm return date."

She nodded, a mechanical, jerky motion. "Do you travel every week?"

Sizzling from the stove captured his attention, part of it, anyway. "No. The new season of my show premieres in two weeks, so I'm traveling a lot right now to promote it. I guess I do have appearances every week, but only for the next month. Things aren't usually so hectic."

The flame on the stove died. Drew lifted the pan and used a spatula to remove what turned out to be an incredibly large omelet. Thank goodness he divided it between the two plates. Nobody should eat that many eggs at once.

Sophia busied herself with pouring orange juice, the only thing she had that wasn't water, into glasses. They sat down together. Omelets were nothing new to her, but she'd never had one that smelled so good. One bite had her mouth watering for more. She didn't know what he put inside, but it was damn good.

Hunger overrode anything she might have said about his travel schedule. She was going to miss him, but perhaps this was for the best. If she was forced to spend time away from him, then she would have time to process the changes he brought to her life. She'd never been the kind of person who liked change, but now she was manic about her need to keep her routine intact.

Between bites, he watched her eat. "I'm glad I fed you last night."

It was an odd thing to say. "Why?"

Indicating the food on her plate with the wave of his fork, he finished chewing before responding. "This is the first time I've seen you eat slow enough to actually taste your food."

Sophia bristled at this. "I ate your Hawaiian Chicken slowly. And I liked your crepes."

"You threw up the chicken," he said with a grimace. "It doesn't count."

The fork dropped from her unsteady fingers. How could he bring that up? Ellen, Jonas, Daniel, and anyone else who witnessed her breakdowns always had the grace to pretend nothing happened. "That wasn't your fault."

"No?" He continued, unrelenting in his quest for something she couldn't give. "Why don't you tell me exactly what did happen?"

Frozen to her chair, she closed her eyes and willed it all away. "This isn't an appropriate conversation to have over breakfast."

"I get the feeling you'll consider this conversation inappropriate whenever I bring it up." Resentment edged his voice.

How could she close him out after she woke up declaring her love for him? The answer was easy. If he knew about her past, he would look at her in disgust, or worse, pity. She couldn't handle either of those things from him. She wanted him to look at her and see *her*, not what happened to break her.

His warm, strong hand enclosed the cold fist in her lap. "Sophie, you can tell me anything, honey. I am a good listener."

Something in his tone made her look at him. He knew. No. The acceptance in his eyes was too calm. He couldn't know. Nobody would betray her secret. There was no way he could find out unless she told him.

Rising, she grabbed her plate with an outward calmness that surprised her. She paused to place a kiss on his cheek. "I'm mentally unstable, Drew. I thought I made that clear." He would tire of the drama eventually.

She didn't make it more than a step before his arms wrapped around her from behind. "Bullshit."

Though she flinched at his quiet statement, her voice remained calm and steady. "There's still time to cut your losses. I won't think less of you if you run now. I won't hold it against you."

His voice was a hurricane whispering in her ear. "You're not mentally unstable. Something bad happened to you. I'll give you that. It's left deep scars that make you wary of getting close. You had a panic attack Sunday because you're afraid of your feelings for me. Last night, you turned a corner. This morning, you told me you love me. I know this isn't easy for you, but I'm not going anywhere. I won't give up the woman I love just to make things easier for you."

The entire time he talked, he held her close, his arms strong and tight around her. Curiously, she felt peaceful and safe instead of restrained and restricted. She melted against the surety of him. "Still," she disagreed, "I'm mentally unstable. You're in over your head."

Laughing, he pressed kisses to her neck. "I'll be fine, Sophie. I'm not above carting you downstairs and tying you to the bed if you get it in your mind to dump me again. I think I've picked up a few skills from you, and I'm sure Jonas and Ellen can enlighten me as to a few more tricks that'll help you overcome your fear of intimacy."

He made it sound so inviting. She half wished he would do it now. She laughed, chuckling low with a hysterical edge. What kind of a dominatrix looked forward to having the tables turned? When he trained her, Jonas repeatedly insinuated that subs and Doms often experimented with switching roles. It stood to reason that when two Doms entered into a relationship together, this kind of thing was inevitable. Eventually, she would have Drew where she wanted him, but she began to see that he would frequently have her where he wanted her as well.

"If it's any consolation, I'll let you call me your girlfriend now."

He greeted her olive branch with an equally quiet laugh. "I never stopped."

Drew's estimation of their arrival time at the bakery was a little off. She completely missed rush hour traffic, which was a blessing. Driving east or south in southeastern Michigan during rush hour was something she strove to avoid completely. A simple fifteen-minute drive could easily stretch to forty-five.

She was upstairs, completely buried in sorting out the supply orders and payments, before Drew graced the building with his presence. On the way out the door, he grumbled something about needing to keep extra clothes at her house.

He brought lunch. "You need to keep up your strength."

The page in front of her blurred. She wanted to assure him she wasn't pregnant, but she had none of the physical proof he would require. She thanked him for the thick, crusty sandwich that had things she didn't recognize on it. Nothing he'd given her so far had been less than delectable, so she tried it on trust. Delicious flavors burst in her mouth.

Pulling up a chair, he joined her at the lone desk. "My flight is at four. I have to leave right after lunch."

With the lift of her brow, she communicated amusement. "This is a short work day for you."

"Not really." He shrugged, but looked at her meaningfully. "It's a long day for both of us. I'm on Leno tonight."

She nodded and made a mental note to watch. Her television hadn't been getting much attention lately. Between the apparent success of starting her own business and the demands Drew made on her time, Sophia was too busy.

"Will you stay late tonight to make up for coming in late?"

That was a question a boss would ask, so she switched modes, shifting from girlfriend to employee with ease. "I can't. My class starts at six, but I have to be there earlier to prep."

Prep consisted of participating in the group counseling session. She was there to support the women who came to her for strategies to fight back against the violence in their lives. It was the only place she ever shared her story, and she did it so they would know she was one of them. That confidence strengthened the bond they shared and made it more likely the individual women would complete the training sessions. Still, many of them dropped out after a time or two. That was the reason she made sure to cover several techniques each night.

If a woman only came for one session, or if she came sporadically, she could still reap the benefits and not feel like she was missing something when she missed a session. Guilt wasn't an emotion she was looking to add to anyone's load.

Daniel provided the private room for the counseling and the training, but he avoided intruding on the counseling, correctly assuming the women wouldn't talk with a man in the room.

Sophia was glad because she knew reliving the telling of her experience was just as torturous for him as it was for her.

Drew blinked at her. "Class? I thought you worked Wednesdays."

"I do," she said, finishing her sandwich. "I teach a self-defense class for women who've been victims of violence. It's a free class, and we have a grant to pay for counselors to be on hand before and after. We've been able to find the money to provide child care as well."

That was the best idea so far, and she credited Daniel with it. Children weren't a concern that ever crossed her mind. Last winter, Daniel casually mentioned he thought more women would come more consistently if they knew they could bring their kids and not worry about them while they're doing what they need to do. He'd even researched the grants.

Alaina had been Daniel's date. That's how Sophia knew her. She was the new counselor who started in May. The new grant was tied into a research project headed by Dr. Alaina Miles. That's where Daniel met her.

Sophia wondered if Alaina knew about Danny's hidden depths, and then quickly jettisoned the thought. Even if she did, he'd obviously been nasty to her during the date. It was completely unlike Daniel, but every guy was entitled to a bad day.

During her musings, Drew stared, his expression carefully neutral. "You teach it by yourself?"

"Daniel helps. It's kinda hard to demonstrate self-defense as a theory." Daniel was her punching bag. He helped choreograph likely attack scenarios and Sophia showed the women that they didn't have to be afraid of a man who was both bigger and stronger. Being her brother, Daniel didn't spare Sophia, though he did find some of the scenes more uncomfortable than the others. Demonstrating how to fend off a rape was the worst for him, but he never complained and he never went easy on her.

With a brief nod, Drew pushed to standing and cleared away evidence of lunch. "If you ever need a counselor, that's the kind of thing my mom loves to do. She used to spend a lot of time volunteering in women's shelters, but now that she's not practicing anymore, she's not as connected as she once was."

Sophia bit her lip to staunch an outright rejection. Miranda Snow was too perceptive by half. "Maybe she doesn't want to be connected anymore. It's not an easy topic. Maybe she retired to get away from it."

"Maybe," he agreed. "Still, it never hurts to ask."

"I'll keep that in mind in case we run short on counselors." Who was she kidding? The grant covered the fee of one counselor before the lesson and one after. Occasionally, they benefitted from a batch of doctoral candidates needing field time, but that was a seasonal thing, and it came with lots of paperwork for Sophia. Women weren't victims only when service credits were needed. Every two minutes, someone in the United States was the victim of sexual assault.

Volunteers would be more than welcome.

She needed to get over herself. This wasn't about her.

Drew didn't push the issue, and he let Sophia change the subject. She turned it toward his schedule for the rest of the week. With a string of appearances up and down the Pacific Coast, book signings, demonstrations, and parties, which he called meet and greets, he was going to be a very busy person.

When she kissed him good-bye, he admonished her to not spend all her time buried in paperwork.

"I like being buried in paperwork," she said, defending her antisocial bliss. The contents of this office might give Ginny nightmares, but it was a pleasant dream for Sophia.

"I can see that." He smiled. "However, you need to get out of the house. How long has it been since you've had one of your girls' nights out?"

Cocking her head to the side, she looked at him quizzically. While she joined Sabrina and Ellen for a drink after Sabrina's sessions, and she knew they got together with Ginny and Lara and frequently Jonas's sisters for what they termed a "girls' night out," Sophia had never been part of that ritual. Sabrina didn't usually schedule time with Sophia during those nights. "I'm not really part of all that."

He frowned. "Why not?"

"I work Friday nights." Working Friday nights was how she knew about their monthly habits at all. Jonas used to work Fridays with her. He was always a ball of tension whenever his wife was out painting the town with Ellen. At the time, he was keeping his real job there a secret from Sabrina, and he was afraid Ellen would slip and tell her. Sabrina already knew and she had met Sophia, but nothing would have induced Sophia to reveal that piece of information. It wouldn't have brought him any relief.

Drew's frown remained. "I don't understand. I know you're not that close with Ginny, but I thought you and Sabrina were good friends."

"We are." This was the point where he expected an explanation of the nature of her relationship with Sabrina. That was Sabrina's business to divulge, not Sophia's.

After a minute, his nostrils flared as he realized she wasn't going to say more. "You seem pretty close to Ellen. You've known her for a number of years, right?"

"Yes." She answered his concern in backwards order. "Ellen and I are friends."

"So, you'll call her and go out and have some fun?"

Sophia's brows scrunched together. Why did he care what she did while he was gone? Did he think she would stay at home and pine away for him? "Drew, don't worry about me. I promise I'll be fine."

She was still shaking her head Saturday after she finished helping Daniel cover his classes. The same girl had developed a habit of skipping out on Saturdays. He was reluctant to replace her because she was very good.

"She has a new boyfriend," Daniel said by way of defending her actions.

"It amazes me that she still has a job," Sophia returned. "I can't believe you're seriously putting up with this."

He shrugged, rolling his shoulder as if the motion would push her away. "If she does it again, I'll give her a warning."

The acerbic reply died on Sophia's lips in response to the ringing of her cell phone. It was Sabrina, so she gave up on Danny and took the call.

"Oh, thank God," she breathed when Sophia answered.

The schedule on the phone's calendar played through her head. A fitting was scheduled for today, but not for five more hours. Immediately, Sophia was worried. "What's wrong?"

Her relief turned to a severe case of nerves. "Sophia, is there any way you could come by the house today? I really need to talk to you."

It was a good thing she hadn't worked up a sweat. Sophia raced to Sabrina's house without showering. The urgency in her voice didn't hint at catastrophe, so Sophia didn't think anyone was hurt, or that she'd lost the baby. But something was wrong.

When she arrived, Jonas was out front trying to remove a tree. A pest had attacked and killed it, so it wasn't top-heavy with leaves. Still, it was a sizeable job.

She parked in the driveway and paused next to him. He was shirtless and sweaty, which wasn't a new look since she usually saw him at the Club wearing only jeans and beads of sweat. Not that she meant to, but she mentally compared his physique to Drew's. She'd always thought Jonas had a nice build. It was similar to Christopher's, but Jonas was stronger and a little shorter.

Drew was a little taller than Jonas, and broader in the shoulder. For the first time, Sophia realized a distinct preference for Drew's bulkier muscles.

"Hey," he said when he saw her. A gloved hand came up to brush his blond curls away from his face. "I called you yesterday."

She had listened to his message, but not until she checked her phone after work. She had returned Drew's call, but not Jonas's. "I've been busy," she said. Indicating the tree he chained to Ryan's truck, she added, "Looks like you've been busy, too."

"Fucking thing doesn't want to come out."

Eyeing the situation without sympathy, Sophia shrugged. "You don't have the right equipment. Want me to call my dad? He can get it out, stump and all, in less time than you've already spent trying to move it."

He snapped his fingers. "That's right. I forgot your dad did landscaping. I've got a rich wife. By all means, hook me up."

In ten minutes, she had her father's assurance that the tree would be gone by the time Sabrina got home from work on Monday. Jonas wanted the landscaping to look nice for the wedding, which they were having in the backyard. She would have suggested using her father's full range of services, but she knew how much Jonas loved gardening. With a soft, proud eye, Sabrina had informed everyone that all of the flower gardens were the fruits of Jonas's labor.

"Where is Sabrina?" If this were Sophia's house, she would be out front helping with the work.

"You mean, why isn't she out here getting dirty with me?" The grin on his face should have warned Sophia away from the topic.

She nodded.

"She doesn't like dirt. When the lady of the house has sex with the gardener, she makes him take a shower first." His grin grew. "Of course, she joins him and makes it a really, really fun shower, but she still makes him clean up for her."

The dots took a minute to connect in Sophia's head. She'd forgotten that Jonas liked role-playing as much as he liked having sex in front of an audience. The grin on his face left no doubt as to who did the washing in that scenario.

If Drew came to her sweaty and covered in dirt, Sophia would ravish him before, during, and after the shower, no roles necessary. For the life of her, she couldn't imagine him with smudges of soil and grass on his clothes and chest. Marinara or Alfredo sauce, definitely. Those would need to be licked away. In the bedroom, she couldn't imagine him being anything other than himself.

"So, what did you want?"

Now, he tilted his head to stare quizzically at her.

An impatient sigh zinged past her lips. "You called last night. Sabrina called this morning. She said she needed to talk to me. It sounded urgent."

His face assumed that guarded look she knew all too well. He lifted a hand to indicate she should follow him around the house. "Before you see Sabrina, you should know I haven't told her anything about your past that you wouldn't want me to tell her."

"But?" It was there, dangling silently from his declaration.

"But she's been asking a lot of questions, and she knows I'm not telling her all the answers. Drew called her yesterday and the day before. They talked for a long time both nights. She's tried to get information from Ellen, but Ellen's even better at stonewalling her than I am."

Behind him, Sophia tensed. "Jonas." It was as close to a plea as she could manage.

He led her to a refrigerator in the garage and snagged two beers. "Help me finish these."

She took the one he handed her, but she didn't open it. The unused pregnancy test was still in her purse. Her period was late, but that wasn't unusual.

Jonas twisted the lid from his and tossed it in an open trash bin. "Sabrina's in the pool. She always swims when she's anxious. She'll be out soon."

"Why is she anxious?" And what the hell had Drew said to her? Sophia put the beer back in the refrigerator, exchanging it for water.

"I hear things are going well with you and Drew."

The look she gave him was enough to let him know the change in subject wasn't going to last. "Yes and no."

"No? Tell me about that." He leaned against a workbench along the inside wall of the garage.

"It's none of your business." Really, what did he expect? He used to be just as closed to new relationships. Just because falling in love changed his perspective didn't mean it changed hers.

"You're my friend." That iron stare fell on her, but it wasn't effective.

Sophia waited, but he said nothing more. "It's still none of your business. I've been honest with Drew. I can't help it if he's stubborn and won't listen to me."

"Honest, how? I know you didn't tell him anything significant." He patted the bench next to him. Like a good girl, she obeyed his command. She would have been upset with both the gesture and her response if he hadn't made it obvious he only wanted her closer to have a quiet conversation.

"I told him I was mentally unstable, and he should get out now. I told him it wouldn't end well, and that it would definitely end."

He chuckled softly, mirthlessly. "Then you kissed his cheek and sent him off to Los Angeles for four days."

"I tried breaking it off, but it didn't work." She wanted to say he didn't take no for an answer, but that wasn't entirely true. He didn't believe her when she pushed him away. Or his ego was too large to believe she could mean it when she rejected him. Or he was incredibly stubborn and single-minded. "I don't understand what he would have to say to Sabrina. When he left, things were fine."

A shadow caught her attention. Looking up, Sophia spied Sabrina standing in the open door to the garage. She wore a pink swimsuit, the serious kind, not the sunbathing kind. Over it, she had thrown some kind of white terrycloth wrap that was wet from her body. "Is this a private conversation, or am I invited?"

She didn't make it sound like she would be hurt if either of them asked her to give them a few more minutes.

Licking her lip in a defiant nervous gesture, Sophia waved her closer. "You're fine. I'm dying to know why you're upset, though." She wasn't really, not after knowing Sabrina had spent hours on the phone with Drew.

With a lightning flick of her eye, she dismissed Jonas and his bottle of beer. He didn't take the silent hint, so she verbalized it. "Jonas, I would like to speak with Sophia alone."

He shook his head. "Not this time, honey." Before either woman could protest the need for his presence, he held up a hand. "I won't interfere until you're both upset and crying, okay?"

Immediately, tears sprang to Sabrina's eyes. "That's not fair. I cry at the drop of a hat."

The dread clenching Sophia's stomach was the distinct desire to not have to deal with those hormones raging through her own body.

"Sophia doesn't," he said by way of compromise.

"Fine," she sniffed, directing her attention to Sophia. "I thought we were friends."

Sophia's head started to hurt. "We are."

"I didn't ask you to come out with us because you always work on Friday and Saturday nights." The tears came faster. "I thought that was your primary source of income until Ellen told me you worked as an accountant."

Jonas sipped his beer.

The string of curses wending through Sophia's thoughts was impressive. Only a few escaped through her vocal cords. "What did Drew say to you?"

"He said Ellen and I were your only friends, and that we did a horrible job at it."

The throbbing in the center of her forehead felt a little better when she pressed the heel of her hand against it. "Why do you listen to him?" If they talked for hours, she wondered how long it took him to say that to Sabrina. He wouldn't come right out and say something so nasty, would he?

"Isn't it true?" she asked. Her question ended with a hiccup. "You never mention other friends, or going out with them. Jonas says that when you say you have plans, you're usually doing a scene with a submissive, and that they don't mean anything to you. Even you say you have lovers, affairs, not relationships."

She was not accountable to Sabrina or anyone else for her sex life. She answered what should have been the primary concern. "You're a good friend, Sabrina. Don't listen to Drew."

"Why don't you have any other friends? Why do the friends you do have tiptoe around you?" She paused to blow her nose on a tissue Jonas offered. "Don't think we haven't all noticed that Jonas and Ellen are careful with you. Like the other night when Drew followed you upstairs at Ellen's house. Your brother wanted to go after you. Jonas convinced him to give you some time, but he kept his eyes on the stairs and his ears tuned to any sounds coming from that direction. He lost more hands than he should have."

The ache settled behind Sophia's eyes. She pressed the cold water bottle against her forehead and closed her eyes.

Sabrina moved closer to Sophia and captured her free hand, pressing it between her smaller ones. "Sophia, he put on a good front. They all did. But they were all jumping out of their skins with nerves until you and Drew came back downstairs and everything seemed to be all right."

"Jesus, let it go!" Sophia snapped. The ache subsided, assuaged by the release of emotion. "My life hasn't been sunshine and roses, but I fail to see why that's any of your business!"

Tears tracked down both of Sabrina's cheeks. Sophia made the mistake of looking at Jonas. Her pain tore him apart, but he was sticking to his promise to not interfere.

This was a mistake. She couldn't be friends with both of them without coming between them. Jonas didn't want to keep secrets from Sabrina, and Sabrina would blame the distance Sophia kept between them on whatever he wasn't telling her, and so, on him.

Slamming the water on the bench behind her, Sophia muttered several curses under her breath. "Sabrina, this was a bad idea. I think it was a mistake for us to try to be friends. I'll stay in your wedding to keep your numbers even, but that's all."

She tried to leave, brushing between Jonas and Sabrina, but they closed the distance and trapped her. Well, Jonas held her in place, and Sabrina threw her arms around Sophia's neck and sobbed.

This was the most miserable day of her life.

"You can't leave like this," she managed to gasp between gulped breaths. "You can't just end our friendship like this."

"Yeah," Jonas said quietly in her ear. "We're not going to let you take the easy way out this time."

"This time?" When had she ever been given the option of an easy way?

"Yeah, this time," he echoed. "I watched you throw away every friendship you had before we met, and I was too caught up in my own problems to call you on your cowardice. I've watched you reject every person who showed a romantic interest in you. I thought you were going to kill me when I pushed you toward Drew, but Sophia, it's time to let the past go."

"He's a good guy," Sabrina said. Her sobs were a little less vehement. "I wouldn't have encouraged you if I didn't think you two were perfect together. Drew has his quirks, but they seem to complement yours."

"And if I thought he was capable of hurting you, I wouldn't have let you start anything with him." Jonas's mumbled assurance worked to soothe her nerves. "You know I've got your back, Sophie. Always."

Chapter 19

The rest of the day hadn't gone much better. Sophia managed to let Jonas and Sabrina extricate a promise that she would try with Drew. The entire time, she shot covert, curious looks in Jonas's direction. She *was* trying with Drew. She was giving him a chance, but the deck was so stacked against him that it wasn't fair. She didn't want this thing with him to end, but it would eventually.

Somehow, she managed to leave without having to divulge her shameful secret to Sabrina. Thinking back to some of the sessions in which she participated before and after the self-defense classes, Sophia realized her behaviors were self-destructive.

Telling her family and friends once had been difficult enough. Enduring the range of reactions, from revulsion to fear to pity, wasn't an experience she ever wanted to repeat. When would it stop mattering?

She tossed and turned for most of the night before dropping off into a troubled sleep close to dawn. Before too long, she opened her eyes to a horrible smell.

"Daniel, you're so gross." She pushed his face away and rolled over to get away from his odor. "I can't believe you're a year older than me."

He laughed wickedly. "It's noon. Get your lazy ass out of bed. Mom and Dad will be here soon, and you'll never hear the end of it if they find you still asleep."

It was her turn to host the monthly family gathering. David and Anna DiMarco would be in the kitchen no later than one thirty, finishing the dessert that both preceded and followed dinner. Sophia desperately wished for chocolate.

"What did you eat?" The disgusting smell that disturbed her sleep had been his breath. "I have extra toothbrushes and a brand-new bottle of mouthwash. This is why you don't have a girlfriend."

"Garlic pickles. You had them in your fridge. And I could have a girlfriend if I wanted one. There are too many beautiful women out there to settle for just one." He was uncommonly happy. Sophia experienced a sinking sensation.

Ignoring the last part of his statement was the wisest move she could make. She flung back the covers and gathered her clothes for the day. "You ate the whole jar, didn't you?"

"I was hungry."

"You're always hungry. Did you check the expiration date? I've had those for a long, long time." Not even Drew had touched them. Sophia disappeared into the bathroom.

The door opened and closed again. The bang of cupboards told her Daniel was rummaging around for that toothbrush, or at least for the mouthwash. The smell that woke her was far worse than the onions Drew had burped in her face. That man was too mired in the sibling torture minor leagues to compete with the things Danny put her through. His mom was a shrink. She probably made them play nice.

He gargled, and she endured the temporary spike in heat as he rinsed. "It's not like you to keep food once it's gone bad. You know how much I trust you."

She showered quickly, not worrying about details like double-checking her legs after she shaved them. Drew wasn't due back until tomorrow. Even then, their sex life might not survive the coming fight. Interfering with her friendships and making Sabrina feel like shit weren't nice things to do.

Danny left. Having finished showering, she dressed and threw on shorts and a light cotton shirt. The trail of toothpaste that leaked from her mouth necessitated a change in shirt. She opted to forego makeup, a little treat to herself. Her father would be happy.

Daniel lounged at the foot of the bed. He had straightened the covers. She studied him for a moment before rifling through a drawer.

He was twenty-six. Except for his family, he eschewed anything that might tie him down. He lived in a loft above his studio instead of purchasing a house, even though he could easily afford one, and he never dated a girl for more than three weeks unless he really liked them. Once he had gone as long as three months with the same girl, but he had broken it off when she talked about exchanging keys.

He had broken the hearts of more than a few of her friends. She had warned them, but Daniel DiMarco was an exceptionally handsome man, and her friends invariably ignored the warnings. During her sophomore year of high school, Sophia became aware of the number of girls pretending to be her friend as a way to wrangle an introduction to Daniel.

It made her wary of making new friends. That wasn't a new thing.

The few friends Jonas watched her push away were college friends. Nothing beyond sharing a beer or a bra had ever developed, so losing them didn't matter so much. Letting those friendships lapse meant nobody was looking at her as if rape was a disease that could be transmitted through contact.

"You don't look so good," he said.

"Neither would you if you woke up to that smell," she shot back.

He stood up, but didn't come any closer. "No, I mean, you look…disturbed. Restless. What happened yesterday? What did Sabrina want?"

With a sigh, she spilled the story. Daniel was one of the few people to whom she could say almost anything. By the time she got to the group hug portion of the story, his mouth was twitching with the attempt to not laugh.

"Danny, this is serious. He can't go around calling my friends and telling them they suck. She cried forever. I didn't get away from her until after the fitting."

That smirk didn't fade. "But you're still friends. You let her stop you from throwing that away. Sophia, you're making progress. Drew has been good for you. I wasn't sure at first."

A month ago, she would have flounced out of the room to get away from the idea a steady man could be considered good for her. Now, she wasn't sure. The urge to flee was still there, but it wasn't insistent. It was manageable. No headache pressed behind her eyes, and her stomach looked forward to whatever pie her mother would to make that night.

"Still," she said in an effort to salvage her pride, "I'm going to kill him."

Daniel hugged her cheek to his chest and pressed a loud, smacking kiss to the top of her head. "You have to invite him to dinner, Sophia. Mom is going to piss herself when she finds out you're dating a chef."

In the kitchen, she made a cup of tea. Daniel looked at her sideways because he'd already started the coffee before cleaning her out of pickles. The early pregnancy test languished somewhere in the bottom of her purse, and none of the usual signs her period was imminent appeared.

A killer headache waited just behind that thought. She was only twenty-five. Her fledgling business was only a couple weeks old. Her relationship with Drew wasn't much older. He'd made it clear a pregnancy wouldn't drive him away, but she couldn't help but think he wasn't ready for a child, either. He was twenty-nine. His business was successful, but his show was only in its second season.

Daniel knew Sophia was a coffee junkie. Maybe the headaches were caffeine withdrawal. Ignoring the questions in Danny's eyes, she ate a bowl of cereal and sipped decaffeinated tea. Her phone rang, interrupting the silent interrogation. She ignored that, too.

"Aren't you going to get that?"

"Nope."

"It's Drew, isn't it?"

That was his ringtone. She was a firm believer in giving the people who called the most their own ringtone. "He's in Los Angeles. Let him stew."

"Head games," Daniel hissed. He had more fire in his eyes than she'd ever seen. "I can't stand women who play these kinds of head games."

That caught her interest. Ignoring Drew's calls sent a pretty clear "I'm pissed at you" statement. Daniel's anger was personal. Somebody was getting under his skin. "Who is playing head games with you?"

His eyes narrowed. He confided in her as much as she confided in him. "Alaina."

The pretty, little brunette who drove Sophia's car home from Drew's house the night she had a meltdown. She was spunky. Sophia liked her. "I didn't think she was your type."

"Why?" He seemed offended. "I date all kinds of women."

"As long as they're tall, skinny, and blonde," she clarified. "I don't think Alaina is the kind of person who'll put up with your shit."

She hit something because he came back with a low blow. It was true, but low. "Like Drew puts up with yours?"

Unfortunately for him, she wasn't feeling charitable toward Drew. "I warned Drew several times that he was in for a world of trouble. He said he isn't going anywhere."

Daniel leaned back in his chair, hooking one arm over the back, and studied her curiously. "You're in love with him."

Sophia shrugged. "It won't last. Nothing good ever does."

Doors slammed in the driveway. The sounds of their parents' chatter drifted through the open front door and windows, interrupting anything Danny might have said. The conversation was saved from taking an irreparable downturn.

They met their parents at the door eagerly. Each carried a fruit pie. Anna had baked apple-walnut with a caramel topping for Sophia and cherry for Daniel.

She planted a kiss on Danny's cheek and handed the pies to Sophia. "Danny, go and get the rest of the groceries from the trunk."

Sophia took the pies to the kitchen and put them on the table. Her father followed her through the living room, his arms full of things that would turn into a huge dinner. He tossed the bags on the floor and turned toward her with his arms spread.

Like Daniel, David DiMarco was a tall man with dark coloring. However, Danny's muscles were longer and leaner because his workouts consisted mostly of practicing the martial arts. David's business involved a lot of heavy lifting. The sheer bulk of him testified to that kind of life. She'd witnessed her father lifting huge boulders that three of his crew struggled to scoot along the ground. He'd hoisted it as if it had been made of Styrofoam.

She stepped into her father's tight embrace. No matter what anyone said, she was her father's little girl. He squeezed her tight and pressed a kiss to her temple. "I don't see you enough, Sophia. You call your mother like a good girl, but it's not the same."

There wasn't an answer to that. Italians were masters of giving guilt. This was his way of saying he missed her. Stretching to the tips of her toes, she kissed his freshly shaven cheek. "I missed you, too, Daddy."

He let go, and Anna swept her up next. She was the odd duck in the family. David, Daniel, and Sophia were dark Italians. Anna was light.

Blonde hair, light brown eyes, and a light complexion made her seem like she didn't fit, but she did. Her people originated in northern Italy, whereas David's were more centrally located.

"Baby, you look tired." She patted Sophia's shoulder, and then pushed her back to pinch at her stomach. "And you're too skinny. We bought extra food, Sophia. You never have anything to eat in the house."

"I eat fine, Mom. I just had a bowl of cereal." The assurance was lost on her. Sophia refrained from mentioning that she worked out. In addition to wielding the whip, she ran at least four days a week. She preferred to run outside, but she had a treadmill in the basement for when it was too cold or too hot or too dark outside.

Sophia absolutely hated weight discussions with her mother. She thought working out was akin to a cardinal sin. It was her unrelenting opinion that the Pope didn't work out, so neither should anyone else. Daniel and David were excused from that unissued edict because they were doing their jobs. Sophia bit her tongue every time the urge to tell her that being a dominatrix was physically demanding work. She would spend the rest of her life crossing herself and muttering prayers under her breath, pleading for Sophia's soul.

Anna's build was rounded with generous curves and a large rack she neglected to pass on to her only daughter. At least she inherited something in the hips.

Daniel came in with the rest of the groceries. Anna wasn't kidding when she said she went grocery shopping. Sophia didn't mind. It saved her a trip. An impish part of her wondered if Drew would give his shopping list to her mother. Anna might smack him upside the head, but she would probably get him the things on the list.

Laughter and talking filled her modest house. Anyone listening in would probably guess there were ten people inside, but it was just the four of them, all talking at once and interrupting one another.

They finished off the two pies in no time, and Daniel brought mugs of coffee for everyone. Her mother spooned four sugars into her coffee and handed the sugar bowl over to Sophia. David and Daniel drank it black. It was a man thing. Sophia and her mother loaded theirs with sugar.

Absently, she fixed the cup how she liked it, but all she did was stir it. It smelled really good, and she wanted some badly, but she refrained.

Casually, she wandered to the sink and poured out her cup, rinsed it, and filled it with water before popping it in the microwave.

"What's wrong with the coffee?" Anna asked, sniffing her cup suspiciously.

"Nothing. I've been on a tea kick lately. Do you want some?"

Mom frowned, thinking. "Let me see what kind you have."

They were discussing the sampling of tea Sophia had when there was a knock on the front door. David was the closest. He lumbered to the door with the attitude of a man who knows it's someone selling something he doesn't want. Her father's size made him forbidding. His attitude only sharpened that image.

"Whaddaya want?" It amazed Sophia how his accent morphed from Michigan to Brooklyn when he was trying to be unwelcoming. None of them had ever been to the state of New York, much less that specific part.

"Sophia."

That was Drew's voice. Her head swung around as the fact he just told her father he *wanted* her registered in her head. She knew for a fact that her father saw her as a virgin, not as a sexually active woman. It wouldn't matter if he caught her in bed with a dozen men, he would still insist his Sophia was chaste.

Daniel tactfully shouldered his dad aside and pushed open the screen door. "Drew! Sophie said you were in Los Angeles until tomorrow."

"I came back early."

While Daniel invited Drew inside and introduced him to their father, Sophia busied herself with the canister of assorted tea bags. "Which one do you want, Mom?"

Anna stared at her daughter, her head cocked to the side. All efforts at diversion were futile. "Sophia Anna-Maria DiMarco, who is that man?"

Drew made it to the kitchen in time to answer that question himself. "I'm Drew, Mrs. DiMarco. I'm Sophia's boyfriend." He took her mother's hand and greeted her with a respectful handshake.

The aloof look Sophia gave Drew failed to quell his determination.

He didn't bother to hide his displeasure. "You can't break up with me if you don't pick up the phone when I call."

"You flew back a day early because I didn't answer the phone?" She infused her voice with disdain. She was angry with him, but she didn't want to have it out with him in front of her parents. She hadn't even wanted him to meet her parents. All she really wanted to do was wrap her body around him naked. "Maybe I was busy."

He parked his hands on his hips in a gesture that radiated danger. God, he was sexy. "I'm not stupid, Sophia. I talked to Sabrina last night. Jonas, too."

Her temper reached its boiling point, both with her libido and his attitude. The growl that came out of her was a precursor to yelling and screaming, two things she hadn't done in front of her parents since she convinced them she was done having meltdowns four years ago. "You had no right."

Black pupils dilated, and the ice in his eyes burst into flames. "Excuse me?" Inherent in his statement was a reminder that he'd known Sabrina for more than half his life. If either of them had more claim on her friendship, it was him.

From the corner of her eye, Sophia watched her mother and father exchange looks of interest. The fact she hadn't called him a liar when he introduced himself as her boyfriend spoke volumes.

"This isn't the time or the place, Drew. Go back to Los Angeles."

"No way. I flew four thousand miles to have this argument, and we'll have it now."

Now, her hands were on her hips. She leaned forward, unafraid of him. That told her parents even more about their relationship. With a curt nod toward the hallway, she gritted her teeth together. "Fine. In my office."

She stalked off, leaving him to follow. He entered the room on her heels, closing it firmly behind him. She would have slammed it.

Whirling, she lit into him, punctuating every word with her pointed finger stabbing at the air. "You had no right to call Sabrina and upset her like that. You have no right to interfere in my life!"

She was yelling, and she had no doubt her parents and Daniel heard every word, and she didn't care. "I like my friendships the way they are, thank you very much. I do *not* need you to call up my friends and tell them they don't treat me right. It's none of your goddamn business!"

Arms crossed, Drew leaned against the door and waited for her to finish yelling. He took the wind out of her sails pretty quickly. She was used to arguing with people who fought back, or at least reacted. Interruptions and counterarguments were helpful in fueling her temper.

When she was done, he took a step closer and dropped his arms. "It *is* my business, Sophia. Everything that concerns you is my business. I'm not going to stand by and watch you hold every person who cares about you at arm's length."

"You don't know anything about my life," she shot back hotly. Damn him for sounding so reasonable.

He leaned closer, stopping inches from her face. The minty scent left over from his gum fanned across her skin as he breathed heated breaths on her. "Because you won't tell me anything. You keep *me* at arm's length."

That was a slap in the face. She'd let him get closer to her than anyone else in the past five years. She stepped back, stumbling over a box of printer paper on the floor. Drew caught her by the arm. Once she was steady, she pushed him away.

"Sophie..."

Retreating across the tiny space, she leaned against the desk and crossed her arms. "So you called up my friends to pump them for information?"

His mouth tightened, forming a grim slash from those lush lips. "I refuse to apologize or feel guilty for pumping Sabrina for information. Something made you afraid of letting me close to you. If she could tell me, then it would help me break through to you. Christ, Sophia! I don't even know if you're afraid of me because of something I did or because of something that happened in your past."

No hot replies formed in her head or on her tongue.

"And I didn't tell her she was a bad friend," he continued. "I asked her questions, shared some theories, made her think. She's the one who jumped to the conclusion she was a bad friend. I tried to talk her down, but she...she was...a little irrational."

He seemed genuinely puzzled by her unreasonable behavior. Sophia wasn't about to enlighten him. Sabrina asked her to keep the pregnancy secret, and Sophia assured her that she would.

Silence was her friend. She used it now because her suddenly poor impulse control wanted to confide the gory details of her past to Drew. An unfamiliar optimism argued he would understand. Then, logic and prior experience took over. The looks of pity and disgust people couldn't hide haunted her still.

"Sophia, I'm flying blind, and I don't like the feeling. You use every opportunity to push me away. Even when you have answered the phone these last few days, things have been different. You've been distant. I don't want to lose you."

With a sigh, she dropped her eyes to the floor and studied her bare feet. She had wanted this time away from him to put things into perspective precisely because she felt too close to him. Had she been distant? Yes. Had she been trying to push him away? Hell yes.

"You haven't done anything, Drew. I've been very honest with you from the start. I have panic attacks and migraines. I'm a mess. I haven't had a real relationship in five years. I don't even want this one, but I can't seem to get you out of my system."

Her body prickled with an awareness of him, leaning forward automatically. His arms came around her. She rested her head against his shoulder. Instantly, all felt right with the world.

"Why do you sabotage relationships?" His voice was muffled by her neck.

"Drew, do you remember when Jonas told you to give me time and space?"

"Yeah."

"Give me time and space."

He didn't say anything. He just held her close for a long, long time.

The clank of pots from the kitchen made her aware of the time. Lifting her head, she smiled sheepishly at Drew. "You shocked the hell out of my parents when you told them you were my boyfriend."

"Does that mean you're inviting me to dinner?" His smile was that lush, relaxed one that made her want to feel it moving over her entire body.

"Now that they know you're here, they won't let you leave. Prepare to be interrogated."

They were ambushed the second they appeared in the kitchen, which was technically only a few feet from her office. David pulled out a chair from the kitchen table with menacing slowness. The brief inclination of his head ordered Drew to sit. Though Drew wasn't quite as tall as her father, he was nearly as bulky. Still, her father was overprotective. Sophia was a little afraid for Drew.

"It got awfully quiet in there," he said pointedly as Drew followed orders. He remained standing, hovering over Drew like a brick wall threatening collapse.

"I can get my point across without shouting, and so can Sophia."

David DiMarco took that as a threat and crossed his arms forebodingly over his chest. "And what point was that?"

Drew turned, staring down her father's toughness with a casual, yet respectful demeanor. "Sophia has a volatile temper, Mr. DiMarco, as I'm sure you know. She needs to understand that she can't push me away just because she's upset with me. She also needs to understand that I will not pussyfoot around her alleged frailties. She's a strong, intelligent woman. I refuse to treat her as anything less."

Sweet Jesus. He hit every one of her father's macho buttons with one assertive statement. Her father would be the last person to admit that Anna DiMarco wore the pants in the family, yet she clearly did. He didn't dare do anything without her approval. He might argue with her on many issues, but he always caved. His life's goal was to keep her happy. Even with his daughter, he was a giant marshmallow.

However, he perceived himself as the dominant, uncompromising male. Drew just set himself up as one of the guys. He might have been born with a silver spoon in his mouth, but he had the innate ability to identify with any group of people. It was what made him so successful.

Sophia's table was oval. She hovered nervously in the doorway. Her father took the seat around the corner from Drew, planting his body squarely between them. "Is 'Drew' your real name, son?"

"Andrew Snow," Drew supplied.

"What do your parents call you?"

The easy charm that came as second nature to Drew served him in good stead. His smile was genuine and friendly. "Drew. My mom occasionally calls me Andrew."

Finding her vocal cords at last, Sophia piped up. "Dad, Drew's staying for dinner. You can spread the interrogation out over several hours. You don't have to do it all now."

It wasn't so much that he held up his hand that stopped her. It was the look. Her father needed to know he could trust Drew with Sophia or he would not be sleeping at night. Her eyes dropped, and she studied the floor as she held back the tide of shame threatening to overwhelm her.

Anna put her arm around her daughter's shoulders and guided her to the counter. She thrust a pile of potatoes in her direction. "Your brother's getting the grill set up. He's going to need these soon."

A pot of Vernors boiled on the stove. Barbecued ribs were on the menu tonight. Anna boiled them in ginger ale before releasing them to Daniel for grilling. Sophia wondered if Danny volunteered for grill duty, or if their father had pushed him out the door so he could confront Drew.

She scooted around to the end of the counter so she could have a better view of her father and Drew. The position put her right behind Drew. Her eyes traced the outline of the broad shoulders against which she wanted to rest the complicated feelings swirling through her mind and upsetting her stomach.

Drew, for his part, understood the gravity of the situation. Whatever scared Sophia away from relationships affected more than just her, and somehow he knew that. Facing her father, Drew folded his hands together and leaned forward.

"What do you do for a living, Drew?"

The sliding door leading from the family room to the patio opened and closed. From the corner of her eye, Sophia recognized and dismissed Daniel.

"I co-own a successful bakery and catering company."

Daniel came into the kitchen and snorted. "He's a chef, Dad. Sophie found herself a man who cooks."

"Good," her mother said. She took the pile of potatoes Sophia had peeled and set them on a cutting board in front of Drew. "Let's put him to work."

With casual grace, he replaced the knife she handed him and got another, larger one. In response to her mother's narrowed glare, he shrugged. "Big hands, big knife."

Sophia had seen him use a tiny paring knife with ease, but she knew when to keep her mouth shut. Chefs were particular about knives.

Danny didn't have the same sense. "He has a cooking show on TV, Mom. He cooks better than you."

"Is that so?" Her question was directed at Drew, as if he had challenged her standing as one of the best cooks in existence. Their father had always raved about his wife's cooking, which was very good. Sophia and Daniel learned all they knew from Anna, and David wasn't bad in the kitchen either. Drew's skills put them all to shame, but Sophia wasn't stupid enough to say that to a woman whose cooking was part of her identity.

She kicked Daniel, but he kept going. "He has medals from winning contests all over the world. I think he should be in charge of dessert."

Drew narrowed an eye at Daniel. "Sophie told me you all cook together. I'm happy to do my part." He transferred the cutting board and potatoes to the counter to have more freedom to maneuver. With quick, expert movements, Drew cubed the peeled potatoes. Her parents watched in amazement at his speed and accuracy. Even Danny was impressed.

With a tiny smile on her face, Sophia finished peeling the remaining potatoes, rinsing them and adding them to Drew's pile as she went.

One by one, the rest of her family got to work on their portions. David peeled the corn, fastidiously removing every piece of silk. Anna added ribs to the simmering pot of Vernors. Daniel readied aluminum foil sheets and loaded them with Drew's cut potatoes.

It was quiet, which was strange for her family. Also strange was the fact that being next to Drew, working in silence, filled her with contentment. It was a foreign feeling, but one she liked.

"So, Mrs. DiMarco, what's in the pot besides those ribs?" Drew framed the question in an offhand manner, as if they had been conversing the entire time.

Anna bristled a bit, shifting the racks of ribs in the pot more than necessary. "Family secret."

"My Anna is protective of her recipes," David explained as he bent over the growing pile of corn guts on the table.

Drew grinned at her mother's back. "Sophia already showed me the red wine in the tomato sauce thing. I added it to a new dish I've developed. I'm featuring it on an episode this season."

A hand fluttered to her chest, pressing tight. Her mother had her emotions under control before she turned around. If she had been pissed at him, she wouldn't have worried about it. But she was pleased, so it made a difference. "My grandmother taught me that. Sophia's always loved my sauce."

"With good reason," Drew said. Though he only appeared to glance casually at her, and not notice how happy she was, he knew exactly what he was doing. Sophia struggled not to laugh at the game the pair played. "Do you want to come to the taping? It's Tuesday at my house. Noon. Sophia can bring you."

"I'm working," she said, handing Drew her last potato.

His brows drew together. "Ginny said you weren't working tomorrow or Tuesday."

"For you. I have other clients."

"She working for me," Daniel supplied. "I had her first."

Drew knew about the proposal Sophia had submitted to Christopher's firm. The question in his eyes stewed there for an indecisive minute. Though he was supposed to get back to her Friday, she hadn't heard from Chris at all. Tomorrow, she would place a follow-up call just to see where things stood. Likely, she hadn't been chosen. They were probably waiting to confirm with their primary choice before informing the rest of the bidders that their bid wasn't accepted. Still, a friendly call would have been nice.

"You need to know how to do your own books." David's admonition boomed from the table. It had been a point of contention between Daniel and him for many years. It was an old, worn-out argument any of them could have lip-synced.

Mom chimed in, defending Daniel as she always did. "David, leave the boy alone. This is Sophia's business."

"I can do my books, Dad, but then I'd be denying Sophie the pleasure. What kind of big brother does something like that?"

Their mother ended the argument before it could get into the fact Daniel finished college with a degree their father considered useless, political science. If he'd gone on to become a lawyer, David would have been okay with it. But when their grandfather retired and left the studio to Daniel, he jumped at the chance to follow his dream.

"Danny can give you the afternoon off, Sophia. What time are you picking me up?" Anna couldn't have been more pleased.

Drew didn't understand her glare. She sighed in exasperation.

"I'll pick you up at eleven, Mom." Before Daniel could say a word, Sophia held up a hand to him. "I'll come back after dancing lessons Tuesday, and I'll finish up Wednesday night after class."

Because Drew wanted her to watch him film all afternoon, he was going to lose two nights with her. She watched as he ran the rest of her weekly schedule through his head and he realized he wouldn't see her alone again for an entire week.

He swore under his breath, but only Sophia was aware of his foul language. This time, it didn't make her laugh.

Chapter 20

Daniel popped in a Bruce Lee DVD and camped out on Sophia's couch. Taking that as their cue to leave, her parents kissed Sophia on the cheek and invited Drew to call them by their first names.

The rest of the day had gone extremely well. Drew found an easy fit with her family. He grilled the meat with Daniel, talked preseason football with David, and charmed Anna out of her culinary secrets by gushing over her ribs.

Of course, Drew made the barbeque sauce, which was sweet and tangy, so she wasn't sure if her mother's simmering marinade or Drew's sauce made the meal. It was tasty, and that's all she cared about.

She closed the door behind her parents, ready to turn her wrath on Daniel. As she prepared to kick him out so she could be alone with Drew for the first time in four days, he stretched and grabbed for his phone and keys.

"You're welcome," he said.

"For what?" She wrinkled her nose at him in confusion.

"For acting like I'm staying late tonight, Sophia. Do you really think they would have left before Drew?"

"Oh," she said. He was right. "Thank you. Are you leaving?" She had to make sure.

"After you answer one question."

Drew wrapped his arms around Sophia from behind and pressed a kiss into her neck. Danny needed to leave.

"Make it quick."

"Are you pregnant?"

She froze, her arrested attention fixed on Daniel. "What?"

"You're a coffee addict, yet you won't drink it, or anything else with caffeine. You refused beer twice today. Drew doesn't seem surprised. He didn't even offer you any coffee after dinner, though the rest of us were drinking it." He stared at her expectantly. "And I found a pregnancy test in your purse the other night."

She swallowed the lump in her throat. "I'm not pregnant."

The shock running through Drew manifested physically. His body jerked against hers, and he let go of her. "You're not?"

"I told you I wasn't." Her body was stiff, and her voice was a whisper.

If Daniel saw her lie, he didn't call her on it. With a brief nod, he squeezed a hand on her shoulder and bid them good-bye. He locked the door behind him.

Sophia turned to Drew and pulled his face to hers. She wanted to drown in his kiss and revel in the feel of his strong hands roaming her body.

He had other ideas. "Sophia, does this mean you've started your period?"

With her mind firmly on the fun she wanted to have that night, she shook her head. "Not yet."

Those hands held her shoulders firmly, thwarting her efforts to get romantic. "The test was negative?"

Stepping back, a low growl escaped to illustrate her frustration. "I didn't take the test yet. My period is only a few days late, which is not at all unusual. Don't push it, Drew. I'm being careful."

And she was being careful. Everything Daniel said was true. Even though she desperately didn't want to be pregnant, she was taking every precaution to protect something that was a maybe.

Frustrated, he glared at her for the longest time. His internal struggle played over his features, shades of anger and defeat turning to acceptance and patience. When he pulled her to him, his kiss was rough, ravaging her lips with repressed passion. His hand wound in her hair, and he jerked her head back to suck and bite at her neck.

She let him have her this way, reveling in his barely restrained ardor. Treatment like this from anyone else would have scared her. She never thought she would be able to trust anyone enough to really let herself go, to just accept the things he made her feel. Drew shattered almost all of her boundaries. She would do anything to keep him from looking at her with disgust or pity. Her resolve to keep her past from him strengthened as her love for him grew.

Suddenly, he broke away. "Let's go downstairs, Sophia. I have a surprise for you, and I'm sure you don't want the neighbors calling the cops over all the screaming you're going to be doing."

That didn't sound good. "Screaming?"

He grinned. "Yeah, you know. Faster. Harder. Oh God, Drew. Yes."

She blushed, sure those words and more were going to flow from her in profusion. Drew was the only lover who had ever moved her to be desperately vocal. She'd always directed her lovers with gentle commands, not frantic demands.

Turning out most of the lights, she left the one over the stove lit as a nightlight. It was doubtful they would make it back upstairs before dark.

Drew had most of her clothes off before she locked the door to the playroom. His lips were everywhere, lighting fires that would never be quenched. He wore a polo shirt today, which he helped her remove, but he stopped her when she went for his pants.

She looked up at him, puzzled.

He smiled, a sly, cocky curving of those luscious lips. "Time for your surprise."

She didn't move.

"Trust me?" It was both a question and a request.

There was nothing tentative about her nod.

Lifting her with ease, he threw her to the mattress, and then he bound her hands above her head. Her heart beat so fast she thought it would burst from her chest. She struggled, fighting the restraint and a panic attack. "No, Drew, don't do this to me."

His response was to kiss her until passion took over, calming her. Then those clear blue eyes met hers, unflinchingly intense. "Trust me, Sophie. I'm only going to make you feel good. I promise."

Her nod was tentative, but she was determined to trust him. She didn't protest when he slipped a blindfold over her eyes and finished undressing her.

His weight eased off the bed, and the door opened. She heard his footsteps moving up the stairs and echoing through the kitchen. Icy breaths caught in her throat, stabbing the sudden dryness there. Rationally, she knew he wouldn't leave her like this, yet her vulnerable position made her nervous and unsteady.

Moisture rushed to her pussy. It swelled in anticipation and scented the air with spicy arousal.

Drew's returning footsteps only heightened the tension. By the time he secured the door and the bed dipped under his weight, she was as tight as a bowstring. One touch would send her over the edge.

"Miss me?" he whispered before plundering her mouth with a demanding kiss.

She met his demand, matching his passion and whimpering with need. The nights at work had begun to take a toll on Sophia. She no longer wanted to spend her evenings whipping or binding strangers, even familiar strangers. Every second she spent at the Club was a second she wished she was spending with Drew. The procession of naked bodies, which used to fuel her passions, did nothing for her anymore.

But now she needed the job for the income, not the emotional outlet. God, how she missed Drew!

"Yes," she whispered back. "I'm glad you came home early."

His lips curved happily as they traveled down her body. Wispy caresses cascaded down her arms, across her breasts, and down her stomach. He skipped her pussy, as he had skipped her nipples, to concentrate on her legs.

The breath sucked out of her when she felt his mouth close around her smallest toe. The rhythm of his sucking and the scrape of his teeth created a curious sense of urgency. She pressed her legs together, trying to concentrate the swirling as he gave each digit the same treatment.

Taking one ankle gently in his hand, he wrapped cold leather around it. In the darkness under the mask, she realized he was binding her ankles. She didn't fight him. Her legs were spread, and she couldn't close them, and she didn't care. She wanted his face there. She wanted his mouth sucking her clit the way he sucked her toes. She wanted to come in his mouth. If she was running the show, he would be bound in this position while she rode his face. Maybe they'd do that next.

His weight shifted to make the bed dip near her hip. Something feathery brushed her nipple, swirling around the areola until it puckered. Air rushed across, hardening it to the point of pain. It burned pleasantly, aching for the pressure of his mouth or the pinch of his fingers. Moaning, she arched toward him, offering her breast.

But he shifted again, leaning across her. Part of his arm grazed her stomach lightly, sending tingles rocketing in all directions. Silently, he repeated the motions on the other nipple.

Now both of them burned. She moaned, squirming against her bonds.

"Like that, honey?"

The brush swept lightly across her bottom lip, leaving something sticky there. Darting out her tongue, Sophia tasted sweetness that left a light tingling behind. She caught his play on words. "Honey? What did you mix in with it?"

He chuckled lightly. "A chef never reveals his secrets."

With that, he left her quivering, aching body to settle between her legs. She didn't get her hopes up too high. The denim scraping her leg said he was still clothed.

The outward push on her thighs had her spreading them wider. The bindings on her ankles slackened as she gave him what he wanted. His hot tongue licked long and deep, tracing a trail along the inside of her vaginal lips and circling her clit. She arched into him, wishing the situation was reversed and she could ride him as fast and hard as she wanted. He licked for a while longer, keeping his pressure light to let her know this was still the warm-up.

Then he was gone. The brush replaced his tongue, lightly flicking over and around her clit. The sticky substance burned there more intensely than it did on her breasts. When he blew on her to dry the honeyed mixture, she lifted her hips from the bed, crying out in frustration. Yes, this was very stimulating. It made her want to rub her entire body on him and fuck him blind.

Wetness spurted into her pussy, but he kept her spread open, forcing it to pool somewhat south of her clit. He wasn't going to give her relief any time soon.

Even as she bucked and squirmed, he tightened the bindings, forcing her legs further apart and limiting her upper body movement even more. "Drew!" He was right, she was screaming his name, but not in the way she thought she would.

"Patience, my love."

She heard him rummaging through the containers on her shelves. One of the reasons she selected her toys and props beforehand was so that if her submissive was blindfolded or tied with their back to her, which was frequently the case, they could not be aware of exactly what she was doing. Not knowing heightened the tension.

For Sophia, knowing heightened the tension. Drew wasn't trained on using the other kinds of bindings or the whips, not that she thought he would try to use them. He'd promised he wouldn't hurt her, and he didn't have any special love for the whip himself. He was unfamiliar with many of her toys, not that he couldn't figure them out.

Foil packets dropped on the bed next to Sophia and she sighed. Finally, he was going to get down to business.

His big, warm chest pressed against hers as his lips reminded her that she belonged to him. Arching as much as she could, she offered her body to him. The honey on her nipples had dried to a hard shell, pulling the skin taut. Whatever spices he mixed into the honey tingled tantalizingly against her sensitive skin. Her breasts were on fire for his mouth, and her pussy was an inferno.

She writhed with need.

He pulled back, and she felt the tip of a fairly wide, textured toy nudge her opening. "I love to watch you come, Sophia." The vibrating length slid into her. She rocked against it, wanting it faster, harder, and rubbing against her clit. He did none of those things.

Whimpering, she begged. "Please, Drew. 'Upon thy eyes I throw all the power this charm doth owe.'"

He chuckled, and she knew he found amusement in the reversal of their roles. "Oh, honey, the power of your charm is definitely upon my eyes. Tell me how you want it, sweetheart. I want to make you come."

The easy solution was to bury himself deep inside her. He wasn't going for easy tonight. "Fuck me with it, Drew."

It wiggled inside as he pressed it up and down. The increased pressure of the vibrations against her vaginal walls lifted her hips the few inches allowed by her bonds. She cried out, so near an orgasm. He pumped it in and out, up and down, rotating the curved head inside as she screamed out her first orgasm.

The clenching and pulsing of her pussy did little to alleviate the burning on her clit, but Drew paid little attention to that need as he continued to thrust the vibrating toy deep into her. No man had ever pushed her the way

Drew did. He didn't let her orgasm wane before forcing her to the next one. The sensitized muscles of her vagina only pulsed faster. Tension coiled, a hurricane swirling toward that ultimate release.

She screamed again as she shattered. The many parts of her body littered the bed. She was aware they existed, but she had no control over anything anymore.

Drew planted a kiss on her slack mouth and dialed down the setting on the vibrator, but he didn't turn it off. "I love you, Sophie. I love watching you come. You'll come again for me, won't you?"

She didn't know if she had it in her. She lacked the ability to move or to respond to Drew's question.

He laughed lightly, the dissonance of the rumble transferring easily to her chest. The moan that escaped when his hot mouth closed around one nipple was involuntary. Juices ran down her legs, smearing across her thighs and itching down the crack of her ass. The sheet below her was sopping wet. Her body was languid and liquid.

With just one more touch, Drew turned her molten. She couldn't find the energy to fight the leather straps binding her in place.

She heard whimpering, moaning, and begging. The voice was hers, but the need was primal, bypassing her brain completely. When he gave the same attention to the other breast, licking the honey slowly to soften it up, then sucking hard to cleanse it away, she was out of her mind with need.

She swore at him, threatening bodily harm if he didn't give her clit the same treatment. It wasn't that she wanted the feeling gone. She just wanted the burning need assuaged. She needed to rub against him in the worst way.

Drew shifted over her. The straps binding her legs disappeared. His jeans hit the floor. She never thought she could want someone like this. The need in her eclipsed everything she'd ever felt for Drew before.

He lifted her, turned her over, and pushed her knees underneath to lift her ass in the air. The bound hands stretched out above her head relegated her to having to accept this position without modification. She couldn't lift her torso to push back against him. She would be forced to accept what he wanted to give.

Gravity caused her thick, creamy juices to flow toward her clit, wetting the nearly dried honey mixture and sending the tingles zinging over a much wider area. She bucked backward as much as she could, begging for him to fill her and knowing it wouldn't happen. For starters, he hadn't removed the softly pulsing vibrator from her pussy. In this position, it pressed forward and down, heightening her arousal. She was near orgasm, again.

The head of his cock nudged against the muscle closing her anus. Anticipation flooded her.

A hand traced along her spine, trying to chase the tension gripping her body. "Relax, Sophia. Let me inside you."

"I can't," she gasped. "I'm going to come."

"Not yet." The vibrations, already soft, muted further.

She knew how this was done. Breathing deeply, she shoved backward against his tip. "Now, Drew. Don't hold back."

He didn't. With a shuddering groan, he impaled her. His hips pistoned, thrusting into her with uncontrolled passion. One hand crept around her thigh to turn up the vibrator. It stayed to massage her clit.

Sophia's body was no longer her own. She had no control over the way it bucked and the sounds that tore from deep inside. Dimly, and from a distance, she heard the wet slapping of his hips and balls against her ass, and the animal grunts and moans they both made.

Drew said her name over and over, and that was her last semi-coherent memory. Black spots dotted her vision seconds before a blindingly white light obscured it completely. The orgasm ripped through her. The long, low cry went on and on and on until her knees gave out.

He held her in place for one last thrust that sent him over the edge. He collapsed next to her, rolling to his back and reaching up to release the straps binding her wrists.

The burning in her pussy was not assuaged. It motivated her to rip the vibrator from inside and throw it to the floor. Energy flowed through her, fresh and urgent. She had no idea where it came from.

The walls of her pussy still wept and clenched. She straddled Drew, facing him with iron determination.

Sweat glistened over his chest and shoulders. She was right about how arresting he looked this way, but she didn't let it distract her. Sophia's body heaved up and down with the large breaths moving his chest and stomach.

With one finger, she tested the folds of her pussy. Because he had ignored her clit for so long, it wasn't the least bit sore or oversensitive. "You're not finished."

He grinned, something both cocky and meaningful, and ran his hands up her thighs. "With you? Never."

"What did you put on me?" The potency was waning, but it still burned pleasantly, firing her passion when she should have been exhausted. "And don't give me that line about being a chef when you weaseled two of my mother's cooking secrets from her and are about to profit from them both."

"Weaseled?" He bit his upper lip in an attempt to hide that grin. "I prefer 'charmed.' It sounds so much nicer. Besides, I'll give her credit on-air. Now, tell me what you want, honey. I'm all yours."

Lazily, she gave his nipple a light tweak. "You better believe it, mister." Scooting her way up his body, she made her intention clear. "I want your mouth on my pussy. I want you to lick away every drop of that stuff until I come in your mouth. Then I'm going to fuck you until you pass out."

Amusement lifted the corners of his mouth and crinkled his eyes. "I love how you make that sound like a challenge." Parking his hands under her thighs, he lifted her into place. "I'm up to the task, honey. I've dreamed about you for four agonizing days, and you didn't even kiss me when I came back an entire day early just to see you."

She refrained from mentioning how pissed she had been at him. "I'll have to work on greeting you with more enthusiasm when you return from a trip."

Discouraging any further conversation, she lowered her pussy to his mouth. He opened, licking long and deep with that hot tongue. His teeth nipped at her clit and other places she never considered bitable. Winding his arms around her thighs and gripping her ass with those large hands, he held her to him and feasted on her flesh.

The first orgasm took her by surprise, coming fast and hard. She shuddered and screamed, falling forward, but he didn't stop. She gripped the headboard for balance, and the second orgasm rocketed through her.

That man had a magic mouth.

Lifting her from him, he set her on his freshly sheathed, rock-hard cock. She slid down him hard and fast, riding him to that same rhythm. The burn caused by the mixture was gone, licked clean away. Now it was replaced with another burn, this one originating low in her abdomen.

Electric heat shot through her nervous system, sending cold sparks through her arms and legs to short-circuit those muscles. She lost the rhythm at the threshold of the largest orgasm she'd ever had.

Drew flipped her over. Lifting her legs high to hook over his shoulders, he drove into her, pounding to the rhythm she set. She'd always forced her lovers to be gentle. Drew was nothing of the sort right then, and she loved it.

From a distance, she heard a shriek and a roar, and then everything went black.

Chapter 21

The playroom had no visible windows. Though they were still accessible, she'd covered them with the soundproof foam that hung on the walls and ceiling. When she woke sometime later, she had no idea how much time had passed. It could be morning for all she knew.

The only certainties were twofold. First, Drew had passed out at the same time she did. He was still inside her. Second, breathing was challenging because he had collapsed on top of her.

Surreptitious wiggling didn't work. She tried shoving him gently, but that only made him groan and tighten his hold.

"Drew."

He didn't stir.

A pressing need in the region of her bladder urged Sophia on her mission. She shook his shoulder insistently. "Drew."

One eye cracked open. That ice-blue orb barely focused on her before closing again.

"Honey, I need you to get off me."

"I got off on you," he mumbled without moving. "Let me rest, and I'll do it again."

God, she loved his sense of humor. She sent up a prayer now. "Lord, 'do thy best to pluck this crawling serpent from my chest.'"

That got his attention. "Did you just call me a nightmare?"

Whoops. Her sleep-addled brain chose the wrong quotation. Her smile was sheepish. "I just meant you're heavy, and I have to pee."

"You're lucky, DiMarco," he said, narrowing his eyes in false vexation. "'The more you beat me, the more I fawn on you.'"

Interesting choice of words for a man who didn't respond to the whip. "Can you fawn on me in ten minutes? I wanted to jump in the shower, too."

With a resigned sigh, he removed himself. Because they had dried together, it was a little painful. "Sorry," he said when she flinched.

She rolled from the bed as soon as she could.

"Oh, shit. Sophie, I'm sorry."

That didn't sound good. Glancing back, she saw the color had drained from his face. "What's wrong?"

He looked up at her, lost. "You're bleeding. I hurt you."

Then she saw it. The wet spot on the sheet was stained pink with fresh blood and darker with dried blood. Peering down at herself, she saw the smears coating her thighs. She breathed a sigh of relief for more than one reason. "You didn't hurt me, Drew. I'm all right."

Realization dawned on him rather quickly for a man.

"I'm going to jump in the shower," she threw over her shoulder as she headed to the next room.

The hot spray washed away her worries. She shed a few silent tears, both in sorrow and relief. The curtain opened, and Drew joined her. His arms came around her from behind. She let her head fall against his shoulder, and he buried his face in her neck.

"You were right," he said. A sad acceptance permeated his words.

She thought back to the day the condom broke. He hadn't been upset by anything other than her refusal to have a reaction. He had loved her then.

She crossed her arms over his, twining their fingers together. "Are you all right?" The question was gentle and not judgmental.

"Yeah. You?"

Taking a deep breath, she plunged forward. "I want kids, Drew, with you. But not yet. I'm not ready to be a mother. I've already contacted my doctor about starting the Pill."

He nodded, a small movement that didn't take his face out of her neck. His arms tightened around her. Then, he pressed a kiss to her shoulder and let go. "I feel a little guilty about being relieved. I want kids with you, but I want a few years of having you to myself first. It's selfish, but I don't want to share your attention just yet."

She turned in to his arms, meeting his lips in a tender kiss that communicated exactly how serious this thing was between them. She thought she could get him out of her system. Now she knew that would never happen. He was part of her, and she was part of him.

When they finally made it upstairs, they found it was late morning. Drew didn't have to be at work, but Sophia had plenty to do. As she scurried around getting ready, he caught her in his arms.

"Sophie, do me one favor this week?"

This week, she wouldn't see very much of him. Though they would work three days in the same building, she would be busy upstairs, and he would be busy downstairs. According to the receipts she saw, his catering business didn't seem to have a slow season, and neither did the bakery. If their growth rate kept up, they would need to greatly expand their staff and facilities.

She nodded in response to his question, indicating he should ask the favor.

"Stay at my house. It's closer to the bakery, Daniel's studio, and Ellen's club. I'll teach you the alarm code so you can come and go as you please." When she opened her mouth to protest, he continued. "You have an exhausting schedule this week, and the drive back and forth might just kill you. I can't have that happening. Just pack up what you think you'll need, and I'll take it home today."

Her protest died as she thought through his reasoning. He was right. She nodded and set off to select her wardrobe for the week.

He was right about how bad the week was. She rushed to Daniel's studio and worked until dark. The only reason she left when she did was because Drew called Daniel and told him to kick her out. She fell into bed next to Drew and slept like the dead.

Tuesday wasn't any better. Her mother loved watching Drew tape his show. Sophia found the process interesting and odd. He was so busy with preparations, makeup, lighting, and retakes, it didn't seem to matter that she was there.

Ginny as a producer was an interesting thing to watch. She commanded the crew with finesse and ease. Filming went off without a hitch.

That evening, she leaned against Drew, dozing on his shoulder as they danced. He made excuses to leave early, but she insisted on going to Daniel's. Again, he kicked her out when Drew called.

Wednesday, she worked all day at Sensual Secrets, taught her self-defense class, and worked on Daniel's accounting. It was well after midnight when she finally finished. Drew had called again, but Sophia growled at Daniel to grow a pair, and he left her alone after that.

Thursday, she was dead on her feet by the time she finished her shift at Ellen's. Friday was worse because she dragged herself from bed exhausted in the morning, and she worked all day and most of the night.

Saturday, Drew growled and threatened to tie her to the bed when she tried to go into Sensual Secrets to make up some of the time she lost working at Daniel's Monday and Tuesday.

Saturday night, she was awake at the club for the first time that week. Though she was alert, the joy had gone out of the job. She no longer harbored the vast reserves of guilt and pain and fear for which this had become an emotional outlet.

Ellen didn't look surprised when Sophia handed in her notice. She smiled, a move that transformed her face into something beautiful. "You don't have to give notice, Sophia. I'm glad your business is doing well, and I'm ecstatic that you're in love with a good man. You deserve to be happy, and I'm glad you can finally see that."

She went home that night, to her own house. She hadn't been there all week. Daniel had come by to collect her mail, and a large stack was piled on her kitchen table. After staying with Drew for a week, it was too quiet. Her cozy house had become a lonely place.

Yet, she needed some time away from Drew to breathe. He had been very understanding all week, not complaining that she crashed in his bed well after midnight and rose near dawn the next morning to start everything over. He cooked for her, making sure she didn't skip meals, which she totally would have if he'd left her to her own devices.

And each night, he wrapped his body around hers and held her close.

The unrelenting pessimist inside her was cautiously optimistic. Instead of convincing herself that it couldn't possibly last, she could see herself growing old with Drew. She loved him, and he loved her. The future unfolded before her, bright with promise.

It lasted three weeks.

Drew was delighted Sophia quit her job at Ellen's club because it gave them evenings together. Ironically, he worked many nights. Clients often paid extra to make sure Drew Snow catered their event. He limited these appearances, but they still took him away several evenings each week.

She finally introduced him to Christopher, whose relationship with Janelle probably wasn't going to last the way they were going, and the three of them had a very satisfying evening together. She went hard on Chris, probably because she didn't get the contract with his firm and he took more than two weeks to get back to her about it. Drew went easy on him, for the same reason. He thought she had enough to do.

One sunny Wednesday evening a week before Jonas and Sabrina's wedding, Sophia was in the process of teaching the self-defense class at Danny's studio.

He had two training arenas. The back one was private, and that's where Sophia held her sessions. Most of the women had been through a lot already. The last thing any of them needed was to have an audience.

Tonight's session focused on close combat techniques. Only six women came, which was an average number. Sometimes there were as many as fifteen, but that didn't happen often.

The women stood in an uncertain line, watching Sophia demonstrate on Daniel. He always made himself available to help demonstrate. Some of the positions she made him assume were ones he found distasteful, but he was a good sport about it, citing the greater good.

"Only one in twenty rapists will ever spend time in jail. Thinking the law will be on your side is a mistake. Rape is hard to prove, partially because 73 percent are committed by someone you know, especially someone with whom you're involved."

She didn't know everyone's stories, and they didn't all know hers. Sometime in the past two months, she had stopped sitting in on the group sessions. Alaina sat off to the side, watching. Her failed date with Daniel hadn't scared her away. She still ran a support group meeting after the training session. She had bonded with some of the women who were now beginning to come regularly. Sophia wasn't too caught up in her own life to miss the way Daniel looked at Alaina when he thought it was safe.

Daniel moved into position without being told. He wore padding and a cup because Sophia did not pull her punches. The women all had a chance to practice on him as well. He was good about telling them when they needed to hit with more force or when they needed to alter their stance.

"You have to know how to defend yourself. Stop thinking about how much you don't want to hurt his feelings or damage his face. Once a partner attacks you, the relationship is over."

Moving behind her, Daniel slipped his arms around Sophia's waist. "Hey, baby, I paid for dinner. It's time for you to show me how thankful you are."

She turned a sweet smile on him. "Not tonight. I have to get up early for work. I had a great time."

"Let me in, just for a little while." He did his best imitation of flirting.

"Okay, just for a few minutes." Turning back to the group, she raised her brows. It was a familiar situation that every woman has found herself in at one time or another. "At this point, most of us aren't thinking anything bad would happen. They had a good time on their date, and he appeared to take no for an answer."

Using a very uncomfortable wicker sofa, they playacted a typical scene, minus the actual kissing and fondling. "You get the idea," she explained.

Nervous laughter and twitters of apprehension rippled through the small group. For her part, Sophia hated this. She hadn't fought Charlie when he raped her. Her mind spent the entire time grappling with the fact that her date, someone she had literally known since she was in second grade, was raping her.

"The hardest part is keeping a presence of mind," she said. "When you know your attacker, when you have feelings for your attacker, it's difficult to wrap your mind around the fact that he's actually treating you this way."

Daniel pressed his advantage.

She went for a groin kick with her knee, but he blocked her. Reflexively, she brought her hand up, shoving the heel of it into his nose. She pulled this punch. Used full force, a swift, upward blow to the nasal cartilage could result in permanent brain damage or death.

He reeled as if she hadn't pulled the punch, falling to the floor.

Leaping up, she assumed a defensive position. "Now I can put enough distance between us to use some of the other techniques I've shown you tonight. Most of the time, your date will call you a bitch and leave. Some men will keep it up, becoming more and more violent."

Daniel peeled himself from the floor. "Run to a neighbor's house, or grab your keys and get in your car. If you grab your phone, call emergency.

Don't stick around just because you know a few moves. Most of the men who attack you are bigger and stronger. Maybe you can't beat them, but hopefully you can buy yourself some time."

Glancing up, Sophia caught sight of Drew in the doorway. He was supposed to meet her at Ellen's later for the continuation of her sporadic poker night. What was he doing here? She wasn't sure how much he'd seen or heard, but he needed to leave.

Several of the women caught her inattention and stared openly at Drew.

Nudging Danny's shoulder, she leaned close. "Get him out of here."

"You done with me?" There were only a few minutes left of the hour, so she could do without him. He frequently bowed out before the session ended. It was a lesson he learned early on. Women knew a good man when they saw one. They frequently hit on him. He didn't have anything against dating a woman who has been through a traumatic experience, but he wanted these women to see him as a teacher, a resource, not fresh meat.

With his track record, Sophia was glad he refrained. The last thing she needed was for a woman to stop coming because they'd run through Daniel's three-date limit and lost his interest.

"Yeah."

"I'll take him up to the loft."

"Thanks."

After they left, one of the ladies, Colleen, gaped at Sophia. "Do you know who that was?"

"Yeah," she said, recognizing the tone of a fan. She had obviously seen his show.

"Figures," another woman, Angel, snorted. "Someone as hot as Daniel would be friends with someone as hot as Drew Snow." She sighed. "You're so lucky, Sophia."

She was losing their interest. "I'd like you all to practice the punch I used on Daniel. It's effective, even in close quarters."

Colleen tilted her head to the side and studied Sophia. "Are you going out with Drew Snow?"

Titters of excitement moved through the group. Those who didn't know about Drew's quasi-celebrity status were enlightened by those who did. Sophia wasn't going to get anywhere with them now. "One minute, and then we drop the subject. Yes, Drew is my boyfriend."

They fired off questions as to the duration and the seriousness of the relationship, and Sophia answered most of them. Exactly sixty seconds from the starting point, she called a halt to the questions. "Let's get some practice in before time expires."

Alaina intervened before too long, suggesting Sophia absent herself from the group session because they didn't want the focus to be on her. She was fine with that.

She wanted to know why Drew came by the studio instead of meeting her at Ellen's house.

The stairs to Daniel's loft apartment were at the end of a hallway by the locker rooms. A sign on the door warned people that the door was not part of the studio and that they would be trespassing if they went inside.

The steps terminated in a small landing that had two doors. The first door was to a small storage closet. The actual door to his loft, dead bolts and all, was across from the closet. It wasn't properly closed.

Male voices carry so much farther than female voices. It's the increased bass, giving the sound vibration more energy so it could travel farther. It was simple physics.

Something in Daniel's voice stopped her about halfway up the stairs. Being a dominatrix, she'd long ago mastered the art of moving quietly about a room. She hadn't meant to sneak up on them, but that's exactly what she did. To compound matters, she eavesdropped.

Her original goal had been to see if Daniel was confiding in Drew. Alaina was definitely under his skin. While he acted like he was okay with the fact their date was a disaster, Sophia knew her brother.

He was out of his league with her. She wanted him to confide in her, but he was reluctant. Maybe he needed a guy's perspective. Drew certainly could teach Daniel a thing or two about patience and perseverance.

However, they weren't discussing Daniel's failed attempt at dating Alaina. They were discussing Sophia.

"You blame yourself." Drew's voice was grave, the statement meant to clarify.

"It's my fault. He was my best friend. We hit it off the first day of school in third grade. All those years, he didn't look twice at her. Then, Thanksgiving break our junior year in college, he asks me if I'd be okay with him asking her out."

Sophia's stomach dropped. That sounded dangerously like her story. Daniel wouldn't tell Drew about that. He couldn't betray her like that.

"If I'd told him no, he'd have backed off."

"You have no way of knowing that." The voice of reason was carefully neutral, yet every word stabbed at her heart. *He knew.*

"I didn't come home for Christmas break because I wanted to show my parents how grown up I was. If I had come home, that would have been a double date, and nothing would have happened to her." Daniel's voice scraped the words, scratching at the old wound to make it fresh. "I failed her. I was supposed to protect her, and I failed."

Stabbing pain pressed behind her eyes. He told Drew the one thing she'd never intended for him to know. Panic compressed her chest, and she couldn't breathe. Blood drained from everywhere. Pins poked at her fingers and feet. She must have made some sound because the door to the landing flew open.

Daniel stared down at her. The pain in his eyes was no match for the riot inside her.

Her lips moved to form words. Finally, some squeezed out, bringing a few tears with them. "How could you? You had no right to tell him any of that."

The color drained from his face. Now they matched better. "I...He knew, Sophie. I thought you told him."

She shook her head in denial, the movement slow and manic. "I can't stay here."

She ran. By some twist of fate, her car keys were under the counter displaying the clothing embossed with the studio's name. She grabbed them on her way to the parking lot.

Drew caught up to her before she made it to the front door. His lips moved, but she couldn't comprehend the sounds coming from them. Reaching out one hand, he tried to stop her.

He was no match for her. She'd programmed herself to react without thinking, to never be the silent, disbelieving victim again. She elbowed him hard in the stomach and flipped him over her shoulder, tossing him to the ground.

Her car exited the parking lot before he was able to get to his feet.

She drove on autopilot, heading straight for her parents' house. She would have gone to Ellen's, but she had company. The last thing Sophia needed was to have a breakdown in front of all those people. Sabrina was already "concerned." She'd been making more overtures of friendship since her conversation with Drew. He still hadn't told her what they discussed, and she was too much of a coward to press the point.

The modest, colonial-style house where she grew up had always been a refuge. She was sobbing by the time she rang the bell. Her father's face fell when he saw her.

Wordlessly, he pulled her through the door and onto the nearest sofa, holding her as she cried. She was too distraught to speak, to explain anything.

Her father was a big man, but the sight of his daughter crying reduced him to a helpless mass. Sophia hated doing this to him, but she couldn't help it. She buried her face in his strong shoulder and drenched his shirt. Beneath the fabric, she felt his tension, and she knew his mind automatically went to the worst-case scenario. Behind Sophia, the couch dipped as her mother sat, lending her soothing presence and a box of tissue.

Forcing her emotions under control, she pulled away from her father. "I'm fine," she squeaked. She needed to assure them nothing physical had happened.

"David, why don't you put on some tea?" Anna suggested. She took Sophia's hand in hers, holding it like she did when Sophia was little. "Sophia and I are going to the computer room, and we're going to have some girl-talk time."

The computer room was her old bedroom. They'd remade it into a catchall room. It now contained their ten-year-old computer that hated the Internet, a bookshelf full of how-to books and abandoned projects, and a futon folded into a couch. They sat on that, and Sophia spilled her guts.

The story was hiccup-filled, convoluted, and probably didn't make a ton of sense, but Anna possessed a mother's amazing listening ability that helped her figure out the pertinent facts. Sophia loved Drew, and she never wanted him to know she was raped.

When Sophia finished, she found she had been maneuvered so that she was lying down with her head in her mother's lap. Maternal fingers fanned through the hair at her temple, soothing the way they'd always done.

Sophia felt safe. In the silence, her tears dried.

"I don't want to lose him." Her throat was raw, and the words rasped painfully. "I can't see him again, Mom. I can't face him knowing he knows."

Sophia's heart hurt something awful, but she was cried out. If she looked in the mirror, she would see that her face was puffy and her eyes were pink and swollen.

"Let's have some tea, Sophie," her mother said. "I'll make up the guest bedroom, and you can sleep here tonight. Everything is clearer in the morning."

Numbly, Sophia followed her mother downstairs to the kitchen, where her father waited. He'd probably heated and reheated the water, wearing a track in the linoleum where he paced. David DiMarco was a hands-on man, a man of action. He didn't know what to do with himself in situations like these. The family counselor they saw after Sophia's rape helped him realize it was okay to just hug her.

Still, he needed something to do, someone to blame, a face to smash.

When the doorbell chimed, he left his women in the kitchen making tea to answer it. Sophia expected Daniel. He would easily guess her destination.

Drew followed David into the kitchen. He wore his usual Sensual Secrets T-shirt and jeans. The shirts always stretched tightly over his shoulders and chest, showing off his sexy build. She noticed that, but it was his eyes that held her attention.

They were somber. The determined set of his jaw and the grim press of his lips communicated clear and present danger. He wasn't going anywhere until he said what he had to say.

Drew set her purse and phone on the island counter. She had forgotten them in her haste to escape. Her father ushered her mother out of the kitchen. The cup of hot water in her hand splashed out, scalding the delicate span of skin between her thumb and forefinger.

Drew took it from her and set it on the counter.

She watched him, wondering why he drove all this way just to make their breakup clear. She waited for the pity or the disgust and revulsion.

It didn't come.

Resting one hand on the counter, he both faced her and blocked her escape. "A successful marriage is built on a solid foundation of trust and honesty."

She had no idea where he was going with this.

"Sophia, you don't trust me, and you haven't been honest with me."

Okay, she got it now. He was explaining why he couldn't continue their relationship. In her defense, she honestly told him she would sabotage this thing. One way or another, they were doomed from the start.

Not a muscle in his face moved. "I've spent a lot of time trying to figure out what it was about me that made you need to keep things from me. I wondered if my reputation for playing the field was to blame, but then I reasoned that your reputation wasn't much better. I wondered if you had a problem with having threesomes, but you're the one who sets them up. I wondered a lot of things, Sophie."

He moved one step closer, and she flinched.

"I suspected you were the victim of violence in a relationship ever since that night you freaked out at my house. My mom brought up the possibility that you'd been raped. She told me to be patient. Jonas told me to be patient. Ellen, in her roundabout way, told me to be patient. You asked me for time and space. I've given it to you."

He took another step. She backed away. That low, husky voice of his was lethal to her well-being.

"But I'm not going to wait forever. That's one of the reasons I came to pick you up at Daniel's instead of meeting you at Ellen's. I knew there was a reason you kept me away from there. I knew there was a reason you don't talk about what you do there."

She backed away from his verbal and physical proximity, halting abruptly when her ass crashed into the stove.

"When I saw you tonight, when I heard the way you said the things you said to those women, I knew you were talking about a situation you had experienced. I knew you'd been raped. Things began to make sense. This need you have for control, especially where sex is concerned. You have an incredible fear of getting close, of letting anyone in."

Another step put him inches from her.

"You run away from me any time I get too close." His head dipped down, putting his lips inches from hers. She wanted him to kiss her, and she wanted him to move so she could run away screaming. "You've come so far, honey. I know this is hard for you, but I'm not going anywhere. Not now, not ever."

She shifted, turning her head away from temptation and closing her eyes so she wouldn't have to see his face, the face she knew would haunt her dreams for the rest of her life. Still raw, her voice was tiny and scratchy, strangling in her throat. "I didn't want you to know."

A light caress began at her temple and traced her hair back from her face. She wanted so badly to turn her cheek into his hand.

"Why? Do you honestly think it'll affect my feelings for you?" He exhaled, hard. "Maybe it does, a little."

That admission felt like a punch in the gut. She flinched.

"It makes me angry that someone could treat you like that. If I ever met the guy, I wouldn't think twice about beating the shit out of him, but I think I wouldn't be the only person in that line."

Her eyes opened, focusing on the gold pattern in the floor that screamed 1985. She couldn't quite find the courage to face him.

"Sophia, look at me." It was an order, something she'd rarely heard from him. Even at work, he framed everything as a request, not just to her, but to everyone.

Reluctantly, she met his eyes. Their ice-blue color was warm and blazing with love.

"When I look at you, I see an intelligent, beautiful, witty, strong, wickedly sexy woman who can quote my favorite Shakespeare play at will. I see the woman I want to spend the rest of my life with."

She couldn't speak. She wanted to think he could give her a happily-ever-after. She'd wanted to believe in fairy-tale endings for so long. Fragile hope pounded at her walls, working the cracks with frantic precision. She loved this man, and he loved her.

"I see the woman who ignores me every time I ask her to marry me."

That got her. She laughed. "Yet you keep asking."

"One day, you'll say yes." His smile was a bit sad. "'The course of true love never did run smooth.' Should we be subject to different rules just because we're both extremely good-looking?"

Tension left her. She laughed again, loving his sense of humor. This was the man she wanted to wake up with every morning. She framed his face in her hands. "Yes."

His jaw dropped, but his mouth closed as confusion clouded his eyes. "I'm going to need you to clarify, Sophia. Which question were you answering?"

Smiling, she said, "The one that gets me a giant house and an extremely good-looking husband."

Lifting Sophia to hold her tight against him, Drew kissed her, gently and deeply.

When he set her down, tears streamed down her cheeks. Squaring her shoulders, she looked at him with undisguised emotion. "I'm not afraid, Drew."

"It's about damn time," he said, turning that charming smile on full blast. "I want a midsummer wedding, and I want you dressed to rival the fair Titania."

She laughed at him, loving the idea and the vision. "I want a wedding planner."

Taking her hand, he swept a low bow. "As you wish, my queen."

THE END

www.sirenpublishing.com/MicheleZurlo/

ABOUT THE AUTHOR

Michele moved to a pond, a beautiful little pond, where she dreams of replacing the aeration pumps with fountains, but she knows the association will never go for it. Until then, she'll keep her feet on the ground as she reaches for the stars.

Also by Michele Zurlo

Awakenings 1: *Letting Go*
Irrepressible Force

Available at
BOOKSTRAND.COM

Siren Publishing, Inc.
www.SirenPublishing.com

9 781606 017975